ARTIFICE

ARTIFICE

SHARON CAMERON

Scholastic Press
New York

Library of Congress Cataloging-in-Publication Data
Names: Cameron, Sharon, 1970– author.
Title: Artifice / Sharon Cameron.
Description: First edition. | New York : Scholastic Press, 2023. | Audience:
Ages 12 and up. | Audience: Grades 10–12. | Summary: Isa de Smit grew up in
her parents' art gallery in Amsterdam, but in the middle of the war she surives by
selling fake paintings to the Nazis while trying to help her friend, Truus, smuggle
Jewish babies to safety—but in 1943 it is hard to know who to trust.
Identifiers: LCCN 2023009263 | ISBN 9781338813951 (hardcover) |
ISBN 9781338813982 (ebook)
Subjects: LCSH: Art dealers—Netherlands—Amsterdam—Juvenile fiction. |
Art—Forgeries—Juvenile fiction. | Holocaust, Jewish (1939–1945)—Netherlands—
Amsterdam—Juvenile fiction. | World War, 1939–1945—Underground
movements—Netherlands—Amsterdam—Juvenile fiction. | Amsterdam
(Netherlands)—History—20th century—Juvenile fiction. | Netherlands—
History—German occupation, 1940–1945—Juvenile fiction. | CYAC: Art
dealers—Fiction. | Art—Forgeries—Fiction. | Holocaust, Jewish (1939–1945)—
Netherlands—Amsterdam—Fiction. | World War, 1939–1945—Underground
movements—Netherlands—Amsterdam—Fiction. | Amsterdam (Netherlands)—
History—20th century—Fiction. | Netherlands—History—German occupation,
1940–1945—Fiction. | BISAC: YOUNG ADULT FICTION / Historical /
Holocaust | YOUNG ADULT FICTION / Religious / Jewish | LCGFT:
Historical fiction. | Thrillers (Fiction) | Novels
Classification: LCC PZ7.C1438 Ar 2023 | DDC 813.6 [Fic]—dc23/eng/20230306
LC record available at https://lccn.loc.gov/2023009263

10 9 8 7 6 5 4 3 2 1   23 24 25 26 27

Printed in Italy   183

First edition, November 2023

Book design by Elizabeth B. Parisi

Quotations on pages ix, 86, 186, and 368 from *Twentieth-Century Latin American Poetry:
A Bilingual Anthology*, edited by Stephen Tapscott. *Decálogo del artista | Decalogue of the
Artist*, translated by Doris Dana. Austin: University of Texas Press. Page 79. 1996.

For the creators of beauty,
and those who rebuild it

"You shall love beauty, which is the shadow of God over the Universe."

—Commandment I, from *Decalogue of the Artist*,
Gabriela Mistral

ARTIFICE

"Thou shall not be passive only, but shalt turn thy soul to the permanent risk of life."

—Commandment Seven, from *The Dutch Ten Commandments to Foil the Nazis*

1

Amsterdam, The Netherlands
— September 1943 —

EVERY EYE FOLLOWS when you walk like you have something
to hide.

So Isa de Smit slowed her steps. Hummed. Dug for a handkerchief
in the pocket of her tatty wool coat. Blended into the background.
Faded into a landscape of steep-stepped gables and moving feet. And
the gazes passed her by on the morning-misted street, glancing across
her cheeks with the barest of brushstrokes.

Isa wanted to be seen and remain unnoticed.

Because Isa had something to hide.

She tucked her package tight beneath her arm.

Amsterdam was a colorful city. Blue boats and blue doors.
A butter-framed window in marmalade brick. Leaves that were
autumn-tinted, fog-frosted, marbling the pale acid-lime of a copper
patina. But there were new shades on the city's palette now. Spattered
on the walls, dripping down the flagpoles.

Black on bloodred. Army olive. Khaki brown.

Nazi brown.

A German soldier leaned against the iron railing of the canal
bridge, rifle in one hand, cigarette in the other, a silhouette against
waters of rippling viridian. His gaze flicked to Isa once and away.
The package under her arm was awkward—flat, square, and

slippery—wrapped in brown paper and tied up with string. As if she'd decided to truss up a window and take it for a stroll. Isa adjusted her grip. The soldier studied the curling smoke of his cigarette. And her feet changed their rhythm.

Faster. Closer. A little faster.

She was eyeing the middle button of the soldier's jacket, a spot of gleaming brass set squarely in the center of his drab brown chest. Imagining the coolness of the metal. How it might press into her palm when she gave it a sharp and sudden shove. Imagining the indignation. The surprise.

The splash.

Her feet went faster. Closer.

And now the Nazi was watching her walk, a line between his eyes. And then the number 14 tram rolled to a stop and Isa took it. She made her way down the narrow aisle, to the very last seat, package perched on her knees. The tram lurched, and the electric motor purred.

It was not the tram she had meant to take. Now she would have to change. Now she was late.

But she had removed temptation.

The polished wood interior was dim where it should have gleamed, dull where it should have been cheerful. The passengers rode in silence. And then four Nazi soldiers climbed on, taking the two front seats on either side of the aisle. The tram was loud with German. Laughing. Joking. Isa saw her stop, and let it pass. She let the next stop pass, and the next. She did not want to thread the narrow way between the soldiers. Not with her package. They might as well have formed a blockade.

The tram bumped and leaned around a curve. No one got off. Some elected not to get on. Shoulders brushed, umbrellas knocking against knees, until the soldiers finally stood and left the tram at Plantage. The passengers breathed a collective sigh. Then the tram hurtled around the corner to the next stop and disgorged.

Isa stepped down to the sidewalk with her package. Chin up. Eyes up. Invisible.

She walked past burnt-umber roof tiles. Wine-purple pansies spilling from their pots. The clean lead-white of a grocer's empty shelves. Around the corner, and the trees were torches lit with russet-gold. Across the street, and the windows were smoke-stained, blackened teeth of broken glass, soft gray soot smearing the cinnabar bricks of the Records Office, firebombed five months ago by the Resistance.

Arondeus had done that, with thirteen others—artists, musicians, and students—burning up records so the Nazis couldn't uncover false identities. So they couldn't find Jews. Only, the Nazis had found someone. They'd found Arondeus. And ten more.

And they had shot them.

Isa had liked Arondeus, a shy man—odd, but funny—a favorite in her mother's studio. She missed him. She missed them all. And then she turned the corner and there was the stop where she could catch the number 4. And there was the brown again, Nazi brown— too much brown—the soldiers who had been on the tram now passing a bottle with the guard of a derelict theater on the other side of the street. The theater had been gutted, windows boarded over, the handles of its grand doors chained.

It was a deportation site. A holding place. A prison for Jews.

And here came the tram, the number 8, clattering down the center of the pavement, blocking the view of the soldiers. And here came Truus, quick down the steps of the teaching college, the soles of her sensible lace-ups making a bright, smart slap against the stone. She had a leather overnight bag gripped by its handles, swinging at the level of her skirt hem.

Truus was supposed to be away. Living in a forest. Blowing up train tracks and cutting telephone wires.

Isa was supposed to be at home. With her father. Making sure he didn't burn down the kitchen.

The people locked in the theater should have been at home, too, and the Nazis should have stayed in Germany.

No one was where they were supposed to be today.

Isa paused on the pavement. "Truus!" she said.

Truus froze, one foot behind her on the step.

"What are you doing in the city?" Isa asked.

Truus had eyes as soft as a new spring sky. Isa could remember a time when they were innocent. The leather bag in her hand squirmed. Once. Twice. And then Truus walked away, fast down the street. Shoulders hunched. Eyes down, locked on her path. Like she didn't want to be seen. Like she didn't want to be seen so much that she was going to make herself be seen.

Isa turned her back. So she couldn't watch Truus go. She breathed, and didn't let the air out again.

The tram squeaked and rumbled away, and there were the Germans, still milling in front of the prison-theater, leaning against the columns. Two of them were laughing, one unlocking the chain looped through the handles of the building's front doors. And one soldier had his gaze fixed on Isa, with her awkward package and a lock of flame-red hair sticking out from a hole in her knitted hat, standing stock-still and staring on the opposite side of the street.

Exposed.

Memorable.

Isa released the air from her lungs, and she walked slow—too slow—hesitating down the sidewalk. Looking back. Looking front and looking back again. Letting the soldier see. Letting his eyes follow her instead of Truus. Remember her instead of Truus. Two steps. Three. Away from the teaching college, clutching the package against her side.

There was a drawing inside her package. A Rembrandt. Irreplaceable and priceless.

Or worthless, depending on who you asked.

Because the picture inside Isa's package was a fake.

What Truus had been carrying was priceless, too. Or worthless, depending on who you asked. Only what Truus had was real. All too real.

Because what Truus had been carrying in that bag was a baby.

Isa glanced back. The soldier was still watching her while the others chatted. She met his eyes over the slick, black metal of a slow-moving car. And then she hurried. Let him remember the girl half running down the street with a strange, window-shaped, paper-wrapped package. So the memory of another girl—a girl with a precious leather bag—would fade, bleached like a print left too long in the sun.

It must have been a Jewish baby. There was no other sort of baby Truus would need to smuggle. But what was a Jewish baby doing in the teaching college? And where was Truus taking it?

One cry. One whimper. One wrong glance from the wrong person. One soldier watching Truus walk like she had something to hide and she would be caught.

Truus would be shot. Or worse.

If Isa was caught selling forgeries, then the Nazis might shoot her, too.

Or worse.

And if Isa was found selling away her country's artistic heritage, feeding the greed of the invading Nazis with the art treasures of the Netherlands, then Truus might be the one doing the shooting, because shooting was what could happen to a collaborator in Amsterdam. Or a bomb. Or a rope around the neck. A quiet drowning, at midnight in the canal.

The Nazi gaze on her back felt like a rubber band—stretching, stretching—until a truck, its tall back draped in olive canvas, cranked to a stop in front of the theater, snapping their connection. The truck motor chugged, brash over the rattle of the door chains, and Isa risked a last backward glance. Truus and her bag were gone, lost to the color and the thinning fog. The rear gate of the truck screeched down onto the pavement, a metal tongue scraping the street. An open mouth.

The guard who had been watching her was fully occupied now, beating and bullying prisoners out of the theater. She could hear the sound of sticks and rifle butts, the soft, sickening thwack of wood against flesh, the cries and the protests. Dutch. Yiddish. The bark of a German order. And the prisoners vanished into the wide, dark mouth. Like Moshe had. Like Levvy and Hilde.

She knew what *deportation* meant now. What it really meant. Everyone knew what the trucks meant now.

Damn the Nazis. Damn them straight into the flames of Goya's hell.

Isa walked to the next tram stop, package held tight against her side.

Blending. Fading.

Invisible.

There were so many different ways to die today.

2

ISA STEPPED OFF the number 4 tram at the Herengracht. The buildings on either side of the canal stood tall, skinny, red-bricked and honey-stoned, with yellow shutters, navy shutters, no shutters, leaning this way and that way, out and in, like old men who had dropped a guilder.

She knew these buildings. She knew them in every light.

The fog rose. The smell dampened. Water lapped in a sudden rain of rusty leaves. Isa passed the guard on the bridge without a glance, and at number 458, she climbed broad stone steps to a set of double doors, paint rubbed elegantly from their edges. There was a guard beside the doors, eyes forward, back erect in his repellent brown, as if the cargo rope dangling from the roof peak was the most fascinating thing Amsterdam had ever shown him. Isa opened a door.

And stepped into the smell of old things and money. The familiar creak of floorboards beneath shuffling feet. The soft running static of whispers. Rumors. Who? When? And most important, how much? The auction houses had been her world before the war. The world of her childhood, holding her father's pigment-stained hand. The world of her teenage years, a pencil stuck behind one ear, calculating commissions in the shadow of her papa's sun.

It was not her world now.

This was the world of collaborators.

Isa stood to one side with her package.

Paintings sat propped against the walls, frame to frame, some stacked two or three deep. Goudstikker would have never allowed a painting to be treated in such a fashion, but this was not Goudstikker's auction house. Not anymore. Goudstikker had caught a ship. So he couldn't be put on the back of a truck. Little groups of threes and fours hovered around the leaning art—all men, no women—rubbing their chins, muttering. And they were strangers. Not one dealer she knew. Isa looked them over, assessing.

Buying at an auction was like walking down a Nazi-laden street. Best to pass unnoticed, nondescript, with your fat pockets hidden. But selling was different. When you were selling, you should look like mink is something you snatch off your coatrack. Like diamonds live in your side drawer. Like you ate gilded nuts for your breakfast. Or, alternatively, you could put on tatty wool and a knit hat barely fit for a sewer and come through the door wide-eyed, just out of Grandmama's attic. An innocent eighteen-year-old with a cobwebbed masterpiece you really don't know very much about.

Isa tucked a bright, stray lock back into the hole in her hat, displaying the frayed end of a coat sleeve. She'd only just stopped short of rubbing soot on her nose. She knew how this game was played, or she used to. When she wasn't a criminal. When she'd only been playing with her livelihood, not her life.

The whispering men looked her up and down. Assessing.

There was a table at the far end of the room, where Goudstikker had taken registrations for his auctions, a row of Dutchmen with long coats and longer faces now lined up in front of it. Isa caught a hint of gold from a blanketed frame. A pale marble elbow peeking out from beneath butcher paper. Art leaving Amsterdam. By the crate load. By the trainload.

A man left the desk, trudging past Isa and out the door, hat pulled low, a fistful of reichsmarks disappearing into his pocket. The next in line stepped forward, a blue-and-white vase cradled in his arms like a child. The man was so thin Isa could guess the shape of his skull.

Collaborators. That's the name Truus would have given them. Isa would have called them desperate. Both terms were probably accurate.

Damn the Nazis. Damn the Nazis straight into the nightmares of Giovanni's hell.

Isa took her package to the last place in line.

There was a man standing behind the desk, hair slicked back, lips pursed, exquisitely dressed in a navy striped suit with a watch chain and a pocket square of mustard-print silk. No one else could look so well fed and satisfied in wartime. No one but a Nazi.

Isa watched him examine the marble statue emerging from the butcher paper, a woman with a water jug on her hip. A nice piece. He looked down his nose at it, peered with a loupe held against one eye, speaking quiet German to a young soldier seated at the desk. The soldier's pen scratched in a ledger book, then onto a label that went around the marble woman's neck.

A guard watched the proceedings from the shadow of the back wall, stoic, alert, a pistol at his side.

The soldier at the desk unlocked a metal box, reached inside, counting, and then handed the Dutchman a fresh stack of reichsmarks. The sound of a rumor rose, speculating. The tagged woman with a water jug went to stand against the wall with the other art, and the lips that had been pursed stretched flat. Smug.

This was not an auction, Isa realized. It was a sale. A sale where the Dutch took whatever the Nazis would give them.

It was better than what they had given to Goudstikker. Which was nothing.

And then she heard a whisper, a clear word in the hum. "Goering."

"Goes to Goering," said another.

Isa glanced behind herself, but she couldn't see the whisperers, so she stared fixedly at the floor. Hermann Goering was second-in-command of the Reich. The head of the Luftwaffe. The man who had ordered Rotterdam bombed into a fiery oblivion. Was this smug little dealer Hermann Goering's agent?

Hermann Goering deserved to be sold a fake.

"Fräulein? Name, please?"

Isa looked up and there was no one in the line ahead of her. Only Goering's oily-headed agent, the soldier with the gun, and the soldier at the desk, who was now looking at her steadily, pen hovering above his ledger. He was young, neat and clipped, with heavy brows over eyes in a shade of brown that clashed with the Nazi of his uniform. There were shadows beneath those eyes. The rape of Holland must be heavy work. He looked her over, one dark brow rising ever so slightly.

"Papers?" he tried again, in decent Dutch.

Isa set the package on her scuffed shoes and reached into her ridiculous coat. She let herself be nervous. Big-eyed. Allowed her little identity booklet to shake when she handed it over. Which was not that difficult. Her papers were as fake as her art. The soldier glanced at them and at her. That brow was very high now.

"Elsa Groot?" he confirmed. She nodded. The pen scratched. The Nazi against the wall adjusted his pistol.

"You will unwrap the paper," Goering's dapper little agent said. In German. But the message was clear. Isa began picking at the string.

"I was looking . . . in the attic," she stuttered, working at the knot, "looking for . . . for something to . . . so we could . . ."

Pick. Pick.

"Looking for something so we can . . ." She let them fill in the blanks with "looking for something to sell so we can eat."

Pick. Pick. Pick.

The soldier translated what she was saying while he wrote down the fake address from her fake papers. The agent got irritated. The hoverers watched from the edges of the room, whispering.

"Grandmama," she went on, pulling slowly, painstakingly at the newspaper, "it must have belonged to her. It might not be worth . . . but perhaps . . . I heard, maybe, you would want to buy . . ." She let the brown paper slither into a heap and turned the frame.

The soldier at the desk must have known art as well as Dutch. His German slowed and both his brows were up over his tired brown eyes, hiding beneath the brim of his cap. His gaze darted to Goering's agent, who was leaning forward over the table, the loupe already against his eye.

Isa watched, and she waited.

"Imagine the art, my child," her father would say, her legs dangling from a high stool in the reek of turpentine, her chin in hand, watching as he washed out his brushes. Her father's beard had been brown then, instead of gray. "Imagine the lost art, hidden away in closets and storerooms, unknown and unloved. Paintings tossed aside because the widow or a banker had no regard for them. Because the artist thought them flawed. Unworthy. Imperfect . . ."

Her father's eyes would glisten then, dreamy with love. Not for his daughter, but for art. But Isa had not been offended. She had been enraptured.

"But art has no imperfection. You must remember this, my little Sofonisba. Art is imperfection. And when the light shines anew on what has been lost, when our eyes behold the glory, then all we shall see is the hand of the master . . ."

Theodoor de Smit was an excellent artist, better at imitating a style he loved than finding one of his own. Content with re-creating his imagined lost treasures. He'd done Michelangelo's studies of the Sistine Chapel. A set of Dürer's first watercolors, spectacular in their detail, but with a less-sure hand, as if in childhood. And he'd drawn this picture, a Rembrandt self-portrait, black and red chalk on paper, the pretended inspiration for a well-known copper etching made more than three centuries earlier.

A lost masterpiece.

Rembrandt's face stared out at them from the frame, with a tall black hat and bulbous nose, an open book lying on a stack of books in front of him. Rembrandt had not been a pretty man. He'd never tried to make himself one. But his expression was . . . thoughtful. Melancholic. With a little lift of humor at the corner of his mouth.

The face might be Rembrandt's, but the expression was every bit Theodoor de Smit, which had likely been his own private joke when he drew it, when his second love, Isa's mother, had still been alive, running their small gallery, her chin on his shoulder while he worked. The drawing had lurked in their back hallway for years. And three days ago, Isa had taken it off the wall, thrown coffee grounds on it, then left it on the floor beneath the dining room curtains while she stood on a chair, shaking out the dust.

This had been the extent of her plan. Her ingenious method of fooling the Nazis. Coffee stains and curtain dust.

It did not feel like enough, here, in front of soldiers with guns and Hermann Goering's agent in the whispering auction house that should still belong to Goudstikker.

Not nearly enough.

Isa's pulse did what her feet had done at the canal bridge. Moved faster. A little faster. She kept her gaze down.

"Maybe . . . it isn't worth anything . . ." she said, taking a small step back, allowing her voice to quiver. "I should not have come . . ."

The soldier behind the desk stood, holding out his hands. "May I?"

Isa hadn't known a Nazi knew how to ask. She let him take the picture.

And now her moment had come.

The soldier and the agent leaned in, peering at the surface, tilting it beneath the light. The agent's upper lip was flattening, the young soldier's mouth taking the shape of a whistle. And Isa knew.

They wanted it.

They wanted to believe.

Which was as good as believing. And what would be this smug little man's reward for bringing a Rembrandt to Hermann Goering? More than what Isa would get. Much more. But what Isa would get was so much more than the nothing she had right now.

Isa felt the tiniest release of tension from between her shoulder blades. Nearly let a sigh blow from her lungs. And then she raised her eyes, and her breath stilled.

There was a painting hung on the wall behind the desk, at the level of the guard's stiff chin. A woman with a wineglass in her hand, tilting on the edge of her fingertips, the still, frozen moment captured just before the glass fell. It was a pensive painting, intense, lush with vermilion. Shimmering in shades of ultramarine. Full of pure, clear light.

Isa knew this painting. She knew it intimately. It was a Vermeer. And it should not be in Goudstikker's.

It could not be in Goudstikker's.

Then her eyes snapped back to the table, to the young soldier still bending low over her Rembrandt. His brows had come together, two furrows across his forehead. His head gave a tiny shake, and then another. His gaze lifted.

Isa blinked. Big-eyed. Innocent, the way Truus used to be. It didn't work.

He knew, damn him. He knew. Something had given her away.

Her pulse revved like an engine.

There were so many ways to die today.

The agent was muttering excitedly in German, while the soldier stared steadily at Isa. His eyes were brown and yet translucent, strong tea poured in a cup of porcelain. He translated, "Herr Hofer would like for you to tell him where this artwork has come from."

Isa played with her coat collar. "My grandmama . . . in the attic . . ."

The agent chattered.

"What family? Were they wealthy?" The soldier's eyes were not tired and they were not like tea, Isa decided. They were brown glass. Smooth and cold.

"No. Or maybe . . ." she stuttered. "They . . . they arranged sales. For estates . . ."

It was a good story. Probable and yet difficult to verify. And what a shame this young soldier translating her answer so fluently into German knew that it was a lie. But the agent didn't. He was hooked, touching the paper with ginger love beneath the curtain dust, gazing at the hasty, confident strokes. Rembrandt's strokes. Her father would have been meticulous about that. How soon would the agent discover what the soldier had? And what would happen when he did?

It would be the truck.

Or something worse.

She should run. Right now. Before this soldier at the desk could say what he knew. Before the soldier in the shadows could draw his gun. Before they could alert the staring Nazi outside the door. She knew the back alleys of Amsterdam better than they did. She knew how to disappear, and she would do it as soon as the young man holding her forged Rembrandt made a move.

But he did not make a move. He just looked at her, asking the little agent's excited questions.

"Has anyone else seen this painting, Fräulein? Has it been appraised?" He didn't bother to translate the shake of her head. Goering's agent straightened, pleased. Smug. The rumors in the room crescendoed to a buzz.

And suddenly, the whispering hushed. The agent stilled. The young soldier half turned, chin jerking sideways to look behind him. Because the door to the back room had opened—Goudstikker's former office—and now another man was approaching the desk.

Heavy-lidded and unassuming, with wire-rimmed glasses and a suit in soft, coal black. Understated. Expensive. Perfect, Isa thought, if you're selling. But she didn't think this man was selling. This man exuded something more important than tailored elegance. It was in the set of his mouth, the flagpole stiffness of his spine. In the very stride that was bringing him to the desk to examine her forgery.

This man was not invisible. This man walked with power.

Dutch police, Isa thought. SS or Gestapo. Only he had no uniform.

Higher, then. Much higher. Isa dropped her eyes.

And so it would be more than a truck. It would be blood and fists. Clubs, pliers, needles, and knives.

A rope or a bullet.

The soldier against the wall stood alert, hand hovering near his pistol.

Goudstikker had a door in his office, stairs down into a cellar, a cellar with more stairs that led back up again to the street. They would not expect her to run that way. Straight into this powerful man's lair.

She didn't think she could get there faster than a bullet.

The man in the dark suit lurked behind the young soldier's shoulder. The soldier who knew. He held the Rembrandt stone-still, rigid. The man looked. And looked. He adjusted his glasses. And then he leaned down, whispering something into Herr Hofer's ear.

The tip of Hofer's ear turned pink. The lips pressed. Livid, Isa thought, and trying very hard not to show it.

Goering's agent must know now, that he'd nearly been taken. The brown-eyed soldier hadn't even needed to tell him. Duped by a little girl with a hole in her hat. Made to look a fool.

Sweat trickled down Isa's neck. She let it trickle. Her left foot twitched, inching toward the office.

Then the man in the dark suit reached out and lifted Rembrandt's self-portrait from the soldier's grasp, giving the room one sweeping glance before he walked away, slowly, carrying Theodoor de Smit's imagined masterwork to the inner sanctum of Goudstikker's back room. The latch clicked.

The room broke into whispers, rumors, a hum, a buzz of speculation that rose into discord. The young soldier sat down behind the desk, mouth tight. He didn't look at Isa anymore, and neither did Goering's little agent. He was flushed with rage. Or indignation. Or fear, wiping his forehead with the pocket square. The soldier made a note in his ledger and opened the metal box, arms moving as he counted, hands hidden behind the lid. He held out a stack of reichsmarks to Isa.

She took the money. And met his eyes. Brown. Translucent. Murky glass.

Isa could have sworn they were telling her to run.

She didn't run. She shoved the money and her fake identity card deep into her coat pocket, slowly gathering up the paper and string she'd let fall to the floor. Gaze down, expression blank, past the line of new collaborators who had queued up behind her, shuffling through the door with her arms full of rubbish. Past the guard, along the street, creeping around the bend of the Herengracht until she'd turned the corner, out of sight of the canal guard.

And then Isa ran, darting quick into an alley. She dropped the brown paper into a rubbish heap, stuffed the money and her false identity card into her bra, yanked the cap off her head and tossed it to the trash along with the coat. Just like she'd found them.

Over the bridge and across the Singel, where a chill breeze blew and collars turned up and feet moved. Where she blended. Where the sun hung like a slice of lemon above her head, floating in a pool of frosty water. Then left and onto Kalverstraat, quiet where it should have been busy, past open and shuttered shops, bolting left again into the Rozenboomsteeg, a lane so narrow that passersby had to turn to avoid a collision. Isa ducked beneath the awning of a tiny café—dark and empty, not yet open for the day—flattening beside its pane of gilded glass. Waiting. Watching for pursuit.

And fear, Isa thought, was like a paint pot spilling, crawling, creeping, obliterating the colors in its path.

She was far from the theater, where there was one Nazi soldier who would remember her face. Far from the auction house, where everyone would remember it. Where she could never go again. So

Truus would not find out she was a collaborator. So the Nazis would not find out she was a forger. A fraudster. A criminal.

Only what she'd done had been worse than a crime. Because Isa de Smit hadn't just sold some dubious painting to a German officer looking to surprise his wife. She hadn't even sold a faked Rembrandt to Hermann Goering, the arsonist of Rotterdam. There was only one man whose agent could have superseded Goering's. Only one who could have walked with such power.

Isa de Smit had just sold a forgery to the Führer himself.

3

WHEN THE NARROW lane remained empty and no one came to arrest her, Isa ventured out from beneath the shadow of the awning. Before Mrs. Breem could unlock the café and ask what she thought she was doing. Rozenboomsteeg veered off-kilter, angling into an alley, leaving the corners of the buildings sharp, triangular, the bricks beneath her feet a pattern of herringbone. To her right were the long sides of two empty houses. To her left the high wall of a convent, spanning as far as she could see, a blank brick canvas cut only by an archway surrounding a pair of thick, wooden doors.

Isa had never seen a nun from inside the walls. She'd never even seen the door opened. But her mother had told her a story once, about Sister Cornelia, who had objected so strongly to the use of their chapel by Protestants that she'd demanded to be buried in the street gutter. The other nuns must have actually liked Sister Cornelia, her mother had said, because when she died, they laid her out in the chapel. Only in the morning, Sister Cornelia was in the gutter. And she put herself in the gutter every night until the nuns gave up and buried her there.

"But which gutter?" Isa had asked, reaching up for her mother's hand.

"Why, the clean one, of course," her mother replied.

Isa looked down at the gutter she was standing in. It was not clean. She looked up and down the alley. She did not want to be followed home.

And then she heard footsteps, echoing between high walls, approaching from the café on the lane.

She dug in her skirt pockets, pretending to look for a handkerchief. Utterly confounded by that lack of a handkerchief. Listening to the click of heels on the herringbone. The reichsmarks prickled, poking against her skin, and a woman passed her by without a glance, a shopping bag on her arm, hair wrapped against the fog in a green-and-gold kerchief.

Isa stilled, and as soon as the woman had disappeared down the alley, stepped right and slipped through a chink between the houses. A place where two sharp-cornered walls hadn't quite met. A crack that led to a weedy, cobbled gully running along the back walls of everything.

And then she hurried, past two gates in the high brick wall on her left—one for a teacher, out of work and fled, one for the deserted home where all three sons had been conscripted to a labor camp in Germany—past the back gardens of three houses on her right, all Jewish, all empty. Then came Mrs. Breem's and the rear door of the café, and straight ahead to the two buildings facing Kalverstraat—a radio repair shop, now closed, and a seller of antiquities, now dead.

The gully was inconvenient. Damp and unpleasant. A space no one bothered with. No one but Isa. She could have dodged its puddles in the dark. She opened her gate, the third in the wall on the left, shut it fast, and put a shaky key to the back door of the Gallery De Smit.

The lock turned behind her with a comforting snick. And there was no tromp of boots on the gully stones. No shouts. No rifle butts splintering the wood of her door. No one had followed her. No one knew her real name, or where she actually lived. No one knew who had sold a fake Rembrandt to Hitler.

Isa leaned against the wall, where damp grew up the plaster like vines, in the dim light soaking through the blanket she'd tacked over the door's glass transom. The silence was thick. Soft. A velvet glove.

And Isa felt a shiver. A thrill. Like a streak of pale blue paint over cucumber green, cool and delicious. Because she had outsmarted them. Tricked them. Shown the world that the Nazis were fools. Or, if not the entire world, at least she had shown Isa de Smit. Because she knew what the Nazis didn't.

She knew that their Rembrandt was a fake. And *Woman with a Wine Glass*, the exquisite Vermeer hanging on Goudstikker's back wall, she knew that painting was a forgery, too.

Isa straightened, smiling at the satisfaction. Listening to the tap of her own footsteps down the hall, to the echo of her shoes in the dark, empty space that had been the Gallery De Smit.

The house had been two houses once, in some far-off day of black suits and lace ruffs, when a grandfather of a grandfather had been a successful spice merchant. Doors had been knocked through walls, steps built where the floors didn't meet, and then her mother had come along and the walls had come down—leaving the oak-blackened beams and supporting columns—creating two open spaces on the ground floor. The big gallery, for the public, with floor-to-ceiling windows, and a smaller gallery behind it, a more intimate space that could be closed off with a curtain, for private events and showings. Perfect for display.

And it had been perfect. Full of art and artists. Lessons in her mother's studio. Inspiration in her father's garret. Loud. Busy. Bright with creativity and color.

It had been unique.

Beautiful.

And then, when she was fourteen, her mother had died, and the sun inside her father had dimmed. Their business slowed. When she was fifteen, the Nazis came and confiscated her city. A year after that, they confiscated her art. Because the art in the Gallery De Smit was modern. Different.

Imperfect.

Degenerate.

Isa walked to the opening of the big gallery, where picture wire hung nail to nail like a mockery of tinsel, where the front door was barred, the windows tacked over with quilts for the blackout, hiding their emptiness from the street. The German attack on the Netherlands had offended her father; their attack on art had bred a hatred in him that knew no bounds. And something inside him had been snuffed, a cord disconnected. He stopped paying their accounts. He stopped leaving the house. He painted for three days straight and then slept for four.

And there had been no point in going back to school after that. Her teachers at the Lyceum had been replaced with Dutch National Socialists eager for the new Nazi rules and curriculum, and Isa had been a waif who wore orange hats and dreamed of marrying the north wind. Not because she'd read Ovid, but because she'd seen a painting and liked the sound of it. Other than Truus, Isa's friends had been artists, sculptors, and the occasional poet. If she hadn't stayed home to manage the gallery's remaining assets—to manage her father—she supposed they would have starved.

Isa lifted a hand to the bricks beside her, the partial wall between the big and the little gallery, feeling the rough grit of mortar, the blank, butter-pale smoothness of Jacobean brick. There was no leftover picture wire here. Not in this place. This wall was clean and bare.

Because the Nazis hadn't found everything.

She smiled again. Shivered. And then she frowned, wrinkling her nose. That faint, sharp tang in the air of the gallery wasn't emptiness. It wasn't even the smell of sadness.

It was cooking gas. From the stove.

Three long strides through the little gallery, and Isa took the spiral stairs up and around, making the wood creak and protest. She could smell coffee now, as well as the gas, and when her head rose up above the level of the old oak boards of the kitchen floor, she said, "Papa! Did you leave the stove on? I . . ."

But her words trailed as she slowed, teetering at the top of the stairs. Her papa was sitting at the table, innocent in his smoking jacket—tartan slipper on one foot, a pigment-spattered scarlet on the other—his long, gray hair loose, silver beard trimmed to a point from his chin. Two steep black brows were aimed at a card in his hand, a printed painting of a forest scene in twilit snow. He looked up.

"It is the brushwork of Van Gogh, I think, but with the brooding of a Caravaggio!"

"Yes, Papa," Isa said. "I see . . ."

Only she didn't see. Because she wasn't looking at her father anymore. She was looking at Truus, making herself comfortable on the blue-and-yellow cushion of the window seat, feet propped on the ledge like she'd done when she was ten.

"Hello there, Isaatje," Truus said, using Isa's nickname. A nickname for a nickname. "Having a busy day?"

Isa shrugged. "Not as busy as yours, I imagine."

Her father's gaze jumped up again, startled, dark eyes bright beneath his brows. "Daughter," he said. He held out a hand and she went to him, letting him kiss both her cheeks like a duchess just arrived. "How nice to see you. Do come in. But do you see this light? It is not correctly placed . . ."

And his attention was reabsorbed by the problem of the card, the back of which proclaimed "A Happy Christmas."

"Cup of coffee?" Truus asked, hopping off the window seat.

Isa pulled out the chair across from her father while Truus opened the painted cupboard in the corner, where the mugs were kept. She'd cut her hair short sometime in the past year, a blond bob. Practical. And she'd taken the tacks off the blackout curtain. Sunshine was pouring through the leaded glass above the window seat, glowing on the glaze of blue-and-white tiles, brightening the marigold walls. And what drawer had Truus found that card hiding in, ready-made for distracting Theodoor de Smit?

Truus set two cups on the table. There was no milk, not even powdered, no sugar, and the coffee she poured was not even coffee. No one had seen real coffee since the invasion, though the grounds had worked well enough on the Rembrandt. What poured into Isa's cup was thin, watery, and more ochre than umber. She sipped it all the same.

It would have all been very cheerful, sitting in the kitchen, drinking bad coffee with Truus, if her father hadn't been stroking his beard, muttering about Botticelli and perspective. If Truus hadn't been going through their drawers. If the reichsmarks hadn't itched in her bra.

Truus sat with her own cup, drank once, winced, and crossed her legs.

"So. What have you been doing today, Isa?"

A bold question, considering what Isa had seen in that leather bag.

"Selling off the last of the gallery's assets," she replied. "There are still one or two people in Amsterdam with money tucked away."

Truus frowned. "And how do you imagine they've managed to tuck money away from the Germans?"

"Degenerate," her father muttered. Bitter.

Isa didn't answer. Truus swirled the contents of her cup.

"Does it not occur to you, Isaatje, that these people have money because they are working with the Nazis?"

And there was the word, looming between them. Like an unwanted guest in the table's fourth chair.

Collaborator.

"Should I ask everyone I sell to for a financial statement?" Isa snapped. "The ground tax is due. Three years of it, plus six percent. We have no business. Either I pay or we lose the gallery."

Truus glared into the coffee, brows hunched over stormy eyes. There had been a time when Truus was her best friend. Two girls who giggled and wrote notes, played the phonograph and went to the cinema. They'd snuck into the cinema once, when they were twelve, to see *Blonde Venus*, a film of such scandalous reputation that Mr. Peeters had stood daily guard outside the Corso, shooing children away with a broom. Which, of course, made seeing it irresistible. "Operation View *Blonde Venus*" had involved stealing Mrs. Oosterhof's key to the hat and glove shop next door, climbing through her upper window, down the connecting rooftop, then lowering themselves into the cinema through the skylight.

It had been Isa's plan, a reckless plan, but well executed. Though they had not considered pigeons. Or the dust. Or the fact that the film was in English, with German subtitles, languages neither one of them spoke. They also hadn't considered exactly how they were supposed to get back out again.

The incident had left Isa without pocket money or Truus's company for an entire month. Though she'd heard her mother telling

Papa about it, whispering behind their bedroom door. Laughing and laughing. Until she'd coughed . . .

Truus had gone right on with such antics when the Germans came, starting fires and stealing distributor caps—saving the Netherlands, she'd said—and she'd taken it for granted that Isa would want to do the same. Would do the same. Had been so furious when she hadn't. Not harrying Nazis, Truus said, was tantamount to disloyalty to the Dutch. It was treason.

Truus had two older sisters and a brother-in-law to care for her parents if she was caught. When she was caught. And executed. Like Arondeus. Isa's papa had no one but Isa. The gallery had no one but Isa.

What was behind the brick wall of the gallery had no one but Isa.

It was a cage without a door. A beloved cage. But a cage all the same.

"If the tax is due," her father said suddenly, "we should plan an exhibition! Something new! Tell your . . ."

He looked up, stricken. His words gone like the flip of a switch.

Tell your mother. That's what he had almost said.

Papa knew there was no art on the walls of the gallery. He knew there was a war and that Francina de Smit had died of cancer the year before it. Except for every now and then, when he didn't. Truus dropped her gaze to the table, embarrassed.

"Papa, did you say something about the light?" Isa asked, nodding toward the card. "Where it hits the snow? Shouldn't that be on the other side of the tree?"

Isa watched the mundane thoughts of taxes and war take off from her father's mind like a fluttering bird.

"It could be better," he said, "so much better . . ." He pushed back his chair, and then he remembered Truus. "My dear," he said, reaching for her hand. "What a pleasure to entertain a woman of such rare and delicate beauty. Do come again."

He kissed her hand with the flourish of a courtier—a role he enjoyed, much like the mismatched slippers—and made a beeline for the kitchen door. In two minutes, Isa thought, he would be in the garret, painting snow, unpleasantness banished, and he wouldn't come back down again. Probably not until tomorrow. Or the next day. Or the next. While Isa took care of everything else.

This was the arrangement.

Truus watched the swinging door to their dining room thump softly back and forth behind Theodoor de Smit. She ran a hand through her short hair and looked back at Isa. For a moment, her eyes were the summer sky.

"I only want you to be careful," she whispered. "You will be careful?"

"Will you?" Isa asked.

Truus gripped the coffee cup, her voice barely a whisper. "You can tell no one."

Isa shook her head. As if she would. What did Truus take her for?

"It's life and death, Isa."

Of course it was. "Where did it come from?" she asked.

Truus didn't answer.

"Where were you taking it?"

Truus hesitated, and then she leaned forward, voice coming out in a breath. "There are women who will pretend they've had a baby, families willing to say they've adopted a nephew or niece, or have a visiting cousin. We take as many of the children as we can, with permission, if we can, and erase them off the rosters. Retype the lists every night, so that to the Germans, it's like they never existed. But there aren't enough people willing to hide them, and if we take too many, we're caught. We can only choose a few . . ."

Isa closed her eyes. Damn the Nazis.

Truus shifted in her seat. "Do you really know people with money? People who could be . . . trusted?"

Isa ran a finger over the scarred surface of the table, a piece of thick oak that had probably been seeing the bottom of plates since the time of Vermeer. She didn't know how to answer. The only people she knew with money were not going to adopt Jewish babies. Far from it.

"There are papers to be forged," Truus whispered. "Ration cards for the milk. Food and clothes. No one will take another child if their own are going to starve. There's an . . . arrangement to get them safely out of the city, but now that arrangement is requiring a bribe. A big one."

Isa looked up. "Can you trust someone to help who needs a bribe?"

"As long as we're paying a lot more than the Gestapo's bounty to turn in a Jew, and as long as they keep thinking there's more money to be had, then yes, I believe so. But we don't have any money, and it's impossible to ask, because there are collaborators out there who would hand a Jew over for nothing. And Isa . . ." She clung to the cup between her hands. "They're only babies . . ."

And shame hit Isa like the canvas-topped truck. The reichsmarks in her bra might as well have been staining her blouse.

"How much do you need?" she whispered.

"About fifteen hundred guilders."

Nearly twice what she'd gotten for the Rembrandt, and that was for paying the tax and possibly the winter's coal.

"Could you find out?" Truus said. "Could you ask? Discreetly?"

Isa hesitated, and then she nodded. It certainly would be discreet, because she wasn't going to ask anyone anything at all. How could she? There was no family to go to; their friends were either dead or in prison or fled. And she had nothing left to sell.

Then Isa asked, "Does Willem know you're here?"

"No. But he will. He's . . . not in the city right now."

Willem had been the first wedge driven into the divide of their friendship, though not because of Isa's preference, but because of Willem's. Which had been a confusion to everyone. Willem was two years older and every girl's ideal. Every girl's but Isa's. His family was strict—church three times a week, no cigarettes, no alcohol—and Isa had grown up in an art gallery where not everyone wore their clothes. Though now, Isa realized, her lack of enthusiasm might have had less to do with her romance with the north wind and more with a refusal to like the same boy everyone else did. When Willem and Truus had become a couple, it had seemed natural. Truus had always been the beauty. But Isa still found her friend's choice . . . unimaginative. Willem would follow a rule to its last letter.

"He's a good person, Isa," Truus said, suddenly defensive. "And he's done incredible things for the Resistance. He's brave. Too brave. He's just . . . rigid, when he knows he's in the right . . ."

Isa would have said ruthless. Ruthless when he thinks he's in the right. If Willem's morals and ethics hadn't clashed so thoroughly with Hitler's, he would have made an excellent Nazi.

She wondered what Truus meant by "too brave."

"He won't like it that I've involved you. We keep our circles small. So if one of us is caught, we can't give away the others. But we don't have time to wait. They're going to take the children. We don't know when, but they will take them. All of them."

Isa didn't answer. She just nodded. Again.

Truus pushed back her chair and opened the window latch. The frame of leaded glass swung outward as she sat on the sill, cool air, a little sour, drifting in from the back gully path.

"I'll come back in two days," Truus said, "to see what you've found out."

Nod number three.

"And, Isa, the stove was on when I got here. I think he forgot."

Nod number four. Isa looked up.

"It was good to see you, Truus."

She smiled. "Day after tomorrow, then."

And with that, Truus swung her sensible lace-ups out the window and onto the wall's outer ledge, fingers clinging to the gutter as she edged over and across, toward the little roof above the gallery's back door. Her preferred method of coming and going ever since the *Blonde Venus* affair.

Isa went to the window to watch Truus shinny down the porch post like she was stepping down a ladder, her skirt hem brushing the enclosing bricks. Truus landed lightly on the ground, in the scanty, grassy patch Isa's mother had always grandly referred to as "the Garden De Smit," a place probably meant to house an outdoor toilet.

And then, Isa saw a hat appear. Through the crack between the buildings, moving along the brick wall that ran behind the houses on Isa's side. A hat riding someone's head. A brown hat.

Nazi brown.

And when Isa turned, Truus was reaching out for the gate latch.

4

ISA DUCKED DOWN, out of sight from the open window, covering the warning in her mouth with a hand. She couldn't shout. She couldn't make a sound. Not without alerting the Nazi. And Truus hadn't seen. The wooden gate was solid, the wall too high, and he was coming quietly, head down, picking his way around the puddles.

The hat paused, looking up at the windows on the other side of the gully, some dark and broken, some blank for the blackout. Truus bent down to tie her shoe. Isa held her breath. What was a Nazi doing in the back gully? A place to nowhere. A place not easy to get to. Little more than a running gutter every time it rained. A place only a local would know.

But this Nazi knew.

Isa watched from just above the sill. Truus straightened. And the hat turned. Going fast now, the way it had come, back down the gully. Truus put her hand on the gate latch. Isa made a little noise, and Truus tilted her head, listening. Isa caught a glimpse of a square shoulder, the clipped hair above a stiff-collared neck, hesitating at the space between the buildings. The hat looked left, then right.

Truus opened the gate.

And the hat went right, disappearing into the alley.

Truus hurried off down the gully, looking out carefully between the buildings before she slipped away. To the left.

Isa moved her hand, and let out the breath she'd been holding.

Then she latched the kitchen window and ran.

Out the door and through the dining room, grabbing a silver candlestick, up a step and into a hall startlingly papered with scarlet poppies. Past her parents' bedroom, down the straight stairs and into the big gallery, shadowy behind its blanketed windows. She pressed her cheek against the wall, putting an eye to the space between the blanket nails and the window glass. She had a sliver of a view of Kalverstraat and the bakery across the street.

No German.

Isa gripped the candlestick, and moved quietly to the opposite side, peeking around the blanket edge. And there was her Nazi, walking away, square-shouldered, one hand in his pocket.

He had already passed her door.

Her relief moved the heavy cotton.

And then he stopped, glancing at a slip of paper in his hand. Looking up. Across the street. He marched smartly to the empty bookshop on the next corner, a building leaning dangerously to the left, the breeze toying with the pulley rope swinging from its upper gable. He lifted a hand, and Isa watched him knock. Three times. Quick and precise.

He waited, the dry leaves swirling nut-brown and speckle-gold around his sleek, shining boots, the uniform a smear of drab against the warm cinnamon of the house bricks. A woman coming down Kalverstraat crossed to Isa's side to avoid him. He took no notice. He stepped back. Studied the house. Noted the darkness behind the empty windows. Took off his hat and scratched the back of his head. And then the Nazi soldier turned on a heel, and looked directly at Isa.

Her breath sucked in. Pulse skittering, jumping inside her temples, her chest, her wrists, the tips of her fingers against the cold and heavy silver. She didn't know what good a candlestick would do her. The Nazi had a pistol.

The Nazi who knew how to come the back way.

The Nazi who had just walked straight to the false address on her identity card.

The soldier who had sat at Goudstikker's registration desk that morning, saying nothing while she sold a forgery to the Führer. Who'd had eyes the color of tea. Only they were not tea now. They were two holes in a head, black and empty, staring at the space above the door, where a sign still hung, faded and weathered. A sign that read GALLERY DE SMIT.

And the Nazi smiled.

Then he put his hat on his head, his hands in his pockets, and walked away, a brisk clip toward Spui and the bridge over the Singel.

She waited, blinking at a street that should have been bustling, now a study in sunshine, in stillness, an exploration of the tones between brick and gold. She took a step back, and another step, across the wide, wooden floorboards, to the clean wall between the galleries, the wall with no wires. And Isa slid down and sat, knees huddled to her chest, her silver candlestick left on the floor.

Blackmail. That's what his game must be.

Blackmail was quiet—no bringing the Gestapo, no shooting down the doors—and Isa wouldn't be the first Dutch girl it had happened to. Caught hoarding sugar. Caught with a bicycle. Wearing nylons not overpaid for in a German-controlled store. Even the smallest infraction could ensure a girl would do what a soldier wished of her. There were the babies to prove it.

Selling art forgeries to Adolf Hitler was the opposite of an infraction. It was treason.

What Truus had once accused her of, when she'd chosen her father and the gallery over the Resistance.

What Truus would accuse her of now, if she'd seen her walking into Goudstikker's. Isa traced a line along the bricks behind her, squat and square, rubbing a finger between them. Where the mortar was still just a little too soft.

She remembered when Moshe had mixed that mortar, at three o'clock in the morning, ransacking the house for something that could be used as a stain. They'd settled on iodine, and Moshe had tinted the mortar so skillfully, rebuilt the wall so cleverly, that the difference between the old and new was nearly imperceptible.

Moshe had been a talented man, with a biting sense of humor and a flair for the dramatic that had made Isa roll her eyes. They'd sold several of his paintings, mostly to tourists, one to a more serious critic, works he'd slapped down—by his own admission—with haphazard strokes of a brush. But he'd worked all night on the wall, feverish and exacting, tapping the last brick gently into place with the sunrise.

Three days later, and the truck had taken him.

Isa pressed her palm on that last, tapped brick.

Damn the Nazis. Damn them to the most inventive of tortures in Bosch's pit.

And now the soldier who knew what she'd done was looking for her. But the girl he was looking for was named Elsa Groot, wasn't she? She lived in the deserted bookshop across the street. He couldn't know Isa de Smit. Where she was. Who she was.

And if the Nazi couldn't find her, he couldn't blackmail her.

Isa looked down. She had dug her nail into the too-soft mortar, tiny crumbs scattered along the floor. She remembered it wet, heavy and sandy, crusting on her fingertips. She could see the veiled lantern, the long, flickering shadows in a gallery still hung with art. The dust rising as Moshe chiseled, prying away one brick, then another, opening the space inside the wall.

And Isa had rolled her eyes. She'd been fifteen and thought Moshe was being dramatic. She hadn't known then what was to come. She'd complained of how tired she was going to be, all the dusting that would have to be done. She'd worried about what would happen if Papa woke and found Moshe chiseling a hole in their gallery. But Moshe's eyes had been so haunted.

If it is nothing, Isa, then we will laugh, yes? I will joke and you will laugh and I will fix your wall. But if it is not nothing, then you will promise . . .

So much fear, in the hunch of his shoulders, in the corner of his mouth.

Promise not to let them have it. They take our city, they take our country, but they cannot take this. Two hundred and fifty years it has hung on my family's walls. It is Dutch, Isa. It is who we are . . .

And Moshe had unwrapped the painting.

And Isa had seen the hand of the master.

And she had promised. Because it was Dutch. Because it was beautiful. Ultramarine and vermilion. Pure, clear light. A woman with a wineglass just tipping from her fingers, a moment so real Isa had wanted to reach out and catch the glass before it fell. Originally one of a set of three, Moshe had said, made for a wedding gift. A Vermeer that was not currently in Goudstikker's former auction house, being crated for its trip to Germany.

A Vermeer that was here, safely hidden inside her wall.

And Moshe, as it had turned out, was not being dramatic after all.

But he had outsmarted them, and today she had outsmarted them.

And someone else had done it, too, and done it even better. Someone had forged *Woman with a Wine Glass*, and the Nazis did not suspect a thing.

Isa smiled in the shadows of the gallery. Shivered once at the cool touch of the brick.

The Nazis thought they could have everything. They thought they had everything.

They did not have this. They would not have it.

Isa hugged her knees. And then she tilted her chin.

But what if she could make them think they did? What if she could outsmart them again?

What if she could do it one more time? Sell them one more fake and make enough money to give to Truus. What if she used the Nazis' own ignorance—their greed—to trick them into paying for the rescue of the very children they were trying to kill?

The idea was a shudder up her spine. A soldier off a bridge.

Dangerous. Reckless.

Delicious.

And then Isa stiffened. Because a sound had severed the silence of the gallery. Three taps. Knuckles on wood. A sharp and sudden echo.

Someone had just knocked at the gallery's back door.

It could be Truus. Bringing a stroopwafel and a record and a magazine. A Truus who'd suddenly decided that doors might be more convenient than a window.

Isa waited, and the knock came again. Three smart taps.

That was not Truus. She knew it wasn't. She'd seen that rhythm just a few minutes before. On the Groots' derelict door.

And fear, Isa thought, was like a pool of spreading paint, viscous, bile-yellow, oozing sick through her stomach.

She thanked all the gods in all their heavens that her papa was three floors up, in the garret, absorbed by the deficiencies of a Christmas card. He wouldn't hear the door.

Surely, he would not hear the door.

And what would her papa do if confronted by an angry Nazi in his gallery? Would he be insulted? Be insulting? Rise up in the defense of "degenerate" art? Or babble on about Botticelli until they lost patience and shot him?

Isa waited, nails digging painfully into the skin of her knees. For the shout. The splintering of wood. For the bullet that would destroy the old iron lock.

What she heard was three more taps. Louder. Insistent.

She pushed the shoes from her heels, leaving them where they lay beside the useless candlestick, stealing through the gallery and up the straight stairs. Lightly in her stocking feet, across the poppy-scarlet hall, past a square of clean, blank wall, where the Rembrandt had hung, up three narrow steps and into her bedroom.

She could just hear the knocks. Three more. An even dozen.

Her bedroom had been meant for a maid, more than likely, with just enough space for a dresser, a mirror, a chair, and a bed boxed into the wall, hung with fading curtains of raspberry velvet. But at the moment, her room's best feature was the excellent view of the little roof over the porch in the back garden.

Isa dropped to her knees, getting an eye around the edge of her blackout blanket. And there he was, the soldier from the auction house, stepping out from beneath the porch roof. If her window had been open, she could have stretched out an arm and dropped her water jug straight onto the top of his Nazi brown hat.

But her window was not open, and so she watched as he stood, contemplating—her door, the weather, art, she didn't know what a

Nazi thought about—craning her neck to see as he reached down, tilted a flowerpot, and put something underneath it.

The soldier straightened, slid a hand into his pocket, and turned on his heel, a military move. The back gate banged closed, and the hat was on the move again on the other side of the wall, away down the gully to disappear between the buildings.

An edge of creamy paper stuck out from beneath her empty flowerpot.

The lure of a snare.

The bait in a trap.

Damn, damn, damn the Nazis.

Damn this Nazi.

She was not going to be tempted into opening her door.

Isa stood, took the reichsmarks and the fake identity card from her bra and stuffed them both beneath her mattress. She checked the lock on her window. She checked the locks on every window, meticulously, on every floor, latching the leaded glass in the kitchen with wire before double-, triple-checking the bar on the gallery's front door.

She would not think about the flowerpot.

Isa scrubbed the dishes, boiled a potato, and took it up two flights to her father in the garret. He was not painting, to her surprise. He was asleep, nested in pillows and blankets on an old relic of a sofa, his ivory pallor flushed, chest moving deeply up and down. He had a lavender scarf wrapped around his neck, an unworked canvas on the easel beside him. At least he hadn't taken the blackout curtains down. Theodoor de Smit resented a lack of natural light almost as much as he hated a narrow view of art.

She left the potato beside him, went down the stairs and dusted the dining room. Did an inventory of the groceries, their money, and their ration books. She could stretch for three, maybe four days without leaving the house. They would use blankets, she decided, and not the boiler. To save the coal. Maybe until the first snow. She tacked the blackout over the leaded glass in the kitchen, while the saffron sun slid away behind the chimney pots of Amsterdam.

Curfew came down with the sunset. No light and no voices. A deep-set silence in a dead and soulless dark. Nothing like the Kalverstraat of her childhood, with music and the restaurants and the late-night tapping of leather-soled shoes. Laughter and a lady's high heels. It was almost a pleasure to block out the quiet.

Isa pulled her raspberry curtains over the blackouts in her room, switched on the lamp, and put a needle to a record on the phonograph—Johnny & Jones, the most un-Nazi swing she had. The only swing available, with the radios confiscated and the Dutch broadcasting shut down. She sat cross-legged on her rug, sketchbook in her lap, and opened a box of pastels.

A pattern emerged from her fingertips, curving, swirling lines that left a meandering trail across her page. Twisting roots and tangled vines, and all in a cool palette. Pale blue on a soft green. Azure and jade. Ice and mint. And then, in the center, a thick line of scarlet.

Isa nearly dropped the pastel, staring at the mar in her color scheme. How had she picked up the red? It was jarring. Wrong. It hurt something inside her to see it.

Isa closed her eyes, and heard her mother say, *Oh, no, my little imp. There are no mistakes in art.*

She could see Francina in her studio, trailing scarves and wearing a messy smock.

Art is a mistake. One big, beautiful mistake. See, when I draw a line here . . .

And she'd painted a thick brown line straight through the center of her picture, ruining a field of daisies. Isa had gasped.

That felt wrong, didn't it, my goblin? But if we accept the mistake, work with an error rather than rejecting it, if we make it a part of our whole . . .

Francina picked up quick color from her palette, and the scrawl softened. The line elongated. A soft yellow, a pale highlight, and the scrawl grew, and changed, and became a tree in the foreground of her field, old and gnarled. A new focus. Much more interesting than what she'd painted before.

Do you see, darling? Now the mistake is beautiful. It un-becomes . . .

Isa opened her eyes. And picked up the red pastel. A few moments, and a flower had erupted from her vines, big and blooming. Tints of scarlet and flame. A hot, rich vermilion. She studied the icy thrill of her blues and greens. The contrast of her flower.

Isa knew what the flower was, and why she had drawn it. She could feel the heat, opening poisonous red petals in her chest.

She wasn't certain she believed in beauty anymore.

When the last Johnny & Jones ended, needle scratching, Isa heard the bombers. Rumbling, flying high past Amsterdam, the pop and crack of the German flak chasing them across the darkness.

Isa set her drawings aside and boiled water in the kettle, lit the gas under the water heater above the tub, boiled that, and poured it all in, steaming. Then she boiled herself. Scrubbing, scouring, pink and sweating. Trying to rub the spatter of freckles from her nose.

Thinking of Moshe. The empty studio above the kitchen. The room on the floor above the bathroom, where Arondeus had once lived, happy in his own world, writing a book. Remembering Hilde and the soft shock of curling brown hair on her baby's head, a baby so new she was still wrinkled and pink. She thought of the bulge of a foot against a leather bag. A Nazi who had come knocking on her door.

The Nazis. Who had made an ugly world. Who thought they had everything.

The steam rose. And still, something in her shivered.

Isa pulled the plug in the tub and tied a thin, printed robe of Chinese silk around her waist, a leaf pattern of bronze-brown, the last gift from her mother. She took a brush to her bright hair, gone springy in the steam, long with the war and no one to cut it. She opened the door while the last of the bathwater gurgled.

The air in the hall was a slap. A block of chill. Isa looked to her right, at the door of her room, where her rug was, and her velvet curtains. Her warm nook of a bed.

She turned left instead. Quick across the poppy hall, down the straight stairs, through the big gallery, the little gallery, and into the damp dark of the back hall. She stood before the locked door that she had so carefully checked. Listening.

Then she turned the lock, threw open the door, and darted out, fleet in her silk, scooping up the note from beneath the flowerpot, bare toes back in the house with the door locked before she'd let out a breath.

Isa felt her way back up the stairs and into her bedroom. The folded paper was crumpled at one edge, dirty from the flowerpot, thin and lightly lined. Ledger paper. She opened it, and saw the name, Elsa Groot, with the address across Kalverstraat. There were other words, too, in German, written along the printed lines in handwriting worthy of an engraver, a copperplate. Isa could read the word *Rembrandt*, numbers that must be measurements, and *800 reichsmarks*. Her payment, printed beside a neat cut, where a sharp knife had slit the page from the ledger book. And over everything was the lead gray of a hasty pencil, written large and diagonal across the page.

Do not do it again

And those words had been written in Dutch.
Isa smiled. And she shivered. A reckless thrill.
Because what she had decided to do was exactly the opposite.

5

WHEN ISA TOOK down her curtain the next morning, the sky was fire, an infinitesimally slow explosion of coral pinks and liquid gold. She tied up her hair in the light of it, put on a pair of paint-speckled overalls, bare feet on a rug that was a confection of needlepoint, leaves and flowers blended into softness by the footfalls of time. She picked up the drawing she had done the night before, the sketch with the fire-flower in its center, and pinned it to the wall beside her bed. A reminder of her anger. For when the fear came back.

She knew it would come back.

In the kitchen, the light was electric yellow on the marigold paint, on the crazed, cracked blue-and-white tiles that had always so delighted her mother—a bear, a cow, a boy with a fishing pole. When she took down the blackout, the room woke and it glowed. She made the ersatz coffee, cut bread, and boiled another potato. She took the cup and plate across the scarlet-poppy hall to the last door on the left, knocked once, and opened the door.

Her parents' bedroom was grand, with a high ceiling and the same footprint as the big gallery below it. The upper walls were papered in cyan and metallic gold, glass-fronted cabinets built in along one wall, gilt along the edges of the lower wainscoting. A fancy room, almost certainly meant to be a living room, a place for showing off to business partners and friends. But beauty, Francina had said, was more fully appreciated by the De Smits, and impressing others had meant nothing to her at all. So why not spend most of your time in the most beautiful room?

What would her mother have done with this ugly world, Isa wondered, if she'd lived to see it?

The bed, an enormous Louis XIV, was a smooth, unwrinkled sea of satin; the sofa where her father sometimes slept, a pile of cushions and nothing else. Isa balanced the coffee cup on the plate and put her finger into a small hole beneath the gilded trim of the wall beside the wardrobe, tripping the latch. A door swung inward on hidden hinges, papered and wainscoted like the rest of the room—not invisible, just unobtrusive—revealing a set of plain wooden steps on the other side. Isa went up barefoot, two steep flights into the garret, into the smell of oil paints and turpentine.

The blackouts were down, the sun filtered by windows that were opaque with dirt, slanting with the angles of the roof ridge, warming the A-frame of black oak beams. And there was her father, in a puddle of pearly light, awake and on the far side of an easel. His brush whisked, the rustle of quick, broad strokes. The sound of an underlayment going on. Yesterday's potato sat cold and shriveled on the plate. He didn't look up.

Isa walked around the easel. She recognized the canvas, an old one with a neatly repaired patch in the upper left-hand corner, overpainted many times, a piece of detritus that had lived in the storeroom for as long as she could remember. But the layers had been thinned now, scraped away, the surface smoothing to a bluish-white.

Blank.

Expectant.

Isa wondered for the thousandth time what was going to happen when her father ran out of paint. It would have happened already, if Moshe, Hilde, her mother's students hadn't left so much behind. The lack of paint was a looming catastrophe. But for now, the brush moved over the canvas, a soft hand over a scratchy chin.

"I know your mother is dead," her father said.

Isa winced. Swallowed. "Yes, Papa, I know you do."

"And I remember the Germans, too. And what they've done. And if the tax is due, you should have said."

Said, and then what? Her father wouldn't have known how to pay the taxes even before the Nazis came. And he'd never understood how to make money. His father had made money. Francina had been born with money. All Papa had ever had to do was paint.

"It's just that . . ." His brush slowed. "It is so much nicer not to think sometimes, isn't it?"

Yes, Isa thought. It really must be.

How nice for him.

She turned to examine her father. Like a specimen in the zoo. He was thin, the collar of his shirt too large beneath his smock and his lavender scarf, a faint stain of charcoal shadowing each eye. And the garret must have been cold last night. Her feet were freezing. She set the plate and coffee down beside his jar of brushes.

"You should eat, Papa," Isa said.

He didn't answer. He picked up a new brush, and with a sweep of his arm, a streak of cobalt appeared, a shooting star, deep and purpling across the expectant white.

Beautiful.

The tension left Isa's shoulders, a knot undone, and she saw her father's joy sparkle. A sun that hadn't risen in some time.

Sometimes, she wanted to change him. Other times, she wasn't sure that she should.

Isa left her father to his canvas and went to the garret's slatted back wall, a place made for drying linens, now a spot for drying paint. And since most of her father's work never came down once it went up, the back wall was a storage place. A private gallery of copied art. An exhibition of invented masterpieces.

And one of them, Isa thought, just might fool a Nazi.

The majority were too new to fool anyone—her papa hadn't been trying to fool anyone, after all. Some were blocks of vivid color, abstract, "degenerate," like Moshe's had been. Others were too obvious. Leonardo da Vinci's *Mona Lisa*, for instance. That was in the Louvre, or had been, before the Nazis took France. It could be hanging in Hitler's bathroom by now for all Isa knew. But the *Mona Lisa De Smit* was quite good. The style, the pigments, all perfectly authentic. Though even Hermann Goering's oily little agent would likely be aware that Leonardo had not painted his mysterious woman with a wink.

How her mother had laughed.

Isa ran a hand along the edge of the canvas. The weave was too regular, too new, the paint soft when she pushed with a fingernail. It took years, a lifetime, for oil paint to truly dry, centuries for it to harden and crack. Goering's agent wouldn't have missed soft paint on a four-hundred-year-old painting any more than he would have missed the wink. His blackmailing soldier of an assistant certainly wouldn't have. The Rembrandt had been chalk, not paint, but he'd caught something on it just the same.

How had the Vermeer forger managed it? You could reuse an old canvas, like her father was doing. But how could you harden the paint?

Isa moved away from the *Mona Lisa De Smit* to look at her father's Vermeer, a street scene, small and sparse, serenely clear. And with soft paint. She passed a Titian nude, bold, large, and—she was very much afraid—a buxom version of her mother. With soft paint. Then she reached for a piece of thick paper tacked to the drying slats. One of the Dürer watercolors, the pretended childhood attempts, a rose, a hare, a fox, and this one, a bluebell, browned and curling at the edges. Watercolors were not like paint. If kept away from humidity, from the sun—kept inside a book, perhaps—then watercolors could stay the same for half a millennium.

Isa looked over her shoulder. A twilight was taking shape on the canvas, her father living, breathing his paint. She quietly unpinned the four watercolors and stole down the stairs.

She filled the kettle in the kitchen and lit the stove, the gas a sting in her nose, then stacked the four papers a little haphazardly on the table. She restacked them this way and that, adjusting, and with one of the pins that had held the pictures to the slatted wall, Isa began pricking round holes all the way through the stack. Punching, enlarging, creating a meandering row, extending one into a path that ran off the edge. The kettle had long boiled before she was done. She took the water off and put it on again, turning each paper over to painstakingly shave away the ragged bits with a sharpened penknife.

The result was rather credible wormholes, bookworm holes, boring their way through the paper. Showing that these pictures had been stacked together for a very long time, with the added advantage of hiding the original pinholes.

Isa held each drawing over the kettle steam, dampening it, and in a burst of inspiration, she fished the wet coffee grounds from the pot and stained the drawings, the top one—the hare—in particular, working the grounds into her wormholes so the cuts would not look clean when examined through a loupe. She wiped the paper scraps and coffee from the old, scarred table and laid the drawings side by side.

Scrutinizing.

Critical.

They looked good. Old. So obviously stored together, lost for years inside a heavy book. The palette was pale but lovely, the drawings imperfect and yet thrumming with movement. With energy. The bluebell looked as if it were twisting in the breeze. They might have tricked her, had someone brought them to the gallery. And yet, Isa thought, they were small. Simple. Not at all showy. And Dürer had not been as much in favor before the war. These drawings were not going to be the payday the Rembrandt had been. They might be barely worth the risk.

But she would risk it. They were what she had and she would use them. Because of Hilde's baby. And a tiny kick in a brown leather bag.

Because the Nazis deserved it.

And there it came. The spilling fear, yellow bile creeping out from some pit inside her stomach. She almost welcomed it. She'd known it was there, lurking. Because there was a Nazi soldier who knew what she'd done. A blackmailer who knew where she lived. Who had told her not to do it again.

But he was also a Nazi who did not know how to play the game.

He'd cut the proof of her forgery right out of the book. And even if he did decide to tell what he knew, now he would have to explain why he knew and had said nothing. Why the entry for the Rembrandt was missing. Giving her up to his superiors was going to cost him something now, and he'd let her know it. That was a loss of power. It was bad negotiation. It was bad business. But he could still hurt her. And her father.

Her father, who was a bitter, angry lamb in the wolf pack of the world. Who had stacks of pretend masterpieces piled up in their garret. And what would the Gestapo make of that, if someone suggested that the Gallery De Smit would be a good place to search? If her father took down the blackouts and left on the lights like he'd left on the stove?

And she had a fake identity card. With a false address.

The identity card had been such a stroke of luck. Elsa Groot had been her age, a student at the Lyceum, a nice girl, with big hands and an unfortunate bout of measles when she was ten. Not a friend, and not an enemy, either. But her parents had been careful, not the sort to let their daughter associate with the comings and goings of the garret. Isa didn't know exactly how they had run afoul of the National Socialists, unless their books were more radical than they were. But one morning, the bookshop had been closed, the family disappeared, and there was Elsa's identity card, damp with some rubbish on the edge of the street.

It hadn't taken much to remove the staples. To put Isa's photograph in place of Elsa's. The official Nazi stamp—a circle of ink on both the picture and the paper—had nearly aligned, the judicious use of a fountain pen correcting any little discrepancies.

It was enough to land her in prison even without the Dürers. Or the Rembrandt.

The Vermeer inside her walls.

Isa gathered her damp, stained watercolors, lining up her wormholes precisely, and put the whole stack between an art dictionary and a French cookbook on top of the yellow-painted cabinet, a heavy ceramic bowl on top of that. Where they would press. Then she went to her tiny bedroom and pulled the false identity card from underneath her mattress and her real one from the dresser drawer. She sat in her chair and picked carefully at the staples, switching the photographs to their proper places, aligning the ink stamps. Then she stood.

Thinking.

Surveying.

She took down her mirror, found a spot for Elsa's card between the wood backing and the glass, and hung it up again. Then she went to the opulent living-room-cum-bedroom-cum-half-deserted-shrine-to–Francina de Smit, and stood, bare toes sunk deep into the blue rug.

Thinking.

Considering.

Dusty perfume bottles still lined the dresser. The enormous scroll-worked wardrobe, a counterpart to the French bed, had the sleeve of an evening gown peeking out from the half-closed door. The black leather case, which had contained her mother's medicine vials, lay on a teetering stack of catalogues, the top one from the Surrealism Exhibition of 1938.

She would never forget that exhibition. Not just because of a glamorous train ride and the excitement of Paris, but because, rather than leaving her to the enjoyable yet often indifferent care of an artist living in one of their guest rooms, her parents had taken her with them. And the exhibition had not just been pictures. There were rows of mannequins, dressed in wire, or with a birdcage for a head. A car that rained on the inside. A room where the paintings and the gyrations of a burlesque dancer could be viewed only by flashlight.

Her father had been fascinated, her mother intrigued, Isa a little shell-shocked. She'd been twelve, a young, fanciful twelve, shaken not by the people or the art—she'd spent her formative years in the garret, after all—but by the idea that the bizarre, sometimes disturbing landscapes of melting buildings or misshapen heads were what the artist really saw. Were what other people could really see.

It is only a daydream, her mother had whispered, hand in hers, eyes on the art. She had been much, much too thin. *Imagination, Sofonisba, is both dark and light. A door within a door within a door. And no matter how dark or how light, there is still, always, another door . . .*

A door within a door.

Isa stood in the empty room.

Imagining.

And an hour later, a blaze of ember hair stuck sweaty to her forehead, Isa had emptied the wardrobe—clothes, dresses, boxes, ties, and shoes, all piled on the unused bed—shoving a thick blanket underneath each side. And then she'd pushed, pulled, sliding the wardrobe away from the wall, and once she'd created enough space, she'd taken a hammer to the back of it, prying off the wooden planks.

The wardrobe was open in the back now, unbraced and a little rickety. But when she pushed it again, slowly, carefully creeping it back across the floor on its blanket slide, it rested flat against the wall. Innocent and unassuming. Right over the door that led to the garret.

A door within a door.

Isa pulled down the folding stair and stepped inside the wardrobe. She could see the shimmery blue that papered the garret door, but it only looked like the wall, the little finger hole for tripping the latch now at the level of her knees. Getting through would require some bending, a hop down or a scramble up. Nothing worse.

It was like the garret had never been.

She stepped out, tugging until the blankets came out from underneath the wardrobe, using them to wipe up the exposed square of dust and fluff where it had once stood. She rolled the rugs back into place and was hanging up the clothes, so many—Papa had always had a penchant for clothes—when she heard a click. And a rustle. Isa spun on a bare heel.

Her father's face was sticking out from between a rhinestone dress and a housecoat. Blinking owlishly.

"Did I come the wrong way?" he inquired.

Isa laughed.

She told her father a story about German raids, about confiscation and burning. It wasn't even a story. But he needed no reminding. No explanations. He just ran back to his canvas as if the Nazis were hot on his heels, instructing Isa to shut the wardrobe when she was done.

The strange had never much fazed Theodoor de Smit. It was normalcy that was difficult.

Isa finished the clothes, went back to the kitchen, and chopped half an onion. She'd fed her father and not herself, and she was famished. Aching, but satisfied. The sun was passing her by, arcing over the roof peaks, slanting onto the sienna bricks of the mysterious convent wall. She slid the onions into a pot along with a beef bone she'd been saving and her father's uneaten potato, pocketed in the garret. She would make soup. Soup was her specialty. Imprecise, versatile, and difficult to ruin. She put water in the pot, a flame in the stove, hesitated, and decided to make a raid on the cellar.

She went down the spiral stairs, the triangular treads groaning beneath her bare feet, past the little gallery, down and around again and into a long, low room a full level below the street. The cellar had been a kitchen once, with an ancient hearth, bread oven, and a decrepit old box bed. Now it housed the boiler Isa was refusing to fire, and a washing machine with a crank that threatened to break her shoulder. It was a dark place, dank. The kind of room that felt dirty even when it was clean. A room she'd avoided as a child, because of its possible proximity to Sister Cornelia's gutter. And Moshe had decided to make it his place, for when he was too busy making art to go home.

Isa had never understood it. They'd had guest rooms, a big one on the floor above her bedroom that often resembled a bohemian dormitory. But Moshe had been a Communist—a Communist with priceless art on his family walls—and he liked the drama, Isa thought, of privation. He'd also preferred men and everybody knew it, like Arondeus, and he was Jewish, so the trucks had come for him first. Isa had packed his things, for when he came back.

She hadn't known then that people didn't come back from the trucks.

The stone floor was unpleasant. Icy. Isa hurried. There were only a few cans left, but she still couldn't bring herself to store them in the kitchen. This way, each time she took one, it felt like Moshe was giving it to her.

She peered at the dwindling labels in the dark, chose a can of carrots—she thought it was carrots—and went up the stairs slowly, silently thanking Moshe. And thinking of soup, and Sister Cornelia, and whether that little space in the unfinished wall of the storage room in her mother's studio, the one that led through to her father's garret, didn't need boarding up.

And so Isa was a swimmer coming up the stairs, deep in the water of her thoughts, rising slow to the surface. Slow to see. Slow seconds for her head to turn. For her gaze to come around. For the figure standing in the open space between the big and the little gallery to come fully into focus. A silhouette, square-shouldered and with a hat. A shadow in brown.

Nazi brown.

"While fighting for victory, the German soldier will observe the rules of chivalrous warfare. Cruelties and senseless destruction are below his standard."
—Commandment One, from *The Ten Commandments of the German Soldier*

6

ISA STOPPED FOUR stairs from the gallery, carrots in one hand, the other on the rail. The Nazi shape took a step, deeper into the dimness of the little gallery.

"Fräulein . . ." he said. "Or 'Miss,' I should say. Miss de Smit, yes?"

Isa blinked, unmoving. He took off the hat.

"I believe that we need to speak. Would you agree?"

And the moment stretched. She couldn't see his eyes this time. He had become one of the gallery's shadows. But there was the outline of a pistol in the holster at his side. And then Isa broke the surface of her deep water and drew in a breath.

"Get out," she said.

He shook his neat head, hat in hand.

"How did you get in here?"

"There was a key," he said, "underneath your flowerpot."

Isa felt her lips part. That would have been her mother's doing. For Moshe. Or the artists. A remnant of a happier time. And she'd been locking all the windows and sleeping soundly in her bed.

The yellow fear was with her now. Spilling. Obliterating. Sickening.

"You will excuse me, please, for letting myself in, but I must speak with you, and you do not answer your door."

"Get out," she said again.

He took another step into the little gallery and turned his back to her, facing the blanketed window. Isa could see through the open space into the big gallery, where the last of the daylight glowed through the blankets. Her two shoes, scattered. The heavy silver candlestick where she'd left it on the floor. The Nazi put his hands behind his back. He was still holding the hat.

"You will not remember me, of course."

Isa wondered if he'd lost his mind. He was the soldier from the auction-sale, holding her forged Rembrandt, leaving notes at her door. And then she realized this was not what he'd meant. She thought again of the square shoulders, the tea-in-porcelain eyes that had gone so hard. Excellent Dutch with a German accent, though the accent was softer, a little rounder. She couldn't place him.

"I remember you well," he said, talking to the nothing of the window, "though you were a child the last time I came here. My name is Michel Lange."

He pronounced it like a German, the last syllable taking on the sound of a Nazi salute. And Isa's mind churned, spun, sifted, and latched on to the memory of a man. A dealer. An Austrian. Herr Lange. Standing ten feet from where she stood now, in a vibrant gallery full of color and light, purchasing one of Hilde's battlefield scenes with a son at his side. A gangly, spider-legged son, three, maybe four years older than her, at the height of an awkwardness and embarrassment that the child Isa had never yet considered.

Thirty pounds, a German uniform, and the ability to shave had made a difference.

Isa glanced through the doorway. She could just see the gleam of the candlestick.

"What do you want?" she asked.

She saw the slight curve in his back, the subtle droop of the shoulders. If she had seen that outline preserved in a painting, Isa would have titled it *Disappointment*. But only for the space of a breath. Michel Lange straightened, did the military turn, facing her, hat on his head, hands behind his back. She thought she caught a smile in the gallery's gloom, a knowing smile, and now Isa would have named his portrait *The Blackmailer*.

"Miss de Smit," he said, "you are a forger."

Isa waited. Listening.

"But I think, perhaps, that we could come to an arrangement. An even trade."

She only just controlled her wince.

"I will say nothing about your crime," he said, voice cool, "and in return, you can give me . . . something that I would want."

He really was terrible at this. He'd already given her the ledger entry. But now he was going to make her ask, and then he would have to say his answer aloud. In her gallery. In her home.

It was ugly, this game.

She thought of Herr Lange buying Hilde's painting. Of Hilde, almost exactly where Herr Lange's son stood now—handing Isa her baby. And the little girl had been so new and sweet, soft in Isa's arms. Hildy, named for her mother, with curling hair the color of an autumn field, sleeping while Hilde hurried, panicked, gathering what she could. Trying to escape.

It hadn't worked.

And the yellow-sick fear began to smoke and smolder. Burning in the blaze of vermilion that bloomed in her chest. The opposite of the shiver.

Reckless.

"And what is it, exactly, that you want, Soldier Lange?" Isa asked. Crisp.

He waited to answer. Embarrassed, Isa thought. As he should be. Maybe the Nazis hadn't stripped away all of his conscience. Though she was sure they would manage it, in the end.

The candlestick was an answer. The heavy silver in her hand, one of those unsuspecting military turns, and the problem in front of her could go away.

A forger and a murderer.

Maybe the Nazis had taken her conscience, too.

"What I want," he said finally, voice dropping low. "What I would very much like is . . . a place to hide."

Isa took her eyes from the doorway and put them on the Nazi in front of her. "What do you mean?"

"I mean a place to hide."

"From whom?" Isa asked.

"From the German army, of course," he said, irritated. "Who else would I hide from?" He straightened, hands tight behind his back. "What I would like, Miss de Smit, is to desert my post."

This was not what she had expected.

"I plan to disappear, and very simply, I will need a place to disappear to. And you are going to give it to me."

Isa climbed the final steps and walked into the little gallery. They stood, two shadows facing, one hot and one cold in the thickening dim. Even barefoot, hair tied up, and with a can of carrots in her hand, Isa thought she might be better at this game. If what this Nazi said was true, he wasn't going to give her up. If he did, he'd have nowhere to go.

He needed her.

He needed her so much, Isa wondered what she could get him to do for her.

"Are you really here alone?" she asked.

"It would endanger my life to speak of this to anyone else."

"And what about . . . Rembrandt. Who else knows?"

"If anyone else knew, you would have been arrested."

"And what makes you think that this would be a safe place to disappear to?"

"There are no safe places," he replied.

They both looked up at a muffled thud, the faint creak and pop of footsteps moving high in the house above them. Like someone had just found their way out of a wardrobe.

"Are your parents here?" he asked.

"My father is. My mother is dead."

He paused. "I did not know that. I am sorry." Another pause. The footsteps had stilled. "Your father, I think, would not begrudge me . . ."

"My father," she said evenly, "would happily throttle you. No matter who you think you . . ."

"Stop it." The force that burst from the neat, cold exterior took Isa by surprise. "This is not . . ." His voice rose. "I am not . . ."

He didn't finish. For a strange moment, Isa thought he might spit on the floor. But the moment passed, and his balled fists relaxed, hands returning to clasp together behind his back.

"It does not matter," he said. "I will need shelter, until I can arrange transportation. Two weeks at most. And I will need clothes. Civilian clothes. So you see, it is a business transaction, nothing personal. A clear exchange, for my silence."

He was so bad at this.

Or, it was all a lie, and he was very good at this indeed, and the Gestapo were about to break down her door.

But Isa was having trouble equating the skinny teenager who couldn't string two words together with the kind of blatant liar it would take to pull off this kind of entrapment. And why entrap her, when he could just arrest her?

He needed her.

He was still the enemy.

But perhaps she could use him. A shiver made its way up her spine.

And then a bell rang, a sharp, friendly clang. Isa's gaze shot toward the passage. Footsteps moved across the ceiling. She looked at the shadow of the Nazi.

"Someone's at the back door," she whispered.

"You have a bell?"

It was a fair point. This was someone who knew the existence of the little bell chain, slightly hidden in the porch roof ever since the pull handle had come off. The outline of Michel's fists had balled up again. Tense.

"Were you expecting someone?"

Isa shook her head. "Were you followed?"

"I am certain I was not. I cannot be seen."

No, he could not. And the only other way out of the Gallery De Smit was directly onto Kalverstraat. The bell clanged again. Requesting.

"Go down the stairs and wait," Isa said. "Don't touch anything. Don't move. Don't make a noise until they're gone."

He was already moving toward the spiral stairs. He hesitated. "I must be back at my post by seven."

Isa waved her arms.

"Seven o'clock," he hissed. "If I am not, then I might as well stay, Fräulein."

Damn this Nazi. Damn, damn, damn him.

She waved again, and his brown hat disappeared below the level of the floor.

She had just sent a Nazi into Moshe's room. Something in her stomach rejected the idea. Isa put an arm around her middle, walking quickly through the gallery to the back hall. She could hear soft voices beyond the door.

Maybe they had come to arrest her. Maybe her Nazi was that good after all.

The bell rang again. Harsh. Insisting.

"Who is it?" Isa called. She stood to one side, in case they shot through the door.

"Isa? Open up."

Isa let out her breath, thinking. Then she turned the lock and cracked the door open just enough to allow herself a view of the other side.

"Willem," she said.

7

WILLEM CROWDED CLOSE, his powerful frame filling the space Isa had opened. He was tense, jumpy, unshaven, a hand up on his side of the door, pushing.

"Let us in, Isaatje," said Truus, peeking over his shoulder.

Isa stepped back and they came through together, quick. Willem shut the door and turned the lock himself, which Isa did not like.

She didn't like any of it. Her pulse jumped. Revved. Faster.

Faster.

"You locked the window," said Truus. Accusingly.

"You said tomorrow," Isa replied, accusatory. She'd forgotten about the wire on the kitchen latch. Truus would think that had been meant for her.

"She ought to be locked in," Willem said. "That's safe. Hello, Isa."

Willem was dressed like a farmer, arms and chest thrust into a ragged jacket that must have belonged to a suit thirty years ago and seemed to have been stored in a barn ever since. It was a smart disguise—farmers were exempt from forced labor—but also unfortunate, because Willem didn't look like a farmer. He looked like a cinema star, and he sounded like the son of a lawyer turned politician, which he was.

If Willem were a canvas, Isa wondered, and she scraped him

down, taking off all the painted layers, what color would she find underneath? She didn't know. And maybe that's what bothered her. Willem was always in disguise.

It wasn't fair of her. Willem's father was somewhere in a prison camp. Willem had left university rather than sign an oath of loyalty to Hitler. Willem was fighting on the side of the angels.

While she had a devil in her cellar.

"Why are you here?" Isa asked.

Truus rolled her eyes. "The friendliness warms the heart. Can we talk?"

Isa opened her mouth and shut it again. She squeezed her arm around her stomach.

"What have you got there?" Willem asked, nodding at her other hand.

Isa looked down. She was holding a can of carrots. "Oh," she said. "Soup. I was making soup. Come up?"

She led the way down the hall and into the gloom of the little gallery and the spiral stairs. They started up, the way below them a round, black hole. Isa could feel the eyes. She thought she could hear the breath. She knew she couldn't.

Her pulse sped faster. Faster.

She put the can on the kitchen counter, watching Willem arrange himself at the table. Watching him ignore the far side of the room, where there was a sofa and a desk overflowing with bills and their disconnected phone. Where there was a rather large nude hung on the wall—Francina again—done in the style of Degas, looking wistful with curlers in her hair. Truus examined the wire Isa had looped and made herself comfortable on the window seat. The soup had boiled dangerously low, so Isa added water. The beauty of soup.

Silence smothered the kitchen.

"Coffee?" Isa asked.

Truus would have accepted, but Willem shook his head, polite in the extreme, and Truus followed his lead. Isa turned her attention to the can opener.

"Isa, we've come to talk about the money," Truus said, "and . . . what you saw."

She'd assumed they had. It was difficult to pay attention, she was listening so hard for sounds from her father above or the Nazi below.

What might happen if everyone in her house happened to find themselves in the same room did not bear thinking about.

Isa worked the can opener, slowly slicing away a disc of metal.

"Willem is . . . not in agreement," Truus went on, "about asking for your help."

Isa turned. "You know I wouldn't speak of it."

"Of course not," Willem replied. "Or you wouldn't mean to. It's just that . . . Truus knows the rules. We don't talk about this. It was reckless."

Isa saw the look of surprise cross her friend's face, and then a forehead wrinkle of irritation. This was not, perhaps, the direction that Truus had thought Willem's argument would take.

Isa's gaze darted back and forth between the two of them. Tall, fair, blond-haired and blue-eyed. Healthy and athletic. A couple that would have warmed Hitler's heart, had they not been so zealously trying to destroy everything he believed in.

A door shut somewhere in the house. From above. Not below.

"What Willem means to say," Truus said pointedly, lowering her voice, "is that it's your father. He's concerned that your father could be . . . that it might be hard for him to . . ."

"Keep his mouth shut?" Isa supplied.

"You know I didn't mean it like that."

Isa met Truus's eyes. She knew she hadn't. And Truus knew that she knew it. Isa turned back to the stove and dumped the carrots in the soup. Stirring.

"I don't mean any disrespect to your father," Willem said. "But a wrong word and people will die."

Stirring. Stirring. She felt the warm, soft head of Hilde's baby against her cheek.

"Children will die," Willem said, "and for no other reason than that they were born. We can't afford . . . recklessness."

She wished he hadn't ended that thought with a dig at Truus. She wished he hadn't used that word. She turned from the stove.

"I haven't spoken to my father about any of this. He has no love for the Germans, but . . ." She searched for words. "He lives in his own world. He hasn't left this house since my mother died. I didn't even tell him the leasehold was due. And even if I had told him something, Willem, he has no one to repeat it to but me."

Truus looked at the back of Willem's handsome head, triumphant. It must have been close to the argument she'd already put to him. Willem drummed his fingers on the table.

"You should step away, Isa," Willem said. "For your sake, and everybody else's."

She turned back to the stove. Stirring. Hot.

"And what about the children?" Truus countered. "You're not asking her to step away for their sake, are you? And if she died saving just one, isn't that worth it?"

"I don't want . . ."

"Because that's exactly what you said to me, Willem. That it would be worth it."

Another steaming silence.

Willem ran a hand through his hair. "She's a babe in the woods, Truus."

"She's the same age as me. And so was I."

They were talking like an old married couple with their child in the room. Isa slammed a lid on the pot.

"I think I should be the one to decide what I risk." She was saying it to both of them, but she was looking at Truus. And Truus met her gaze, worried. Between the two of them, Isa was the one who could be reckless, and they both knew it.

She was about to do something reckless now.

"How many?" Isa asked. "How many can you save?"

"We have places for eleven more, but not the money," Truus replied.

Willem shook his head, resigned.

Eleven more. She didn't want to ask out of how many others.

"And you need fifteen hundred guilders?"

"More like two thousand," said Willem.

That was triple, maybe quadruple what the Dürers might bring. She would need something sought after. Something more showy like the Rembrandt. Or the Vermeer.

Isa's mind jumped up two floors, to her father's Vermeer in the garret, then dropped down to the gallery and the Vermeer behind the bricks, then down again, to the blackmailer in the cellar. She would need to make a bigger sale than she'd thought. Much bigger. But maybe it could be done.

With the right help.

Isa's gaze cut to the clock. Twenty-five minutes after six.

"You need to understand what you're risking," Willem said. "It's not just the Nazis, or even the Dutch police. There are collaborators out there who would trade you for a ration book. Who will pretend to be your friend and turn you in. Nazis who will pretend to be your friend. They're trying to catch us, all the time. And it is more than a jail cell, Isa. They don't want one of us, they want us all. If you are caught, they will make you talk, like they made . . ."

Willem stopped, mouth in a line. His fist clenched open and shut on the table.

And then the kitchen door burst open.

Isa jumped. Willem stood, knocking back his chair. Truus sat frozen on the window seat.

"Hello," said Theodoor de Smit. "Hello, again!"

He aimed a brilliant smile at Truus, coming smoothly around the table to reach for her hand. She slid off the cushion and let him kiss it. He was bright, buzzing, humming like the electricity in the bulb above their heads, shining in his gold satin smoking jacket and mismatched slippers. A good day with the paint, Isa thought. Willem set his chair upright.

"Papa," Isa said. "This is Willem van Bergen. He is a . . . friend of Truus."

"Happy, sir," her father said, "so very happy." He put out a hand, and Willem shook it, solemn.

"Please sit. Did my daughter give you any wine? But you're staying to dinner, of course . . ." As if Isa was just putting the finishing touches on the first course. "Tell me, young man, I am so curious. Tell me your thoughts on Botticelli . . ."

Her father crossed his long legs and lit a cigarette. Where had he gotten a cigarette?

"Which do you prefer," he asked, adjusting his purple scarf, "the mythical or the religious works? Personally, I prefer the eccentricity of the religious . . ."

Willem, fluent in all conversations legal and political, was not,

Isa could see, familiar with his opinions on Botticelli. She caught Truus's eye, and they shared a smile of amusement. Then Isa lowered her voice.

"Stay," she said. "I've got enough." Before Truus could even nod, Isa said, "Papa, why don't you take Willem up to the sitting room, where you can be comfortable?"

Theodoor immediately stood, sweeping one golden arm in a grand gesture toward the door, not bothering to slow his thoughts on *The Birth of Venus*. Isa turned back to Truus.

"I'll get another can. To stretch the pot. Keep an eye on them, won't you?"

And Isa flitted down the spiral stairs, leaving her father's voice and the smell of soup above her. Down past the gallery, into the damp, into the quiet, where the air was a paint pot of ivory black.

"Where are you?" Isa whispered.

A match struck, and there was her Nazi. She could see his features now, the brown eyes weirdly amber, clashing, stark in Caravaggio light.

"I must go," the devil whispered. "Miss de Smit, do we have an agreement?"

She walked straight to him, looking him in the eye. Reckless. "We have an agreement. On one condition. Bring me the name of the person who sold the Vermeer. Not the agent. The owner."

"But . . ."

"Bring me the name and we have an understanding."

Only there would be more to their understanding. Much more. Michel Lange the Nazi soldier was going to help her sell a forgery. But he didn't have to know that. Not yet.

Worth the risk. That's what Truus had said.

The worried furrow in the forehead of her Nazi turned to pain.

He dropped the match and they were alone in the paint-pot dark.

"Do we have an understanding?"

"All right. Yes," he hissed. "Yes."

"And the address."

"Yes. But I must go."

"You can be seen from the back windows," Isa whispered. "Give me two minutes, and then I will keep them away for five. It's the best I can do."

He moved toward the stairs, but Isa felt for the shelf in the dark, grabbed a can, and brushed ahead of him. She took a step up and turned, blocking his way. She could smell the starch in his uniform.

"Give me my key," Isa said.

And Michel Lange slipped back, soft and quick as an alley cat. She could almost hear the smile in the dark when he said, "No."

Damn this Nazi. Damn him to the seventh level of Dante's hell.

Isa turned and hurried up the spiral, careening through the gallery, when she looked up and stopped, a hand leaping up to her chest. Truus was halfway down the curve from the kitchen.

"You startled me," Isa said. Her laugh was a little shaky. Unconvincing.

"You were gone a long time, fetching a can."

"The bulb is out. I didn't think to take a light." She held up the can. "Moshe's."

"Ah."

They stood in another awkward silence. The kind of silence that now seemed to define their friendship so much more than the talkative nights of the past. Isa's pulse was revving. Skittering.

How she wished there did not have to be lies between them.

She followed Truus back up into the kitchen, where the room was steamy, homey with a bubbling pot. Where her father and Willem had not gone up to the sitting room.

"Oh, no, young man," her father was saying, waving the end of his cigarette. "Beauty is not a thing one sees. Beauty is a thing to be felt . . ."

Willem sat listening, stoic. A little stunned. He had his back to the leaded glass window, now clouded with the room's steam. Michel Lange would get his moment.

Truus was watching her. Watching what she watched. Isa looked back.

Reckless.

"Could I talk to you for a minute?" Isa asked.

Truus shrugged, following her out the kitchen door, down a step, and into the dining room. Isa turned the switch on the lamp and the oak-paneled room shone. Honey highlights in burnt umber. She lowered her voice against her father's chatter.

"I didn't want to say, because of Willem, but . . . I already had that conversation. With someone. About the money."

Truus widened her lovely blue eyes. "What did they say?"

"Wait here. I'll show you . . ."

"No, that's all right," Truus said, "I can come with you."

Isa bit her lip, and let Truus follow her into the poppy hall, around the corner, and into her bedroom. She still had the can. Isa left it on her chair and walked casually across the room, glancing once around the blackout. There was a Nazi out there, lifting the latch of her gate in the sunset. She pulled her tassel curtains closed.

Truus had an unhappy crease in the corner of her mouth. "Why did you lock the window, Isa? Really?"

Isa bent down to pick up her scattered drawings. "Because I heard a noise last night. It's a big place and I was frightened." Her story should have a ring of truth, because truth is what it mostly was. With omissions. "I was worried," Isa said, "because I had this in the house."

She left her sketches on the bed, reached beneath the mattress, and pulled out the stack of reichsmarks.

"They said yes. They don't know your name or Willem's. So here." She placed the tax money on Truus's startled palm. "That's eight hundred. How many can you get out with this?"

Truus stared. "How many guilders is this worth?"

"About eleven hundred."

"It's one fifty for the bribe, so five children, I think. With a little extra."

"All right. I'll ask about the rest."

"You think there could be more?"

Isa nodded.

"How much more?"

"Enough for all of them," Isa said. "All eleven, if you still have the places."

Truus nodded, still gazing at the money. Then she went to Isa and put her arms around her neck. "Thank you," she whispered.

Isa hugged her back, surprised at the hot, sudden tears that sprang into her eyes.

This was a gamble. A deal with the devil. If she lost now, she would lose absolutely everything.

It was worth the risk.

Truus stepped back, wiping her eyes. "There's a girl," she said, tucking the money away into her blouse, "working for the Resistance. No one knows her name, but everyone talks about her, because she's fearless. Deadly, they say. The Nazis are terrified of her. Everyone just calls her 'the girl with red hair.'"

Isa watched Truus fiddling with the record she'd left on the dresser. "Wait." Isa touched a lock of hair that was stuck to her forehead. "You don't think . . . You know it's not me?"

Truus chuckled. "No, I suppose it isn't." Then she picked up the can on the chair. "You're putting beets in the soup?"

Isa looked at the label and closed her eyes. "See? Deadly."

Truus laughed, a real laugh, and they walked back together to the kitchen, where Willem and her father had still not gone to the sitting room, her papa gesturing wildly, expounding on the misunderstood nature of the Expressionists. Where the air smelled of soup and the back gully. Where the leaded glass window was thrown open to the sunset, Willem leaning back on the window seat, elbows on the sill. Studying her.

"Hope you don't mind, Isa," he said. "Getting a little warm in here, wasn't it?"

Isa kept her smile and went to the painted cabinet for plates and bowls, asking Truus to go find her some spoons. Her forged Dürers sat pressing beneath the cookbook above her head. And when she glanced past Willem, she could just see her garden gate through the open window. A gate that was now open, unlatched, and swinging free.

8

ISA LOCKED HER bedroom door that night, propping the back of her chair beneath the latch. Because a Nazi had a key to her house. Had walked into her house.

Because the Resistance might know that a Nazi had walked into her house.

The lock didn't help. And there was noise from the garret. Faint scrapes and thumps she thought were her father's stool, thuds that sounded like he was rearranging the furniture. She'd had to put up the blackouts, which he hadn't liked, mood plummeting with the speed of a falling bomb. And now came the quick squeak and squeal of manic footsteps, back and forth, back and forth, creaking two floors up through the beams. Sleep was an absent friend. So Isa pulled back her bed curtains. Climbed out from her box with the quilt around her shoulders, folded herself onto the rug, and picked up her sketchbook.

Another pattern came out of her pastels—lavenders and violets, purple and amethyst—hard sharp lines and narrow angles, making unexpected shapes, unexpected shades. A maze with no discernible path.

She sketched while the garret floor groaned, wondering what Willem had noticed. What he had seen. He'd given no sign, just eaten soup while her father talked. Watching her, closely, slipping away with Truus before the long dark of curfew.

Isa straightened a line with a contrast of burgundy and magenta. Thinking of school. And Willem. When Willem turned in Joop Jansen for plagiarism, for copying an essay from a book. When the essay was part of his exam. When Joop had been away in Belgium for his father's funeral.

Ruthless. Ruthless when he was in the right.

Willem would not think making deals with a Nazi was in the right.

Isa's hand moved, transferring color from pastel to page.

And what should it matter to her if Michel Lange now regretted his decision to enlist? He was an occupier. An invader. A thief of Holland's art. He could even be a murderer. And he was a bad black-mailer. It made no difference if she could remember a time when he'd been awkward, shy and unsure. Even Hitler must have been fourteen. Michel Lange deserved to get blackmailed, didn't he?

Wasn't that what happened in an ugly, ugly world?

She deepened her line with a hint of aubergine.

If Michel wanted a place to hide, he could help her facilitate a sale, a real sale, not the pretend auction bargain hunt at Goudstikker's. A sale that would bring enough money to save the children. All she needed was a forgery. A good one. And she would have that, hope-fully, just as soon as Michel brought her the name of the forger. Just as soon as she learned how to harden the paint on her father's Vermeer.

Isa looked down. She'd filled the page. A riot of rich color.

And purple, Isa thought, was a shade neither red nor blue. It wasn't angry or sad, impulsive or prudent.

Purple, Isa decided, was the color of uncertainty.

She tore out the drawing neatly, tossed it on the floor, and started again. Gradients and axis, this time. A violet geometry.

And what if she did well with the sale, very well? What if there was enough money to restart the gallery? Other galleries were managing, but they were less discerning in their work, less fussy with their clientele, selling standard portraits and landscapes to the Germans. The Gallery De Smit had supported rising artists, new work, catering to dealers and tourists.

Could there ever be tourists again, under a Nazi regime?

Would the Dutch have money one day, enough to buy art?

The illegal newspapers that found their way into everywhere said the war wasn't going as well as the Germans would like. That they'd lost Stalingrad. That Mussolini had been arrested, the Fascist government of Italy fallen. If Truus and Willem and the Resistance had their way, Germany would be driven out of the Netherlands.

A future without National Socialists or the Nazis was difficult to imagine.

What would such a world even look like? Isa knew one way it wouldn't look, and that was the way it had looked before. The world was marred. Discolored.

And these mistakes, she thought, might be too big to un-become.

And when Isa looked up again, she realized the garret had gone still. That it had been still for a long time. That the city was waking, begrudgingly.

She got to her feet in a litter of sketches, stiff, aching, cold to her bones, her fingers every shade of purple. Her father she found on his pillow-strewn sofa in the blue room, sleeping so heavily a shake of his shoulder didn't disturb. Isa threw a quilt over him, drew back the blue-and-gold curtains and pulled down the blanket, to let in the heat of the sun.

A thin sheen of frost was on the window glass, a diamond sparkle already melting where the light shone, and Isa watched four German soldiers saunter together down Kalverstraat, eyeing the gallery's blanketed windows. Then she watched them turn, come back, and eye the windows again.

She got her sketchbook and brought it to the window, settling to one side on the cold radiator, highlighting the shapes of her maze with thistle and mauve. Watching the street. A man wandered by in wooden shoes and ragged pants, a woman with a shopping bag and a kerchief in a bold pattern, green and gold. A kerchief, Isa thought, that she had seen before.

She added a new path to her maze. Grape with tints of mulberry.

Her father slept the day away. Isa ate the rest of the soup, prowling the windows of the gallery like a lion walking the boundaries of its cage. The sun lowered, and she went to do the blackouts, tacking the cloth back up over her bedroom and the kitchen, the blue bedroom, climbing through the wardrobe and up the stairs, in case her father had taken the garret curtains down again.

He had taken them down. Probably trying to open a window. The air in the garret was vaguely unpleasant, like an unused classroom at the Lyceum, and at the same time overly sweet, as if he'd tried to combat the staleness by spraying her mother's perfume. The storage room was open, its contents scattered, the sink and the brushes left in a mess. And when she looked at her father's easel, there was no twilit snow. Four figures had been blocked out on the repaired canvas. Large, in darker tones than he usually liked to work with, on a background that was surely Van Dyck brown.

Old colors, Isa thought. Renaissance.

She was surprised. And then she tilted her head, and was less so. A banal Christmas card had been unusual subject matter to give Theodoor de Smit a case of paint-fever. She thought he'd been hot with it, up here bumping and painting himself into an exhaustion.

But this piece was barely started. What had he been doing last night, to be so exhausted?

Or was it just nicer not to think?

Taking down those curtains with a light on was like sending up a flare. Firing up a road sign in the night sky. Offering a bomber an invitation. Inviting the police to their house. For a fine or a search. A jail sentence.

He could have taken them down at dawn, she supposed, but he wouldn't have gotten them back up before dark. He wouldn't have woken. He wouldn't have remembered to do it if he had. And the stairwell bulb was still glowing.

What would happen, Isa wondered, if she wasn't here to do the blackouts?

Isa got the ladder and tacked up the curtains. Considered cleaning his dirty brushes, and decided not to. She climbed out of the wardrobe. Her father was on the sofa, twitching in his dreams. He needed a comb. And a bath. Isa went to her room, locked her door, propped the chair beneath the latch, and sat in a sea of purple drawings, sketchbook balanced on her knees.

She was still sketching when the bombers came. British probably, and American. Much closer this time. Coming in low, fast. Wave after wave. Shaking the sky. The crack and boom of the German flak became a rhythm she could draw to.

Iris. Fuchsia. Lilac and petunia.

Iris. Fuchsia. Lilac and petunia.

And vermilion. Isa picked up the red. Crimson and flame. Blooming.

Isa did not think they would drop bombs on Amsterdam. Though they had done it before. These planes were probably on their way toward Germany. Or France. Though sometimes they dropped their bombs on the airport. Or the docks at Rotterdam.

Sometimes they made mistakes. Isa set down her pastel.

And a different boom sent a tremor through the ground. Through the house. Gentle, like a nudge. Somewhere close—but not too close—a plane had hit the ground. Or a bomb. Isa stood, treading through her amethyst ocean to the window, tying the belt of her Chinese silk, peeking out beyond the curtain. Looking for a fire. For a glow on the horizon.

What she saw was a chink of light blaze out across the ground. A match lit. A beacon in the deep dark of Amsterdam.

It was the light from her own window.

Isa dropped the curtain. Pushed the tack of the blanket into the wall, and stepped back, horrified. Reached out and switched off the lamp, just in case. How could she have done it? Lifted the curtain with a light on? She hadn't been thinking. She'd been distracted. Stupid. Angry at her father. And now she'd done something so much worse than he had.

She waited, tense in the dark. Listening. But the rumble above her was unbroken, moving in straight lines, deeper into Europe, and the flak did not change its trajectory. But she had seen something in her beam of misjudged light.

Paper. Creamy-pale against the flagstone, sticking out from the terra-cotta shadows of the flowerpot.

Isa scuttled down the straight stairs in the blackness, through the big gallery, then the little gallery, pulling back the heavy, precautionary table she'd left crammed against the back door. She listened, but the air was all engines and propellers and crack and boom. It had no room for other sounds. She wouldn't know if someone was there.

The lights were out. Isa threw open the door, stepped out, snatched up the paper by feel, and locked herself in again.

A plane passed so close it shook the house. It was being

machine-gunned. And somewhere, a little closer, something big hit the waterlogged soil of the Netherlands. Isa felt the echo of its earthquake in the bottoms of her feet. One more like that, and she would wake her father and put him with Sister Cornelia in the cellar. If she could wake him up. She'd dunk his head in a bucket if she had to.

She tucked the note in her robe and pushed the table back into place, only knowing it was there when it bumped the door. Up the spiral this time, finding a way through the dark with her feet, through the kitchen and poppy hall, a quick listen to the breath of her sleeping father, and into the bathroom. The bathroom was interior. No windows. Nothing to tempt a bomber. Isa turned the switch.

And swore, squinting, eyes watering against the attack of the glare. She fished the note from her pocket, forcing her eyes to open, to adjust, to blearily make out a pencil scrawl worthy of copperplate.

She read the name and was surprised. She rubbed her eyes and read it again, and was less so.

Isa tucked the paper back into her pocket, grabbed a match, and lit the gas beneath the water heater perched above the tub.

Waiting. Thinking.

When the water was warm, she filled the tub, soaping and soaking.

Thinking. Planning, while the sky sighed above Amsterdam and fell silent.

She went to bed in the dark, skittish about turning on her lamp, and when the room took on the slate-gray light of sunrise through a blanket, Isa got up and rolled a pair of stockings up her legs. Buttoned up a red-and-brown tweed suit with a white blouse, her best before the war, sliding her toes into leather pumps. She brushed her hair, pinned it, and the face that looked back at her in the dim was ivory and a little freckled. Grim and ready. Spoiling for the fight.

She needed to speak to her father.

Her heels sounded odd on the creaking wood floors. Loud. Authoritative. But their echo was wrong. Altered in a way she couldn't put a finger on. Isa knocked on the blue room door, and when she opened it, the room was empty, the sofa an abandoned nest. She stepped up through the wardrobe, difficult in her pumps, and up the stairs, but she knew before her head crested the level of the floor that no one was in the garret. The sloping shadows of the beams were silent. A quiet that was more than quiet.

Her father was not in the bathroom, the dining room, or the kitchen. She went up the spiral stairs from the kitchen to her mother's studio. Down and down again to the galleries, the back hall. Moshe's cellar. Her footsteps sped. Faster. Calling. Up the straight stairs to the third floor and the sitting room, the guest rooms. Opening every door. Up again to the garret, the storage closet, just in case she'd missed her father asleep in some corner.

Isa went down again through the wardrobe, where there was one tartan slipper, and one yellow. Where her father's street shoes were missing.

Theodoor de Smit had left the house.

It was a strange, unsettled sort of feeling. The subtle presence of an absence.

And he must have done it during curfew.

Isa pinned on her hat, pulled on gloves and a copper wool coat. She grabbed her purse and ran downstairs to the gallery. The table at the back door was in place, but the wooden bar had been removed from the front.

Unlocked. While she slept.

She stepped out the front door of the Gallery De Smit, set at the diagonal across the corner of their triangular block, and locked it behind her. Isa looked left down the lane to the brick archway of the convent and its impenetrable doors, right to the shops and one or two early risers moving up Kalverstraat. She didn't see any soldiers. She didn't see a woman with a kerchief. She turned right and walked.

Eyes up. Chin up.

Looking.

She tried her mother's favorite paint supplier on the Spui, open, though with wares they could no longer afford, then cut over to the Arti, the club for artists, though she didn't think they would have let her father in, not since he'd refused to sign his declaration of Aryan birth. She hurried up to Rokin, where the trees were a blaze of orange glory, flaming leaves blowing like sparks, faster, past cafés and hotels, the smear of German guards and Dutch police. Past a spatter of swastikas printed on posters. Past Vlas, and Douwes and Eisenhoffel's, the wonderland auction houses of her childhood. They wouldn't unlock their doors for hours. And he couldn't have gone to the museums. They were closed other than the Stedelijk, and the Stedelijk had been taken over by Nazis. She turned left and ran back across to the upper end of Kalverstraat, where the buildings were dressed in the last century's finery.

She was not invisible.

Isa ignored the interest of a German soldier, watching her run like she had something to hide. Leapt out of the way of a midwife on a bicycle with wooden wheels. She was thinking of the prison on the Leidseplein, an unspeakable place where the Nazis took the unfortunate they had arrested. Where they'd taken Arondeus. And then she was thinking of the waters of the Singel. Thick and black-green, lapping at algae-brushed walls, rippling with the bob of a boat or the breeze. Imagining the flash of floating silver hair. The trailing end of a lavender scarf.

And then Isa saw the scarf.

In Dam Square. On a bench in front of the Royal Palace.

It was strange, seeing her papa in the daylight, against the backdrop of a city instead of their own four walls. Easier to see the smudges beneath his eyes. The pallor of his skin. Isa sat down beside him, and she was a kaleidoscope—relief, fury, love, and curiosity—all vying for the privilege of choosing her first words.

She settled for a mild "What are you doing, Papa?"

He lit a cigarette. Where had he gotten cigarettes?

"I am studying the reflection of early autumn light in the windows of the New Church," he replied.

He'd said it with none of his eccentric sunshine. But Theodoor de Smit's courtly charm had always been reserved for guests, or artists, or Francina.

"I was worried," Isa said.

"I am not a child, Sofonisba."

Isa bit her lip. Of course he was a child. He'd always been a child. And now Isa was the adult. This was the arrangement.

She stared up at the enormous, empty, soot-stained Neoclassical palace in a square that was nothing like it used to be. The organ grinders were gone, the queen gone, the man selling dates and roasted nuts was gone, the church bells melted down. Even the pigeons were nearly gone, killed by the Nazis so they couldn't carry messages. But it was the faces that were the biggest loss, expressionless, varying shades of buff tinged with gray. The color, Isa thought, of misery.

Two Nazi soldiers strolled by, rifles strapped across their backs, looking over the bench before they moved on past a woman in a green-and-gold kerchief, lugging her shopping bag. A full bag. When the shops were barely open. When the shops had bare shelves.

Her father threw down the cigarette—not even half-smoked—crushing the glowing butt beneath his heel. "There is nothing worth seeing here," he said. "I am going to sleep."

As if sleep had been unfairly denied him. As if the weight of his responsibilities was too much. He wrapped the scarf more firmly about his neck, hunched his shoulders, and walked away toward Kalverstraat.

Isa watched him go, clutching her purse on her knees, wondering what was wrong with him. If he was sick, like her mother. Why he'd left the house. If he even had a key to get back in.

She wondered where he had been. How often he was out during curfew.

She wondered why he was walking like a man who had something to hide.

The soaring face of the New Church glowed in the early sun, hundreds of stained-glass panes in crimson and cobalt, catching the rose-gold light in thousands of glints. No one had ever captured such glitter in paint, and the New Church hadn't been new in nearly five hundred years.

It was worth seeing.

Isa wondered if she could ever count as something worth seeing.

Heat opened up inside her chest. The poisonous bloom of a vermilion flower. It left the breath trapped in her lungs.

The wind was cold, but Isa was hot.

She got up and walked across the square as slow as she wanted. As fast as she wanted. Reckless. Letting the woman with the kerchief watch. Letting the Nazis watch if they felt like it. She paused at a shop window to read a pasted poster, one of the swastika kind, explaining the shopping restrictions for Jews. As if the Jewish people left in Amsterdam had homes to take shopping to. As if they had money to shop with that hadn't been stolen from them.

Beside the poster, Isa watched the tram come, emerald green in the reflection of the window glass. The tram slowed to a stop. The door whooshed open.

And Isa turned. And took it.

The door shut and the tram rolled and rattled as she lurched to a seat. The woman in the kerchief—who'd been studying the shop window next door—had been left behind. Isa smiled. She felt cooler, better, riding the number 4 down Rokin and across the Singel, like she should have done the day she went to Goudstikker's.

Resistance, that's who the woman in the kerchief had to be. Someone Willem had sent, to make sure that she and her father were worthy of trust. Only, her father had been wandering about Amsterdam at night. And she had a Nazi leaving notes underneath her flowerpot.

But if they'd seen that, surely they would have tried to slip her into a canal already.

Isa passed the Herengracht, waited one more stop, and this time, stepped off the tram at the Keizersgracht.

It was quieter here, in the neighborhoods ringed by water. The trees were raining leaves, speckling the canal with auburn and saffron, the tall, gabled houses leaning out and in—navy and brick and cream and stone—an unbroken hodgepodge curving with the water's path. It was hushed. Even serene. And with absolutely nowhere to hide.

Isa stepped smartly to the canal bridge and its German guard. Not invisible but with eyes up, purse beneath her arm, as if she knew her business, traversing the gentle arch without meeting the man's eyes or pushing him in. She turned right, counting the numbers, past another bridge and halfway to the next before she stopped, craning her neck. A four-story house made of bricks the color of clay and claret, with large, Georgian windows painted in bright white trim. Neat and formal. A mansion. Isa pulled a slip of paper from her glove, dirty from the bottom of a flowerpot.

Han van Meegeren
Keizersgracht 321
ten days

In handwriting worthy of a Dutch engraving.

In ink that was Nazi brown.

The name of the man who had forged a Vermeer and sold it to Adolf Hitler.

But ten days was too soon for Michel Lange to hide in her gallery. He had to remain at his post. Because Michel Lange was a Nazi who—whether he knew it or not—was about to help Isa de Smit save the lives of six more Jewish children.

Isa tucked the note into her purse, straightened her hat, and climbed the steps of the imposing facade. She put out a gloved finger and pushed the button of the bell, an electric bell, just below a shiny brass plate that proclaimed the name HAN VAN MEEGEREN.

The painter who—whether he knew it or not—was about to teach Isa de Smit how to forge a Vermeer.

"You shall create beauty not to excite the sense but to give sustenance to the soul."

—Commandment III, from *Decalogue of the Artist*,

Gabriela Mistral

9

ISA LISTENED TO the buzz of the doorbell. She knew Han van Meegeren, or at least knew of him. He'd been a successful dealer in Amsterdam, a moderately successful artist before that. She'd never heard of him selling dubious art. She'd never even heard of him brokering a shady transaction, much less blatantly forging a Dutch masterpiece and selling it to the Führer. But he did have a reputation for rumor-worthy finds. For the occasional gossip-inducing sale.

Maybe Han van Meegeren wasn't a forger at all. Maybe he was stupid. Maybe he'd been duped and passed on someone else's nefarious work unaware.

Isa pushed the bell again.

She hoped he was a forger. She hoped he was a damned good one. If he was, then she was going to learn, and she would be the one to outsmart them.

The thought sent a shiver down her spine.

Isa put out a finger, to push the bell again, and the door to Van Meegeren's house opened. A woman stood looking down at her, stiff as the guard at the bridge, with dark, salted hair and a ring of keys hanging from her belt. She eyed Isa like an odor that had become visible.

Isa smiled. "Mr. Van Meegeren, please?"

"He will not come," the woman said, heavily accented. And with that, she began shutting the door. Isa put out a hand.

"Perhaps you should ask him," she said. "My name is Isa de Smit."

"De Smit?" The housekeeper looked down her nose with more interest. And more disdain. She said, "You should come."

Isa raised a brow and followed the woman and her jangling keys inside.

The Gallery De Smit had always had pretensions of grandeur. But the Van Meegeren residence was not pretending. A staircase wound its way up from the entry hall, not the steep, narrow, wooden spiral but a wide, elegant affair of white marble, sweeping up and sideways, leading the eye to the ornate plasterwork and the crystal chandelier hanging from the ceiling. She let the woman—Isa assumed she was the housekeeper—lead her into the living room on the left, where there was more plasterwork; pure white walls and a marble mantelpiece; sleek, pale furniture in the modern, chrome-edged style.

The room was flooded with light. No trace of a blackout. Isa supposed that's what a housekeeper was for.

The woman held out a hand. Isa unbuttoned her coat and gave it to her. She thought about sitting on a fur-lined chair when the housekeeper left, but decided not to.

The place reeked of money.

And it stank of collaboration, too.

Big deals indeed.

It was a good thing she'd lost the woman with the kerchief, because Willem and Truus did not need to know she was here.

Isa wandered over to the fireplace, where an enormous, rather gruesome painting of Salome with the head of John the Baptist was displayed. She didn't recognize the artist. But to one side and lower down, much smaller, there was a tronie, a character painting, a woman in a white linen hat and lace collar, sturdy, even bawdy-looking, holding up a stein as if eliciting a cheer. Classic Hals, surely. A Dutch master.

She walked closer, nose to the paint. Where the light hit, she could see the craquelure, the minuscule lines and spaces that made their way into paint over time, like marsh mud dried out by the sun. The Vermeer's paint must have looked like that. If it hadn't, Hitler's agent wouldn't have bought it. But how?

Isa thought about mud. And heat.

Could paint be baked?

"You like that one?"

Isa straightened and found Van Meegeren in the doorway. She knew it was Van Meegeren because a memory came back to her, floating up from some sea of things she'd forgotten. The ringing of the front bell at the Gallery De Smit, a balding head and a bright yellow tie, her mother slamming the door with the words "What an odious little man!"

Van Meegeren was thin, older than she'd remembered, the hair that was left gray and wispy, a drooping mustache hung above a drooping mouth. He was shirtless, barefoot, wearing an open, untied, flame-stitched, kimono-style robe paired with red satin pajama pants and a bemused expression.

His attire did not concern Isa. She had grown up in the garret.

Van Meegeren took another step into the room. "I said, girl, do you like it?"

"Um, yes," Isa replied, treading carefully. "Of course."

"Then tell me what you think of it."

She looked again at the painted woman's smiling, sweaty face. "She looks very real. Like someone you would meet on a back street, and . . . that maybe you wouldn't like very much. But the wrinkles on the face, the detail of the linen, they're particularly well done. You can see the dirt on . . ."

Van Meegeren had stopped listening. He was looking her up and down.

"You're Theo's daughter, eh?" He tilted his head to one side. "Grown up, haven't you? Did your father send you here?"

"No."

"No? You interest me." He plopped onto the sofa, soft with creamy, crushed velvet, leaning back and crossing his legs as if he were a debonair thirty. She could see the gray chest hair, the skin of his neck like thin paper creased and flattened. She could also see the woman through the open doorway behind him, creeping down the elegant stairs, shoes in hand, a dilapidated flower pinned to her low-cut dress, long, red hair loose and disheveled. Not Mrs. Van Meegeren, Isa presumed.

"So," he said, bobbing a bare foot. "Who painted it?"

She looked back to the woman on the wall.

"Come now, girl, you must have some opinion."

"Hals," Isa replied.

"Hals, huh? That's what you say, is it?" But he seemed pleased. The front door softly closed, and Van Meegeren grabbed a gold box from the side table, opened it, and popped a chocolate into his mouth.

Isa hadn't seen a chocolate since 1940.

"So, Theo de Smit's grown-up daughter," he said, mouth full. "What do you want, eh? Or perhaps there is something I could offer you?"

The underlayment beneath those last words had been heavy. Isa went to the fur-covered chair and sat. Her mother had been right.

What an odious little man.

Isa arranged her smile. "I am looking for work," she said, "and was hoping you might need an assistant in your studio. I am very competent with oil preparation and—"

"Please," Van Meegeren said, holding up a hand. "I prepare all my own canvases and paints."

Isa found that interesting.

"I am also well versed in running the business side of a studio," she went on. "If you need bookkeeping, or correspondence—"

"Your father put you up to this, didn't he?"

She didn't answer this time. Van Meegeren tilted his head the other way.

"I suppose your little gallery is struggling?"

Of course it was.

"In need of extra money, are you?"

Of course they were.

"Then I can give you some work as a maid. My housekeeper says she needs help in the scullery."

He was trying to insult her. To drive her out the door. And the harder he pushed, the harder Isa was going to dig in the heels of her good leather pumps.

"I would be happy to, thank you," she said. "How much would you pay, and what time of day would you be needing?"

Van Meegeren looked at her. And then he laughed. Too loud. Two spots of color shone in his cheeks. He clapped his hands together and leapt off the sofa, fingers stroking the end of the mustache, walking a slow, full circle around her chair. "What is your name again?"

"Isa," she replied. Reluctantly.

"Stand up, then, girl."

She stood. Reluctantly.

And he walked another slow circle, chin pitched one way, then the other, considering her from different angles. Isa was considering whether or not to put a foot in the man's path. But then he stopped, clapped again, and hopped back onto the sofa, legs on the table, arms languidly behind his head in his satin finery. Isa could see the dirty soles of his feet.

"Instead of my scullery maid," he said, "maybe you would like to be my model."

Isa only just kept her eyes from rolling. "Why?"

"Why not? You won't make the cover of a magazine, my dear, but what of that? You are expressive. Especially when you are angry. I like you when you're angry, and I would much rather paint interesting than lovely. And besides, I have a penchant for red hair."

A rivulet of revulsion slid through Isa's chest, pickle-green and tobacco-brown. It must have showed, because Van Meegeren laughed again. Uproariously.

She'd let this man get under her skin. And suddenly, she was quite sure Van Meegeren was trying to get beneath her skin. She wondered why. Maybe he had his reasons. Maybe it was a hobby.

But being his model meant time in his studio.

Isa wanted desperately to see his studio.

She sat down primly on the edge of the chair, purse on her knees. "How much do you pay your models, Mr. Van Meegeren?"

"Fifty," he said. "Per project."

"It would be fifty per sitting. And we will have a contract."

"A contract, eh? I see no need for—"

"Do you want to paint me or not?"

He studied her face. And chuckled. "All right, girl . . . what was your name again?"

"Isa," she replied.

"Come with me, then. To the office," he added when she hesitated. "You said you are capable with correspondence?"

Isa followed him up the elegant stairs. He had a typewriter in his office, a dingier, messier place than the pristine living room. Van Meegeren sifted quickly through a drift of letters and receipts, invoices and bills, until he found a blank sheet of paper, which he handed to Isa with a flourish. She sat in front of the typewriter and rolled the paper in.

She was a slow typist—very slow—but accurate. She typed meticulously, stopped frequently to tap a tooth, to consider her terms, to sneak a peek at the piles of paper around her before deliberately clicking the keys again. A little bell dinged each time she changed lines.

Van Meegeren got bored. He poured himself a drink. Smoked two cigarettes. They were the same brand her father had. He dozed off on the sofa, and Isa ran her eyes over an entire letter from a man named Gurlitt, promising to pay a visit to view a painting of Van Meegeren's, a possible new acquisition for something called the Führermuseum.

So Hitler was creating an art museum. A shrine to his own glory. No wonder there was so much Nazi interest in the Dutch masters. Hitler had a whole museum to fill with stolen history. With stolen beauty to bask in, beauty he thought would reflect on himself. She wondered if Gurlitt was the man who had bought *Woman with a Wine Glass*. If he was the one who had purchased her Rembrandt. And the thought of the *Rembrandt De Smit* hanging on the walls of the Führermuseum gave her another little shiver. Made her smile, cool and brisk.

She hoped the place would be riddled with fakes.

"Are you reading, girl, or typing?"

Van Meegeren was still on the sofa, eyes closed. But he was noticing everything she did.

"I am creating my terms," Isa said. And she typed. Slowly.

Van Meegeren got up and poured himself another drink. He'd had another and a third cigarette before she was done, splayed out in his chair in an attitude of amused disdain. Isa pulled the paper off the roll with a zip and handed it to him.

He read aloud, haphazardly. Contemptuously.

"'Model will be paid fifty guilders per two-hour session, payment due each session, yes, yes. Sessions will take place at Keizersgracht 321. Sessions with the model will be chaperoned . . .'"

He looked up at that one, and Isa crossed her arms. She hadn't grown up in the garret for nothing. He read on, faster. The paper was shaking in his hand, just a little.

"'Model will be fully clothed. Model will approve all clothing. Model will approve all poses. Model will be painted as posed, in the approved pose, and as clothed, in approved clothing, or ownership of the painting will transfer to the model.'"

Van Meegeren sighed dramatically. "You really know how to suck the fun out of things. Well. In that case . . ." He picked up a pen, struck through the fifty guilders, and wrote in twenty-five.

"Fine," said Isa. She was pleased. Fifty had been ridiculous, and twenty-five still might buy her a sack of coal. "When would you like me to begin?"

"Tomorrow," he said, waving a hand. "I've had enough of you for a day, and I don't get up early. Come at one."

Isa nodded. "And where is your housekeeper now?"

"What do you want with her?"

"As a witness. For the signatures. I assumed your wife was not home."

He laughed again and rang for the housekeeper, whose name was Mrs. Martinelli—from his villa in Italy, Van Meegeren said—a woman who had seen a thing or two and did not blink an eye.

They signed, and Isa watched the shake in the lines as Van Meegeren wrote his name, the telltale tremors in the ink, the manic movements, and the flush on his face. Van Meegeren must be an alcoholic. And a yellow stain began spreading inside her, mottling her cool blues and greens.

She had to learn how to forge a Vermeer.

And the man who could teach her could not even hold a pen straight.

When Van Meegeren's door shut behind her, Isa buttoned her coat, passed up the tram, and walked home in air that smelled of cold instead of chill, a slow wander over worn brick and cracked stones. She missed her bicycle—confiscated for the rubber—the wind of speed freezing her cheeks and blowing down her hair.

She always had loved a north wind.

And there was no woman with a kerchief on her way home, and nothing underneath her flowerpot. Nothing on her father's sofa bed but the pillows. She kicked off her shoes, climbed through the wardrobe, and found him on the garret sofa. Asleep. Again. A heap of long limbs and garish clothes.

The flower was still blooming inside her chest.

She went quiet in her stocking feet and stood before the makeshift gallery hanging from the drying slats. Her father's pretend Vermeer was small, like so many Vermeers, a street scene of a bygone Amsterdam, where the rooflines were the focal points, the sparse, tiny people relegated to the details. It was a lovely piece. Pure and serene. Just like a Vermeer. Isa looked back at her sleeping father.

An artistic mimic, Francina had said. That's what Theodoor de Smit was. As talented as all the rest of them put together. When Isa was young, watching her father paint, she'd thought of him as the sun, a blaze of color and passion around which the rest of them had circled. It was only now that she was beginning to realize what a distant star she had been in her parents' universe. Isa leaned in, studying the painting.

If this picture had been genuine, it would have been worth thousands before the war. Tens of thousands. A large Vermeer, an early, religious work, had gone for three hundred thousand to a museum in Rotterdam. So what would it be worth to the Nazis now, with their desire to appear as cultured as the Dutch?

A vast sum, if Van Meegeren's lifestyle was any indicator. It would have to be, to be worth the risk.

Hers would have to be good enough to be worth the risk.

She wished she had asked Michel Lange what he had seen on the Rembrandt.

Isa touched the paint of the *Vermeer De Smit*. Dry, without the first hint of the telltale craquelure. And when she pushed in a fingernail at the corner, it made a tiny dent.

Isa went to the storage closet, still a mess from her father's rummaging, and found a small canvas. And then she hesitated. She didn't want to use her father's paints, not while his supplies were so low, and he would have given up art altogether before he touched Francina's. Francina's paints were holy.

But this, Isa thought, was a holy cause.

She picked up her mother's battered, dusty paint box and took it downstairs with the canvas, changed into her spattered overalls, and spent the rest of the day baking.

The first trial blistered the paint. Isa lowered the temperature. The next attempt turned the white pigment the color of rye, toasting the exposed canvas like a piece of bread. It was fiddly, turning the canvas to a clean side, painstaking because she was impatient, interesting because the browned paint cooled and turned white again.

Her next try was more successful. The paint hardened, but it didn't crack. She did it again, and this time tried creating the cracks, pushing the canvas with her finger while the paint was still warm. Flakes fell to the table like confetti.

Isa baked longer. Shorter. Hotter. Cooler. Wasting her mother's paint and running up the bill for the gas. Making a mess of the kitchen table. She sat in one chair, propped her feet in another, and examined the cooked rainbow she had made, shrinking on the canvas, chunks entirely missing.

What if the problem was the paint?

Francina's paints were premixed tubes of pigment and linseed oil. Would they react differently, maybe, with more or less oil? Or if they were hand-mixed, mortar and stone, like a Dutch master would have done? Or perhaps the problem was because the paint was fully wet. Would the paint crack if she had started with a drier surface?

Should she put the *Vermeer De Smit* in the oven?

Maybe baking wasn't even the answer.

Or what if nothing was the answer, and she couldn't alter the *Vermeer De Smit* at all? What if she couldn't get the money? What if she'd agreed to let a Nazi stay in her house for nothing?

Truus was going to dump her in a canal. Or Willem would. Or she could be arrested, and no child would be saved, and the gallery would be lost.

Isa looked up at a familiar thumping from far above her head. Her father—awake, apparently—repeatedly throwing a shoe against the floor of the garret, a favorite method for requiring one's presence. She went down the hall, through the wardrobe, his voice coming to meet her as she climbed the stairs.

"Have you brought food?"

Isa paused, her head just above the level of the paint-dotted floorboards. Theodoor de Smit was bright, upright, and behind his canvas. She could see one stocking foot and one street shoe through the railing.

"What are you waiting for, child?" he yelled. "Didn't you hear me? Breakfast! How can I be expected to work if I am famished?" His brush moved in tiny, rapid strokes, brows pointed down in concentration.

"Papa," Isa ventured. "You'll remember to leave the blackout curtains up, won't you? In case the bombers come?"

He didn't answer. He leaned forward, living his paint.

"Papa, you have to remember that if you take down the curtains at night, then someone will call the police."

That got his attention. The dark eyes flicked upward. "Yes, yes," he said. "But I need food. And I will need the ultramarine, if you please. Before this afternoon."

It was already afternoon. It was nearly evening. "Couldn't you use cobalt, Papa?"

"No! Ultramarine. Pigment, mind you. Not the synthetic."

Isa blinked. Pure ultramarine had been too expensive for anyone even before the war. Would they test her father's Vermeer for ultramarine? Cobalt hadn't existed in Vermeer's time. Isa felt her brows scrunch. "What are you working on?"

"Nothing," he snapped.

Nothing. He just needed a paint worth its weight in gold, and she was supposed to wave a wand and get it for him, right along with his breakfast. At dinnertime. When he didn't even know if there was food downstairs. They could be on the point of starvation, for all her father knew.

He didn't even know if the tax had been paid.

And she was hot. Ruby-red. Crimson and scarlet.

Isa went back down the stairs, boiled a potato, ate it, and tidied the kitchen. She looped the wire over the latch on the leaded glass, checked the rest of the blackouts, and made sure the table was tight against the back door. Then she positioned the chair beneath her bedroom latch, slid on her robe, and unpinned her hair while her father threw his second shoe—and other things besides.

She sketched while he thumped and complained through the ceiling, calling in the hallway, tromping up and down the stairs. Isa ignored him, drawing purpling twists around an enormous red bloom, a hothouse flower, exotic, poisonous, filling the page. She didn't notice the cold that reached through the window cracks and along the rug. She started again, this time in shades of sky and sea foam.

If the secret of craquelure could be found, she would find it.

She would be careful. And reckless. And the Nazis would pay. For everything.

And her father would never even notice she'd been gone.

10

THEODOOR DE SMIT had gone quiet by the early morning, as usual, but Isa slept late, just in case. Enjoying the warmth of her bed so she wouldn't encounter him. She put on a plain, blue-print dress, loosely pinned her hair. She didn't know what Van Meegeren would want, and when she looked in the mirror she was grim again, a few pale freckles standing out on her nose.

Did she always look like she was spoiling for a fight?

Or was this the way everyone looked in an ugly world?

Isa slid on her coat, checked the flowerpot, and walked beneath a sky made of granite. Past powder-frozen windowpanes and frosted leaves, taking the long way around, back and forth, over and down, skirting the icy iron rails. Walking in circles to the mansion of Han van Meegeren.

She didn't see the woman in the kerchief.

She could only hope the woman in the kerchief hadn't seen her.

Isa was early to her appointment, and Mrs. Martinelli let her know it. She was not allowed to wait in the studio, or even in the office, and now that she was a model, she was no longer living room material. The housekeeper sat her at a table in the kitchen, a shining kitchen, with blue-and-white tiles—in the old style, but brand-new—with a geometric pattern and a glossy glaze. The icebox did not run on ice; it was plugged in, but Isa was sizing up the oven. Big enough for some paintings, she decided, but not for *Woman with a Wine Glass*.

She probably needed to stop this foolish idea about baking paintings.

"Would you like the coffee?" asked Mrs. Martinelli.

Isa nodded, surprised. The tone had been friendly, even kindly. Maybe Mrs. Martinelli wasn't used to Van Meegeren's models being so quiet and good. A rattling cup and saucer was set in front of her. Isa sipped, and then she closed her eyes. It was real coffee, the coffee of three years ago—staying up late to watch the painters in the garret kind of coffee—and miracle upon miracles, there was sugar in it. Isa couldn't help her sigh. Which seemed to further please Mrs. Martinelli.

Mrs. Martinelli, Isa guessed, wasn't often complimented.

"This is a beautiful kitchen," Isa tried. "It must be a pleasure to cook in."

"Cooking the food is my joy," she said. "The cooking is . . . my purpose."

Her purpose. What an interesting thing to say. Other than being her father's caretaker and her mother's amusement, Isa wasn't sure she'd ever had a purpose.

"Today we have guests," Mrs. Martinelli went on. "So there is a lot of the cooking."

Isa was glad to hear it. At least there would be people in the house. She looked up at the ceiling, with its circle of grape-leaf plasterwork. This room had not been made to be a kitchen.

"I suppose Mr. Van Meegeren had this kitchen put in for you? When he moved to Amsterdam?"

"Sì, yes," she said, stirring something floury in a bowl. "He likes for his things to be . . . not cheap. The old one, down the stairs, it is . . ." She shook her head, showing her disapprobation rather than voicing it.

Isa nodded understandingly.

There was another kitchen. Probably in the cellar, like Moshe's room. A kitchen that could have an oven.

And then something buzzed and lit a little bulb, a bulb in a row of bulbs, the sign above it marked STUDIO. Mrs. Martinelli told her to finish her coffee.

They went up the elegant staircase, and up again to a third-floor room that ran along the back of the house, where windows had been cut along the entire wall, made for capturing the light. It was as if blackouts didn't exist on the Keizersgracht. The granite light was pale, a bleak wash from a cold sky, gray with blue undertones. Much like Van Meegeren's face. His beret sat lopsided. He looked a little ill. He glanced up at Isa from behind the canvas he was working on and then at the clock.

"Here, eh? Late, I see. We'll have to work a little longer."

"I was here early," Isa replied. "You called for me late, and our session will end on time, as per the contract. Though I will be happy to be paid for a second session."

Van Meegeren pouted for exactly five seconds. And then he laughed, shook his head, and seemed to regret it. He left his palette on a stool and went to wash his hands.

"You also remember the other stipulation, about a chaperone being in the house?"

"What was that?" Van Meegeren said, but Isa met Mrs. Martinelli's gaze and knew they had an understanding. Mrs. Martinelli nodded, tapped a finger beside her eyebrow—a move that meant she had an eye on things—and made her way back to her cooking.

And then Van Meegeren was bustling. Arranging a chair, finding a sketchbook, judging the light. Isa stared at a plaster head sitting on the table. It was a severed head, with upturned eyes and stringy hair and red ribbons trailing from its ravaged neck.

Not Salome, Isa thought. Anything but Salome.

"You can dress in there," he said, tossing her a bundle of chiffon. "Or here," he added, "if you've decided to stop being so fussy."

Isa found the little closet he'd pointed to and turned the skeleton key in the lock. She was out in five minutes. It wasn't the worst of costumes. Better, probably, than she had expected. A long, flowing, classical sort of dress with a high waist and gold braiding that made thin straps to show her shoulders. A little loose, but Isa had brought a packet of pins.

She had, after all, grown up in the garret.

Van Meegeren was with her in a second, walking his circle, stroking his mustache, taking down her hair and adjusting the straps. But this time, it was impersonal.

It was business.

This was art.

"I want your face done," he said, pointing back to the dressing closet. "Kohl around the eyes, lipstick, probably nothing else. You'll find what you need."

"What is the subject matter?" Isa asked, looking at her dress. "The time period?"

"Judith," he replied, "with the head of Holofernes."

Isa sighed. Why did artists have to be so fascinated with a woman holding a severed head? Probably because they were mostly men.

Fifteen minutes later, Isa was standing on a chair, her eyes painted, a sword propped against her shoulder, the plaster head held out like she was using it for a lantern. The window was open, to stir both her hair and the head's. It was freezing. Van Meegeren sat on the floor with his legs crossed, sketching from an upward perspective. Isa used her time to study the studio of a forger.

And she saw nothing unexpected. Vases and urns for props, canvases and easels. A sink full of jars of soaking brushes, and a wooden cabinet with filing drawers for paint. She would look at that as soon as she could, though there was nothing unconventional about the palette he'd left behind on his stool. Cadmium reds and yellows. White and a Van Dyck brown. A blue that was probably cobalt. But the palette, Isa noticed, was new, the freshly varnished wood still visible under the pools of spurted, blending colors. Her father's palette was a mess, a mix of everything. An old friend.

And then Isa began to fully understand why models got paid. The arm holding the severed head ached. Her back ached, and her legs, from holding her balance on the chair. The sword was digging a hole in her shoulder, her nose starting to run from the chill. She sniffed and tried to distract herself, to study Van Meegeren's sketch from her vantage point, upside down. The perspective was powerful, though he was leaving out the freckles on her nose—Judith did not have freckles—and her chest, Isa thought, was not quite as represented.

Van Meegeren's right hand began to shake. He paused, stretched the fingers, and tried again. The ache in Isa's arm progressed to a pain that turned her chill into a sweat.

"A break," Van Meegeren announced. Isa lowered the head, gasping.

She got down from the chair while Van Meegeren got up, the manic energy of before completely vanished. He poured himself a drink, downed it in one, and had another. His form of alcoholism, Isa thought, was different from what she'd seen before. Severe, but more functional.

She set the head on the table, watching him try to control his tremor from the corner of her eye. She thought of Van Meegeren's war. A war of painting and profit, of women and chocolates and silk kimonos. A war with enough alcohol to be an alcoholic, while other people got nothing but the truck. While Holland lost its treasures. While the Netherlands lost its children.

"Your toilet?" Isa asked. The question came out as an accusation.

Van Meegeren grunted, his nod indicating something in the vicinity of the hallway. Isa wandered out, the stairs and the curve of the balcony on her left. And when she looked back, Van Meegeren had stretched full length on the studio floor, arms flung behind his head, eyes closed. She took a step. He didn't move. She took another. His eyelids didn't even flutter.

Isa went quick down the stairs, silent on bare feet, chiffon trailing around the elegant sweep, then down again to the main floor. She was looking for a door, another way down to an old cellar kitchen. A kitchen with an oven. A big one.

She found an entrance to a back corridor. A billiard room, full of the memory of cigar smoke, a larder where the shelves were barely visible for the bottles and sacks and cans. This led through to the shining new kitchen, pots steaming, the smells both tangy and sweet. The second door took her to a dining room where the table was set, then the living room she'd already visited.

Isa hurried back into the entrance hall, rustling over the marble tiles, trying to visualize a house that had been completely redone, wondering where the stairs might have been. Where they would have been preserved. Wondering just how long Van Meegeren would think she needed in a toilet. Then she looked harder at the wall beneath the sweep of stairs, and put a hand on the pure, white wainscoting.

There was a door. Masked by the decoration of the walls, just like in her mother's bedroom. She found the hole beneath the trim. For a finger. For a key. She could feel the little latch inside, but it would not open. The door was locked.

It could be a cupboard, of course. Under the stairs was a convenient place. Or it could be another stairwell.

"You are wanting something?"

Isa jumped. Mrs. Martinelli was standing in the doorway to the living room, a feather duster in hand. The ring of keys hung temptingly from her belt.

Isa tried a weak smile. "The toilet?"

"Up the stair, to the right."

"Oh, yes. I looked, but . . . thank you. I must have missed. I . . . didn't see. Thank you, Mrs. Martinelli."

Isa bit her lip, so she would stop talking, lifted her trailing skirt, and retreated up the stairs, Mrs. Martinelli watching her progress.

Isa stepped inside the little water closet, exactly where she'd been told, and shut the door. She needed those keys. But what kind of pretense would get the correct key off Mrs. Martinelli's belt?

She waited a decent moment and pulled the chain—for the flushing noise—and raced back upstairs, full of excuses. But Van Meegeren was no longer on the floor of the studio.

"Hello?" she ventured.

The head of Holofernes leered with its tortured eyes. The little dressing room was empty, as was a supply closet, filled with haphazard costumes and props. The sketchbook had been left on the floor, and Isa wandered over to it, pretending to gaze at the busty figure of herself. When the hall remained quiet, she bolted to the sink and opened a cabinet.

Turpentine, paint strippers, and, on the other side, varnishes to be applied on top of the finished oil. Isa went through the cans, peering at the labels, smelling the tops. She'd seen every one of them in their own garret. Then she went to the wooden paint cabinet and opened a drawer. Tubes in shades of green, phthalo, and chromium. Drawers of reds, blacks, and all the different types of white. And in a drawer all by itself, a small glass bottle of blue. Isa held it up to the fading daylight. Ultramarine, if she had to guess. Crushed lapis lazuli. Not a synthetic.

How many children could have been saved with the money it cost to buy this one tiny bottle?

She put the ultramarine back, shut the drawer, and stepped away from the cabinet, a knot of tension she hadn't even acknowledged untying between her shoulder blades. A loosening in the back of her neck. She could see nothing wrong with Van Meegeren's paints. Other than the ultramarine, not one tube or brand she hadn't purchased herself. The secret to craquelure had to be in what happened after the paint was put on the canvas.

And surely that had to be about heat.

She glanced into the hall, the balcony with the stairwell. Van Meegeren's house was white and silent, solemn as a church.

She went to the painting he'd been working on when she arrived, a half-finished nightclub scene of slinky, smoking women—a completely different style than what he was doing with Judith. She could see that from the sketch. Then she went through the canvases stacked along the wall. Classic, impressionistic, one scene almost illustrative, even comic in its style. She picked up a self-portrait, done in bleak, sepia tones with tints of turquoise and cerulean. A face that was fun-loving and yet tormented.

Van Meegeren was good, quite good when he wanted to be. A bit of an artistic chameleon, like her father. But not one of these paintings showed craquelure. They were all soft.

She needed that key.

Isa looked up at the clock. Van Meegeren's "break" had stretched to well past an hour. She climbed one floor down and opened the door to the disheveled office. And there he was, splayed on the sofa, an arm thrown across his eyes, a half-empty decanter on the table at his side.

Asleep. Or passed out.

He had an open box, only just held by the slack hand on his chest, gold-plated and engraved with initials, a few white tablets spilling out to the floor. Isa crouched down and picked up one of the tablets, holding it to the dim light filtered through the heavy curtains. It didn't look like an aspirin.

So more, maybe, than just an alcoholic.

She laid the tablet on the carpet where she'd found it. Francina hadn't allowed addicts into her studio or the garret. They were unpredictable, she'd said. More trouble than they were worth.

Unpredictable, Isa thought.

Or dangerous.

Isa stole quietly to the desk, where the untidy piles of paper lay strewn and intermingled. If Van Meegeren woke badly, she'd run and shout for Mrs. Martinelli. If he just woke, she'd say she was tidying his papers, since he was paying her anyway. She wanted to see bills. Receipts. A supply list. Anything that would explain the hardness of paint.

Isa sorted and assembled. She saw a purchase for canvas, paint. A painting from an antiques dealer, seventeenth century. A new easel.

German beer. An order for kerosene and carbolic acid from a chemist. Ten new palettes and twenty badger-hair shaving brushes. Isa paused.

No one needed twenty shaving brushes. And paintbrushes of badger hair were used by the masters.

She saw a grocery bill. A tailor's receipt. A doctor's bill, for a huge amount. An arrangement, maybe, for his drug supply? An order for formaldehyde. Was he interested in taxidermy? And an absolutely staggering bill for Belgian chocolates.

Isa sat back, tapping a fingernail, looking at the sprawled little artist with one foot hanging off the sofa edge. She knew he'd done it. She knew he was a forger. He would have known Moshe, at least slightly. He could have seen that Vermeer on Moshe's walls. Might have even guessed that Moshe would have hidden it. Van Meegeren had forged *Woman with a Wine Glass*, and he'd gotten away with it. Based on his house and the astronomical amount of his bills, he'd gotten away with it to the tune of a fortune.

He must be clever. Very clever.

And if someone was clever, and had a locked door, a door that was hiding the means to make forged paintings, forgeries that were being sold to the highest levels of a Nazi government that would imprison you, torture you, or shoot you without a qualm, would a clever man leave such an important key on the belt of his housekeeper?

No. He would not.

She watched the dried paint on Van Meegeren's smock rise up and down. He really hadn't moved an inch, but he'd appeared to be asleep last time, too. Isa waited, and then ransacked the desk. Quietly. Only now she was looking in envelopes, between pages, even sliding out the drawers and peeking underneath. Wherever it was, the key would be in the safest place. And the safest place was out of sight. Somewhere personal. Convenient.

Isa pushed back the chair, soft in bare feet across the carpet. Van Meegeren's eyelids were still, wispy hair mussed. She could see the nicotine stains on his teeth. She reached down, slowly, carefully sliding her hand into the large front pocket of his paint smock.

And she came out with a key.

11

ISA STOOD IN the hall, key in hand. She looked back through the office door. Van Meegeren hadn't moved, and the glorious smell of onions and bread wafting up the stairs made her think there was a good chance Mrs. Martinelli was safely distracted in the shiny kitchen.

Her time was now.

She flitted down the stairs. Like Daphne running from Apollo. Like the hundreds of paintings of women fleeing the sack of Troy, or Jerusalem, or Rome. Light and fast, loose hair flying, with a quick glance over the shoulder, looking for pursuit. The key was clutched tight, her mind focused, intent on the lock of a half-hidden door, on the secret of cracked paint, down and around the elegant curve.

And there was a man standing in the hall, where Mrs. Martinelli had been, hands behind his back in the doorway to the living room. A medium sort of man, with a stiff spine and impeccable suit, heavy eyes behind round glasses, watching the chiffon of her dress trail behind her down the steps.

No one looked that neat and well fed, not in wartime.

No one but a Nazi.

Isa slowed. And slowed, hand dragging down the rail as

if her fingers were trying to stop their own progress. And only now did the significance of the set table in the dining room, Mrs. Martinelli's cooking, and her reference to "visitors" become evident. Mrs. Martinelli just hadn't mentioned the level of importance of these visitors. Because this was the man from Goudstikker's back room. The man who had walked with such power. The art agent for Adolf Hitler.

The agent who had handed her eight hundred reichsmarks for a piece of Theodoor de Smit's fakery.

Isa's feet stopped three steps from the bottom. She could feel the pulse in her throat. Her fear spilling yellow. Sickening.

How long would it take for him to realize that the girl with the wild hair and kohl around her eyes was the same girl with a hole in her hat, the girl who had sold him a Rembrandt? Had they seen it yet, whatever Michel Lange had seen? Did they know yet that the Rembrandt wasn't genuine?

Damn the Nazis.

Damn Van Meegeren.

Damn everything.

Hitler's agent watched her with the heavy-lidded intensity of a hunting cat.

There were voices in the room behind him, German voices, smears of olive and brown against the white, clustered to one side of the fireplace, looking at the Hals. Hitler's agent lifted a hand, eyes still on her, and snapped his fingers.

The German chatter paused. A uniform broke away from the cluster, boots crisp on the parquet, shoulders square, dark hair shaved short on the sides. Isa knew who it was. She knew even before he lifted a pair of translucent brown eyes.

Their gazes met, and for an imperceptible moment, the rhythm of his boots stuttered. Then Michel Lange stepped forward, turning smoothly to the agent, listening as the man said a few words, low and guttural.

Michel straightened his back and said coolly, "Herr Gurlitt would like to know who you are, please?"

"Elsa," she blurted. "Elsa Groot."

She saw Michel press his lips together. She felt hers part. That had been silly. Profoundly stupid. She had no papers with that name, not with her, and it was not the name Van Meegeren was going to use whenever he woke up and came down the stairs. And it was Elsa Groot who had sold this very man a forgery, not Isa de Smit.

But she could not bring these men to the gallery. To terrorize her father. To search. To break down her walls.

If the wall was going to be broken, then she would be the one to do it.

And she wasn't caught yet.

Isa smiled, came down the steps, and held out a hand, the empty hand. The one with the key was behind her back. "It is very . . . nice to meet you."

Michel translated softly. Gurlitt, apparently, had no Dutch. And he did not take her hand. Isa let it drop to her side.

Herr Gurlitt spoke again, slow and deliberate, and Michel said, "He would like to know what you are doing here?"

And that question, Isa thought, probably went for all of them.

"I am Mr. Van Meegeren's model," she said.

She might as well have said "prostitute." She saw the brows go up on both of them. Their little scene had now gained the attention of the other men in the living room, three more uniforms and a suit watching from their conclave.

Gurlitt spoke, and Michel translated, "And where is Van Meegeren? We are waiting."

She thought of the artist sprawled on the sofa in a litter of pills. They might wait long. Isa forced a smile.

"We have just finished a sketch, a level of light he wanted to capture . . ." Michel began translating, speaking low German while she talked. Her pulse was pounding. Pounding. "I'm sure he will be down soon. I'll just go change, and tell Mr. Van Meegeren . . ." She took a backward step while Gurlitt muttered.

Michel said, "Herr Gurlitt says you will join us now, please, while we wait."

Isa met Michel's gaze, but he could offer her no way out. Gurlitt extended an arm, ushering her into the living room with her bare shoulders and made-up eyes. A living room full of Nazis. She made a show of holding up her trailing dress, key trapped in a web of chiffon. And they watched her come, all of them, listening as Gurlitt introduced her. She heard "Elsa" and "Van Meegeren" and some laughter. Some contempt. But much interest.

Too much interest.

"Sit here, please," said Michel, indicating the sofa. "And Herr Gurlitt says you would like a drink?"

It wasn't actually a question. A bottle of wine was on the chrome-trimmed bar, a glass already being procured by the man in the suit. The blackout curtains had been put up, tall, heavy, and pinned down, a geometric pattern of white and black on the interior. It made the room smaller, somehow, chic and intimate.

Herr Gurlitt sat beside her, his arm along the back of the sofa, Michel in the fur-lined chair. Ready to translate. The others hovered, listening.

She was sitting on the key.

Michel had his hat in his hands, one knee jiggling. He stilled it, and said, "Herr Gurlitt would like to know the subject of your sketch?"

"Judith," Isa said, "with the head of Holofernes."

It had the ring of truth. Because it was. And because no one would have chosen a Jewish heroine as their preferred lie to a Nazi. She saw the information enter Gurlitt's head, along with a spark of recognition.

The pounding in her chest paused, skittered. Her yellow-sick fear pooled. He'd remembered. He knew who she was. His low voice came out soft. Like a growl.

"Herr Gurlitt says you will make a good Judith," said Michel, a hint of apology in his voice. "Your hair . . ."

And Isa's pulse jumped back into tempo. Faster. He did not remember.

She smiled her thanks at Herr Gurlitt. She'd heard of the association of Jewish people with red hair. She'd seen it in art. And here it was again. One more belief that made absolutely no sense. Like the whole of Nazi philosophy. Like the war. Like her father. There was no logic to any of it. There was no logic left in the world.

A drink was put in her hand, a clear purple wine, sparkling.

The color of uncertainty.

She stared through the wine, at the shadows of her own fingers, pressed against a surface of purpling crystal.

Or was it the color of recklessness?

Because she had the key to Van Meegeren's cellar. Right now. And unless she could put it back before it was missed, Van Meegeren would know who had taken it. There would be no more pretense of modeling. No more chances. If she wanted to give the Resistance the profits from a forged Vermeer, she needed to get into that cellar tonight.

The idea of doing it in a house full of Nazis was more than reckless. It was ridiculous.

The idea of doing it under the nose of an arrogant Nazi she'd already swindled gave her a thrill that cast away reason.

She glanced at Michel. The brown eyes were the color of amber in the low electric light. Full of warning. She sipped her wine, and Herr Gurlitt turned a little on the sofa, speaking German, the other men gathered at a respectful distance. Listening.

Michel said, "Herr Gurlitt wishes to know if he may call you Elsa?"

"Ja, danke schön," Isa replied, getting a laugh from the room.

"Do you speak German?" Michel translated.

Isa sipped her wine and smiled. "No, I'm afraid that's all I've got." Michel repeated this for another laugh.

Isa said, "Would you ask him if anyone speaks Dutch?"

Michel translated quickly and answered for them. "No. No one speaks Dutch other than me."

"Not at all?"

Michel shook his head. Gurlitt crossed his legs, speaking softly, looking Isa over beneath heavy-lidded eyes. Michel said, "Herr Gurlitt wishes to know if you have been an artist's model for long?"

Isa shook her head, smiling idiotically. "It's my first time, but it's very exciting, isn't it?" And without taking her eyes from Gurlitt, she added, "How soon will you all go into the dining room?"

Michel paused. Then he translated, listened, and said, "Herr Gurlitt says he is sure you will be successful, and we are waiting for our host. Have you done something to him?"

"Of course not, and tell him I hope that he is right."

What did Michel Lange think she was, a murderer?

"I need to leave the room before your host comes," Isa said. "He knows my other name. And ask Herr Gurlitt about his line of work." She was all innocent smiles.

Michel spoke soft German, listened, and said, "Herr Gurlitt is a collector of art . . ."

More like a thief.

". . . and is acting for someone very important, one of the most important men in Europe though he cannot say who, and I cannot say who will remember who, so you should pretend to be ill and go."

Isa ignored Michel and smiled at Gurlitt, remembering the letter on Van Meegeren's desk. Gurlitt wasn't just collecting for Hitler personally, but for Hitler's new museum. The agent was still speaking, soft and satisfied. Purring.

Michel said, "He wants to know if this is truly your first time as an artist's model. He thinks he has seen your face before. In a painting."

She glanced once at Michel. He was cool, collected. Smooth. His uniform pressed and boots polished. But there was a stiffness in the corner of his mouth, in the set of his jaw. Tonight, Isa would have named his portrait *Fear*.

Fear was good. A steadying influence. It kept you out of danger. It kept you alive.

Unfortunately, Isa had lost hers.

She lowered her lashes and shrugged, coy. She might have even managed a blush. She said, "As soon as everyone goes to eat, I have to get through the door below the stairs and then I will go. Ask him which piece is the most exciting that he has collected so far."

She saw the narrowing of Michel's eyes from the corner of her vision. His German seemed almost reluctant. But Herr Gurlitt sat up, lip curling. He wanted to brag. To crow about his accomplishments. He started in, and Michel began his translation without a break in speed or tone.

"Herr Gurlitt says he has just been fortunate enough to bring an astounding find to his client. Tell them you are ill and go through your door another day. I will pretend to look up your name and give the other address. You do not understand what kind of party this is. The painting is from one of the best artists of your Netherlands. An unknown Vermeer . . ."

A Vermeer. It was *Woman with a Wine Glass*. Now Isa sat up straighter. Leaned toward Gurlitt with her glass.

"Really? Is Vermeer very famous?"

Quiet, condescending laughter from around the room.

Michel translated with tight lips. "Yes, he is very famous. The painting will be the jewel of the collection."

Isa tucked a bare foot beneath her pinned dress, her gaze on the fat cat of an art agent. "I will disappear when I have done what I came to do. Ask him how much he paid for his prize. His client must be very wealthy."

Michel's German was becoming stilted, but everyone was suddenly focused on Gurlitt, who was carefully examining the gold of his cuff link. When he spoke, Isa could almost understand. She looked to Michel for confirmation.

Michel's voice was cool when he said, "One-point-six million guilders."

Isa nearly choked on her wine, too stunned to speak. No wonder Van Meegeren was living like a king. The oily Gurlitt would be living like a king just on the commission. She sipped carefully. Hitler must have wanted that Vermeer for his museum badly. Knowing that the

Führer had paid such a staggering amount for a painting that was as fake as his Rembrandt gave Isa a shiver of contentment that was difficult to conceal.

But would he pay it again?

How many children could be saved with a million and a half guilders? How many people? How many bribes paid? Weapons purchased?

Could they take back the Netherlands?

Was that even possible? To get the country back with a painting? And even better, with a forgery.

They couldn't do anything if she didn't get through that door.

"Fräulein Groot," Michel was saying, leaning forward. She'd obviously not been paying attention. "Herr Gurlitt says he believes you are very impressed and will you please go."

"Oh!" She put the wine on the table. It was becoming too difficult to remember who was talking to who. "Ja. Yes. Please say that he must be very good at his job."

Michel translated this, giving her the Dutch back as Gurlitt spoke. "He says, yes, there was another agent who wanted a Vermeer very much, but that his own client was more important, so he was able to broker the sale . . ."

Isa glanced up. Hofer. Goering's agent. The smug little man who was not here. The rivalry between the two had been obvious.

". . . and tonight," Michel went on for Gurlitt, "he is going to be outdone again . . ."

Hitler's agent was smiling beneath his lids. Confident.

". . . and these men are dangerous and will you please get ill right away."

Isa didn't look at Michel. So, Goering wanted a Vermeer, too, did he? A collection not to be outdone by his Führer. This meant that

Hofer would want to believe. He would believe whatever was put in front of him.

And if he believed, he would pay.

"Hello! Hello, everyone, and welcome!"

The room turned as one, and there was Van Meegeren, arms out-stretched in the doorway. He was pale beneath a flush of color on his cheeks, but wide awake, buzzing, dressed in a neat, navy-striped suit with a smoking jacket over top, velvet and silk, hair combed and rings on his fingers. A contrast that could not be more different from the sofa sprawl.

Isa felt the throb she'd nearly forgotten, pounding a staccato in her chest. She thought she could feel the outline of a key beneath her chiffon.

Van Meegeren's eyes landed on her, shiny and sharp. "So you're here, too, eh? Has everyone met . . ." He waved a blank hand at Isa.

"Elsa," Isa supplied.

"Right, right," said Van Meegeren. "You've all met my Judith, then?"

She really couldn't believe her luck.

"The cook says our dinner is served, so, gentlemen, if you would join me . . ."

And then Michel was standing, and Herr Gurlitt was standing, bending over her gallantly, both hands extended. She had no choice but to put her hands in his, no choice but to let him pull her to her bare feet. To leave a silver key exposed on the white velvet. Michel came to stand on the other side of her, ready to translate.

"Herr Gurlitt says that of course you will join us for dinner."

Isa smiled. And there came her fear, a paint spill, an oil slick spreading, joining the brown-green trickle of revulsion sliding down her spine as Gurlitt kissed the back of one hand, and then the other, slipping her arm through his. Michel leaned down, removing fuzz from his pants, left from the fur-lined chair, and as Isa was led firmly into the dining room—a butterfly on the arm of the spider—she looked back. The little silver key was gone, and Michel Lange was taking his hand from his pocket.

12

MRS. MARTINELLI SENT a maid Isa had never seen to set another place at the table, to hurry and make room for another chair. The housekeeper looked at Isa askance, a feeling Isa could not disagree with. She was made up like a circus performer, only just on the correct side of decent, insinuating herself into a formal dinner. Their understanding, Isa could see, was at an end.

Isa attempted to wriggle away by suggesting that she change her clothes while the table was reset. That at least she could put on her shoes. But Gurlitt only smirked and told Michel to tell her she was fine as she was.

Van Meegeren chuckled, rubbing his hands together. Bright-eyed.

Mrs. Martinelli must have gone upstairs and thrown cold water on him.

They found their places at a table that was long and narrow, chrome and glass, a row of tall, thin silver vases running down the center, filling the space above their heads with fresh roses. An extravagant amount of roses, clouds of them bursting from the stemlike vases, like sitting beneath a bloodred storm. It smelled like a funeral.

Van Meegeren was at the head, Herr Gurlitt to his right, Isa reluctantly beside him, after Gurlitt had pulled out her chair. On the other side of Van Meegeren was the suit she'd taken no notice of yet, a man with a paunch who was obviously embarrassed by her presence, introduced as the German Minister of Culture in the Netherlands. Beside him sat Michel, ready to facilitate conversation, while the other three uniforms filled in the table. They were SS, the two across from Isa young and arrogant, leering with a blend of interest and condescension, showing off for the officer to her right. He was older, quieter, and, Isa thought, probably more deadly.

She was in a web full of spiders.

A little silence fell.

Michel sat straight in his chair, making a minuscule correction to the placement of his spoon. Isa studied him, here in his natural surroundings, the Nazi who had managed to pilfer two of her keys. And he was exactly as he ought to be. Dark-haired and brown-eyed—but so was Hitler—average to look at and physically strong. He was well educated, his demeanor polite and impersonal. He had no rank, but an enviable posting, a far cry from marching in the Russian snow or riding roughshod over Poland in a panzer. That spoke of influence, someone high in the hierarchy.

And he wanted to leave it all behind and hide in her gallery. At the risk of a firing squad.

The boy-officer next to Michel put an elbow in his ribs, saying something low and possibly insolent based on the lift of his cheek. He was dark like Michel, but more handsome. And he knew it. Michel's response was stiff, formal, and, Isa could see, highly irritating. The young man repeated it to the soldier at his side for a laugh, eyes searching to see if the older officer had heard and approved.

She couldn't decide whether Michel Lange was an ally or a blackmailer. If he'd wanted her gone from this dinner to protect her, or to protect his potential hiding place. If he'd taken that key to thwart her, or to prevent the key from being found. She didn't know what Michel Lange was, and she couldn't ask him, not even in Dutch. Not with Van Meegeren in the room.

She wanted that key.

Gurlitt leaned toward her, murmuring, and Michel said, "Herr Gurlitt wishes to know if you are comfortable."

Isa smiled through her lashes. She could see her own bare feet through the table glass. "You can tell him I am just about as comfortable as Holofernes."

She didn't care if Van Meegeren heard that much.

Michel translated without an outward sign, the fear she'd seen in the living room tidied up, folded, and put away. Though obviously he changed the meaning of her reply, because Gurlitt's eyes half closed behind his glasses, pleased. Van Meegeren chuckled and lit a cigarette, smoke rising to mingle with the roses.

Then the door swung open, and Mrs. Martinelli and the young maid came through with a soup tureen on a cart, and the scent of flowers and tobacco was cut with the odors of mushroom and garlic. The three SS officers talked low amongst themselves, waiting to be served, while Van Meegeren started in on Gurlitt.

Van Meegeren knew enough German to have a conversation, or at least enough to sell a painting, which—with the occasional word from Michel—was exactly what he was attempting to do. Isa listened, trying to look as if she wasn't listening, and caught the word *Vermeer* three times. Another Vermeer must be the reason Gurlitt had come here tonight, a dinner to view his new find, to celebrate his out-maneuvering of Hofer and Goering.

But the painting, Isa deduced, was not present to be viewed. This was interesting, though Gurlitt found it vexing in the extreme. So vexing that, for a moment, she thought things were going to go badly for Van Meegeren. But the very inability to see what he'd come for—the curiosity denied, the deferred gratification of uncovering an unknown masterpiece—was making Gurlitt want the painting all the more. Isa could see the desire growing, a greed that suffused his neck with a salmon-tinted flush.

Van Meegeren knew exactly what he was doing, gesticulating with his ringed fingers, leaving Gurlitt and the Minister of Culture struggling to follow. He had a fish on a line—a fish too arrogant to even know there were hooks—and he was reeling it in, slowly. And enjoying every minute of it. An enjoyment based not only on the size of his profit but on the fact that this new Vermeer he was selling was probably just as forged as the last one.

Isa couldn't blame him. She'd enjoyed selling this man a forgery, too.

It gave her an unsettled, queasy sort of feeling, to be in sympathy with Van Meegeren.

And then, for a split second, she imagined handing 1.6 million of the Führer's guilders to Truus, and a shudder ran up between her shoulder blades.

She wanted that key.

Michel reached down to retrieve his napkin, and when he came up, Gurlitt was leaning toward her, bridging the space between their seats to put a hand on the back of her chair.

"Herr Gurlitt apologizes for being inattentive," Michel said stiffly. "The painting he wished to see has not arrived, and he is anxious, because both he and his rival will be leaving Amsterdam next week. But he is sure that he will be the one leaving with the prize."

"Oh, no!" Isa said stupidly. "You're not leaving so soon?"

She didn't want them to go. Not before she had milked them for every guilder she could get. Gurlitt practically purred, leaned closer to pour wine into her glass.

Michel barely opened his lips when he said, "He wishes to know just how sorry you are."

And Isa felt a hand on her knee, caressing.

Her trickle of revulsion erupted in disgust. Gray-brown.

Streaked with a blaze of vermilion.

"Bread?" she said, as if Michel had mistranslated. "You would like the bread?" She put on a face of sudden concern and half stood, bumping the table, shaking the roses, stretching right over the plate of the SS officer beside her to grab the bread basket, removing her leg from Gurlitt's roving hand in the process. "Please," she said, sitting back down and offering the basket. "Have some."

The whole table had gone silent, the young officer beside Michel staring. Gurlitt took a roll, straightening his glasses, his returning smile a little more chilly. The man beside her said something low and contemptuous to his fellows. Michel's eyes flicked briefly to him, to Isa, and away.

She didn't want to know what had just been said.

Michel began some kind of German apology to Gurlitt, while the officer who had probably just insulted her was picking up little white tablets off the tablecloth, returning them to a tin box, a box she had knocked sideways in her haste to get away from Gurlitt. He washed two of the tablets down with wine and passed the box to the arrogant boy-officer across the table. Then he gestured at Isa, and they laughed.

Isa didn't want to know what they'd said this time, either. She didn't want to know what Michel was saying. She didn't want to know what sort of pills were in that little box, or what effect they might have on officers of the SS.

Her fear churned and pooled. Oil-slick. Bile-yellow.

The revulsion still clung to her spine. Sticky.

One more rejection of Gurlitt's attentions, one flash of the man's memory, one slip of her true name from Van Meegeren, and she wouldn't just lose her opportunity to get through a door. She'd lose her opportunity to escape this house.

And then Isa's gaze darted up. There was no clock in the dining room, the only window covered in its chic blackout. Even Van Meegeren's office had had the curtains drawn. When was the last time she'd seen the sun? She would never get back to the gallery after curfew, not without being arrested. Not from here, where bridges were guarded, where it was impossible to be invisible. If she didn't leave before dark, she'd be trapped.

And she was afraid it had already happened.

The moment was snapped by Mrs. Martinelli, coming through the door with the second course: plates of sausages and sauerkraut and potatoes, buttered carrots and pickled onions. Sweet, stewed apples. The amount, the variety, the smell, after months of bread and potatoes and the occasional can from the cellar, was overwhelming. Platters covered the glass-top table as the maid came plate to plate to serve.

The mood at the table lifted, though whether that was sausages or the little white tablets, Isa wasn't sure. The boy-officer beside Michel began talking diagonally across the table to Gurlitt. He was wearing a watch, but it wasn't close enough for Isa to see. Van Meegeren jumped into the conversation with enough half-Dutch for her to understand that they were discussing new postings. Everyone except the cultural minister, it seemed, was leaving in eight days. The Friday after next, some kind of governmental changing of the guard. And then the officer who had been talking so eagerly about *Neiderlande* said the word *Judenfrei*.

Isa knew what that word meant. It wasn't that far from the Dutch. *Free from Jews.*

Was that why these SS officers were in Amsterdam? To hunt Jews? And now they were leaving because their work of making the city Judenfrei would be complete? Isa reached out for the wine Gurlitt had poured.

Eight days, and the children would be gone.

She didn't think it was enough time. It wouldn't be enough time.

Damn the Nazis. Damn them to the fiery blazes of Munch's hell.

They all deserved a Judith. Or a Salome.

And then Isa jumped a little. Flinched. There was a foot on her foot. A warm sock brushing against her bare toes.

Isa set the goblet down too hard on the glass, jerking back her foot. The officer beside her looked around, but he was intent on some story they all found very amusing involving die Juden, Gurlitt deep in a conversation with Van Meegeren.

And Michel Lange was settling his napkin in his lap, leaning back a little in his chair, like he'd eaten too much. Gazing at the roses, the German minister. The gleaming, sparkling crystals of the chandelier. Anywhere but at Isa. He was not looking at her so hard that Isa was afraid it was very obvious that he wanted to. She could see the shadow of his leg through the table glass, a glimpse through the numerous platters. And there came his foot again, soft against hers, only this time, she felt the cool smooth surface of metal.

It was a key.

Michel Lange was giving her the key beneath the table. With his toes.

The gazes met and glanced away, one dot of a brush. And now Isa leaned forward over her plate, as if buttered carrots were all she could think of—the only things worth paying attention to in the world— sliding her foot over Michel's sock, trying to get a purchase on the key.

She knocked it to the floor, a nearly inaudible *tink* below the surface of the conversations. But she found it, got it underneath the ball of her foot, sliding it back and back across the tiles and beneath her chair. Michel sat up a little straighter, dabbing the corner of his mouth, interjecting a word of help for the German minister. Pretending to scratch a leg when she knew he was trying to get his boot back on.

How had he managed to take off that boot when it went nearly up to his knee?

She gave a little cough, and then a bigger one, instantly bringing the attention of Herr Gurlitt and the SS. Drawing it away from Michel and his boot.

"I am so sorry," Isa said. "I think . . . I am a little ill."

Michel translated, but no one was looking at him. Isa pushed back her chair, key beneath her foot, then leaned suddenly forward like she was going to vomit.

The officer on her right leapt back, pushing his chair sideways, while Herr Gurlitt knocked his over with a clatter. Van Meegeren rang a bell. Everyone talked at once. Isa bent double, made a swipe for the key, caught a glimpse beneath the table of Michel with a foot balanced, tying up his boot. She came up quickly with the key in her palm and a credible imitation of a stomach heave. She might as well have given every Nazi in the room a shove, they moved so fast. Even Van Meegeren looked surprised.

"Please . . . excuse me," she said. And ran from the dining room unhindered.

A butterfly that had snapped a web with the beating of its wings.

Through the white living room, a glance at the clock on the mantelpiece, and into the hall, where Isa paused. At a crossroads.

Use the key?

Change her clothes and risk a trip home in the dusk?

Or hide in a toilet?

Mrs. Martinelli came hurrying into the hall, a buzz of male speculation emanating from the dining room. She saw Isa standing, dithering.

"I need to go," Isa whispered.

Mrs. Martinelli hesitated, and then she nodded. They had reached another understanding. The housekeeper turned and walked briskly back toward the dining room, and Isa had decided. She ran to the door below the stairs and put the key to the lock.

The door opened, silent on its hinges. And Isa stepped inside.

Into the darkness.

13

ISA STOOD STILL, letting her eyes adjust, the buzz of consternated German from the dining room suddenly muffled.

She was relieved to find that she was not in a cupboard.

There were stairs stretching down in front of her, just as she'd guessed, the old kind, wooden, steep and narrow, ending with black and terra-cotta floor tiles only just glimpsed in the dim. Isa took a step down, holding the key and the chiffon, edging toward the wall, where the wood was at its strongest, where the grit of decades— maybe a century—dug into the soles of her feet. The treads still popped. And there was a smell, heat and chemicals, something sickly sweet, getting stronger as the sounds above her faded and fell silent. By the time Isa stepped onto the tiles, the odor had wormed its way deep into her nose, fetid, stifling, the air warm enough to have leeched the cold from the floor.

The room was being used for storage, trunks and old furniture with its upholstery hanging loose, broken easels and opened crates. The light was odd, ambience rather than illumination, tinted to orange instead of yellow, and it was coming from behind her, from a partially open door. Isa pushed the door to the wall, and was unsurprised by what she saw.

A kitchen, with its box bed to one side, no mattress, a table covered in jars, and . . . an oven. The old kind, enormous and made of bricks. Orange light glowed from around the edges of an iron door badly sealed, an unreal, steady sort of light that spoke of electricity and embers. The smell was so bad she had to cover her nose.

She set the key on the table and tiptoed to the oven, cautiously, gently, as if it might startle into flight. She put a glancing fingertip on the iron handle. Only warm, not hot, but it must have been that way for a long time, to take the chill from the floor tiles of a canal house cellar. She cracked the door open, looking into the electric orange shadows, bright and dark at the same time. There was a heater inside—modern, glowing, the kind meant for wet feet on a cold day—with a thermostat set to low.

And above it, laid flat on a grate at the top of the oven, there was a canvas.

Baking.

Isa shut the door. The shadowy interior had obscured the subject matter—figures, a portrait, maybe—but she didn't dare move the painting or take it out. She'd used a low temperature when she experimented at home, and it hadn't worked. Maybe it needed longer. An afternoon? A day?

Eight days to prepare the painting, make a deal, take a payment, and get the money to Truus. And they would probably start taking children before then.

Isa turned to the table, covered with brush bristles and colored dust, a pumice stone and the handle of a shaving brush, bristles snipped. So Van Meegeren had been making his own paintbrushes from badger hair. She'd been right about that. She examined the glass jars, where the worst of the smell was coming from.

The lilac oil was easy to identify, sickly sweet. Then she picked up a jar of rubbing alcohol, and a small bottle that stained the tip of her finger. Surely that was India ink. As for the other jars, she didn't know her chemicals well enough to guess what type of foulness each might contain. The invoices upstairs had probably told her, but the cloying smells had gone from her nose to her head, and she couldn't bring the names to mind. It was incredible that the odor hadn't been detectable upstairs. But the fumes seemed to hang in the low places, like some kind of noxious mist.

And then, on a stool pushed below the table, Isa noticed a paint palette. Freshly varnished, new, with just a few small blobs of bright, vibrant color, their edges mixing into tints and hues. The paint looked almost wet, as if the artist had just stepped away for a coffee.

Isa shot a glance over her shoulder, even though she knew she was alone. She'd seen no way in or out other than the stairs, and no one had come down them. She picked up the palette, peering closely at the paint in the shadow light, took a finger and brushed the tip against the pool of Van Dyck brown.

Smooth. Her fingernail clicked on the shining puddle.

Hard paint. More than hard. It was completely dry.

She rummaged through the jars and found the alcohol, dipped in her finger and rubbed. No paint came off the palette. She poured a little on the Van Dyck brown, but it only shone. She couldn't find water to test with, and so she gave up and spit on the blue, a blue that might be ultramarine. Real ultramarine. She rubbed it, and spit again.

And there was not the first smudge of pigment on her finger.

Isa took the palette and sat on the hard wooden edge of the boxed-in space that had once been someone's bed. She was staring at the paint.

This paint had not been in an oven.

And then the door at the top of the stairs rattled.

Once.

Twice.

She sat where she was—there wasn't much of anywhere to go—leaning forward and straining her ears. But she could feel no change in the air from an opening door. No feet on the creaking stairs. Someone had walked by and tested the strength of the lock. Michel Lange, seeing if she'd gone through, perhaps, or wondering what might be behind it? Or Van Meegeren, discovering he had lost his key?

Herr Gurlitt. Looking for her.

She tried to dig a thumbnail into each bright circle. She knew she couldn't do it.

And hopelessness, Isa thought, was to be without color. It was a hole in the palette. An empty nothing.

Because she was not going to free the Netherlands or save the last six babies or even hand Truus another coin. She wasn't even going to pay the taxes. Because the secret to Van Meegeren's *Woman with a Wine Glass*—his fabulous 1.6 million–guilder Vermeer—was in the paint. Paint that had been mixed with chemicals to make it harden, then put in the oven to crack and create craquelure. And that was not a process she could duplicate, no matter how long she heated the *Vermeer De Smit*. The undoctored paint was already on the canvas.

Isa looked up. There were footsteps above her head now, floorboards protesting like the stair treads. She wasn't sure exactly where she was in relation to the rest of the house, somewhere behind the hall. Maybe the billiard room she'd noticed earlier. But dinner was obviously over. Other festivities had begun.

Isa put down the palette and examined the room, making sure she hadn't missed another door, another way out, another hiding place. She did the same in the storage room before she came back to the kitchen to sit on the hard edge of the bed. She could hear the murmur of voices now, a gramophone playing jazz—she supposed no one would be mentioning that to their Führer—the clod of dancing boots, and the brisk, dainty click of at least two pairs of heels.

She was trapped in a place she should not be. On a bed that had no mattress. Beside a table covered in chemicals. In the light of an oven where a painting was baking. And she had only learned what she could not do. A process she could not replicate.

Only, she didn't have to replicate it, did she?

Because she already had a painting with hard paint and craquelure, where time had done the job Van Meegeren had so cleverly imitated. And all she had to do was break down a wall.

It felt wrong. It was wrong. Vermeer's masterpiece, Moshe's birthright, sacrificed on the altar of Nazi greed. Even the idea was a promise broken, a betrayal of everything Isa de Smit held sacred.

But the whole world had betrayed everything Isa de Smit had ever held sacred. She lived in a world that had created the time, and the reason, for such a betrayal.

Such an ugly world.

Isa scooted back across the bare wood, propping herself in the dirty shadows of its corner, letting the terrible idea of breaking her promise to Moshe sink down into the marrow of her bones. She wondered about the color of her bones. If she were a painting, scraped down, what color would one find underneath?

It would be vermilion. She was made of vermilion.

And if she was going to betray Moshe's sacred trust, become the true collaborator that Truus hated so much, if she was going to sell a Dutch treasure to the Nazis, then she would first have to prove that Van Meegeren's painting of *Woman with a Wine Glass* was a fake.

It shouldn't be difficult. She was surrounded by the evidence. She could tell Gurlitt to have his men raid the house, break down the cellar door. But how would Gurlitt react to the news that he had paid

1.6 million guilders of Hitler's money for a forgery? He would have to admit that he'd wasted a fortune. Acknowledge he'd been a fool. It would be scandal and embarrassment, the end of reputation and career. He wouldn't want to believe it. And if Gurlitt didn't want to believe, it was going to take more than an artist's model who had just threatened to be ill all over his dinner plate to convince him otherwise.

He might, Isa realized, actually prefer to keep the fake. And Hitler's favor.

She leaned her head against the wooden wall of the box bed. She would need Michel to convince Gurlitt he'd bought a forgery, and to facilitate the sale. Acting for an anonymous third party, perhaps. But would he do it? Was the hiding place of the gallery enough incentive?

Maybe Gurlitt would pay just to keep her quiet.

Maybe she would teach Michel how to blackmail someone properly. Or maybe, for a million guilders, he would cut her out of the deal entirely and never be seen again.

If she scraped Michel Lange down to the underlayment, what color would he be?

She had no way of knowing.

The party went on above her head without a lull or break in intensity. It went on for hours—it felt like days, with no way to mark the time—which must have had something to do with the little box of pills. Isa couldn't smell the chemicals anymore. She tried not to be able to hear.

The art world was full of hedonists. She was used to them. She'd grown up with them, spent her life in a city where prostitution was a well-organized business. She was still shocked. Maybe she'd been more sheltered in the garret than she'd known. Or maybe she just wasn't used to hedonists who were so pious about a completely different set of twisted principles in the daytime.

She knew she was lucky not to be up there.

She wondered if Michel still was. Participating. If anyone had noticed her clothes were in the studio, or if they thought she'd gone running down the canal in a trailing chiffon. If her father had ever noticed she was gone. Or maybe he'd run out of things to throw and had starved in the garret.

Isa must have fallen asleep at some point, in the dim, orange-flavored light, the stale air and heat from the oven. Maybe the smell had filled her head with fuzzy dreams. But she found herself waking, curled into her corner nook.

Because someone was coming down the stairs.

Slow and unsteady.

She only just kept herself from jumping. Moving. Leaping up to run away. Instead, Isa kept perfectly still, a mouse in unexpected light. The opening of the bed was small, she could see the opposite corner of the kitchen and the back of the storage room door. She reached out and quietly gathered up the dress, tucking it around her legs, and then the door was shoved open, and she caught a brief flash of a small figure with rumpled hair and an untucked shirt.

Van Meegeren.

He must have had another key.

Damn him, Isa thought. And the Nazis. And doors and lock-smiths and the inventor of keys. Because the key she'd stolen from Van Meegeren's smock was still sitting among the glass jars and paint litter of the table.

Her fear came back, crawling. Seeping.

A million and a half guilders, Isa suddenly realized, was well worth killing for.

She kept her breath short, shallow. She did not move the first muscle. Listening as Van Meegeren coughed, the gentle rasp as he turned the oven handle, his hiss of hot fingers as a canvas came out of the heat. Then the wooden chair legs scraped, dragging across floor tiles, and Isa heard the click of a switch.

Light flooded the little kitchen, white and glaring, pouring through a crack where two boards of the box bed had shrunk apart.

Isa wished she'd known about the light. She wished that all those times she'd pretended to need the toilet, she'd actually gone.

Glimpses of movement flitted across the lit crack. A canvas propped unceremoniously between two chairs. The quick motion of a broad brush. She smelled the varnish, heard the faint, familiar rustle of bristles. And then she could see Van Meegeren turning the canvas, bending, reaching below it, swaying every time he straightened to examine the paint beneath the light. Bending and pressing.

Van Meegeren was cracking his paint.

This had to be the Vermeer, Gurlitt's exciting new discovery that had been so disappointingly not present. Because it was still in the oven. And Van Meegeren was working on this one-hour-old, seventeenth-century masterpiece while the man he was planning to defraud with it—defraud for an astronomical sum—was presumably somewhere upstairs, passed out cold.

She wished she could get a good look at it. It really was ingenious, what Van Meegeren had managed, but after watching his movements, even the slivers she could discern through the wooden crack, Isa knew that this was not merely the second time Han van Meegeren had cracked baked paint. He was practiced, sure of himself, even when he was stumbling drunk. And that meant Hitler's art agent was not the first he'd fooled.

Just how many Van Meegerens were out there?

Isa thought about the Hals, the bawdy woman hanging on his pristinely white living room wall, with her nicely painted linen and craquelure. The way Van Meegeren had pushed, goading Isa into saying who painted it. It almost made her laugh.

And then she thought of his profits, and where they came from. How he was living a life of extravagance and debauchery while others lived on a potato ration. While others lost their children and their lives. How he was somehow able to sell fakes while she was forced to part with a treasure. How he had corrupted the beauty of art to build something ugly.

Van Meegeren embodied the ugliness of her world.

Isa listened to him mutter. Heard the soft squeal of a hinge. The painting was going back in the oven, one of the old wooden chairs was protesting beneath a weight. Her legs were cramped, her neck hurt, and she desperately needed a toilet. She hoped Van Meegeren found her and tried to kill her, because she didn't know how much longer she could sit still. And she would quite like to hit him.

"You should go," said Van Meegeren into the silence.

Isa didn't move. The form she could see slumped at the table through the crack hadn't moved, either.

"No need to . . . hide . . . in the dark," he said. His voice was low, slurred, like he was dreaming. "All gone, you know. They've all gone . . ."

The oven door ticked as it cooled. Isa moved her head, a tilt to the left, a little lean, and got an eye past the opening of the box bed. Van Meegeren had his elbows on the table, head propped in his hands. She moved an arm, carefully shifting her weight. He didn't make a sign. The wood creaked softly, gently, as she lifted her body, scooting out from the corner, then forward and out of the opening. Isa got her feet on the floor tiles and stood.

She wasn't certain if Van Meegeren knew she was there or not. If he did, she was fairly sure he was too incapacitated to stop her.

Isa took a step. No movement. She reached out and took the key from the table. The key he hadn't even noticed. His breath came deep and rattling. She took a step backward, and another. Then turned to creep out of the cellar.

"Judith," Van Meegeren said.

She looked back over her shoulder. His eyes were open, and now, Isa thought, she knew the true color of misery. It was waxy pale, with red rims.

"Judith," he murmured, "are you going to cut off my head?"

"Not today," Isa whispered.

"Good," he slurred, and his eyes fell shut.

Isa fled up the stairs. The white and marble entrance hall was tomb-like, a mausoleum filled with stale smoke and possibly the smell of vomit. The party must have been all over the house, because there were champagne bottles that had rolled, whiskey bottles broken, a stocking on a cushion and a man's shoe on the step. She could see the man who went with the shoe, hands crossed, one foot bare, laid out on the sofa like he was in a coffin. The SS officer she'd sat beside the night before. She assumed he was alive.

She didn't wait to find out.

Isa ran silently up the curving steps, found a toilet, and threw the key on the floor of Van Meegeren's office, where it might have slipped from a sleeping man's pocket. Then up again to the studio dressing room, where she pulled off the hated chiffon, pins and all, rolled on her stockings and buttoned her dress. She found a jar of cold cream and a silk handkerchief, using both to wipe the black lines from her eyes. Three pins in her hair, her pumps in hand, down the stairs in her stocking feet, and out the front door.

And Isa breathed. The air was fresh, damp, the sun rising over the rows of gables, shades of apricot deepening to orange-red above a slate-dark line of clouds. A passing woman stared. At the coat hanging half-off one shoulder, watching her slip on her shoes on a front stoop at the crack of curfew. Isa knew exactly what she looked like. But so many people had thought she was a prostitute in the last twenty-four hours that Isa gave the woman a smile. Insolent. Brazen. From a redhead standing on the steps of a known collaborator. A smile the woman could not fail to remember.

That had been reckless. And satisfying.

Isa followed the woman down the Keizersgracht, a soft wind stirring a rain of russet leaves, sending them to collect on an awning of the deepest madder red. A girl stood below the awning, buttoning a faded poppy coat beside a pot of geraniums, flushed with crimson petals even after the frost.

The whole world was red. Colored with a vermilion brush.

Left past the butcher's and the wax cherries still perched on an out-of-date hat, across the canal, and there was Michel Lange. Clean and crisp and not appearing hungover, leaning against the bridge rail, smoking with the German guard. His gaze slid over her, impersonal. But she kept her eyes on him as she passed. He glanced again, and betrayed the slightest look of surprise. Isa stepped off the bridge, and when she looked back, Michel was stubbing out his cigarette, ending his conversation.

She needed to talk to him, and now he knew it. And he would come, and she would convince him to help her sell Moshe's Vermeer, and it was infuriating.

Because it was heartbreaking.

She turned the corner, crossing over toward the Singel, and a plane roared across the sky, German this time, racing ahead of the storm. Chins lifted to watch it pass. And when Isa brought her gaze back down to the street, there was the woman with the kerchief—why did she never change her kerchief, it was so recognizable—strolling with her shopping bag on the other side of the canal.

Had the woman seen, or not seen, Isa spending the night in the house of a known collaborator?

Who would kill her first? she wondered. Nazis, Van Meegeren, or the Resistance?

Isa passed the turn that would have been her quicker way home and walked instead up to Rokin, where there were shoulders and feet, more eyes, more German guards, more trams to jump on as needed. The woman kept pace. Isa felt compelled to lose her. She sped up, darted across the path of a horse-drawn cart—more common than cars, with petrol in such short supply—and jangled the bell on the door of a bakery.

She dug out her ration book from her purse and bought bread. As if bread buying was the purpose of all her walking. She came out with her sack, walked the opposite way, and ducked into a side street. Around the corner, around again, and back onto Rokin.

The sky was getting darker instead of brighter. She couldn't see the woman with the kerchief now. She seemed to have gone the wrong way. Isa couldn't see the German guards, either. A piece of the canal had been filled here, making the road wide, no bridge to watch over. She hurried past a tram expelling its contents, and then Isa's head jerked up.

She'd heard a scream. And now the wailing of a child.

Three houses in front of her, a little girl was crying on the sidewalk, sitting at the bottom of the three stone steps she'd just fallen down, her palms and knees scraped bloody. A factory worker clomping in his wooden shoes had already bent down to help, one or two of the people from the tram coming forward. But others turned their faces. Lowered the brims of their hats and kept walking. Because the whole family, Isa saw, was being forced down the steps. A broad, middle-aged woman still in her housecoat, a grandfather with a long, peppered beard, and two more children, none of them more than ten.

An SS officer stood above them, waving. Shouting. He had a pistol in his hand.

Isa stood still, frozen. The man in wooden shoes stepped back from the crying child, the gathering crowd edging away like they'd discovered a disease. She saw the long, gray curls hanging on either side of the grandfather's beard, the lips that muttered a prayer, the hands of the two children he was holding. He was Jewish. They were Jewish.

This family had been hiding Jews.

And the officer at the top of the steps was raising his pistol, aiming it down, straight at the little girl with the bloody knees. His finger was on the trigger.

Isa dropped her bread.

The mother screamed and threw herself in front of the child. The Nazi yelled in German. Slow. Deliberate. A pronouncement.

And then Isa was bumped hard from behind, a bag thrust into her startled hands. And she saw a woman marching toward the scene on the steps. Truus. Isa knew her by her walk, by the anger in her stride. By the back of her neck beneath her short blond hair.

The Nazi with the pistol was still shouting his judgment, enjoying his audience. The Jewish grandfather rocked as he prayed. The crowd leaned back while the mother cried, shielding her child.

Truus walked to the bottom of the stone steps. She pulled a gun from her coat pocket. Isa felt her lips part. The Nazi turned, and opened his mouth. And Truus shot him.

Once.

Twice.

A body fell.

A thin haze of smoke rose from the barrel of the gun.

Parts of the Nazi were spattered on the door.

An apocalyptic silence came down on the street. Truus put the gun in her pocket and looked back. Her gaze met Isa's. Two blue eyes that were ice. And then she walked away, hands in her coat pockets, fast down the sidewalk. Like she had a tram to catch.

No one in the crowd stopped her. No one even looked at her.

They didn't want to know.

Then someone spoke low, a word, and everyone moved. The mother, the Jewish grandfather, and the three children were absorbed into a crowd that was dissipating like late fog. Not one scream. Nothing to alert the police if the gun hadn't done that job already. Isa turned her back and began to walk the other way down Rokin. She looked down at the bag she'd forgotten was in her hands.

She was holding a baby.

"Thou shalt pursue light even in the darkness, for light remains light."

—Commandment Nine, from *The Dutch Ten Commandments to Foil the Nazis*

14

SHOCK HIT ISA like a bullet.

She stared down into the bag. Closed eyes, soft hair, a small hand reaching upward. Isa zipped the bag, not quite all the way. And then she walked. Faster. Pulse hammering in her throat. Half running down the street. The bag was leather, large, and with handles, like last time. She held it in both arms, unnatural. Around the corner and she slowed, adjusted, holding the bag carefully by the handles, straightening her coat. Strolling like she had a bag of clothes, a bag of tools, a bag of shopping. She turned onto Kalverstraat, moving faster, faster, her breath coming in gasps, like she had something to hide.

She had never had so much to hide.

If someone was following, she didn't see them.

If they were following, she might not be able to see them.

She took the back way, through the gully, pushing the garden gate shut behind her. The blank, dead eyes of the blacked-out windows stared. She tried to fish her key from her purse, but she couldn't put the bag down. She heard a fuss, and then a soft cry. Isa found the key. She turned the lock, pushed her way inside, set the bag gently on the table, and quickly locked the door behind her.

She looked at the bag. The leather squirmed. Isa slowly pulled the zipper. She reached up and switched on the light.

The baby wrinkled its face, kicking and waving two fists, fighting the sudden brightness. It was wrapped in a blanket, with hair the color of a winter chestnut, the button-end of a nose, a tiny mouth opening, ready to cry. And then the baby changed its mind and stilled, looking back at Isa. Blinking. As if life in a bag was something it had come to terms with.

Isa braced herself on the table. There was a shake beginning in her middle, a burst of bright orange. A pinwheel of sick yellow, purple, and scarlet, spinning, swirling into a shade she couldn't recognize.

Truus had killed a man.

Truus had saved a family.

Truus had handed her a baby. And she didn't know what to do with it.

She started at a soft knock on the door behind her. If she had a pulse, it was too rapid to feel.

"Isa?"

It was Michel.

"Are you in there?"

She couldn't speak. She looked around and couldn't find her bread.

"I'm using my key," he said through the door. The lock clinked, and Michel tried to slide inside, only to find himself bumping her with the door. There wasn't room, the table was in the way. Her father must have a key after all, Isa thought, because the table hadn't been pushed against the door. Then her mind caught up with her circumstance and she spun on her heel, leaning back, shielding the bag.

"You should not leave me standing outside. Not in the daytime," Michel chided, getting the door shut and locked. "I cannot be seen coming here."

She agreed. But she'd gone mute.

"Did you see what happened on the street?" he asked.

She nodded.

"I was two blocks back. I only heard. The Gestapo are going house to house. Working their way back from the Singel. They will be shooting people now, whether they are guilty or not. They might even come here."

She nodded again. The shaking from her middle had moved to her hands.

"Did you see who did it?"

She couldn't answer.

"Did you do it?"

She blinked and shook her head. Why did he think she was a murderer?

Was Truus a murderer?

"What were you doing there? It is not on your way home."

She didn't want to say that she was being followed. By the angels. Because she was in league with the devil, and that everyone thought the devil was him. Michel took a half step forward, head to one side.

"What happened last night?"

For a moment, Isa couldn't remember last night. Then the bag behind her moved, and there was a squeak. A gentle cry. Michel raised his chin, looking over her shoulder. He sucked in a breath.

"Is that . . ." He looked at her. "Is it from the family that was hiding?" His eyes were like glass, unreadable. He took another step. "Is that a Jewish baby?"

The pinwheel inside Isa whirled. Spun. And she could see nothing but red. Red like a poison flower. Red like the pieces of the man on the door. She could see nothing but bloodred and Nazi brown. Michel lifted a hand toward the bag.

And Isa shoved him. As hard as she could, two hands flat on his chest. He stumbled, caught off guard, bumping backward into the door. He righted himself. Straightened his jacket. Cool. Jaw clenched. The baby cried, a mewing wail. And then Michel grabbed the crisp hat from his head and threw it hard against the wall. He picked it up and threw it again.

"Do you think I would hurt that child?" he said.

She couldn't answer.

"Tell me you believe I would hurt that child!" Michel yelled.

The baby cried full voice. And the colors spinning inside Isa slowed. Separated. Became pieces she could examine.

She looked at Michel Lange. And shook her head. She didn't believe he would.

Michel swiped up his hat. He moved Isa to one side and picked up the bag. "It is too cold down here. Push that table against the door. Who is at home?"

"My father," she whispered, moving the table until it hit wood. "Or . . . I don't know . . ." She followed Michel into the gallery.

"Did anyone see you come?" Michel asked.

"I don't know. I don't think so." ·

The baby's cry was insistent. Plaintive. Michel looked at Isa and said, "Where?"

She led the way through the big gallery, up the straight stairs, past the poppy hall, and into her room. Where it was smaller. Warmer. She shut the door and Michel set the bag carefully on her chair and scooped out the crying baby, bouncing up and down with his knees, holding its head upright against the Nazi insignia on his chest. The baby fussed and kicked and then quieted.

It was the most unlikely sight in her room that Isa could have imagined.

"Can you see anyone outside?" he asked.

She went to the window and loosened the blackout to examine the empty gully, the bricks and the dead windows, the first drops of rain hitting the glass. She shook her head, pushed the tack back into the wall, pulling the velvet curtains over the blanket.

"If you know who did it," Michel said, "tell no one. Ever. Especially me." He cradled the small head, bouncing, and said, "Klaus was a pig."

She assumed it was Klaus who had ended up all over the door. She didn't correct him on whose child it was. It didn't matter. The shake in her middle was a chatter, like she'd been left in the cold.

"Do you have diapers?" Michel asked.

She looked in the bag and shook her head again.

"Do you have a towel?"

She found one. Michel draped it expertly on the center of her bed, one-handed, and laid the baby down. Underneath the blanket, it was wearing a tiny white shirt. Everything about it was tiny. The baby wrinkled its face, turned red, and cried louder than Isa knew a baby could. Michel looked up.

"Do you have clothes yet? Civilian clothes?"

She'd forgotten all about his request for clothes. Her mind was heavy. Sluggish.

"Do you have whiskey?" The baby wailed and Michel sighed. "Bring me what you can find, then. Quick."

Isa ran out the door and straight to the blue bedroom to ransack the wardrobe, glad for a clear directive, to be doing something that made sense. The baby stopped crying after a moment, or maybe she just couldn't hear. She couldn't hear her father, either. He was probably asleep in the garret, or painting in the garret, or starved in the garret. Or not home at all. She found a pair of black trousers. A blue shirt with an embroidered leaf pattern. A black zippered jacket with a wide collar. And in the dining room, there was a half-full bottle of whiskey in the cabinet beneath the sideboard.

She took it all back to her room, a hurricane through the door, and Michel looked up from the edge of her bed. He had his pinky finger in the baby's mouth, letting it suck, looking at a piece of paper in his other hand. A sketch, one of the many that lay scattered over the rug, lavender and a crimson bloom. There was a wet diaper in her wash-basin. She held out the whiskey bottle and the clothes.

He set down her drawing, pulling his finger from the baby's mouth slowly. The baby's mouth worked, but it didn't cry. It was nearly asleep. Michel stood and took the clothes. Isa held out the whiskey.

"Turn around, please," he said. "And the whiskey is for you."

Isa sat on the edge of the bed, her back to Michel, the bottle in her lap, looking at the baby. She could hear buttons being undone, the rustle of a loosening tie. A glance in her mirror showed someone she barely recognized. Vivid, messy hair. A few freckles dark against a complexion gone to chalk, with a trace of kohl still darkening her eyes. Not ready for a fight. She could see Michel in his undershirt, sleeveless. He had freckles, too, on his shoulders, a little scatter of sand. And then she remembered to look at the baby.

"How old is it, do you think?" Isa asked.

"She," he replied. "It is a she."

A girl. Like Hilde's baby. The miniature hand flexed open and shut.

"Four months, I would guess," Michel said. He sounded angry.

"Have you taken care of babies?"

It took a moment for him to answer. "I have eight sisters."

Isa almost turned before she remembered not to. She could not imagine such a thing as eight sisters.

Then Michel said, "Perhaps you could . . ."

She looked back. He was dressed. The shirtsleeves were too long and the white leaf embroidery a little startling—her father's eccentric taste—but that was mostly covered by the jacket. The pants only just managed to button and were at least four inches too long.

"Wait . . ." She left the whiskey on the floor and found her purse—had she actually carried her purse up here?—digging out the packet of pins she'd used on the chiffon. She knelt, folding up the hems of the pants and pinning them underneath, where it wouldn't show. Where they covered some of the polish of his Nazi boots. She did it with difficulty; her hands were still shaky. But she did it. She stood, and Michel Lange didn't look near as much like a German soldier as he used to.

"Are you leaving Amsterdam?" she asked.

"Of course not," he replied, sharp. "You have nothing and you cannot go into the shops around here, where you are known, and suddenly buy milk and diapers, can you?"

She hadn't even thought of that. Not that a young man in an embroidered shirt buying baby bottles might not cause just as much comment.

"Can you get out quickly," he asked, "if they come searching?"

"I have a place to go," she whispered, thinking of the wardrobe. "Do you have . . . don't you have to be back? At a certain time?"

"The advantage to accompanying Gurlitt to a party is that you invariably get the next day off." He moved to the door. "Give me an hour. And drink some of that whiskey."

He looked her over again, hesitated, then quietly shut her bedroom door.

She sat back down on the bed. The baby was fully asleep now, nested deep in the towel and Isa's quilt, eyelids incredibly delicate and thin. She was a beautiful little thing. And everything in this world had been taken from her.

Killed for being born. That's what Willem had said.

Isa covered the baby's palm with the tip of a finger, felt the little hand clasp reflexively. It had broken her heart before, to think of selling Moshe's birthright. And now, looking at the baby, she thought Moshe would have wanted it sold. For this.

He would have given up his treasure for this.

It was almost like he had given her permission.

Her shaking stopped. She lay down on the bed beside the baby, slowly, so as not to move the mattress, letting her hold on to her finger. There was a family somewhere who had agreed to raise her. Maybe Truus had been able to tell someone, or maybe the woman with the kerchief had seen, and someone would come and get the baby. To take her where she could belong. Isa had no idea how to reach anyone, not even Willem.

She prayed that Truus had gotten away, that the Resistance would know how to get her out of the city. That the Gestapo would not find a likely scapegoat for her crime. That she wasn't arrested already. That the family had found a new place to hide.

Was Truus sitting in a darkened room somewhere with her smoking gun, shaking? Or would she sleep still and dreamless tonight, resting in the certainty that she'd done the right thing?

And then Isa was opening her eyes, instantly aware that time had moved on without her. The room was dim, a little chill, rain spattering the window, soft behind the curtains, and the baby was no longer beside her on the bed. She sat up, stiff, startled, and found Michel sitting in her chair in her father's pinned pants and his undershirt, a clean diaper thrown over his shoulder, giving the well-wrapped baby a bottle. He'd switched the lamp on beside them, the soft, yellow light surrounding the baby's head like a halo. Like a painting of Madonna and Child.

Only different.

"Feeling better?" Michel asked.

Isa nodded and put a hand to her temple. She had a piercing headache. Her hair was falling down, her dress wrinkled and up around her knees. She took out the three pins she could find and pulled her quilt around her legs. The room had been tidied, her drawings stacked neatly on the dresser beside the whiskey bottle, her records, and a small pile of folded diapers. A Nazi uniform hung from her clothes pegs. The baby sucked and kicked.

"I couldn't see anyone watching the house," Michel said. "Not Germans, anyway. If there was . . . someone else, I might not have seen."

By someone else, he meant Resistance.

"The house-to-house search is from where Klaus was killed and to the north," he said. "They believe the shooter did not pass any of the bridges, and are concentrating their search between the Singel and Rokin and up to Dam Square. If they widen the net, or receive different information, they still may come this way."

Isa nodded. Someone had talked to the police, because that was the direction both Truus and the family had fled. She rubbed her temple. The way through the storage room wall in the garret needed to be boarded up and hidden. There was more to think about now than just her or her father.

Michel took the bottle from the baby's mouth, making her protest, turning her upright against the diaper on his shoulder, patting her back like an expert.

"So tell me, Isa de Smit," he said, patting and bouncing, "do you often forge art?"

She almost laughed. And then she couldn't. It was time to make a decision. About how much to say, and who to say it to. About who to trust.

It might be too late to make that decision.

"No," Isa replied softly. "I do not often forge art. The taxes on the gallery were due. We were going to lose it. My father doesn't know."

Michel gazed upward for a moment. "I heard someone above us earlier."

So he was home. And alive.

"His studio is in the garret," Isa said. "He . . . doesn't come down often, when he's painting."

"I remember," Michel said.

The baby burped and Isa realized that's what the bouncing had been about. Michel settled her down and gave her the bottle again. He was waiting. To see if Isa would fill the silence on her own. Explain herself. About kohl and a stolen key.

She played with the hairpins and said, "Why do you want to leave the army?"

"The answer is not obvious?"

She didn't reply, and Michel watched the baby drink, his dark brows down over his eyes.

"My family does not have a gallery," he said finally, "just a brokerage. Buying and selling. And because I am the eldest, and a son, my father began training me to take over before I was out of short pants. Before the war, our clients were government officials in Vienna, Salzburg, wealthy, well connected, and when the Anschluss came and the Austrian government changed, our clients did not. Only now they were Nazis, or those who sympathized with the Nazis, or those who just knew how to keep a position of power. My sister married one, though she was only sixteen. You met him last night. He has been made the cultural minister of the Netherlands."

She pictured the man in the suit beside Michel at Van Meegeren's dinner, paunchy, balding. In his sixties, at the least.

"Yes," Michel agreed, "it is disgusting. My sister does not love him. She doesn't even like him. But for my father, everything is business.

It was the same when he signed the papers volunteering me for the army on my nineteenth birthday. It looked bad to our clients, you see, to have a healthy young man of age out of uniform. And he knew I would get consideration, because of my skills, and my brother-in-law.

"I tried to make the best of it, to wait out my time, but no one . . . we did not understand Hitler's true intentions. My father will not admit the truth of it even now. He cannot. I have been spared the worst, because of my position. I only steal art. The lifework of collectors like Goudstikker, people I knew and liked, handing over the creativity of centuries to men who care more for the beauty of their bank accounts. And every day, I must do what I cannot condone, in Berlin, in Paris and Warsaw, and there are things I have seen in those places that I would very much like to forget. Every day, I do what I detest."

He paused, eyes still on the baby, adjusting the emptying bottle in her mouth.

"I am not making an excuse, and I do not ask for your sympathy. I am only trying to . . . make a correction. When I go, it will be a scandal, and I will ruin the business I was supposed to inherit. I will lose my father and my sisters, most of whom are too young to understand, and my mother will have no power to change my father's wishes to never again see my face. I will be a fugitive. I may face a firing squad. But wearing that"—he glanced up at the clothes pegs—"is impossible to bear. I will not bear it."

He set the finished bottle on the floor and lifted the baby to his shoulder again, gazing down at nothing, rubbing her back in the lamplight. It would have taken a fine painter to capture what Isa was seeing. She might have named it *Condemnation*.

"Hofer and Gurlitt leave Holland in one week," he said. "Gurlitt is going first to The Hague, sending me ahead to Hamburg with a shipment of art. I have bribed a man at the dock to post a letter from me, from Hamburg in ten days' time, so Gurlitt will think I have arrived when I have not. Instead, I will stay behind, with you, while they look for me in Hamburg or somewhere along the train tracks in between, and then I will make my way out of the city."

He lifted his gaze.

"There are rumors," he said, "among the other soldiers. Whispers about downed pilots—American, English—who escape through open flat country. Who disappear. Germans who go out and do not come back again. They say that there is a girl, a girl with red hair, who makes these things happen."

This must be why he kept asking who she'd killed. Isa almost smiled. "I'm not the girl with red hair."

Michel nodded, and said carefully, "Then I want to ask if you might know someone who could help me get to Switzerland."

Isa made a shape with the hairpins on her palm. She had intended to offer Michel Lange a trade, her help for his. An arrangement like he had offered her. Business. Impersonal.

Impossible while he was sitting in her bedroom with bare arms, gently rubbing the back of a sleeping Jewish baby.

She was worse at blackmailing than he was.

"I don't know if they'll do it," Isa said finally. She wasn't sure how Truus felt about deserting Nazis, whether she would believe Michel's story. She didn't know whether she should believe Michel's story. Willem, she thought, would have pulled the trigger ten minutes ago. "I'm not . . . one of them," Isa said. "But I can ask."

He closed his eyes, and for a moment, Isa saw him without the stiff correctness that controlled his movements. His edges softened.

"But I need to ask something, too. From you."

His hand stilled on the baby's back, wary. Isa scooted to the edge of the bed and leaned forward, elbows on her knees.

"I need to sell a Vermeer," she whispered. "For as much as I can possibly get."

A little frown appeared between Michel's eyebrows. "A forgery?"

"No. Genuine. To Hitler or Goering. Either one will do. And I need someone who can help me facilitate . . . that kind of sale."

She watched the frown on Michel's face smooth, emotion dissolved and wiped clean like solvent over paint. He stood and brought the baby to the bed, laying her gently in the center of the mattress, still wrapped in her blanket. Then he straightened, shoulders square in his undershirt, hands in his pockets as he looked down at her.

"That," he said, "is something I will never help you do."

Then they both turned to a noise, sudden and sharp, from the glass behind the closed curtain. Michel stiffened, tense. Isa jumped to her feet. Another tap, with a snick, this one so loud Isa wondered if the window had cracked.

"Step back," she whispered. When Michel was pressed against the wall beside her door, she went softly to the window, peeking around the tassels and the blackouts.

A pebble clicked. Isa winced. But she could see who was standing in the protection of the wall of her back garden, throwing rocks at her window in a silver sheet of soaking rain.

Willem. Gesturing for her to come down.

He was holding a baby bottle.

Isa turned to Michel and said, "Hide."

15

ISA RAN DOWN the spiral stairs to let Willem in. There was nothing else to do. Willem was through the door the instant it opened wide enough.

"What happened?" she asked. She got the lock turned, pushing the table back into position. Willem was leaning against the plaster in the gloom, hands on his thighs, dripping a puddle onto the oak planks.

"Do you have the baby?" he breathed.

"Yes. Where's Truus?"

"Gone. Out of the city."

"Is she safe?"

"For now."

Isa nodded, relieved. She wanted to know more, but she probably shouldn't.

"The Dutch police, soldiers, Gestapo, they're stopping everyone between here and Centraal Station," Willem said. "Double guards on the bridges and the corners. I had to swim . . ."

"Do you have an identity card?"

Willem was supposed to be in a slave labor camp in Germany.

"Yes, a false one. It's got a stamp for labor exemption, but I've got other false ones on me, too. Or I did, if they're not ruined. I only just made my delivery. Had to hand him over a hedge and through a window."

His delivery. She looked at the baby bottle, clutched in his hand with a small cloth bag. Willem had just saved a child. And if he had been caught with false identity cards, he would have been shot.

"What happened today, will this change things for . . . getting the children out?"

"It will change everything," he said, eyes down.

And the officer at Van Meegeren's had said Judenfrei in eight days.

Willem straightened, blond hair running rivulets. He really was a sort of Titian's Adonis, the kind of mortal the goddesses of myth would run around falling in love with. He was also a hero. And he was shivering. "Isa," he said, "I'm sorry to ask, but the safe house is . . . I need a place to stay for the night."

She hesitated. She would have to sneak Michel out. Again. Willem was watching her think, a little vertical line appearing between his eyes. She'd waited a second too long.

Isa shook her head, as if she'd been lost in thought. "Yes," she said. "Yes, of course." She couldn't send a man who had just saved a child and swum a canal out into the rain. "Come. Leave your shoes . . ."

She watched him bend down, obediently tugging off his muddy boots, and she was thinking. Thinking.

"Where's your father?" Willem asked.

"Painting. In the garret. He doesn't even know the baby is here."

"Is the baby all right?"

"Sleeping," Isa said.

She led Willem through the big gallery and up the straight stairs. If Willem knew anything about collaboration, or Nazis in the house, he wouldn't leave the baby here with her, not even in this weather.

Isa took him straight across the poppy hall and opened the door to the bathroom.

"There should be soap. Take what you need, rinse your clothes out in the tub and I'll find you something dry. And you'll have to light the gas under the water heater. The boiler's not on."

Willem nodded, stepping past her through the door, then he turned and handed her the bottle and the bag. "I really am sorry to have just come like this. It's probably not convenient."

As if he could have preplanned his sleeping arrangements for when Truus shot a Nazi and put the city in an uproar. He looked at the floor tiles, the frown still on his forehead.

"I'm glad you're with us, Isa."

Isa smiled weakly, standing where he'd left her when he shut the door.

Maybe the woman in the kerchief didn't know where she'd been last night. Maybe she knew but hadn't had a chance to tell Willem. Maybe she still would.

Collaborators who will trade you for a ration book. Nazis who will pretend to be your friend. They're trying to catch us, all the time. They don't want one of us, they want all of us. That's what he'd said.

More than a jail cell, Isa.

When the tap turned on, Isa moved silently around the corner, up the three steps and into her room, where Michel was standing just behind the open door in his undershirt, the baby still asleep. He'd tucked the quilt around her. The Nazi uniform had disappeared.

She lifted a finger to her lips, and when the water was at full blast, she whispered, "He wants to stay. You'll have to go."

"It is the same one as before?"

Isa looked away. *Nazis who will pretend.* What if she was being a fool?

"Is he Resistance?"

Isa hesitated, and Michel made a very German noise of impatience.

"I want to meet him."

Isa looked up. "No!"

"Tell him I am your cousin," Michel said. "From Austria. That I am escaping forced labor . . ."

"He's escaping forced labor!"

"Then he will understand."

"I don't think he will. I don't think he will understand at all!"

"Why not? Will he be jealous? Is he your boyfriend?"

"No!"

That had been too loud. They both turned their heads, listening to the splash of water running into the tub.

"He knows which window is yours," Michel pointed out.

"And yet he is not my boyfriend. Let me handle this!"

"Like you did last night?"

She knew he had a point. And Michel didn't know the half of how close she'd come to disaster last night.

"I don't have time to argue," Isa whispered. "Go down to the little gallery and change and then slip out as soon as you can. I'll keep him away from the windows, and . . . I will ask him about Switzerland, I promise."

"What about the baby? You don't know the first thing . . ."

"What about the Vermeer?"

He turned his face away, jaw clenched. "Do not talk to me about that."

She saw the disgust. He thought she was greedy. A collaborator. Like them.

"It's not for me," Isa blurted. "The money is not for me."

He turned his gaze back on her. "Who, then?"

She stared up at him, searching his face while he waited patiently for an answer. He still had the towel over his shoulder. And she made the same decision she'd made downstairs. She didn't know what color Michel Lange might be underneath, but she just didn't believe he would hurt the baby on the bed.

"It's for them," she said. "To hide the children."

Michel's brows crooked. A blink over amber glass.

And then the bath tap slowed.

"Hurry," she said. "Where's your uniform?"

He retrieved it from the clothes peg, hidden underneath her robe, gathering up the embroidered shirt and jacket. Isa opened the door and they stole down the hall to the short steps, which creaked so badly that Isa stopped in front of the bathroom door.

"Willem, do you need anything?"

Michel slid by while Willem was calling out an answer of no, he was fine, Isa pointing a finger, miming Michel's turn into the dining room. Michel was hesitating, she could see that he wanted to argue, but Isa waved him on. The dining room door shut with a soft click, and Isa breathed. It was dusk, but a German uniform would have no problem being out after curfew, especially tonight. While they were searching.

And what, Isa thought, if she was wrong. What if she'd just sent a Nazi soldier out of her house, knowing there was a Jewish baby and a member of the Resistance inside?

She didn't think she was wrong.

At least not yet.

She crossed the hall to the blue bedroom for a second ransacking of the wardrobe. Willem was so much bigger, so much broader than her lanky father. In the end, all she found was a pair of ocean-blue pajamas printed with bursts of sunshine paisley. Garish but forgiving, with a drawstring that would loosen at the waist.

Isa heard a muffled thump above her head, like a stool adjusting. A proof of life from the garret. She should check on her father. Or perhaps he was a grown man who should check on himself. He didn't seem concerned about where she had been all night.

She found some socks and some underpants—the fit of those she left up to Willem—and left it all outside the bathroom door, where she could hear the slow gurgle of water draining. Then she went to look at the baby.

Her room was cozy in the lamplight. So tidy, so filled with the sound of a baby's sleeping breath, she barely recognized it. The wet diaper was gone. Michel must have washed it out.

Surely someone intent on betrayal would not bother to wash out a diaper.

She chose a drawer, a deep one, full of winter sweaters, and laid the baby's towel inside. Then, gingerly, carefully, she lifted the baby from the mattress—like she was transferring an unpinned grenade, a nest of hornets—and laid her in the drawer, mildly triumphant when the baby stayed asleep. Isa carried the drawer into the kitchen.

Michel had been boiling bottles. There was one with milk already in it, standing upright in a pot of water, ready to warm. Isa set the drawer on the table and got water to start the last of the coffee. The thought brought a tremble to her fingers, to her middle. Not from shock, she realized. She hadn't eaten since the soup at Van Meegeren's dinner, and barely before that.

She went to the yellow cupboard for bread and remembered that she'd dropped it. It would have to be the last potato, then, divided, and whatever cans of Moshe's she could plunder. She opened the cupboard and found a sack of potatoes, and bread, and two tins of meat. There were also two onions, a block of cheese, a pound of flour, a pound of ersatz coffee, and—praise the heavens—a little packet of sugar. She went to the icebox and discovered a slab of butter, a dozen eggs, and four cans of powdered baby milk.

Isa shut the icebox door. She didn't think milk powder needed to be chilled, but she wasn't going to quibble. She was afraid Michel had robbed a grocery. He couldn't have the ration coupons for this, or the kind of money the black market would demand. Could he? And if he did, where did it come from?

Someone turning you in to the Gestapo, Isa thought, did not bring groceries first.

Unless they very much wanted you to trust them.

And then Willem came into the kitchen in paisley pajamas.

"Well, it's not my fault," Willem said, not as amused as Isa thought he could have been. He went to the drawer and glanced at the baby while she stifled her smile and lit the burner. Willem pulled out a chair, putting his back to the nude on the wall.

It was strange, to be in the kitchen with Willem like this, with the rain drumming against the windows.

"How are the identity cards?" Isa asked.

"Not as bad as I thought. They were in a leather pouch. I've got them hanging in the bathroom." He set a towel-wrapped bundle on the table.

"How soon will you be able to get her to . . . where she was going?" She meant the baby.

"She was going to the family who got caught."

Isa glanced at the little girl over the coffeepot. So that's why Truus had been there. The family in that house had intended to hide one more.

"They were all leaving the city. We had a place ready. It's lucky Truus was running late, or the baby would have been caught, too."

If Truus hadn't been there, they would have all been killed.

"And now we don't know where they are, of course. Truus was the contact."

"So they can't take her," Isa said. The little girl in the drawer had lost again. "How did they get caught?"

"Someone informed. For the bounty, probably."

Informed at the moment that Truus was bringing them another Jewish baby. Isa didn't like that. She didn't like that at all.

Isa looked at Willem in his silly pajamas—handsome, stoic, almost expressionless, the mask that went with his disguise tightly tied and fully in place. He opened the toweled bundle and spread it out on the scarred oak. There was a gun inside. He began taking it apart, examining each piece and wiping it down, drying it out. The baby in the drawer threw up a hand in her sleep.

And yet another sight today that she could have never predicted. She got two potatoes and an onion and a knife.

"I've heard a rumor," Isa said carefully, "that the Germans plan to have all Jews out of the city in a week."

"Where did you hear that?"

"In the tax office," she lied quickly. She slid her knife through a potato and chopped.

"We've heard the same. It's going to be hard to get them out now. Maybe impossible." He hesitated. "Truus mentioned, about the money . . ."

"It's coming," Isa said.

She would sell the Vermeer on her own if she had to. To Hofer, as Gurlitt was unlikely to forget her. She'd have to come in like she had with the Rembrandt, take Hofer's bargain price for the desperate. A pittance, more than likely, compared to the painting's true worth. But even a pittance was more than she had now. Maybe it would be enough.

Willem shifted in his seat. She could hear his discomfort. "What I need to ask, Isa, is . . . where is the money coming from?"

Isa froze. It was just what she'd been wondering about Michel, and for a moment, she thought Willem knew she'd been selling to the Nazis. But the disapproval rolling off him was of a different kind. She closed her eyes. Money. A suddenly full icebox. And that damned kohl still clinging to the corners of her eyes. Isa struggled between incredulity, laughter, and offense. Humor won. She turned her back, chopping. But when she answered, there was still a little frost in it. "I am not a prostitute, Willem."

She felt him flinch at the word behind her.

"I told Truus that I knew people who might . . . invest. It's purely a business dealing. Aboveboard." Not strictly true, but true enough for Willem.

"I didn't mean to . . . I didn't . . ."

"No need to apologize."

She started in on the onion. The chop of the knife was the only cut in the silence.

"What if you got more money?" Isa asked. "What would you do with it?"

"How much more?"

"All the money you could want." Isa smiled over her shoulder. "A million guilders. What would you do with it?"

"I'd buy a fleet of bombers and an army of tanks and drive out the Germans," he said without hesitation.

"Or you could just bribe them all to desert," Isa said. "It's easier on the architecture."

Willem shrugged once, wiping down the barrel.

"Do you ever help deserters? Do German soldiers ever . . . try to leave?"

"The last deserter one of ours tried to help wasn't a deserter at all," Willem said, eyes on his work. "He was a spy."

Isa put a pan on the stove. It clanged a little harder than she'd meant it to. "What happened?"

"Our man was arrested and they shot him. After three days. If he hadn't stood up to the torture, we'd all be dead with him. He was . . . a hero. So much better . . . than the rest of us . . ."

Isa turned. Willem was staring at the pieces of the gun. And this, she thought, was what really lay beneath the mask. A scarlet wound, soul-deep and still bleeding. If Isa could have painted his portrait, she would have named it *Blame*. Except that all the blame seemed to be directed at himself.

"Who died, Willem?" Isa asked.

Willem looked up. Stunned. A little horrified. And then the mask clicked back into place. Clamped down. Tight. "Sorry," he said, eyes dropping to his work. He picked up the gun barrel. "And don't worry about tonight. We should be safe. I've got someone watching the house, so there will be warning, if we needed to get out . . ."

Isa turned and bit her lip, bracing herself against the counter. Someone from the Resistance was watching the house. And she'd sent Michel out the door in a Nazi uniform. How could she have been so stupid? She should have known. She should have thought. Where were they watching from? It was dark, raining. What had they seen?

And what would Willem do about it?

"Isa, are you all right?"

She looked over her shoulder. Threw Willem a smile. "Sorry. I was . . . lost in my thoughts."

The coffee was starting to boil. She turned the gas down. Maybe Michel hadn't dressed yet. Maybe there was time to stop him.

It was far too late to stop him. She turned abruptly.

"I'll just get something from the stores downstairs. Would you watch the baby for a . . ."

"Oh, hello."

The door from the dining room had swung open with barely a sound. Isa didn't move. Willem didn't even have time to stand, just folded the towel over the pieces of the gun.

"Hello," Michel said again. He stepped into the kitchen toward Willem, her father's jacket zipped to hide his ill-fitting shirt, holding out a hand. "I'm Michel." He looked back and forth at the stillness between them. "Isa's cousin? She didn't tell you I was here?"

"No, she didn't," Willem said slowly.

"I was just about to," Isa said quickly. "I thought you were . . . still asleep."

What she really thought was that she might put Willem's gun together and shoot Michel herself. Isa smiled, devastatingly polite.

"Michel, this is Willem. My boyfriend."

A brief second of silence, and Willem half stood, giving Michel's hand a short shake. "Have a seat," he said, indicating the opposite chair.

Michel tucked the baby's blanket as he passed. "A beautiful baby," he said. "I told Isa so myself. I was surprised, of course, but these are strange times, and I am no judge. You must be proud of her." He looked at Willem expectantly. As if she had told Michel that this was their child. Willem and Isa's.

Willem's blue gaze rose over Michel's head, to where Isa stood frozen against the sink. He looked absolutely staggered. Scandalized. She mouthed the word *Sorry*, and turned her back. It was probably as good a story as any she could have come up with, had she known she needed a story to explain a baby and Willem's pajama-ed presence in her kitchen to a previously unknown cousin.

Or perhaps it was revenge for "boyfriend."

Or maybe Michel was a spy. Pretending. Maybe he was sitting at her table, waiting for the Gestapo to come and arrest them.

Or maybe he just wanted out of the German army more than pride or life or limb.

"I'll just . . . make us something to eat," Isa said. She grabbed the second potato and started chopping.

"Cigarette?" offered Michel.

"No. I don't smoke."

Isa heard the click of the lighter as she chopped. And chopped. The baby sighed.

"So where are you from again?" Willem asked. "You see, I didn't know Isa had a cousin."

"Yes," Michel agreed. "We're about all there is, as far as family goes. Our mothers were sisters, you see. But they had a falling-out. Years ago."

"Your mother fought with Katrina? What about?"

She could almost hear Michel's smile. "You mean Francina, Isa's mother, yes? My mother was Dorcas. She didn't like it when Francina married Theodoor, and they haven't spoken much since."

Isa chopped. She'd been wrong, that first day in the dark of the little gallery. Michel Lange had gone from a teenager who couldn't speak to the smoothest liar she'd ever heard. It was a disconcerting thought.

"Do you have an ashtray, cousin?"

Isa put a plate in front of him. The two young men were sitting on opposite sides of the table, sizing each other up like cats in an alley. The gun was still in pieces, wrapped inside the towel at Willem's elbow. If the Gestapo was coming, then they were coming. If they weren't, then Michel needed help.

"Michel's father was Austrian," Isa said, grabbing the coffeepot before it boiled the second time. "Aunt Dorcas lived there until the Nazis took over. We barely heard from her. I didn't even know they'd been in Rotterdam."

There. Michel could do with that what he would.

She set two mugs of coffee on the table and put butter in the pan. The baby was sleeping better in the noisy, smoky kitchen than she had in Isa's quiet room.

"So where are your parents now?" Willem asked.

"Dead," Michel said. "Bombs. But no, there is no need to console. They were not very nice people."

Isa bit her lip, and slid the potatoes and onions into the pan, where they sizzled.

"What do you do, Willem?" Michel asked.

"I was a student before the invasion. I'm . . . unemployed now."

"Ah. So am I. I was working the docks in Rotterdam. The Germans invited me to do so. It was very hard work, dropping engine parts into the sea every time our supervisor turned his back. You would not believe how difficult it is to keep them from splashing."

Isa closed her eyes and stirred.

"But my time in Rotterdam became unpleasant. So I thought of my cousin in Amsterdam and came in by boat, underneath a canvas tarp. I prefer not to have any German associations right now. Where I would quite like to go is Switzerland."

He was overplaying his hand.

Isa got the plates. She got them noisily. But it didn't stop him. Michel stubbed out his cigarette, leaning closer to Willem.

"I was asking my cousin earlier, if she knew anyone, someone who could help me get to . . ."

Isa fumbled the plates and dropped one, shattering it against the edge of the countertop.

It was a shame. She liked those plates.

Chairs scraped. Isa apologized. The potatoes popped. The noise woke the baby, who tuned up immediately to an indignant cry. And from somewhere in the house above them came a thump, and another, a series of thuds that shook the light fixture hanging from the ceiling. They all looked up.

And that, Isa thought, was her father. Falling down the steps from the garret.

16

ISA RAN DOWN the hall and into the blue bedroom, just in time to see her father stumbling out of the wardrobe, coming down onto the carpet on his hands and knees.

He was sickly pale, in the same clothes he'd worn the last time she'd seen him, blood running down the back of his head and over his forehead and into his eyes. He tried to get upright. He couldn't do it. Isa dropped down beside him.

"No, Papa, sit where you are. Let me see what happened. Did you fall?"

She unwound the lavender scarf, trying to sop up the blood, and saw that he had a scratch on his neck, deep, like nails had been digging into the flesh. The place was raw and a little infected. The reason, she realized, for wearing the scarf. His skin looked papery.

"When was the last time you drank anything, Papa? The last time you ate?"

"Dizzy" was his response. "I am . . . dizzy."

His words were slurred, his lips cracked. And then he shook, for just a moment, like he had a chill. He needed a doctor. They couldn't afford a doctor. They couldn't afford to have anyone else come into this house.

And guilt, Isa thought, was almost the same color as revulsion, but tinted, shaded, dotted with hot reds and sick yellow, with the deep, deep cobalt of regret.

Guilt was so many things.

Then Willem was standing in the doorway, the baby crying full voice in the kitchen. "Where did he fall from?" he asked, staring at the enormous bed and the gilded trim.

She had no time to answer. Michel came up on her father's other side with a damp towel, and she wiped away the worst of the blood and put pressure on the wound. They each took an arm and helped her father to his feet, stumbling together to the piled sofa, where he sat, swaying. And then his eyes focused, wandering upward to where Isa stood, pressing down on his bleeding head with the towel.

"Sofonisba," he whispered, voice hoarse. "Where have you been?"

The guilt spilled. Poured.

Then he turned and blinked at the young man on his other side.

"Do you remember me, Theo?" Michel asked.

"Michel," he said. "Michel . . . Lange. What a very . . . sneaky child you were."

The comment almost made Michel smile. Isa looked back at Willem, whose hands were on either side of the doorframe, spanning the open space. Whatever Willem thought was going on, she could see that he had not expected her father to recognize Michel or call him by name.

"I would say it is good to see you, Theo," Michel said, "but I think I will say it to you tomorrow."

"I am . . . I think I am finished . . ." Theodoor whispered.

"You're just exhausted, Papa, and you hurt your head . . ."

"Painting," he croaked. "I am finished . . ."

Isa sighed. "Willem, could you get him a glass of water? And the baby? And turn off the stove?"

Willem went, and as soon as she heard him move down the hall,

Isa turned to Michel and hissed, "What are you doing here? I told you to leave."

"I did . . . I did leave . . ." her father mumbled.

"And yet," Michel whispered, "I decided it would be wiser to stay. You have someone watching your house." He bent down to take off her father's shoes. "And I have one week before I disappear, and I will need his help."

"This is not a game, Michel!"

He looked up, suddenly still. "I know."

Willem brought the water and another damp towel, and Isa cleaned the wound well enough to see that the cut was superficial despite the amount of blood, a small split in his scalp that was beginning to swell. The rest was bumps and bruises.

Her father drank the water greedily, and was immediately ill all over the carpet. They cleaned him up again, and the carpet, and changed his shirt while he muttered. The second time, Isa made sure her father sipped, and slowly ate half a slice of bread. He was breathing hard, eyelids drooping, his entire body seeming to say that life was too much work.

Michel got her father settled, long limbs propped on his pillows, while Isa laid a clean towel under his bandaged head. Willem watched from the doorway, the baby in his arms, a little rubber comforter stuck in her mouth.

"Finished," he muttered. "Tell him . . ."

"Who, Papa?"

"Tell him I am finished . . ."

And then he shook once, violently, like he had before, head to foot. It was unsettling, and gone as soon as it came. Isa put a hand on his cheek, but he felt cool. If this was paint fever, it was the worst she'd ever seen.

His muttering slowed. His eyelids closed. When Isa was fairly certain he'd fallen asleep, she tucked the blanket, and went to rinse the bloody towels in the sink. The water ran salmon, shades of pink and blush. Willem's clothes were dripping from the towel bar, but there were no identity cards. He must have hidden them just as soon as her father fell.

What must Willem think of her? Giving sanctuary to a member of the Resistance and a Jewish baby, and somehow forgetting to mention that there was a stranger in the house? And on the same day that someone had betrayed that family.

Or was it Truus they had betrayed?

It was unforgivable.

In the kitchen, Michel had lit another cigarette, and Willem had the baby. Someone had cleaned up the shards of plate. The baby was fussing even with the comforter, searching Willem's shoulder while he sat ramrod straight in his chair. Isa turned up the heat beneath the food and the bottle.

"Is Theo sick often?" Michel asked.

Isa shook her head. He didn't say anything more.

She decided they could eat the food as it was, put three plates of the potatoes and onions on the table, and took the baby from Willem. Michel tested the heat of the bottle on his wrist and handed it to her. Isa sat, trying to find the right position. The baby cried, kicked and squirmed. Michel reached over and tipped her elbow into place beneath the baby's neck, a move that made Willem frown. But the bottle popped in and the little girl's mouth started working.

Willem began snapping the pieces of his gun back together.

Michel watched, thoughtful, all of them cramped around the mugs and plates and Isa's sweater drawer. It was a silence so heavy, Isa could feel the pressure in her head. When she looked up, there were two sets of eyes on her. Tea and ice.

"I'll sleep in the blue room tonight," Isa announced, "to tend to my father. You can have a guest room," she said to Willem.

"Doesn't he sleep in your room?" Michel asked innocently, smoking.

She gave him a withering glance. "You can sleep where you were."

Which was nowhere. The corner of Michel's mouth softened, just a little. She hadn't thought it was possible for Willem to sit up any straighter, but he did. Neither of them moved, and Isa was not going to leave a devil and an angel together in her kitchen. Though who was who was getting harder to tell by the minute.

At least the Gestapo hadn't come.

At least Michel had seen the watcher outside, though she couldn't think how.

The barrel clicked into place and Willem spun the chamber.

And Michel said suddenly, "Willem, could I speak with you in the dining room?"

Willem stood immediately, solemn. Isa's eyes darted to the towel, where the gun had been, but she didn't see any bullets. That didn't mean Willem didn't have them. He went to put the gun in his back pocket, but he was wearing pajamas. He started toward the dining room door, and Isa said, "I'll just come . . ."

"No need," Michel replied. "I am going to tell him everything."

Isa's mouth opened. She couldn't think of a scenario where that could possibly mean anything good. She also didn't think she should take a baby into a room where it was happening. She sat where she was. Willem followed Michel into the dining room without another glance.

She could hear their voices, a male murmur beyond the door. More Michel than the bass of Willem. A tinge of unfriendliness at first, leveling into what sounded like short conversation. Then the door opened, and Michel came out.

"I have explained the situation, and we are understood," he said.

Willem came through and pulled out his chair again, relaxed. "You should have said, Isa," he chided, but gently, picking up his fork.

"It's hard to know what to say," Isa replied.

"That's true," Willem said. Then Michel sat and they ate, discussing bomb damage in Rotterdam.

The milk was warm inside the glass, the baby solid yet delicate in her arms. She was also, Isa thought, wet. Willem and Michel moved on to an animated discussion of the fall of Italy. And Isa left them to it. She put the baby over her shoulder, like she'd seen Michel do, went to the blue room, and learned how to change a diaper.

It wasn't that hard. She was already good at pins. The little girl kicked her bare legs, arms waving in her small white shirt, cooing and gurgling, her dark eyes big and open in the soft light. Rain pecked the windows behind the blackouts, and Isa built a barricade of pillows on the satin ocean of a bed, enjoying the feel of rumpling her mother's untouched covers. She popped the comforter into the baby's mouth. The little girl relaxed all at once, and Isa watched her fragile eyes fall closed.

Her father was still sleeping, and she did not see him shake. But his face was bruising, two violet half-moons darkening beneath his eyes, his breath coming through dry, cracked lips. He looked emaciated. And she had spent the day flippantly considering whether he had starved in the garret.

Why couldn't he just take care of himself? Why, Isa thought, did he have to be such a child?

Why couldn't she be the child?

She had a wet diaper and washcloth she didn't know what to do with. She had dirty towels everywhere. She left them all on the floor of the bathroom, lit the flame of the water heater gas, and locked the door.

It felt good to be alone.

She scrubbed, washed her hair, removed the last remnants of kohl from her eyes. She cleaned the grimy bits of Van Meegeren's cellar from the soles of her feet and from underneath her nails. But when she sank below the surface, into the still-warm world of water, where the noise in her ears became a whir and hiss, she thought she could hear a pop. Short. Sharp.

Once.

Twice.

And in the dark behind her eyes she saw drops of red paint on a palette. Red spatter on a black-painted door.

Isa came up out of the water, gasping.

She pulled the plug from the drain and tamed her hair. Put on pajamas, slippers, and her bronze silk robe.

Her father and the baby were sleeping. Rain pummeled the chilly house, and there was a light underneath the dining room door. Isa approached it with caution. She was half expecting to find a body. She pushed the door open just a little, and peeked through the crack.

And there was a body, Michel's, bent over the table, studying four pictures aligned with perfect symmetry on the dark polished wood of her table. Her Dürers. The chandelier was on, the paneling lit bark-brown and honey, and there was a place set with a linen mat, napkin, and a knife, fork, and spoon. Michel straightened, hands sliding into his pockets.

"Will you sit?" he asked.

Isa sat in the chair at the end, before the linen mat, robe slick on the soft, green upholstery. Michel went to the kitchen and brought the food she'd made and never eaten, holding the edge of the plate with a dish towel. He'd had it in the oven.

Isa unfolded her napkin. "Are you trying to apologize?" she asked.

"Only a little," he replied.

He didn't ask about the Dürers.

She ate her potatoes, Michel quiet in the next chair around the corner, hands folded, elbows on the table. She allowed herself one more bite before she said, "What have you done with Willem?"

"Sent him to the guest rooms, as you suggested. He intended to choose the small one, without electricity, though I told him the bed is short, he may not fit, but . . ." Michel shrugged.

Arondeus had loved that room and its need for a candle. He'd called it "the monastery." Isa looked up.

"Have you slept here?"

"Yes, once."

"Why don't I remember?"

"Because I was not much more than six, and you were busy being a toddler. I saw you two other times. Once when I was a teenager on a buying trip, and once when we were both at an exhibition at the Stedelijk. You chose to skip the line, as I recall."

She'd chosen to skip the line by entering the museum through the open basement window where the coal was being delivered. Sandberg the curator had delivered her to her mother, covered in coal dust and disgrace. She'd been eight.

Sandberg was gone now. He'd been with Arondeus at the bombing. One of the two that got away.

Isa ate another bite, eyeing Michel, and asked, "And who are you now, exactly?"

"Do you mean who does your boyfriend Willem think that I am? I am surprised you have to ask. I am Michel, your cousin from Rotterdam, originally from Austria, and I would quite like to go to Switzerland, just as soon as I finish my work for the Resistance."

Isa sighed. "How did you convince him you were with the Resistance?"

"I showed him this."

He lifted the long collar of her father's jacket, showing an orange *V* pinned underneath. *V* for victory, orange for the royal family of the Netherlands, exiled to Britain.

"When I saw someone light a cigarette in the window of the empty house across the back, I decided that a form of friendly identification might be in order. And before I forget, the can without the label in your cellar is carrots, and you are missing a hairpin. I was also able to give Willem information about where the Germans are searching for the killer of an SS officer this morning. He was grateful to have it, and for the advice to stop wearing the *V*, as it is known now, and has become a way for the police to find Resistance workers, not just for Resistance workers to find each other. All of which was true, and I was happy to do."

He was more than happy to do it. She could see that. The edges of his mouth were considering a smile.

Isa sat back from her empty plate, and Michel stepped into the kitchen, coming back with her mug of coffee. It was hot. It had just a little sugar in it. It had a little whiskey in it.

"Will you be in trouble," Isa asked, "for being out all night?"

"My services are shared by Gurlitt and Hofer, and it is not unusual for Gurlitt to be . . . unwell after a dinner party. If the two do not speak, I will get away with it. If they do speak, I will not."

"So where did you spend last night?" Isa asked, sipping.

Michel raised a brow. "My brother-in-law and I excused ourselves after dessert, as is our custom. Last night, however, I sent Pieter on, because our driver said you had not come out of the house. So I spent a chilly night chatting with a pig of a bridge guard. Waiting to see what had become of you." He picked up the dish towel and folded it carefully. "Could I ask you the same question?"

Isa peered over the rim of her mug. "You're not asking if I'm a prostitute, are you? If so, it's the second time tonight."

"Did your boyfriend ask you that?"

Isa grimaced. "I used the key you passed me and spent last night locked in Van Meegeren's cellar. My modeling career was short-lived. About three hours."

He undid the towel and folded it again. "Could I ask you another question?" This time he didn't wait for her response, just looked down the table. "I would like to ask why you keep four Dürer watercolors underneath a bowl in your kitchen?"

Isa slid out of her chair, mug still in hand, and went to look at them in the light. A rose, a hare, a fox, and a bluebell. The paper had flattened out nicely, and the wormholes, she thought, were good. She glanced at Michel.

"What do you think of them?"

"I think they are beautiful, of course." He leaned his elbows on the back of the chair. "Not quite as sophisticated as Dürer. An early work, perhaps? The bluebell is particularly good. It has unexpected movement."

He was right. That was exactly why the bluebell was best. The invisible wind.

"I also think your father painted them."

Isa looked up. Felt her lips part. Then she straightened and sipped her coffee. "How did you know?"

Michel almost smiled. "Do you not know that Theo signs all of his work?"

Her gaze darted back to the watercolors. She could clearly see the *A* over the smaller *D* for Albrecht Dürer. She shook her head. "No, he doesn't."

"Yes, he does. Here." He traced a finger along the edge of a grass blade, where it met the leaves of the bluebell. "The highlight is a stylized *T*, and up the stem and into the leaf we have the small *d*, and there, the curling leaf creates the larger *S*."

Isa stared. That couldn't be true. But it was true.

"It is very hard to see, if you do not know to look. And he always stylizes to incorporate the letters. See here, in the fox fur, in the dark tones along the back leg . . ."

She set down the mug, studying the watercolors. The initials were there. In the ear of the hare. Huge and nearly unrecognizable along the edges of three rose petals. Isa straightened and met Michel's gaze.

"The Rembrandt?" she asked.

"In the pages of the book."

Isa closed her eyes. She felt ridiculous. "But how did you know he . . ."

"I saw him do it. In your garret. When I was six. He did not know I was there until I was caught, which is perhaps why I am a sneaky child. I looked at all your father's paintings after that. It was like a game. But I never told anyone. Until now."

"Not even your father?"

He lifted a shoulder. "I suppose if Theodoor de Smit had tried to sell us something under another artist's name, I would have done. But Theo has never made art for money. He painted these because he admired the artist. Because he loves the art." He ran his clear eyes over the *Dürer De Smits*. "The wormholes are nice," he said. "And stacking them, and staining the insides of the holes. Very ingenious. But . . ."

She picked up her mug and waited. For what else she'd done wrong.

"They do smell like bad coffee."

Isa bit her lip. And she smiled, pictured Michel smelling the Dürers, and then she laughed. Michel looked down, his edges softening, though his smile was still a little too reluctant to come out. He straightened the rose picture.

"Do you really have a Vermeer?" he asked. "A genuine Vermeer?"

Isa sobered. And nodded.

"Can I see it?"

"I can get it, but it isn't . . . convenient."

"And you know it is genuine because . . ." He left the question dangling.

"Provenance," Isa replied. "And my eyes."

"A trusted provenance?"

"Unshakable. And documented."

Michel blew out a short breath. "And the money will go to . . ." Another question left to float in the air between them.

"Getting them out. The children. Before Judenfrei."

Michel turned this thought over, examining its perspective. Its angles.

"And just think," Isa whispered, "of who will be paying for their rescue."

She watched the uncertainty leave Michel's face. Watched him come to his decision like she'd taken a trip to the cinema. She saw the satisfaction.

She saw a thrill.

"I will go to Hofer tomorrow," Michel said. "He'll be more eager than Gurlitt. But I have to see it first."

Isa set down her mug. Her weariness had vanished. "Meet me in the little gallery," she said. "I need to get some things."

He nodded, and she was gone, soft across the hall to the blue room, where she ran her eyes over her father and the baby, then stepped up through the wardrobe and down into the garret stairwell.

She needed a hammer and chisel.

The pull-string bulb was glowing, showing the bloodstain where her father had landed on the bottom tread. Isa leapt over it. Her father hadn't touched the blackouts, and so the garret was a shadow study. Deeper black where the windows should be, the shapes of the sofa and the roof beams altered slightly in the faint light emanating up through the floor from the stairwell. She found what she was looking for by feel, a box of sculptor's tools in a corner, rummaging inside for a hammer and the biggest chisel.

There was an unpleasant smell in the garret, faint but familiar. Isa wrinkled her nose. And then she could see her father's easel, standing in the darkness, a square of canvas, sharp-edged against the muted background of grays and black. Isa stood, hammer and chisel in her hand.

And she felt the bloom. The heat. Ruby-hot and fire-red.

What copied masterpiece had left her bereft of a parent this time? What lovely, imagined work of a favorite artist had demanded all her father's love and devotion? Required the sacrifice of food, water, his body, and maybe even his mind? What piece of imitated genius had once again left her alone to face an ugly, ugly world?

Whatever it was, she hated it.

Isa took soft steps across the paint-dripped floorboards, hammer in one hand, chisel in the other. Imagining the ripping. The tearing. The snap of canvas threads. She walked slowly around the easel and turned, facing the canvas. Reaching up with a hand, the hand that held the hammer.

She found the pull chain and switched on the light.

And Isa saw the hand of the master.

"Beauty shall not be an opiate that puts you to sleep but a strong wine that fires you to action . . ."
> —Commandment IX, from *Decalogue of the Artist*,
> Gabriela Mistral

17

ISA LAID THE hammer and the chisel on the floor. And then she turned and flitted down the length of the garret, through the unfinished wall of the storage room, down the short ladder stair and her mother's forlorn studio classroom. A place of quiet and dust. Around the spiral, through the kitchen, down again and into the little gallery.

Michel was running a hand over the clean yellow bricks of the wall between the galleries. He took one look at Isa's face and followed her back up the stairs, unsurprised when they kept climbing to the studio. Unfazed by the scattered cans and discarded canvases of the storage room, turning to slide between the wall studs and into the garret without being told. Because he knew the way. Past the mixing table and sinks and her father's private display on the drying slats.

Until he was standing where Isa had been.

Seeing what she had seen.

Rain drummed the slanting roof, the bulb shining down on the painting in golden rays. Raphael's *Ascension* in electric light. Michel stood still. Looking. Absorbed. Then he stepped back and sat on her father's sofa, all without removing his gaze. He put his elbows on his knees, fingers tented around his nose. Isa sat down beside him.

"It's Christ with the adulteress, I think," she whispered.

Michel didn't speak. The center figure was Jesus—real rather than saintly—one hand reaching out, like a father to his child, and flanking him on either side were the Pharisees. One in the foreground, accusing, the other stepping back in disbelief. In awe. But it was the adulteress who drew the eye. A still profile. A body that spoke of pain. Hands that radiated hope, and all of it painted in the most luminous color. Ultramarine and azurite, madder lake, flaxen-gold and verdigris, bright against a background of green earth and soft, ivory black. The face of the adulteress shone in a shaft of pure, achingly brilliant light.

When Michel finally spoke, his voice was cool. Hushed. "Is there a Vermeer anywhere like this?"

"Not that I've seen. But it is a little like an early Vermeer in Rotterdam, I don't remember the name. A religious work, like this one."

"It is a masterpiece," he said.

Isa nodded. But this time, the master was her father.

Michel got up and peered closer at the paint. "Has he used ultramarine? Is it real?"

"I think so."

"It is even in the underlayment of the face, just like Vermeer. Where did he get it?"

"I don't know."

Isa remembered her father demanding ultramarine, as if it was only just downstairs. Had it really only been just downstairs?

"But look at this," she said, picking up a palette from the floor. It was not her father's old friend. This palette was new, dotted and smeared with puddles and tints of the colors she could see in the painting. She ran a finger over the blue and lifted it, showing Michel the clean tip.

He squatted down beside her and touched the paint, felt the smooth, hard surface of the ultramarine.

"And the brush . . ." she said. It was handmade. Badger hair. Trapped forever in the hardened paint.

Michel went back to the painting. Tried to put a fingernail in a brushstroke. He shook his head. "What is it?"

"A chemical. Carbolic acid, I think, and something else. Can't you smell it?"

Michel went straight to the mixing table on the wall beside the sink, and Isa followed. The mortar and stone showed signs of pigment, where her father had been hand-mixing, like Vermeer would have done. They picked up the various glass jars left scattered, little forests of brush handles poking out of muddy liquid.

"This is formaldehyde," Michel said, frowning.

Isa smelled, and she knew he was right. She'd thought the garret had reminded her of school. It had reminded her of the biology lab.

"I think he's mixing it with carbolic acid and then into the paint," Isa said, "and not with linseed. It's lilac oil he's using. I don't see it, but I can smell that, too. It must react better, to the heat . . ."

"What are you talking about?"

"I'm talking about hardening paint. To make it look like it's been there for centuries."

Michel glanced back at the work on the easel. "You think this painting is meant to be a forgery?"

Her father was the master and the forger.

"These chemicals, they're what I found in Van Meegeren's cellar. It's what Van Meegeren does to his paint. It has to have something to do with him . . ."

"Are you saying to me that Van Meegeren is a forger?"

"The Vermeer that Gurlitt bought for one-point-six million guilders, *Woman with a Wine Glass.* Van Meegeren painted it himself."

Michel frowned, brow furrowed. He put his fingers on his

temples. Then he walked across the floorboards and peered again at the painting on the easel, shining in its electric beams. The lead-white covering on the head of the adulteress glowed. He shook his head. He shook it again.

"That cannot be right. I looked at *Woman with a Wine Glass* myself. Everything was correct. The paint, the canvas. Even the nails in the stretcher . . ."

As if nails couldn't be replaced. Isa walked back to the sofa, curling into its corner, thinking of the seventeenth-century furniture in Van Meegeren's cellar. All that loose upholstery.

". . . and the craquelure," Michel said. "*Woman with a Wine Glass* was cracked, damaged in a place or two. I know it was. There is no cracking here."

"He bakes it," Isa said.

Michel squared his shoulders, listening.

"He puts the paintings in an oven in his cellar. I suppose the paint gets brittle, and while it's warm, he cracks it. I watched him. And the painting I watched him crack, I'm sure it was the Vermeer he's about to sell to Gurlitt. The painting wasn't there for Gurlitt to see because it wasn't ready. It was still in the oven. It's why I wanted the key."

Michel sat back down on the sofa, fingers tented again over his nose. He studied the painting once more. And when he took his hands away, he was smiling, really smiling, the smile that had teased all evening.

It was transformative. A face she did not know.

"There is one thing you have wrong, I am afraid." He turned the smile on her. "I am sorry to tell you, but Van Meegeren did not paint *Woman with a Wine Glass*."

Isa sat up. "Yes, he did. I know he did."

"How do you know?"

She lowered her voice. "Because I have *Woman with a Wine Glass*.

I don't know when Van Meegeren saw it, but he did. He must have."

"I did not say the painting was not forged," Michel pointed out, "just that Van Meegeren did not paint it. The *Woman with a Wine Glass* that I saw was beautiful, a masterwork. And I would bet one-point-six million guilders that it was painted by the same hand as the painting I am looking at now."

Isa turned her gaze to the work on the easel.

"Van Meegeren did not forge *Woman with a Wine Glass*. Because Theodoor de Smit did."

She sat, hands in her lap, trying to think. To remember any hint of her father painting such an epic work. But if he hadn't fallen down the steps, if he'd spirited the painting out of the house like he seemed to be able to spirit out himself—over to Van Meegeren's, perhaps—would she have even known? This showpiece her father had painted, with paint that was hardening while he worked, could have only taken him three days. And he would have seen Moshe's Vermeer. Many times. Studied it, probably.

"Did you never guess?" Michel asked.

She shook her head, still disbelieving. And yet here was the evidence. She sat up straight. "Did he sign it?"

"The hair of the Pharisee," Michel replied.

Isa got up and looked until she found it. It was nearly invisible. "But why would he do it?" she asked.

"One-point-six million guilders?" Michel offered.

"But my father has never done anything for money, like you said. Especially art."

How well she knew it.

"And if even a hundred extra guilders had shown up around here, I would have noticed."

"Does Van Meegeren . . ." Michel hesitated. "Does he have any kind of hold on your father, a way he could force him into forging a painting?"

Isa shook her head. She couldn't imagine.

They looked together at *Christ with the Adulteress*. And then Michel was smiling again, chuckling. A cup running over. A person made over.

Or maybe just a person more himself.

"Gurlitt," he said, "is going to look such a fool."

"So let's do it to Hofer," Isa replied.

Michel raised a brow.

"We won't sell him the original," Isa said. "Not anymore. We'll sell him as big a fake as Gurlitt got."

Both brows were up. "You want to put this painting in an oven?"

"It's what Van Meegeren was going to do, isn't it? That's who this is for, isn't it? This must be Gurlitt's new Vermeer. Look at what it's worth!"

Michel looked. He knew.

"And why should Van Meegeren get rich while the Nazis get our art? And just think . . ." she whispered, "just think where all that money could go."

They both glanced at the dusty garret floor, where two stories down, a baby was sleeping in a sea of satin.

Isa shivered once all the way up her spine. Michel was staring. Thinking.

"Why should he?" he whispered. "Why shouldn't we?" He looked up, suddenly tense. "What about alcohol?"

Isa unfolded from the sofa and went to the mixing table, rummaging until she found a bottle of alcohol. She poured some on her finger, rubbed it hard on her father's palette, and held the finger up. No paint.

"Water?" asked Michel.

She took the palette to the sink and turned on the faucet. The water over the palette ran clear. The paint puddles stayed as they were.

"I'm sure they could test it for something that shouldn't be there," Isa said, "though I don't know what. None of the standard tests are going to show a thing."

"And they haven't even been doing them," Michel said. "Arrogant bastards." He tilted his head at her. "It's a dangerous game."

"It always has been, hasn't it?"

He leaned back on the sofa. "Explain it to me. All of it. Tell me how he does it."

Isa told him everything she could remember about what she had seen in Van Meegeren's cellar. What she had divined from her own experiments baking paint. They discussed it down the stairs, in whispers through the wardrobe, past the sleepers in the blue bedroom, into the kitchen to get a bottle ready for the baby. When the baby had been fed, changed, and put back to bed, Theodoor still breathing deep and slow, they went back to the garret to measure the painting. Then down to Moshe's cellar to measure the oven.

Michel crouched, elbows on knees, scratching at a chin that had gone prickly, considering the dilapidated oven. His Nazi uniform was hanging as neat as he could make it from the clothes wires, hidden behind a set of clean sheets. He was serious about his task. He was always serious. But his voice was warm. His edges soft. Every now and then, he smiled.

It did not change what he had been. It did not change who he still was.

And how, Isa wondered, watching from the edge of Moshe's bed, does a person alter the line of a life? Take the scrawling, messy blotch that has ruined everything, and turn it into something better? Something beautiful? How does a person un-become? Run away, like Michel was doing? Sacrifice? Make restitution? But how much restitution was enough?

When does the moment come when a person can be absolved?

Or maybe, only the person themselves can decide that.

It would be so much easier with paint.

Michel looked back over his shoulder, still stripped down to his undershirt from feeding the baby. Because babies, he had informed her, often spit, and he did not yet have other clothes.

If Isa had been a painter, capturing that moment, she wondered if she could have named it *Friend*. It was a strange thought, unexpected, a current moving slow and deep through her head.

She'd waited a long time for a friend to come to the gallery, when her mother was gone and Truus was gone, her father present, but gone all the same. She would not have expected it to happen now. To come now, like this. In the form of an enemy. From an ugly world. In a day of so many ugly things. But something had changed. Something that had been ugly no longer was. Something had un-become.

Isa closed her eyes.

It could almost make her believe in beauty again.

"Isa," Michel was saying. "Did you hear me? The oven is wider on the inside than the door. If we take out the bricks here, the painting will fit. But we will have to seal it, and that I do not . . ."

"Isa?" Suddenly he was crouching down right in front of her. She'd fallen asleep where she sat, head against the boxed wall of Moshe's bed.

"Come," Michel said. "The rest will wait for tomorrow."

Isa nodded and sat up, ran a hand through hair that had dried wild, letting Michel follow her up the spiral and out of the cellar. The treads protested obscenely at being used in the dead quiet of two thirty in the morning. And then Michel said, "May I ask you another question?"

Isa paused and looked back. Heavy-eyed. Quizzical.

"What is your name?"

She wrinkled her forehead.

"Your full name," he said. "That Theo called you."

"Oh!" Isa smiled. "My name is Sofonisba Artemisia de Smit. My mother had a sense of humor, didn't she?" She started back up the stairs. "I am named for not one but two Renaissance painters. Female painters."

"I did not know there were any," Michel said.

"Neither does anyone else. Which was the point. Mama should have called me Sofie, but she had a student named Sofie that she detested, so Isa is what stuck."

They made their way through the kitchen, the dining room, and into the poppy hall, and Isa opened the door to the blue room. The lamp was switched on, its shade of heavy brocade muting the cerulean with gold. Her father had curled onto his side, and somewhere above, she could hear Willem, not asleep, just pacing back and forth. Rain spit and spattered against the window glass. She took a step toward the bed and realized she'd forgotten Michel.

"Take my room," she whispered, "it's . . ."

But she didn't finish. Michel was standing still in the doorway, looking at the carpet, the edge of his mouth threatening to lift.

"Would you like to ask me a question?" he said, voice low.

She didn't know.

"Would you like to know my name? My full name?"

She half smiled, waiting.

"It is . . . Michelangelo."

Isa felt her smile get bigger.

He raised his gaze. "Actually, it is Michelangelo Donatello Lange."

Now her smile was so big she had to put her hand over her mouth. His smile answered. What was wrong with their parents? Then the baby made a noise, a fussy noise, and they both went to the bed. Her arms were flung back, the blanket squirmed off. Isa adjusted her covering and put the comforter back in her mouth, stroking her head.

"How many people have you told that to?" Isa whispered.

"My name? Voluntarily? You might be the first."

Isa nodded. School registration had always been terrible. The endless spelling. Explanations. The comforter kept falling out. Isa held it in.

"You should call her something," Michel said. "Even if it is just for now. Something better than 'the baby.'"

"Hildy," Isa said without hesitation. For Hilde. And Hilde's baby that was gone.

Michel nodded. "It is a good name."

Willem's soft pace changed above their heads. And then he was moving. Across the room. Down the hall. Coming down the straight stairs. Isa and Michel met him outside the blue room door.

"Someone is here," he whispered.

"How do you know?" Isa started to ask. She wanted to know who was out there, watching, and how they were communicating with Willem. She wanted to ask Willem if he was all right. His eyes were puffy and bloodshot.

And then she heard the faint clang of the back-door bell.

"Hide the baby," Michel said, and he left with Willem, quick down the stairs.

She heard the soft clang again. Isa waited, listening, ready to scoop up Hildy, but she was hesitating. This was someone who knew about the chain. Who didn't want to wake the house. And it was only a few seconds before she heard the scrape of the table in the hall. The voices in the gallery. Isa ran down the creaking stairs.

And threw her arms around Truus.

18

TRUUS WAS DIRTY, dripping, her blond hair slicked to her head. Their hug was short, but Isa kissed both her cheeks. She had a look on her face that Isa wasn't familiar with, at least not on the face of her friend. Truus was uncertain. Frightened. And her skin had been cold to the touch.

"They stopped the trains," Truus said. "I couldn't get out. And the safe house had been searched. I've been out all night . . ."

"Were you followed?" Willem asked.

She shook her head. "Joop is watching, and he's getting his telephone calls. He doesn't think so . . ."

"Joop?" Isa said. "Joop Jansen?" She remembered the lit cigarette Michel had seen across the gully, in the window of an empty house. "Joop is . . . one of you? But I thought . . ."

"Oh, Isaatje!" Truus rolled her eyes, and there, Isa thought, was the friend she knew. "You're not going to bring up that essay again, are you? That was school!"

Even Willem looked slightly amused. But it wasn't her fault if life had moved on for everyone else while hers had stopped. And how was Joop taking telephone calls in an empty house, anyway? And then she saw that Truus was also wet because she was crying, arms crossed over her dirty shirt.

"Greta was arrested," Truus whispered. She looked up at Willem. "She had ration books, and she got stopped . . . they set up checkpoints, because of . . . what I did . . ."

Worse than a jail cell.

"Does she know about here?" Isa asked. It felt selfish to ask.

Truus shook her head, and then she stiffened. Michel was standing to one side, nearly lost in the dark of the gallery. His outline was square-shouldered. Hard-edged. For a little while, Isa had forgotten what that looked like.

"That's Michel," Willem said. "He's with us."

Truus looked at Michel, and then at Isa. And then Hildy tuned up to a cry.

Michel went for the baby while Isa mixed and warmed a bottle. She sent Truus to the bath, Willem to get dry clothes and a bed ready. Willem was uncomfortable with this assignment—Isa could tell because he was too polite—so she went to see to it herself. She climbed up a floor and knocked on the door to Arondeus's monastery, an extra pillow and blanket in her arms. And Willem was in the dark, standing in front of the window with the blackouts down, looking out across the empty gully and gardens to the empty houses. Isa shut the door, quick for the distant light.

"I brought Truus some extra things for the bed, for the . . ."

"What?" Willem said, terse. Almost offended.

And suddenly, Isa realized that she'd made an assumption about where Truus would be sleeping. But it had been a natural assumption. Truus and Willem had been a couple for three or so years, living in the same places for more than two. It had never occurred to her that Willem would follow the rules to such an extent.

Though she supposed it really should have.

Isa sighed. The room was cold, and if she'd been able to see, she probably would have discovered it was dirty, too, full of leftover, lost items from the people who had slept there in the world of before. And the bed wasn't nearly long enough for Willem's legs.

"Willem, are you comfortable up here? I hate for you to do without . . ."

"Isn't that what a monastery is for?" He turned from the window. "We all have to pay for our sins, don't we?"

Isa didn't know how to reply to that. Whoever had died, she could see that Willem considered himself responsible. Maybe Willem also had mistakes in life, lines that needed to un-become. Maybe he had been angry. Reckless.

It was a little hard for Isa to imagine.

She left the extra pillows and blankets, anyway. For him. Because sacrifice, Isa thought, was one thing. Self-punishment was another. But only Willem could decide when he was absolved.

She went downstairs and gave Truus her bed and her nightgown, then found Michel asleep on the sofa in the kitchen, a baby on his chest, an empty bottle rolling on the floor. She took Hildy to the blue room, cuddling her into the enormous bed, and brought Michel a quilt. He turned without waking, pulling the quilt to his chin.

Michelangelo Donatello, Isa thought. Two great sculptors. And a ridiculous name.

He couldn't have looked less like a Nazi.

And in the morning, when the rain was over, a bleak daylight just managing to brighten the clouds, Isa opened her eyes beside Hildy— she felt like she'd just closed them—and discovered that everyone needed her.

Hildy had soaked through her blanket, a towel, and the satin, and she had dirtied a diaper. Isa changed and cleaned her while she got a kettle on the heat and a bottle warmed, Hildy protesting with all the air she could muster. Then Isa got boiling water and all the soiled diapers into the washing machine in the cellar before the next kettle boiled and before someone could take over the bathroom. It was six thirty in the morning. Willem appeared in the kitchen, his eyes bleary.

"Where's Michel?" Isa asked, testing the bottle on her wrist, like he'd shown her. The quilt had been folded, the kitchen sofa deserted when she got up.

"He left just after dawn, he had something to take care of . . . and so do I . . ."

Willem's protest did him no good. She had already thrust the baby and a bottle into his arms.

"Ten minutes," she said, and picked up a glass of water with a plate of bread and cheese and took it to her father.

She had to wake him, even after all the commotion, propping him up on pillows while he groaned. But she was afraid to not have him eat and drink. "Here, Papa," she said.

He sipped obediently, only just able to hold the glass. She looked beneath his bandage—where he had a nasty but healable cut—and then sat on the edge of the cushion while he tried the bread and cheese. Both his eyes had blacked, face showing the skeletal shape of the cheeks above his beard. His silver hair was still stained. He looked terrible.

But her father, Isa realized, had not looked well in a long time. It had just come on so gradually, she hadn't properly noticed. Like it had with her mother.

And a stain spread over the hot, poisonous flower that seemed to have taken permanent root in her chest. A killing frost.

A different kind of fear.

"I saw your painting, Papa," she said. "It's beautiful."

He went still. "Did he come for it yet? Is he here?"

She thought she knew who her father meant. "No, not yet."

"I have to leave," he murmured. "Where is my scarf?"

His hand rose automatically to the wound on his neck. It fit the shape of his fingers. Because he'd scratched that wound there. The thought sat ice-cold in her middle. Then her father began to shake. Isa took the glass and the plate, and he doubled over.

"Tell him to hurry," he said. "It . . . hurts, Sofonisba . . ."

"What hurts, Papa? From where you fell? Are you sick?"

He didn't answer. He wouldn't answer. The shaking stopped, and he curled up again on his side, holding his knees. Isa put a hand on his shoulder.

"Why did you paint it, Papa?" she whispered. "Why paint that for him?"

His eyes fell closed. She thought he was asleep. But his cracked lips moved, and he murmured, "Morpheus."

Morpheus. The god of dreams.

Isa picked up the glass and half-eaten plate. Her father was ill, that was all. He'd made himself ill working in the chilly garret. Exhausting himself until he fell down the stairs. All to forge a Vermeer.

The bloom was there, but the frost had gathered, cold and prickling.

She went to her room, where Truus was still sleeping, changed into her overalls and tied up her hair. She picked up Truus's wet clothes and hung them, grabbed her father's bloodied towels and shirt, and when she passed through the kitchen on the way to the spiral stairs, she said, "Five minutes." Willem sighed, but Hildy was eating, and that was the important thing.

Another kettle of boiling water went into the hated washing machine. Because someone hadn't thought they should buy coal and fire the boiler. She put the kettle on again, and before Willem could speak, hurried up the spiral to her mother's studio.

It was a desolate place. Full of what used to be. A few easels stacked against the wall, one broken, and the empty, raised platform, where the models would pose, men and women half throwing on a robe to come down the stairs for coffee. Isa had been ten before she realized that other people didn't usually condone nudity in their kitchens. She walked the dusty footprints she'd left with Michel the night before, and climbed the ladder stairs to the storage closet. She found the toolbox, another hammer, some rusty nails, and finally, after what must have been forty years, she nailed up the wall planks, one by one, closing up the way into the garret.

The planks looked out of place and surprised. There were discolorations in the wood, where they'd been stacked. Some were cracked. Isa hung old canvases on them. Not pretty, but functional. And when she came down, Willem was in the studio with Hildy, Truus just behind him, still in Isa's nightgown, her short hair standing on end. The hammering must have brought them.

Isa hopped down, rubbing her dirty hands on the overalls. "If you need to hide, go through the big wardrobe in the blue bedroom. Shut it after you and take the stairs up to the garret. I've just boarded up the other end. It's not perfect, but it's a hiding space."

"That's good," Willem said, solemn. "That's really good. Thanks, Isa." He handed Hildy to Truus, and said, "I'll be back after."

Truus nodded.

He was walking away when Isa said, "Willem, I meant to ask. Did you know Arondeus?"

Willem stopped like he'd walked into a wall. Like she was pointing a gun. Truus's messy head whipped around, eyes wide over Hildy's head. Like Isa had done something wrong.

Isa blinked. "I only asked because you mentioned the monastery . . ."

Because that was what Arondeus had called it.

And suddenly Isa realized whose death Willem must blame himself for. Why he had been so upset in that room. How had she never considered it? Willem and Arondeus were both in the Resistance. Both had worked on forged identity cards. And besides Sandberg and Gerrit, and the other artists, the students and musicians, there had been at least one lawyer suspected of planning that bombing, and Willem had been a law student.

Willem had helped bomb the Records Office. Willem was one of the two who had gotten away. And the others had died. Arondeus had died.

Truus was looking at Willem's stiff back, the baby fussing. "Willem," she said. It almost sounded like a plea. But he just shook his head and walked away through the dust, down the spiral stairs, without looking at them.

Truus turned back to Isa, blazing.

"I didn't mean to . . ." Isa began.

"I know you didn't, but you did, Isa! You're just so . . . dense sometimes! You know it won't be enough until he's arrested."

"No, I do not know that." She walked up to Truus and took the baby. "I don't have any idea what's happening with either of you, and that isn't exactly my fault, is it?"

She took Hildy down the spiral before Truus could answer, the darkened window of the kitchen giving it an evening rather than morning feel. Her kettle had long boiled. She couldn't afford that. Leaving the gas on. But were Truus or Willem thinking of these things? Not any more than her father was.

Isa put a pillow in the sweater drawer, propped Hildy into a half-sitting position, covered her with another sweater, and took her into the cellar. Hildy, she discovered, liked dangling things. Like a sock tied to a string and hung over the clothes wire. She batted and grabbed unsuccessfully with her fists, cooing and squeaking, while Isa cranked the clean diapers through the rollers of the mangler, squeezing out as much water as she could before hanging them to dry.

Turning the crank through the ache in her shoulder, Isa found herself wondering if Arondeus could have been in love with Willem. Unlike Moshe, Arondeus had always been open about his preference for men, even outside the gallery. He'd had a boyfriend, but then again, Willem really could have been a cinema star. And Willem was so upright. A rule follower. How would he have handled such a thing?

Maybe not well, Isa guessed.

And then Arondeus was executed. And Willem wasn't.

"Isa."

She looked up. Truus was on the steps, Hildy asleep, the drying diapers decorating the room like strings of white cotton bunting. Truus held out an envelope, the name *Sofonisba* written on the front.

In copperplate.

"A little boy slid it under the front door," Truus said. "Do you know who it was?"

Isa shook her head. But she knew who had written it. She opened the note, rolling her shoulder in its socket.

Café De Dokter
1 o'clock
He is on the hook.
—MDL

Isa smiled. Hofer on the hook sounded intriguing. But meeting in public was dangerous.

Reckless.

He must have a reason. She folded up the note. Thinking.

"What are you mixed up in, Isaatje?" Truus asked.

"Nothing," Isa said. Though she'd said it in a way that meant "nothing more than you." "I'm getting your money, Truus, that's all."

"Leave her with me, then," Truus said, tilting her chin at Hildy. "I'll finish this, and I've got your father as well."

Isa looked at her askance, but Truus only smiled and held out a cheek. Isa came and kissed it.

And they were at peace.

Isa mixed up a bottle and set it in a pan of water, ready on the stove. She made her father drink water. She put on the brown tweed, rolled up her stockings, tamed her hair and pinned it. She put on a little lipstick, like a real person, pulled on her coat, and locked the gallery's front door behind her.

And she breathed. It felt good to escape the trap of the blackout. The air was damp after the rain, a little crisp, the sky blueing behind moray stripes of peachy cloud, the bricks of Kalverstraat reflective with silver puddles. She was only going around the block, but the sense of freedom was the same.

She didn't see anyone watching the house. She didn't see anyone looking at her like she had a gallery full of fugitives. No one who could look inside her head and see her plan to defraud a murdering, Fascist government.

She strolled around the corner to the café on the narrow Rozenboomsteeg and sat beneath its shadowed awning. She chose a table shielded by the rose pots, where she wouldn't be easily seen. Where she could see inside through the glass and out to Kalverstraat. Where she could have stuck out a leg and tripped the next Nazi passing by.

She wondered where Joop was.

Mrs. Breem was surprised to see her, as well she might be. She brought Isa coffee and a roll, which Isa assumed Michel would be paying for.

It was pleasant, to sit at a café.

It was also dangerous. What was Michel thinking of?

She sipped her coffee, ersatz, but better than home. She nibbled at her roll, to make it last. And pretended she was a person sitting at a café when there wasn't any invasion, no occupying army, no need to hide behind blackened windows. It was relaxing. It was nice. And then someone passed her on the lane, passed her by and immediately paused, backed up, and flung themselves down in the chair across the table.

It wasn't Michel Lange.

It was Han van Meegeren.

"Hello there, Judith. You look nice. Out having a little lunch, huh? That's good, isn't it? I was just coming to see you, girl."

Isa set down her cup, wary. Wishing there were more people in the café. In the lane. She had no idea what Van Meegeren might remember about what she'd seen in his cellar.

But a million and a half guilders was worth killing for.

"You didn't show up for your session," Van Meegeren said.

"You didn't make an appointment." She sat back and crossed her legs. "And you never paid for the last session. We signed a contract about that."

"Huh. Well, it's your father I want, anyway. Is he painting?"

Isa raised the cup again. Carefully. "My father is too sick to paint right now."

"I'll bet he is. Surprised he got this far."

Isa frowned while Van Meegeren rubbed a hand over his balding head. Then, all at once, he pushed back the chair. "Well, I need to see him."

"My father is not seeing . . ."

But Van Meegeren was already down Rozenboomsteeg, coat flapping, his walk the speed of another's run. Isa left her cup and plate and went after him.

"I said he's ill and not seeing anyone," she called.

"We'll see," said Van Meegeren.

He walked up to the front door of the Gallery De Smit and rattled the doorknob. Isa was relieved she'd locked it. Then Van Meegeren reached up, slid his hand along the lintel, and came back with a key.

Isa froze. Her mother. Happier times.

No wonder her father had been able to go back and forth.

"Wait," Isa said. "Stop! You can't just . . ."

But he was in. Isa ran after him.

Because Truus and Hildy were worth killing for, too.

"Stop!" she shouted across the gallery, making it echo. She grabbed the key from the open door and shut it. "You can't just come as you please. Leave!"

She was making as much noise as possible. So Truus and the baby would get in the wardrobe. Or at least get out of sight. Van Meegeren looked around at the empty gallery, passed the brick wall, and started up the spiral stairs.

"I said to stop!" she yelled, stomping after him on the creaking, popping treads. The noise was deafening. "You have no permission!"

She might as well have been yelling at the wind. Van Meegeren burst through the empty kitchen, on and up to take a look in her mother's studio.

Van Meegeren knew his way around her house.

"I said to leave!" Isa shouted.

He came down and shoved open the door to the dining room, through and to the poppy hall, where he went straight into the blue bedroom. Isa came running up behind him.

The room was empty. The sofa a forlorn pile of pillows with hints of dirty clothes.

"Huh," Van Meegeren said, eyes searching. "I would have sworn . . ."

He would have sworn the entrance to her father's garret was in here.

"I told you my father is ill." Isa heard the telltale trickle of moving water from the bathroom. "He's in the hospital."

Van Meegeren shook his head. "Don't lie. I know Theo. He's painting, isn't he, girl?"

He looked at her face and laughed, turning back into the hall, satisfied, and then a baby cried. Van Meegeren stopped. Looked around. And he smiled.

"Why, Judith. Oh dear." He gave her a slow gaze up and down. Shook his head. Tsked, chuckled, and went into the dining room.

He thought the baby was hers.

Isa followed him.

"You tell your father that I need that painting by tonight," Van Meegeren was saying. "Tomorrow morning at the latest. I can make trouble for him if he doesn't, you know. Big trouble. And here . . ."

He fished something out of his pocket. A little tin box went sliding across the polished table. "This will help. But only a little, mind. These are strong. And . . . what is this?"

His attention had been caught by the Dürers, still in their neat row.

"Turn on the light, Judith," he said. She switched on the chandelier and watched him. A pair of glasses came out of a pocket and landed on his nose. He bent, studying the watercolors. "Hmmph," he said. "The bluebell is nice."

And Isa felt a tug on a line.

Someone was on a hook.

"Those were my mother's . . ." she began. "I don't want to . . ."

"Nonsense," said Van Meegeren. "Of course you want to sell. You don't have a pot to piss in over here." He picked up the bluebell, examining the edge of the paper, letting the light shine through Isa's wormholes.

"I said I'm not selling them."

Hildy cried, faint in the other room. Helpful.

Van Meegeren smiled. "You mean, girl, that you just don't want to sell them to me."

Isa scowled, reeling him in. "I will not sell."

"Of course you will." He reached back for his wallet, muttering as he counted through the bills. His hand was shaking, just a little. He slammed a stack of money on the table.

Isa looked at it, and then at him. Scowling.

"No? Fine, then." He put two more bills on the stack. "That's the last offer, girl."

She shut her eyes. Humiliated. Resigned. Then she held up her chin.

"And since we have a contract, you can pay me for my session, too. While you're here."

Van Meegeren sifted through the wallet, and threw two more bills on the stack.

Isa gathered up the money and the little tin box, putting them quickly in her coat, while Van Meegeren, well pleased, stacked the Dürers. Their wormholes lined up perfectly.

"Be sure and tell your father I'm expecting that painting. Morning at the latest."

Isa nodded, following him down the stairs and through the gallery. But he didn't leave. He stopped at the front door, not quite looking over his shoulder.

"I had a dream about you, Judith. I dreamed that you had come to cut off my head."

"A dream or a nightmare?" Isa asked.

"I'm not really sure."

He stood in the doorway, thoughtful with his Dürers, and then he chuckled once, shrugged, and walked out the door.

Isa turned the lock. And let the smile come. The satisfaction. The thrill of blue-ice on cucumber. Because she had just out-forged the forger.

And he'd mostly done it to himself.

She wondered if he would ever think to smell them.

Isa felt the money in her coat pocket. She hadn't even counted it. And then she felt the cool metal of the tin box. She took it out—small, plain and unassuming—and opened its hinged lid.

Isa looked at the contents and whispered, "Morpheus."

"Thou shalt not extinguish thy anger, but master it . . ."

—Commandment Three, from *The Dutch Ten
Commandments to Foil the Nazis*

19

ISA SAT BACK down at the table in front of the café, apologizing to Mrs. Breem and promising to pay. Mrs. Breem brought her another coffee, for which she would also pay, and went back inside to prop up her feet on a heater. Isa sipped, considering her life with her father. Her life ever since her mother had died.

And so many things made sense now. So many things that should have never been.

Her bones had a marrow of vermilion. It was a color that made her want to cry.

Michel finally came, more than half an hour late, walking casually around the corner from Kalverstraat to slide into her table's second seat. He wasn't a Nazi today. He wasn't even a young man wearing ill-fitting pants. He had on a light blue shirt and a pair of dark trousers. Street shoes. She barely knew him.

"I am sorry to be late," he said. "But you should look very glad to see me, because I am out with a woman I have taken up with, and I am almost certainly being watched."

Isa had to glance behind her before she realized the "woman he'd taken up with" was her. "What do you mean you're being watched? Who's following you?"

"Hofer, I would think. Not personally, of course. But he is very concerned that I could go to Gurlitt, and that Gurlitt might snatch his prize. We need to be seen, and I did not want them to have your address." Michel smiled. "So say hello, and make my lies look real, please."

Isa sat forward, elbows on the table, smiling, coffee in hand. "Hello," she said, and then, "His prize?"

"Oh, yes," Michel replied. "Hofer is hooked, sight unseen. He did not expect another Vermeer to surface on this trip, and Goering has been . . . insistent. You would think that men who have risen so high in their profession might wonder at the sudden emergence of so many Vermeers, but . . . they do not."

Isa put her chin in her hand. She glanced at Kalverstraat. She couldn't see anyone. Michel leaned even closer.

"I think he will pay more than Gurlitt. He wants to pay more than Gurlitt. So that Goering may brag, the greedy bastard."

He'd said it with a smile. Isa wasn't smiling.

"How much more?"

"Enough to brag about."

Isa tried to imagine handing two million guilders to Truus.

She'd have to get a trunk.

"So, Sofonisba . . ."

Isa opened her eyes, dreamy.

". . . we have very little time. Hofer will want to make sure I am speaking the truth, that I am not acting on Gurlitt's behalf, trying to humiliate him. So I will be watched. I have invented a story about a young woman, to explain how I came across the painting. It also explains my neglect of duty, and my purchases on Gurlitt's account . . ."

So that's where his money was coming from.

". . . and my purchase of civilian clothes. My young woman does not wish me to be identified, because she is married. Hofer was beside himself with glee. I think he was almost proud of me. But he wants to see the painting, of course. And meet the young woman. He must verify that all is aboveboard."

Isa looked up. "He wants to meet . . . me? Can we get away with that? Won't he remember?"

"I doubt that he will. It is art that captures his attention, not people. But we must be careful."

"When?"

"Tomorrow. Two o'clock."

Isa set down her cup, thinking. She would have to look the part, utterly different from when she'd sold the Rembrandt, and her father's painting would have to be baked tonight. There would be only one chance to get it right. "And what if we ruin it?" she asked.

Michel knew what she meant. "Then we break down the wall," he said.

As ready as she had been to sell Moshe's Vermeer, now she preferred not to. She preferred not to like she preferred not to sever her own arm. They would have to get it right. She lifted her gaze.

"What makes you think my Vermeer is in the wall?"

"Please," he said, shrugging.

Her gaze cut to the left, to check on Mrs. Breem, who had her feet propped up, openly flipping the pages of an illegal newspaper. Interesting. Mrs. Breem was also giving them the side-eye.

"Mrs. Breem would like you to order at least a coffee, I think," Isa said. "And you're paying for two of mine and a roll."

Michel lifted a finger, and the woman nodded her understanding. There wasn't much else to order but coffee.

Isa said, "Leave the oven to me."

"Yes. I think I must. I will sleep at the gallery tonight, but I will not come until I lose whoever is behind me. Your watcher is expecting me, thanks to your friends. I just won't arrive in my uniform. I think that would be best, don't you?"

Isa crossed her legs, and let her smile go coy. There was a man at the corner of Kalverstraat, smoking a cigarette. An older man, in no danger of being conscripted for labor. He looked like he was keeping an eye on them. Isa lowered her voice and her lashes.

"How long can you get away with running off at night and spending Gurlitt's money?"

"Not long." Mrs. Breem brought him his cup, and he waited until she was resettled inside, feet up with her treasonous paper. "My foul deeds will catch up with me very soon. It is almost time for me to disappear."

He didn't seem all that unhappy about it. He seemed to be enjoying himself. The smile was teasing his mouth. He pulled out a cigarette, and then offered her the pack.

"You don't smoke, do you?"

Isa shook her head.

"How have you managed it?"

"Thrift," she replied. She picked up her cup, swirling the watery contents. "Did you know my father is a drug addict?"

Michel lit his cigarette. "No," he said. "But I guessed."

"I think Van Meegeren has been supplying him, and withholding. For paintings. *Woman with a Wine Glass*, I would say, and who knows how many others." She paused for her vermilion burn. The ache in her bones. Then she said, "Van Meegeren came to the house today. Not half an hour ago."

"He came inside? Who did he see?"

"He only heard. He thinks Hildy is mine. He was demanding a painting. What painting do you think he could have wanted?"

Michel blew smoke. "No idea."

"He thinks my father is still working. When I told him he was too ill to paint, he left him pills. He wants the painting by tomorrow at the latest."

"So he thinks he has a sale tomorrow, but possibly not after." Michel was thoughtful. "If Gurlitt tells Van Meegeren no, we cannot afford for Van Meegeren to go offering the same painting to Hofer. Even by description. It would be best if we succeed tomorrow, and secure a deposit, at the least. Before any of them find out what we've done. What kind of pills did he give him?"

"Morphine, I think."

"Van Meegeren is dependent on morphine. A lot of them are. Some since the last war. Goering is addicted."

"Really?" Isa remembered her job and leaned forward again, chin on her hand. An intimate conversation. "Have you ever met Goering?"

"Once. He had laurel leaves in his hair, rings on every finger, and had painted his toenails gold. He was wearing a toga."

Isa felt her brows rise. "And you bought that?" she asked, eyeing his plain blue shirt. She saw the corner of his mouth rise. Then he became serious.

"Don't give Theo the pills. Hide them, or flush them away. Men coming off morphine get very sick. He may beg you. But it will pass, and he can get better. They do get—"

And then there was a boom, distant but startling, a wave that made the bricks shudder beneath Isa's heels. Michel turned, Mrs. Breem came to look out the door, and in the crack of sky that could be viewed from the lane, smoke was rising, the color of slate and ash, billowing skyward above the Singel. Bomb, Isa thought, though she hadn't heard a plane, and such an instinctive urge to flee gripped her body, she reached out and grabbed the table. She heard a shout, and another, people talking in the street.

Michel stubbed out his cigarette, and said, very quietly, "I would say our friend has been successful."

Isa glanced up at the smoke. "You don't mean Willem?"

"I sent him the name of a collaborator this morning, and the name and address of his business. As I said I would last night. I told him I had contacts, but could not divulge who or where." Michel looked up, examining her. "It is no more than they deserve."

She wished she could be sure of that. Here she was, Isa de Smit, sitting at a table with a Nazi in disguise, making plans to sell an art treasure to one of the biggest Nazis in Europe. And intending to take copious amounts of money for it, too. Collaboration on a massive scale. And for all the right reasons.

It wasn't just paintings that could look like one thing when they were really another.

Michel said, "The man whose name I gave took a bounty for three hidden Jews, one adult and two children."

Isa met his eyes. Hard glass.

"You know which ones I mean. And would you like to know how much he got for them? Twenty-two and a half guilders. For three lives, and the mother and child hiding them. They were talking about it beside us, at dinner. Even Franz thought that was a bargain, the little swine."

She thought of the young, arrogant SS officer beside Michel at Van Meegeren's table. Laughing when he had said *Judenfrei*.

"It is not as if this man sold a German a picture so he could buy food for his family," Michel said. "He took a bounty. And his shop was closed today. If tomorrow he no longer has a business, this does not concern me."

Michel was right. Collaboration for survival and collaboration for profit—for revenge, whatever the reasons—weren't the same thing. But she wondered if Willem could tell the difference.

Between collaborators and collaborators.

Between Nazi soldiers. And Nazi soldiers.

When everything was a grayish haze, a blur made of every color, how was anyone supposed to see the lines between right and wrong? Or know when they had crossed them?

"It's an ugly world," Isa said.

Michel nodded. They listened to the ringing bell of the fire brigade.

"I will come to you tonight," he said, "when I lose my shadow. Do you see him now? The man in the mouth of the alley with the cigarette?"

Isa glanced over his shoulder. "Yes."

"Is he watching?"

"Yes." She put her eyes on Michel.

"So you will excuse me . . ." He stood, leaned across the table, and kissed Isa on the corner of her mouth, lingering just long enough to say, "Do not let him see you go home."

Then he handed Mrs. Breem a bill and walked away up Rozenboomsteeg, nearly bumping shoulders with his watcher, excusing himself as he passed.

And she had come very close, Isa thought, to knowing what it felt like to be kissed.

It was not exactly how she thought that might happen. Or with whom.

It was strange, this un-becoming.

And when Isa looked to the street again, Michel's trailing shadow was gone, and there, on the opposite side of Kalverstraat, was the woman in the kerchief, her back to Isa, partially hidden by the rose pots. She was talking with Willem. She'd changed her kerchief. A few quick words, and they walked in opposite directions.

Isa wished she could know just how much the woman with the kerchief had seen, and how much she had told.

There was more talk in the street now, people standing in twos and threes, pointing at the smoke. Then Mrs. Breem saw a friend and came out of the café to chat in the lane.

Isa stood. Mrs. Breem's back stayed turned. And Isa slid inside the café and unplugged her foot heater. A quick touch to the handle, to make sure it wasn't hot, and she picked it up and ran straight through to the kitchen. She could only hope the back door wasn't boarded over. It wasn't. It was locked. But there was a key exactly where hers had been, over the door on the lintel.

Happier times.

Isa shut the door quietly behind her, locked it, and put the key over the lintel, this time on the outside. She didn't want to leave Mrs. Breem unsafe. And then she ran across the tall weeds of the gully, awkward in heels and a purse, a hot heater banging against her thigh, hoping she had time to get across before Mrs. Breem noticed her loss.

She would return it as soon as she'd baked a painting with it.

Isa stumbled over the stones, got the back gate open, the door open, and ran into the hall. And Willem was right behind her, coming through before she even had a chance to shut the door.

They considered each other in the damp-stained passage. Willem had a nick on his cheekbone, a small cut on the back of his hand. From flying glass, perhaps. Isa was holding the electric heater, still burning.

They both decided not to ask.

Willem went up the spiral, where she could hear Truus in the kitchen, asking him questions. She took the heater straight to the cellar, ducking beneath the hanging rows of drying diapers, and was relieved to see that the cord would indeed reach the one hanging outlet. That there would be room inside the oven, in the space beneath the grate, once she had widened the door enough to accommodate the painting.

She left the heater where it was and then, on second thought, put it in the center of the room and turned it on. For drying diapers. Nothing liked to get dry in the cellar. When she reached the level of the little gallery she paused, looking up, toward the conversation in the kitchen, and right toward the straight stairs and her father. She needed to speak with her father. She ought to speak with her father.

She didn't want to speak with her father.

She took the straight stairs and opened the door of the blue room.

He was on the sofa, curled on his side, his back to her. He'd bathed, which was something, and he was wearing the only other pair of pajamas left to him, a purple satin stripe. She could see the wound on top of his head, scabbing over.

"Papa," she said.

He didn't move, but she knew he'd heard. She saw the change in his breathing. She knew he must have heard at least some of the conversation when Van Meegeren was in the hall. She wanted to ask how long this had been going on. If Francina knew, or if it was her medicine that had gotten him started.

If Francina knew, she wouldn't have even let him in the garret.

Isa wanted to say, How could you do this to yourself? How could you do this to me?

Can I help you fix it? How do I fix it? Why can't you fix it?

Do you want to fix it?

She didn't say any of it, because her father spoke. Soft, but firm. Words she'd felt but never heard.

"Leave me alone."

And so she did. She went and changed into her overalls. Retrieved the hammer and chisel and his beautiful painting, walking right past his turned back to take it all down to the cellar, gone warm in the heater light. She propped the painting carefully on the table, got on her knees, held the chisel in place at the oven's open mouth, and hammered.

Hard, and not careful like Moshe had been. Mortar flew, bits of brick—clay and sandstone, rust-red dust in the blaze of her hair—a vermilion heat in the marrow of her bones. She should have taken down the clean laundry first, she probably should have covered up the painting, but she didn't.

Swing. Chink. And the fall of a brick.

Swing. Chink. Another fall of a brick.

She worked up a sweat.

And when she was done, wiping the sticking hair from her forehead, there was an opening wide enough for a heater and the *Vermeer De Smit*. She got some of the planks from the storage room upstairs, the kind that were smoothed, ready for painting, finding one that was big enough to fit along the opening, experimenting with a towel on the inside, to seal, and the fallen bricks to hold it all in place. It might work. If she could get the temperature right. When she didn't know what the temperature should be.

She laid the heater on its back and slid it cautiously below the grate—she'd probably scratched it—and propped up her makeshift door. And then Isa waited, looking at *Christ with the Adulteress*, her father's best work, even if it was done in chemical paint, brushing it onto the surface of her memory with delicate strokes. In case it blistered. Burned and ruined.

She still couldn't decide if she loved it or hated it.

Isa closed her eyes, trying to remember the feel when she'd opened Van Meegeren's oven. The degree of the heat. She knelt down, tilting her makeshift door away from the opening, closing her eyes against a hot draft that blew her hair. Too much. She opened the door all the way, letting the heat billow out, and put her hand inside, feeling the air. Deciding.

The light glowed. An electric ember.

And Isa picked up the painting, wondering how the lives of six Jewish children had come down to this moment. Down to a painting and her own ability to forge it. She turned, right or wrong, and slid her father's masterpiece into the oven.

20

TRUUS WAS IN the kitchen, attempting something with flour and a rolling pin, Hildy happy in her sweater drawer, Willem reading an illegal newspaper, like Mrs. Breem had been, the cut on his face a tiny red line. The nearest blackout was down from the window, and they'd brought the phonograph and put it on the desk beside the sofa, playing American swing. Truus looked up.

"Hello, Isaatje."

It was such a homey scene. An advertisement in a magazine. If Truus hadn't just killed a man, and the baby didn't have a death sentence. If Willem hadn't just firebombed a business.

She didn't have room to judge. She'd just met with a Nazi soldier, stolen a woman's foot heater, and was using it to bake a forged Vermeer she planned to sell to Hermann Goering.

She gave Truus a quick kiss on the cheek, startling her into a smile. It was so good to see Truus not arrested. So good not to see her with a gun in her hand. The way she'd found her after Van Meegeren left.

No one, Isa realized, was going to take that baby.

"What have you been doing to yourself?" Truus asked. "You've got dust on your nose."

Isa got a dish towel and wiped her face. It came away brick-red.

Maybe she was even sweating in vermilion.

"You've put too much flour in there," Willem said, eyeing Truus's efforts. She was trying to fold a thin dough around a slice of tinned meat, and it was cracking.

"I think it needed another egg," she mused.

"Water," said Willem.

Isa picked up Hildy, who had been blinking and happy in her drawer, just because it was nice to pick her up. Because her hair was soft and she smelled good even when she didn't.

"Not water," Truus was saying.

"How much did the recipe say to use?"

"What recipe? Why would I look at a recipe?"

Willem sighed. "Because when you follow the rules, Truus, you don't make mistakes . . ."

Isa smiled, her cheek against Hildy's head, and then the treads of the spiral creaked. Announcing. And Michel's head came up from the little gallery. "Are we cooking?" he said.

He was early, Isa thought. He must have lost his shadow very easily.

"Have you seen what this says about Stalingrad?" Willem said, holding out the newspaper. Michel sat at the table and started talking about Soviets and the eastern front while Truus came around to get salt out of the painted cabinet, a little line of frown between her eyes.

"Does he have a key to the house?" she whispered.

"Yes."

Truus let it go at that, but she was watching Michel. Assessing. And so was Isa.

Something was changed since their talk at the café. She could see it in the way Michel was sitting, a little straight, running an amber glance over her every now and then from behind the smoke of his cigarette, while Willem explained why he shouldn't smoke. While

Truus told Willem he should mind his own business. Michel's cheek on hers had been just a little scratchy. And it made her wonder. Especially about Willem and Truus.

She'd seen Truus kiss Willem's cheek before, much like she would kiss Isa's. But she'd never once seen Willem kiss Truus. She'd never even seen them hold hands. And Truus was sleeping in Isa's room like it was the most natural thing in the world.

Her parents hadn't been like that. They'd been embarrassing, at least to Isa's childhood sensibilities. And so were quite a few of the other couples staying in the gallery, where people weren't particularly shy. It made her sad to think of. It made her sad for her father, and a little sad for herself.

Truus loved Willem, that was obvious. She would rise up to defend him at the first wry glance. But Willem, Isa realized, to her shock, did not love Truus. Not like a partner. And he was using some kind of mask of morality to hide his lack of feeling for her friend.

Isa watched them argue over Truus's pastry, bickering like grandparents. Or maybe like best friends. Maybe it had something to do with Willem's wound. His guilt and self-punishment. Whatever the reasons, Willem and Truus were not actually a couple, and Truus didn't seem to know it.

And Truus had accused her of being dense.

Isa set Hildy in her drawer and went to change the record.

Michel came, looking through the offerings, and said quietly, "I saw the oven. Have you been stealing from that woman at the café?"

"Borrowing," Isa corrected. She set the needle down on Johnny & Jones. "You got here fast."

"I have a new lover that claims all of my attention."

"Oh." Isa looked up. "I forgot to tell you. I sold the Dürers."

"Really?" His expression was worried. A little disapproving.

"I sold them to Van Meegeren," she whispered. "He was very happy. Four hundred guilders. He got a bargain."

Michel looked at her. The edge of his mouth came up. And then he laughed. It was a warm laugh. A little unexpected. Truus craned her neck at them, frowning.

Isa was still smiling when she went to make Hildy's bottle.

Truus boiled her creation and sautéed it in butter. It was Polish, she said. Michel brought her the last can of carrots, unmarked. Isa took Hildy in her drawer and they went to the dining room and had a feast. They were ahead of the blackout, so the curtains weren't tacked up, the last of the sun spilling orange-blush between the gable roofs. And the talk was about the underground newspaper. Mussolini. If they would ever get their radios or their bicycles back. The coal supplies for the winter. They did not talk about what any of them had done that day. Or what they might do tomorrow.

Truus watched Michel like a bird about to peck.

Isa watched the clock. She thought she could smell her painting. When Hildy fussed, she picked her up and got her settled in her lap with the bottle.

And then the door to the dining room opened so hard it banged against the paneling.

It was her father, one long arm holding the door in his purple-striped pajamas, haggard and bruised beneath his dark, pointed brows. But he had put on his smoking jacket, a new yellow scarf, and his mismatched slippers. He looked around the table, and then pointedly at Isa, sitting with a baby in her arms.

"Good God," he said. "How long have I slept?"

Truus choked back a laugh.

"My dear!" he said, as if just discovering Truus. "How delightful to see you again." He came and kissed her hand. "And you, what a pleasure." He clapped Willem on the back and shook Michel's hand.

There was something horrible about this attempt at brightness. Like a light bulb flickering. He just didn't have the energy.

"Papa," Isa said. "Do you feel like eating? We saved you a plate."

Theodoor's gaze moved right over her. He sat at the other end of the table, casually, one leg crossed.

Isa felt it like a shove. She'd been meant to. She patted Hildy's back.

Willem's fingers drummed, like he wanted to say something but didn't quite know what that should be. Truus gave Isa a questioning glance. Michel was on her other side. Still. Waiting.

And then her father announced, "I have had a very successful session with the paint. Difficult at first, very difficult. The paint, sometimes, will fight. But I have conquered, all the same. You, daughter. Have you seen my painting?"

He wasn't asking if she had viewed it. He was asking if she had taken it. So he'd been up to the garret, then. Looking. And suddenly she wondered if that's why her father hadn't objected when she moved the wardrobe. Because he'd been up there making forgeries.

"You see, daughter, I believe someone came to view my painting today, at an inconvenient moment. Did you give it to them? Or did they deliver anything? For me?"

Isa stroked Hildy's head. "No, Papa. I don't think there was—"

He smacked the table. Hard.

Truus jumped. The plates jumped. Willem frowned.

Her father took a breath and smiled. "You must have forgotten. I believe my friend brought something for me today?"

"Theo," Michel said. "Do you remember . . ."

"This is not who I want to speak to," her father said. To all of them. Commanding. As if it were everyone's job to keep others from speaking if Theodoor de Smit didn't want to hear. "He is not the man of which I speak. Where is my package?"

Michel glanced at Isa with the baby—there was a warning in it—and then back to her father.

And suddenly, Theodoor de Smit swept out an arm, knocking Hildy's drawer off the table. It hit the floor with a crack and tipped, dumping sweaters on the rug.

"Where have you put my package?" he shouted.

No one answered.

And then her father leapt up and plates went off the table. The glasses breaking. Hildy cried at the sharp, wrong sounds, and Isa moved her away from the chaos, thrusting her into Truus's startled arms. The candlesticks flew off the sideboard, denting the paneling, and Willem was on his feet, Michel at her father's side, trying to reason.

"Theo, you don't have to—"

But he shook Michel off, yanking out one of the sideboard drawers, upending it, and rifling the contents.

"Where is it?" he yelled. "Where? Give it to me!"

What he wanted was in her coat pocket. And Isa couldn't even remember where her coat was.

Her father dropped, hands and knees on broken plate, head in the lower cabinet of the sideboard, pulling out the linens. Isa knelt beside him. She put a hand on his shoulder.

"Papa, stop. Listen—"

He pushed Isa hard enough to make her fall back, sit, bang her head against a chair. Truus ran to the hall with the baby. And then her father was up and off again and into the kitchen. Where drawers were opened. Spilled with a clatter. Willem went after him, Michel just behind, and the sound of a scuffle broke out. Isa listened from the floor.

"Give it to me!" her father was screaming. "Give it to me!"

And when they came back through the kitchen door, Willem had Theodoor by the collar, Michel by one arm, removing her father to the blue room while he kicked and flailed. But his fight was ineffective. He really wasn't very strong, his voice already losing intensity.

He was pleading. He was crying.

Isa sat where she was.

And sadness, she thought, was the silky pale nothing of spilled linen.

She got up and walked past her father's cries to her bedroom, where Truus was huddled with the baby. Where her coat was hanging on the back of her chair.

"What is wrong with him?" Truus asked, eyes sky soft.

Isa found the little tin box in her pocket. "This," she said. "I didn't even know about it until today, but it . . . explains things."

"What is it?"

"Morphine. Michel says that he will get better, but that it is . . . difficult, at first, to stop. I should have already flushed them."

Truus bounced the baby. "Who is he, Isaatje?"

Isa looked around. "Michel? My cousin."

"I really hope that's not true," she replied, shaking her head.

There was a small, uncomfortable silence. Isa chose to fill it.

"I have things I have to do tonight. And tomorrow. It's important. About the money. And I'm going to need help." She looked at Hildy, listening to the noise from the blue room. "With both of them."

They looked at each other. Truus knew it was better not to ask. That she should not know specifics. "Do you trust him?"

Isa looked away. "He gave Willem the name today . . ."

"The name of a collaborator he doesn't care a thing about. Isn't that what you'd do, if you wanted to be trusted, and take down a cell of the Resistance? Or he might have . . . other motives."

"I think he wants to help, Truus. And that he needs to get to Switzerland."

"You know I only want you to be careful."

There was a muffled yell from the other room.

"He'll bring the police, carrying on like that," Truus said. She reached out and took the box from Isa's hand. "You go tend to him, I'll take care of these."

In the blue room, Isa found her father having another fit, shaking and trembling and groaning. She tried to cover him, but it was hard to understand whether he was hot, or cold, or in pain, or none of those things. When it was over, he lay still on his sofa, exhausted.

Willem shook his head. Michel must have already told him what was wrong because he didn't comment when Isa asked, "How much longer, do you think?"

"What I saw was three or four days," Michel replied. "It will pass."

They went to the kitchen, putting drawers back in place and sweeping up glass. The sweater drawer was a little broken, probably not fit for going back in a dresser but still capable of holding a baby. Isa looked at the sky and hurried to do the blackouts while Truus changed Hildy. Michel hung his blue shirt on the back of a chair so nothing would happen to it, washing the dishes in his undershirt, finding dirt Isa had forgotten to notice and somehow making the kitchen spotless. Willem disappeared up the straight stairs, Michel down the spiral.

Isa dried and put away the dishes, thinking about their savings after her mother died—before Isa fully took over the finances—and how quickly it had all disappeared. Her father, actually forging paintings in the garret, using the art he loved to support a habit.

She'd thought she'd been taking care of him. Keeping up her end of their arrangement. Doing what Francina would have done. And all her sacrifices had accomplished was to make it easy. Easy for her father to choose dreams over life.

To choose oblivion over her.

And the crimson heat that blossomed in her chest, the flower that had poisoned her bones, burned.

It ached.

Isa hung the drying towel. And caught a whiff of heat. Of lilac. She went down the stairs, the smell of the chemicals a sting in her nose, and found that Michel had taken the old, decrepit mattress off Moshe's bed, tying it upright to one of the tree trunk columns that supported the cellar ceiling.

"How long does the painting have?" he asked before she could say anything, tightening one of the laundry ropes around the mattress. He was still in his undershirt. She could see the soft sprinkle of freckles across his shoulders.

"Another half hour is my guess, but . . . What are you doing?"

He picked up an old broom handle and held it out. "I would use boxing gloves, but . . ."

And Isa realized what he wanted her to do. She smiled. And shook her head.

"Go on," Michel said, holding out the stick. "Hit it."

She took the stick and hit the mattress. A little. And then she swung back and hit it hard.

"Use both hands," he said.

She did. And the resulting smack into the mattress was satisfying. Better than the hammer and the chisel, because she wasn't making a hole in the house. She did it again. And again. Raising some sort of unholy dust that floated in the air. She hit the mattress mercilessly until she was red in the face instead of inside her chest, until her muscles ached instead of her bones.

"Isaatje?"

Isa paused and looked up, wiping her forehead with a sleeve. Truus was on the steps, peering down into the cellar, Michel on the wooden platform of the bed, smoking in his undershirt. "What time is it?" Isa asked.

Truus shook her head. Michel stood and handed her the stack of dry diapers he had folded. Truus shook her head again and left, hand over her nose. She must have thought there was some kind of fight going on. She might think they'd lost their minds. Michel turned.

"Better?" he asked.

Isa nodded, leaning the stick against the wall. It was better.

"I think it is time," he said.

"Are you sure?"

He shrugged. "Of course not."

Isa knelt beside the makeshift oven door, cracked open to control the heat, and moved a few of the bricks that were holding it up. Michel crouched down, watching as she tilted the propped board, as she closed her eyes against the warm breeze and reached into the heat— it didn't feel like too much heat—making the same hiss of hot fingers that Van Meegeren had when she touched the wooden stretcher. Michel handed her a towel from the laundry and she used it to slowly pull *Christ with the Adulteress* out of the oven. She put one end on the table, held the other with the towel, reached underneath at the corner and pushed upward on the canvas.

The paint cracked.

"Get the varnish," Isa said, excited.

"You are sure he varnished first?"

She nodded. Michel opened the can she had ready and she laid the hot painting fully on the table. She didn't know how much time she had, but she did remember that Van Meegeren had worked fast. She brushed the canvas in fast, broad, shining strokes. Varnishing Christ and the pointing finger of the Pharisee. The adulteress's radiant face. Michel watched, hand on his chin, silent.

The varnish hardened quickly, and when she reached underneath and pushed upward, it cracked in the same pattern as the paint. Exactly as it ought to. She pressed randomly, here and there.

"Wait," Michel said. He pulled a loupe from his pocket, examining the cracks up close. "Different directions. Turn it."

He was right. She turned the painting and pushed, turned and pushed, the way Van Meegeren had done, Michel saying "Here" or "Over here" until the surface had a random uniformity of cracks. A haphazard spiderweb of hair-thin lines. Isa picked up the painting, nearly cool now, and turned back to the oven.

"You are sure?" Michel asked.

She paused. "Van Meegeren did it."

"Do you know why?"

She shook her head.

He stroked his chin, shadowed since the afternoon. "Put it in."

She slid the painting back in and pushed the wooden board shut, propping it up with bricks, but still with a space at the top.

"How long?" Michel asked.

"I don't know. This is when I left."

She waited ten minutes and checked it. There was no change. She waited five more, and the same. Michel paced, hands in his pockets. Hands on his head. Now he was sweating, a V-shaped stain between the muscles of his back. Another ten, and when they looked, the varnish had taken on a yellowed tinge.

"Take it out," Michel said.

She put it on the table, and Michel tilted the shade of the hanging light, directing some brightness onto the surface. Then Isa held the light while the loupe came out. He examined. And examined. And Isa watched the little frown come onto his face, the shake of the head, like when he'd been looking at the *Rembrandt De Smit*.

"What's wrong with it?" she whispered.

"The craquelure is excellent, the paint looks right, even the varnish has a good color for age. But between the cracks, it is clean. New-looking."

Because it was new.

Michel straightened. "Hofer will not miss a surface like that. I would not have, on the last one."

Isa stared at the painting, much duller than it was, but still beautiful. Too beautiful.

"Then the surface must have been different," she said. "Van Meegeren must have done something. Something I didn't see. Another step, after I left."

She sat on the edge of the box bed, fingers on her temples. Whatever the process was, she didn't know how much time she had, or even if it should be done hot or cold.

Michel crouched down in front of her, elbows on his knees. "Think," he said, "about what you saw in the cellar. What was on the table? Tell me. Name the items."

She closed her eyes. Seeing the odd, orange light, her head full of fear and the acrid smells. "A palette of hard paint," she said. "Badger-hair shaving brushes, a pumice stone, and paint dust—maybe he was damaging the paint, to make it seem old?—the jars of carbolic acid and formaldehyde, the lilac oil, like a ladies' perfume, a bottle of ink . . ."

Isa's eyes snapped open. "Ink?"

Michel was thinking. "Perhaps. But it needs dirt. Do you have a bottle of ink?"

"No, I can't think . . ." And then she said, "Wait."

And Isa hurried up to her mother's desk in the kitchen, now with a phonograph and records all over it, and searched the drawers, their sacred disorder no longer sacred. She grabbed every fountain pen she could find, every refill cartridge, stuffing them in her overall pockets, trying to keep the stairs quiet on her way back down. It was nearly midnight.

Michel looked up as she came down. He was gathering brick and mortar dust from the floor into a little bowl that had once held stray buttons. Isa went to the table and started emptying her pockets. "I don't know how much is in them. They could be dry . . ."

He brought the bowl—a pile of what might be coal dust with ash from the boiler mixed in—and started emptying cartridges. Some of them were wet, but the contents were in drops. Then he opened the pens. Two of them were dry. He smashed them open with a brick and dumped in the dry contents. He added a few drops of water, one drip, two, with the precision of a chemist. Then he took a pen and stirred it all into an uneven concoction of blue-black ooze. He dipped a finger and brushed it across the corner of the cracked paint, working it in, wiping it once with the towel.

He got out the loupe and looked. And looked. And then he handed the loupe to her.

The cracks where he'd worked in the ink looked dark, partially filled. Grimy.

She straightened, and saw a smile teasing Michel's mouth.

He knew it looked good.

They worked together, dripping, working in stained grit, inch by inch, dulling the painting down further, blackening, dirtying the spiderweb, then carefully wiping it away. Isa stretched while Michel propped up their work on the table in the light.

It was a Vermeer looking back at them. The most gorgeous Vermeer Isa had ever seen.

One square of beauty in a whole world of ugliness.

And Michel was smiling. Transformative. In delight. In triumph. Because Hofer was going to buy this for Goering. Goering would pay for the children to get out.

Isa closed her eyes. Shivered.

"Oh, yes," Michel's voice said, as if she'd spoken. "I know."

Now all they had to do was sell it to him.

"You must not lie."

—The Ninth Commandment, *Exodus 20:16*

(*The Living Bible*)

21

IT TOOK ISA longer than she'd thought the next morning to get ready to sell a forgery to a Nazi. She'd spent the night alone in the blue bed, her father on his sofa, Michel in one of the guest rooms, while Willem paced the floor above, making her ceiling creak. Truus had taken the baby in with her, but Isa still hadn't been able to sleep. Not well. Afraid of every noise, every move her father made. Afraid of what he might do next.

But unlike Isa, Theodoor had slept deeply, almost without moving, and he'd eaten the food they left beside him. He was still bruised and sickly when he sat up, watching Isa go through her mother's hallowed clothes. He didn't speak, just picked up a blanket, taking his opportunity to climb through the wardrobe and creep up to his garret.

He'd never asked why there were people in the house. Why there was a baby. How much money they had or how they'd acquired the food he ate.

He might, Isa thought, be over the worst.

She sorted through her mother's clothes. Her mother had always been taller, more filled out, while Isa was waifish—as Francina had kindly called it—and Francina's taste had not often run to the conservative that she needed to present today. Isa needed understated.

Like she ate gilded nuts for her breakfast. She was ready with her pins, prepared to button a coat over what pins could not correct.

But Isa, as it turned out, was the one who was taller now, more filled out. She found a soft green wool where the fit wasn't bad, with two rows of buttons down her rib cage, clinging at the hips before it flared. It was a little tight in the chest, but there was a short jacket. Her mother had worn this outfit with a hat of tangerine plaid and a sunflower pin, but Isa found a simple brooch and pair of pearl earrings gathering dust in the jewelry box since her grandmother's time.

She found the makeup box, too, some of which was still good, did her hair into a roll and a knot, and pinned on her own copper wool hat. Her mother's coat with the fur collar went over her arm, after a good brushing, a leather purse with the mold wiped off, a pair of brown leather gloves left inside that fit after a little oil. Her identity card went down her front, unfindable, presumably, unless she wanted it found.

She looked in the mirror. Her hair was ginger-nut and her lips were red, her freckles a touch of whimsy. She wasn't pretty, but she was striking. And she looked ten years older. She could pass for a young, wealthy woman gone wrong. She turned from the mirror, and found her father's head sticking out of the wardrobe. He looked at her, blinking.

"How long have I been asleep?" he said.

It was a joke. An attempt at a pleasantry. She smiled, but her reply had a touch of red that went deeper than her lips.

"Too long, Papa," she said. "You've been asleep for a long time."

"My painting is gone," he said.

"Yes, it is."

"There won't be any more, will there?"

Isa slowed the glove that was sliding onto her newly polished finger-nails. He didn't mean paintings. "No, Papa."

When she looked up, her father was trembling. He had tears in his eyes. If she looked ten years older, he looked a hundred.

"I can't find a canvas," he said.

He might look a hundred, but he was really a lost child. And then Isa remembered that the storage room was boarded up. "I'll ask Truus to bring you one, Papa."

Painting would be the best thing for him.

She turned to tell him goodbye, but he'd already crept away.

When Isa opened the door to her room, Truus was just sitting up, Hildy asleep in the sweater drawer. Truus pulled her knees up to her chest, her short hair in all directions. It reminded Isa of music. Giggling and passed notes. Truus wasn't giggling now.

"Do you know what you're doing, Isaatje?"

"Yes," she replied. It was a ridiculous plan. Reckless. And she was perfectly aware of it. "We'll be back late afternoon with the money, if all goes well. Will that be all right?"

"It will be just in time." Truus was not one to sugarcoat. She looked down. "Greta was shot yesterday. Joop let us know. They took her to the dunes."

Like Arondeus. Like Michel would be, if he was caught. Like all of them could be.

"We were relieved," Truus said, "because it wasn't long."

And what were the chances, Isa wondered, that all of them would come out of this with their lives? Small. Maybe minuscule. There were too many risks.

She looked down at Hildy in her drawer, cuddled in her blanket, deep among the sweaters. Soft-headed. Button-nosed, both arms flung back. Secure and peaceful.

She was worth the risk. They all were.

Because she was the beauty of the world.

"Please be careful," Truus whispered. Because she didn't want to be relieved when Isa died. "I don't trust him. Willem does, and I know you do, and I can't put my finger on what's wrong. Only I know, that there is something . . . I do not understand."

It was, oddly, how Isa felt about Willem.

"I promise," Isa said. "I won't do anything reckless or stupid."

Truus almost smiled at such a blatant lie.

"Papa seems better today. He's in the garret. If you could get him a canvas out of the storage room, your life will be easier. And make sure the doors are locked and barred. That man may come back, looking for his painting."

Truus nodded, and Isa blew her a kiss.

She smiled. And blew one back.

Michel was waiting in the big gallery, thoughtful, sitting on a window ledge. His shirt was neat, and he'd found a way to shave. Isa wondered how he was going to find his way into his repellent uniform. He had a package beside him, wrapped and tied with string. It was painting-sized. Or a trussed-up window. He watched her come down the stairs and stood, shaking his head. Frowning.

"No?" she said, looking down at her skirt.

He shook his head again. "I was just thinking there is no chance in hell that Hofer is going to recognize you. That is all."

She started to put on her coat and Michel took it from her. "You should let me today," he said. He slid the fur collar up, settling it onto her shoulders, and picked up their package. Isa laid a gloved hand on the wall between the galleries as she passed. Seeking its blessing.

"I will go ahead of you," Michel said. "The car will pick me up first, then . . ."

"A car?"

"I did not mention the car? I am setting fire to every bridge I cross today, including using Gurlitt's car. Without his permission, of course, though the driver does not know that. But I do not want him coming here, so we will pick you up on the corner of Spui and Singel." He slid the table away from the back door, making it shudder across the uneven planks. "Wait five minutes and come." He glanced down at her shoes. "You will get through the weeds?"

Isa could have run across those cobbles in heels with her eyes closed.

Michel nearly smiled. "I am almost sorry for him."

"Who?"

"Hofer."

Isa raised a brow. And there was a moment, a fleeting second, when she thought Michel was going to lean down and touch his lips to the corner of her mouth. Like he had at the café the day before. Only more than the day before. Much more.

It would have been natural. Easy.

He didn't do it.

He just said, "Five minutes, yes?" And left with the painting.

Isa stood in the damp back hall, counting minutes in her mother's finery. If he had done it, if he had done it more, would she have let him?

She would have let him.

And she wasn't sure how she would have felt about it afterward.

She took off through the weedy cobbles and up the tiny Rozenboomsteeg, where Mrs. Breem did a double take, and then down to the corner of Spui and Singel. A slick black car was already waiting, engine purring. When she approached, the back door opened, she got in, the door closed, and the car pulled away.

Quick and smooth. A blink and a miss.

And when she looked around, cozy in a soft, leather interior, Michel was still getting dressed, tucking his shirt into his Nazi brown pants. His jacket hung next to him, hat on the seat, and his boots were untied. He was a chameleon changing his colors. Becoming someone else.

Isa glanced forward, but the driver had his eyes on the road, dispassionate. Maybe even bored by a man changing clothes in his car. Probably wondering how shuttling German officers around for their various fiascos—and minding his own business about it—had become his lot in life. And Michel wasn't even an officer.

She turned her face to the window while he buttoned his jacket. The space his uniform created was a chasm she'd nearly forgotten was there.

But it was there.

They were leaving the old part of the city. Driving on streets that were wider and built on a grid, where the buildings were two hundred rather than four hundred years old, some even new, straight-edged and modern. The trees had found room to grow round and thick here, still with a smattering of leaves, little paper hangings of flame and magenta, dangling above grass that had been bronzed by the frost. The Amstel flowed slow and murky on their left.

She turned to Michel. And turned away. He had his hat on. He was a Nazi now.

"Where is our meeting?" she asked the window.

"Oostermeer," he said. His voice was quiet. Cool. The voice of her blackmailer. "It belonged to Goudstikker."

He'd said it like it was nothing. Or maybe he hadn't.

"Hofer uses it when he is in Amsterdam. And so does Gurlitt."

"Really?" she said, casual for the driver. Gurlitt, at least, would not fail to recognize her.

"They have a competition for who gets the master suite. Number of objects acquired. Hofer won this time, so Gurlitt is at the Herengracht office. Recovering." He'd said the last word very low.

"And where do you stay?" Odd that she'd never asked him that question.

"Sometimes with Gurlitt. But here, mostly."

They were driving a lane only just higher than the water now on both sides, glints and ripples made by the sun and breeze, the blades of a windmill turning lazy circles. And then the car turned into a gate—wrought iron and ornate—hung between two stone columns.

And the house on the other side was almost sweet, with even Georgian proportions, a doll's house dropped just so into formal gardens between the river and a canal and a lake. Until they crunched closer on the gravel drive, and Isa realized that the doll's house was enormous. That the two windows on either side of the massive front doors were nearly a full story tall. The driver put the car in park, motor humming.

Isa let the driver come around and open her door, taking his hand, allowing him to lead her to the front steps. She clutched her purse, waiting politely, impersonally, noting the classical statuary of the garden, while the trunk was opened, their package taken out. Michel said something low to the driver in German—why had she forgotten he spoke German?—and then he came across the gravel, square-shouldered, straight-backed, the painting tucked under his arm. Everything a Nazi should be.

She turned to him, to play her part of the straying wife enamored with a young soldier. Someone, she thought, would be watching from the windows. But when she looked up and found the brown of his eyes clashing with the color of his hat, she remembered why he was there, and the smile that came to her face was real. Michel sighed.

"I could use a cigarette," he said. "You?"

"One-point-six million guilders," she replied.

She got the flash of a smile. "Are you ready?"

Isa nodded. "Let's take him."

She went through the door on Michel's arm, haughty but a little bashful. A soldier turned servant took them through to a grand hall and into the front room on the right. The ceilings were overly tall, echoing, the huge window a waterfall of light, the ornate decorations of vine and grape, angel and cherub, making the plasterwork of Van Meegeren's look like a child's first attempt.

The place was exquisite.

The soldier took her coat, saying he would have tea brought— interesting to have a butler who wore a sidearm—while Michel went to the grand piano beneath the window, setting the painting on the stand where the music would be. She knew he was considering the advantages of the light. He pulled out a knife to cut the string, but Isa put a hand on his arm.

"Let him be curious," she whispered.

Michel nodded. And then, "Ah. I forgot to say. Hofer speaks very good Dutch. So no extra conversation."

Isa frowned. "If he speaks Dutch, why were you . . ."

"Translating? Because he thinks the German makes him sound authoritative. Let me handle Hofer. I know which buttons to push."

Isa nodded and took his arm again. And they stood together at the window, a couple looking out at all the loveliness. The opulence. A man doing the last clipping of the roses for the autumn. And this was where Michel had been living. In all the luxury that didn't belong to him. In everything that had been stolen from Goudstikker.

"Bastards," whispered Michel.

They turned together to the bright sound of leather soles, and there was Herr Hofer, just as Isa remembered him, with his dapper suit and slicked hair, smug expression in place. His gaze darted from her to the wrapped package on the piano and back again. Eager, Isa thought. And not the first trace of recognition on his face. He came forward, holding out a hand.

"My dear," he said in Dutch, "how glad I am to meet you. It is so good of you to come to me in my little home."

Goudstikker's. Goudstikker's home.

Isa stepped forward to take his hand, all elegance and sophistication, like Marlene Dietrich in *Blonde Venus*. "Thank you. Michel has said so many nice things about you that I thought I must come."

She gave Michel a look of simpering adoration. He squared his shoulders, a little arrogant, and returned her look with a slight bow of his head.

Oh, Isa thought. He really is good.

"And Herr Hofer," Isa said, lowering her tone, "thank you for your understanding of my situation, and for your lack of questions regarding my name." She looked down, briefly embarrassed. "You are very kind."

"We are people of the world, my dear," he said, "and Michel is invaluable to us. There is no need to let such things affect matters of business. But we shall talk more on that soon. Michel, bring the lady to the sofa. I believe we have tea arriving."

The rattle of porcelain from the hall became a maid rolling in a cart with a teapot and a plate of iced cookies. Hofer threw a look of longing at the package.

"I hope you do not think this is how I like to treat potential clients, my dear," Hofer sighed. "I would like nothing more than to discuss our business over a dinner, a little party in your honor."

"Herr Hofer is very generous," said Michel, accepting a cup.

Isa sipped, demure. It was very good tea.

"We would not want to take advantage of your time," Michel said. "If you would like to view . . ."

"Oh, Michel," Isa chided, smiling. "Let him finish his tea."

Hofer sat back down, curtailing the leap to his feet to unwrap the painting on the piano. He smiled, his smugness a little stiff. There was nothing he could politely do now but wait for her to finish.

Isa sipped, slow, a little at a time, nibbling tiny bites of a cookie. Letting the conversation falter. Watching Hofer's eyes dart. There was almost no question Herr Hofer could ask without disturbing the delicate subject of her identity.

"Michel is very passionate," Isa said, putting a hand on his knee. "About his work. And so knowledgeable about art." She gazed at him like he was her favorite cookie.

Michel took her hand and held it. "You shouldn't speak to Herr Hofer so," he said, embarrassed. The embarrassment might have been real. "He will think I asked you to say it."

"Michel is very diligent," Hofer said.

"How many pictures do you buy and sell in a year, Herr Hofer?" Isa nibbled, holding Michel's hand.

"Oh, that depends on the needs of my clients, of course. My clients, as I'm sure Michel has said, are illustrious. Consummate collectors."

"And what qualities does a consummate collector require?" Isa asked.

Nibbling. Reckless.

"A consummate collector, my dear, only requires an appreciation of culture and taste. And money, of course. It is their agent whom they rely on for sophistication, for an expert knowledge of art, for an understanding of the science and business. But it is the eye of the agent," he went on, "that innate understanding of genius when it is seen, that is the most valuable asset to my clients."

"My," said Isa.

Michel's leg was jiggling just a little beneath their held hands. Either he had heard this revolting speech many times before, or he really needed that cigarette. Isa couldn't make the cookie last any longer.

Hofer set down his cup and said, "Shall we?"

"Oh, yes. Michel, would you show Herr Hofer the picture?"

"Of course." But he lifted her hand first, and kissed it, a gentle brush of his lips before he let her go.

And she felt a shiver.

She sat where she was and let Michel reel in Hofer. Gazing at his uniformed shoulders, where the freckles were hidden, listening to him talk about seeing the painting for the first time, what he thought Gurlitt would have said if he had known, all while painstakingly untying a knot when he had a knife in his pocket.

Isa watched the moment when the paper came away. Hofer's stare. His slightly open mouth. Michel's finger pointing at different aspects of brilliance, the finger with an ink stain still on it. The painting looked even more beautiful in this setting, even without a frame, with the plasterwork and the ebony of the piano polish and the clear flood of Holland's light.

The loupe came out of Hofer's pocket. Peering, examining the surface. Examining Vermeer's signature. Not seeing her father's.

And now their time had come. And then it had already gone.

Isa leaned back and crossed her legs.

Hofer wanted to believe. He had every reason to believe. And he did believe. She could see it in the smile stretching his mouth.

He believed, and he wanted it. Badly.

Michel gave her one quick flash of amber over Hofer's back. He knew it, too. And he knew what Isa was thinking. It was what they wanted, what the children needed, but it was still a little sad.

Her father's best work.

Hofer came and sat down on the chair, Michel beside Isa on the sofa. Hofer wiped his forehead with a handkerchief. "It is a very nice picture," he said cautiously.

"Yes," Isa replied, "isn't it? And it has just been lying around in a storage room. Such a waste. I had to go through our files carefully to find out anything about it. You see, I do not know very much about art, Herr Hofer, but I have seen an appraisal of this piece."

She felt Michel tense beside her. This was not "letting him handle" Hofer.

"Well, certainly . . ." said Hofer.

"And I have done some research with the appraiser, and I know what kind of price a Vermeer can bring."

Hofer chuckled. "Well, I am sure we can come . . ."

"Three million," said Isa. "Guilders, of course."

If Michel had been drinking tea, he would have spit it.

Hofer sat back, reconsidering his nameless seller. "That is a large transaction."

"Is it not within your means?"

Now Michel put a hand back on her knee, cautioning.

"Oh . . ." Isa put a hand delicately to her red lips. "My apologies. I am used to being direct when I do business. I do not mean to sound rude. But I do have other interested parties and would not want to waste your time."

Hofer sat up at "other interested parties," since there could really be only one. Michel did not have to act his distress; he was feeling it. Which Herr Hofer saw. Which is what Isa wanted.

"I feel certain an arrangement can be made," said Hofer. "However, you must understand that I do not act on my own. I must consult my client for any new acquisitions."

Isa saw Michel's brows come down at that. That was new information.

"How long does it normally take to consult with your client?" Isa asked.

"Cables must be sent. And for something this size, my client will not buy sight unseen. However, I am authorized to say that my client is very likely to pay in the realm of one-point-nine million. Once he has seen the painting, of course."

Over Gurlitt's price. For boasting.

1.9 million guilders for a painting. Seven and a half guilders for a life.

What an ugly world.

Isa looked unhappy. "That is a serious undervaluing. Will your client be in the area anytime soon?" she asked.

"I would not think . . ."

"Oh dear." She looked at Michel. "What do you think, darling?"

Michel looked very much like he wanted a cigarette. He squeezed her hand. "I know your time is short, my love."

"Well, thank you, Herr Hofer, for your kind attention . . ."

"Please, please, don't be hasty," Hofer said. He'd practically broken into a sweat. "If funds would be helpful more immediately, perhaps a deposit could be arranged. A payment for the loan of the painting, to be put against purchase, of course."

"Is there a standard percentage for a deposit?"

"Well, in cases of large sums, two percent is . . ."

"Ten percent," said Isa. "With a contract."

Hofer wiped his forehead. "Of course," he said. "Michel, perhaps you could help me in the office . . ."

Isa watched them walk across the parquet floor to a set of French double doors at the other end of the room. There was an office beyond them, not like Van Meegeren's, probably more like Napoleon's, with two gilded desks and scrolling gold chairs. Michel's desk did not have a scrap of paper out of place. He sat and took a black ledger book out of the drawer, opening it while Hofer took a strongbox from a cabinet.

He was seeing how much cash he had, Isa thought. Because ten percent of 1.9 million was 190,000 guilders.

And 190,000 guilders was a lot more than the nothing she'd had before.

Isa got up and walked back to the window, gazing at carved lions and nymphs, little garden bridges and gazebos, trailing with the last of the summer flowers. She imagined handing that cash to Truus. Wondering how many more children they might save. And what if the transaction was approved, and they got the rest of the 1.9 million?

Maybe her father's forgery could help bring down the Nazis.

And hope, Isa thought, is fresh, ivy-green, growing in tints of pine and of spring pear, enshrouding, covering, cooling like ferns in a forest. And there, standing in stolen loveliness, Isa wondered if she could create her own beauty. Build it. Re-create it. Something that was hers.

Was it possible to paint her own beauty into an ugly world?

Maybe she could even go to Switzerland.

She turned, purse behind her back, watching Michel in his ugly uniform, pen in his hand, gaze intent, running a finger down the columns of a large ledger book now open on the glossy desk. Hofer pulled out his chair to count a stack of bills.

Isa didn't know exactly what happened next, but she saw it when it did. Michel's spine stiffened. His jaw clenched. He had read something that disturbed him. That shocked him. He threw a quick glance at Hofer. Read the ledger again, and shut the book. He lifted his clashing eyes and glanced once at Isa, and she knew.

Something with their plan had just gone terribly wrong.

"The civilian population is sacrosanct. No looting nor wanton destruction is permitted by the soldier. Landmarks of historical value or buildings serving religious purposes, art, science, or charity are to be especially respected."
　　—Commandment Seven, from *The Ten Commandments of the German Soldier*

22

ISA WANDERED THE room, studying the pictures on the walls, while Michel consulted quietly with Hofer. Whatever was wrong with their plan, she couldn't see it from where she stood, but she could feel it. In the revving in her chest, the sickly yellow in her stomach. Hofer sat down at his opulent desk, on garnet-and-gold brocade, scribbling quickly in a thin binder. As soon as he was occupied, Michel quietly opened a drawer in his own desk, eye on Hofer, and slipped a small black notebook into his jacket pocket. Hofer finished writing with a flourish, and carefully tore away a small, rectangular piece of paper.

A check.

The check was laid in Michel's hand, along with another folded paper, all of which went into the jacket. Then Michel looked through the French doors and smiled at her—not his real smile; this was a cool imitation—and he came smartly across the parquet, Hofer trailing, smoothing his already slick hair. Isa simpered adoringly, searching Michel's face.

What had happened?

"We've come to a very equitable arrangement," Michel said. "Ten percent. A deposit against future payment."

He looked down into her eyes. He was saying they would take it and run. Isa hooked her arm through his.

"Herr Hofer," said Michel, "would you mind if we took a tour of the house and the grounds?"

"Oh, please do!" said Hofer. "Enjoy yourselves. Take the afternoon, Michel. I will have Heinrich help with the arrangements."

Hofer looked at Isa. The smugness was rising off him like a smell.

"It will be so sad for you, to have him gone at the end of the week. Perhaps you will travel to Hamburg sometime. But we have so few we can trust with our shipments. I will be taking yours personally. To ensure its safety."

Isa looked down, fiddling with her brooch. "I do hope your client is pleased, and that we can complete our business accordingly."

Hofer gave a satisfied little bow.

"Come, love," said Michel. "Let me show you the other rooms."

He let Isa smile once more at Herr Hofer before leading her into the hall, where there was a niche in the wall displaying a small vase, a niche surrounded by scrolling plasterwork of classical motifs that expanded all the way up to the ceiling. Michel chatted about the age of the house, renovations, and as soon as Hofer had gone back to the office, took her by the hand and up the grand staircase, her pumps at a trot.

They passed another soldier coming down as they ran up—dour and with a stack of files, possibly Heinrich—a young man who gave Michel a surprised, and then knowing, look. Michel ignored him, moving straight back through the upper hall to a little door on the left at the rear of the house. He opened it, pulled Isa through, and shut it with a click.

His room. Small, meant for a butler or maid, like hers, with a big window and a bed she would be afraid to wrinkle. There was a picture on the nightstand, a lovely, dark-eyed, straight-backed woman with eight girls surrounding her, their sizes ranging from young woman to the toddler perched on her lap.

Michel pulled the curtains, then went to a little sink in the corner—a razor, shaving brush, cup and toothbrush, all lined up just so—and turned on the water, to cover the noise of a conversation. He sat on the edge of the bed, not worried about wrinkles, elbows on his thighs, fingers rising up to tent over his nose. Isa moved a plain wooden chair to the bed, sat in front of him, and waited.

Finally he said, "Hofer wanted to know what pieces Gurlitt had bought in the last few days. How much he had spent. Hofer has an arrangement with Heinrich to find out what Gurlitt buys, so he knows how much he needs to spend to beat him at their game. It's usually me writing it down in the ledger, but I was not here yesterday, and . . . What I am trying to say to you is, when I looked in the book . . ."

He took off his hat, glanced at it, and threw it across the bed, running a hand over the back of his neck. Fighting to hold his voice down.

"What I am trying to say is that Gurlitt bought a Vermeer. Yesterday. Called *Christ and the Woman Taken in Adultery.*"

"What?" Isa sat back. "Are you sure?"

He was sure.

"How much?" she asked.

"One-point-seven million. And Isa, the seller is Theodoor de Smit, at the Gallery De Smit on Kalverstraat."

She couldn't speak.

"There are two of them. Two! And stupid and arrogant as they are, Hofer and Gurlitt are not going to believe that two unknown Vermeers came to light within one day of each other, and with the exact same subject matter. They are not!"

He got up, pacing. Whispering. "Could Theo have painted another? Before?"

"I don't think so. I mean, no! Why would he paint the same painting twice? And he's been too ill . . ."

Isa put her fingers on her temples. Trying to order her thoughts. Reassembling, like pieces of broken porcelain. And her thoughts took shape.

"Van Meegeren," she said. "He was cooking a painting that night in the cellar. I couldn't see it, but it was a portrait, there were figures . . ."

"Could it have been the same composition Theo painted? Could it have been the same painting?"

"It could have. I don't know." She looked up. "What if it is Van Meegeren's painting that Gurlitt bought? He was shaking, having trouble holding a pen. What if the quality was bad, bad enough to maybe even get him caught, and so he wanted my father to paint this one, too, like *Woman with a Wine Glass*. And when Papa didn't produce . . ."

"He put Theo's name on it," Michel said. "Acting as an agent. Or a third party."

"So if he was questioned, it would all come back on Papa. He threatened trouble of some kind if my father didn't finish, but I didn't think . . ."

"That he would sell the exact same forgery to Gurlitt under your father's name for one-point-seven million? No, I doubt you would have thought of that."

Damn Van Meegeren. Damn him straight into the nightmare of Munch's scream.

Michel sat down again on the bed. "I have to tell you something." His knee was jiggling. He was having trouble looking Isa in the face. "Hofer was not going to let you remain anonymous. Not with this kind of sale."

"He knows my name?"

Michel took a breath. "No, I could not let him know that. That is why I . . . I told him you were Van Meegeren's wife. Or his mistress. Hofer was not interested in the distinction."

Isa felt her lips part.

"It was the perfect story. It gave you access to a painting. None of us have ever even seen Van Meegeren's wife. And everyone knows how much he likes . . . red hair."

Isa touched her hair.

"We were supposed to have the full payment in a day or two. All it takes is a cable from Goering to release the funds. I was going to handle it at the bank, I've done it before. They know me. I would get the money, disappear on Saturday, and they would get my letter from Hamburg on Monday, and it would be the middle of next week before they would know I wasn't where I should be. It would have looked like I stole the money, of course, or ran away with you. It would have broken my father's heart and his pride, and I am not certain which would be more painful for him. But something has changed. Goering must be angry, or not like what Hofer is sending, because there are no more blank checks. Preapproval before the sale is the new policy, and that is going to take time. Maybe weeks."

"So even if he takes the painting," Isa said, "we are not going to be able to collect the rest of the money."

"Not unless I remain at my post, and Isa," he whispered, "do not ask me to do that. I will not get another chance."

She looked at the picture of the women on the table beside Michel and shook her head. No, she would not ask him to do that.

Isa adjusted her mind to the check in Michel's pocket. 190,000 was so much more than they'd had before. All they really needed was nine hundred guilders—twelve hundred, if the bribe went up—to get the last six children with places to hide out before Judenfrei. And possibly, if she was lucky, money for the taxes so they wouldn't lose the gallery. But what would happen when Gurlitt and Hofer compared notes and discovered that they had bought the same painting?

If they decided Gurlitt's was the fake—the one painted by Van Meegeren and supposedly sold by Theodoor de Smit—they would come for her father.

If they decided that Hofer's was the fake—the one painted by Theodoor de Smit and sold by Van Meegeren's anonymous mistress—they would go after Van Meegeren, who would then send them for her father. And the evidence was there, in the garret. The chemicals, the brushes. The oven and the ink in the cellar.

"Change the records," Isa said. "In the books. Take my father's name off the other painting."

"The official book may not even have his name," Michel said. "They keep the paperwork on this end sparse, because they know they're stealing. Hofer's spy book is much more accurate. I'm not sure what Gurlitt's book on Hofer says. Heinrich fills out that one . . ."

"Gurlitt spies on Hofer, too?"

"Of course. Heinrich will put this latest transaction in this afternoon, if he hasn't called it in already. But listen, no matter what the books say, there will be a label on the painting, and official paperwork packaged up with it, for Germany. That will have your father's name and address, and I'm certain this new acquisition will be on the first shipment to Hamburg tomorrow. Just like Hofer's. Neither of them will deliver it personally. They'll send the paintings with Heinrich and the shipment."

They sat. Silent with the water running.

"Then one of the paintings has to disappear," Isa said, "so they can't compare them. What if we went downstairs and just took the painting. Right now?"

"They'd know it was us, and . . . I need to pretend to go to Hamburg."

He also needed the gallery. His hiding place before Switzerland. And he was not going to have that with the gallery's address on a forged Vermeer sold to Adolf Hitler's art agent.

Isa crossed her legs. "So the other painting has to disappear, Van Meegeren's, with Papa's name on it. What if you corrected Hofer's spy book to a different title, nothing about Christ or adultery, and you could do the same to Gurlitt's book, so that neither will realize what the other has bought."

"They will talk, Isa. Eventually, they will talk."

"But what if Gurlitt's painting that he just paid one-point-seven million guilders for gets . . . misplaced? Some kind of clerical error. Would he talk about it then? When he's lost a million-guilder prize?"

"No," said Michel slowly. "It would be an embarrassment."

"And bring the intense displeasure of his Führer, I would think. I think he'd keep it as quiet as he could. I don't think anyone would hear about it, even if he went over to Goering's and saw what we just sold to Hofer hanging on the wall."

Michel rubbed his neck, thinking. "All right. So how does it get lost?"

"We have to take it. That painting needs to be stolen before it leaves for Hamburg. Do you agree?"

He looked up at her. Blinking. Disbelieving. Then his fingers went back over his face.

"If they find out about both paintings, Michel, they will come to the gallery."

They would arrest her father. They would shoot Michel.

"Where do they keep them?" Isa whispered. "Where will the painting be?"

Michel sat back, and now his gaze was steady. "In the Stedelijk."

The only open museum in Amsterdam, located in the Museumplein. Where the Gestapo headquarters were housed. The police headquarters. The government officials', and all the soldiers' barracks.

They put their heads together. And by the time they went back downstairs—having been gone long beyond a tour or the boundaries of decency—there was a plan. A terrible plan. Not careful. It was cobbled together. Both stupid and reckless.

Especially reckless.

Isa took Michel's arm as they entered the front hall, Michel carrying a small leather suitcase that he left beside the door. He spoke to the soldier-butler, and then they strolled through the room with the piano, where there was no longer a painting, and into the gilded office. Heinrich was sorting papers into a wall of metal filing cabinets, startlingly incongruent with the ornate furniture. There was no Hofer.

"Excuse me, please. I will only be a moment," Michel whispered, intimate in her ear, before he sat at the desk.

Heinrich gave her a cold little smile, but his eyes followed her.

Isa wandered over to the window, clutching her purse. She could feel Heinrich's gaze, hot on her legs, her back. She certainly couldn't hear any papers sorting. She turned on a heel, catching him by surprise. "Is Herr Hofer gone? I'm sorry to have missed him."

Heinrich looked at her blankly, and then Michel said something in German from the desk, and Heinrich answered. He had no Dutch. She'd meant to keep him from noticing what Michel was doing, but Michel did not seem bothered. The two had a short conversation instead; the ledger book was gone, Michel screwing the top back onto his pen.

"My love," he said, holding out his arm. Heinrich watched them leave, moving languidly together into the hall. The soldier-butler was there with her coat. Michel put it on her shoulders, picked up the suitcase, and they were out the front door.

"Did you change it?" she asked quickly. She heard the motor of the black car turn. The driver had been waiting all that time.

"Now it says *Christ and the Woman*. I obliterated 'taken in adultery.' It looks like a mistake. Careless. I changed Vermeer to Vermehren, which you can hardly tell, and marked out the last three zeros, for a painting that now sold for seventeen hundred. A good price for a Vermehren."

Isa gave him a glance. In spite of everything, Michel was smiling.

He was never coming back here.

He opened the door for her, set his little suitcase between them on the seat, and gave the driver the address of the Dutch National Bank. The driver crunched the gravel beneath the tires, impassive.

"Heinrich said that Hofer has already taken his new painting to be packaged and shipped. He is delivering it personally, after all. But just to the Stedelijk."

It would be best not to run into him.

Isa caught Michel's eye in the soft, sleek interior and threw a glance at the driver. "Does he . . ."

"No Dutch," Michel replied. Then he opened his little suitcase and Isa saw a few clothes, his shaving brush, the picture of his family that did not include his father. He packed up the blue shirt and pants he'd used to leave her house, already neatly folded on the seat. He was practically humming.

It was a long drive to the bank, not too far from the Gallery De Smit, but Michel needed to deal with a bank manager he knew. He went in, while Isa waited, tense. She felt conspicuous in her finery in the fancy black car with a driver. She looked like a collaborator. She felt like a collaborator, waiting for 190,000 ill-gotten guilders. And Michel did not come back.

Anxiety jumped up and down her spine, little pops of electric yellow.

The driver sat, sullen.

Then Michel came down the sidewalk. Shoulders square, posture correct, the edge of his smile gone. He was more than unhappy. He was angry. She could see it in his jaw, in his walk. Her pops of anxiety became jolts. He sat in the car and slammed the door.

"Bastard," he said. "The check was not good. Hofer does not have the funds. Goering must be very angry. I showed them Hofer's authorization, and they assured me that in two or three days he would have it, but for now, they would only give me ten thousand against the balance of the check."

"Ten?" It was only just over five percent. Isa sat back in her seat.

But ten thousand guilders was so much more than the nothing she'd had before.

"I can't believe they gave you anything at all against a check," Isa mused.

"I had an authorization. And the manager is frightened of Goering." He leaned toward the front seat. "Herengracht 458," he said, using the German numbers.

The car pulled away from the curb. The sun was slanting, their time shortening. Michel took an envelope of bills from inside his jacket—one hundred hundred-guilder notes—and held the stack of money close to the seat. Counting. Dividing.

"You take half," he said, voice low, "in case something happens. So either of us can . . ."

So either of them could pay for the escape of the children.

It was what they had come to do. And she would hand it to Truus as soon as they got the name of the painting they'd just sold removed from Gurlitt's spy book. Hopefully, before Gurlitt ever read it.

Isa put twenty bills into the lining of her purse, then fifteen each in either side of the tight-fitting top of her dress. She saw Michel look when she did it. He put his gaze on the window, knee jiggling, adjusting the little suitcase at his feet.

They came around the corner and into the narrow street along the Herengracht. A word from Michel and they passed Goudstikker's old gallery, where Isa had gone trouncing in so naively with her *Rembrandt De Smit*. Michel pointed to a narrow parking space between the street and the canal several doors down. Gurlitt did not need to walk out and see Isa sitting in the back seat of his own car. Michel straightened his Nazi jacket and his hat, grim. She gave him a smile of encouragement, and he marched down the sidewalk and into Goudstikker's.

Isa watched a boat sail the canal. Weathered cobalt obscured by puffs of cotton-colored steam, the angling sun dappling light through the leaves above it. The way the rays hit the ripple of the boat's wake told her it was about three o'clock in the afternoon.

The driver sat, silent, never once meeting her eyes. She was hungry. She was anxious. She couldn't think what could be taking Michel so long. She watched the street behind her from the passenger-side mirror, a slim, slightly warped view of the gallery steps.

There was coming and going past the armed guard. At first, she thought there must be an auction, but these were uniforms passing in and out, olive and khaki. Nazi brown. She turned to get a better look, and when she turned back, she slid lower in her seat. The young man walking down the sidewalk, passing her car on the way toward Goudstikker's, was dark-eyed, confident. Arrogant and SS.

The boy-officer who had been sitting next to Michel at the dinner.

Franz, that's what Michel had called him. Brought to Amsterdam to ferret out hiding Jews.

He didn't see her.

He ran up the stone steps, quick and upright. And there was something almost familiar about the way he did it.

What had happened to Michel?

She squirmed in her seat. Tapped a tooth. Wondering about her father, and if he would ever heal. If he could be her father once more, or if that time of her life was lost. Wondering if he would ever paint something as beautiful as the painting she'd never see again.

A painting about forgiveness.

She wondered about Truus. And what would happen to Hildy.

And then she was watching Willem walk down the street.

He was coming toward her just like Franz had, approaching the busy Nazi gallery, hands in his farmer's jacket, head down, being as unobtrusive as a muscular Adonis could be. But unlike Franz the hunter, Willem looked up from his reverie, gaze rising as if Isa had given a shout. And he looked right at her.

Sitting in the back of her sleek, black Nazi car. With her lips red and her bra full of money.

They eyed each other as Willem walked past, heads turning to hold their stare. But there was nothing to stop for, and nothing to say. Isa felt blue rise up and take her, the deep blue regret of a sapphire sea. Because there would be no explaining. She and Willem had their differences, but the idea of Willem viewing her as disloyal was as repugnant as Michel's uniform. And he would not think of it as mere disloyalty.

To Willem, it would be utter betrayal.

And then Willem turned his head, and nearly ran into Michel.

Michel in his uniform.

They both paused, a split second of recognition, then moved around each other on the narrow sidewalk. Willem looked back once, watching Michel approach the car. And Isa saw his expression.

No, there would be no explaining it.

They wouldn't help Michel get to Switzerland now. And Michel was so very thoroughly setting fire to all his bridges today.

So it would have to get explained, that's all. As soon as they got back to the Gallery De Smit. Truus, for once in her life, was going to listen. Would have to make Willem listen.

They had no time for it now. The museum would be closing.

But Truus had said getting the money this afternoon would be in the nick of time.

Michel got in and shut the door. He threw off his hat and loosened his tie, eyes out the window. He didn't speak to the driver yet. His jaw was tight.

"Did you change the book?" Isa asked. Soft.

He looked around. "Yes. It was easy. Everyone was distracted. Gurlitt was in a meeting with his door closed. Something was happening. I stayed to find out, but no one was talking, and I could not wait longer."

Isa could hear the thought he'd nearly added. That he should have waited longer.

"Die Spui bitte," he said to the driver. They were going back to Spui. The gallery. Explaining. Giving Truus the money.

The engine turned.

"Wait," Isa said. "Wait!" And she jumped out of the car. A woman had passed by, quick with her shopping bag, not far behind Willem. She was wearing sunglasses, and a green-and-gold kerchief. "Excuse me," Isa called. "Wait, please?"

The woman glanced over her shoulder, startled. She almost kept walking, but Isa had already nearly caught up with her.

"Wait. Please!" Isa said.

The woman stopped and stood, staring, her mouth a thin line, eyes lost behind the dark glasses. It was odd to see her so still and close. What Isa was doing was dangerous. She didn't know what this woman was capable of, or what Willem might have told her to do. Maybe the woman hadn't even realized that Isa knew she was being followed. She reached into one side of her dress and got the roll of fifteen-hundred-guilder notes, took two steps, and put the money into the woman's glove.

"For the rest of the children," Isa whispered. "I have no time. Can you get it to them? Today? Right now?" It was three hundred guilders extra, just in case. Maybe they could even save another. "And if they can place more children, I will get them more. Can you put this into the right hands?"

The woman nodded. And then she nodded again, slipping the money into her purse.

"Thank you," Isa said. "Thank you very much."

They went in opposite directions. Isa got back into the car and said, "Museumplein," to the driver, who immediately put the car into reverse.

"She was one of them?" Michel asked.

"Yes. With Willem."

"Good."

It was the biggest part of their job done. The main thing they had come to do. Six more saved, and they could deal with Truus and Willem after. Assuming they were not arrested.

Michel stared out the window, at the passing hodgepodge of Amsterdam, and Isa thought about the night before, Michel and

Willem talking Italy in the kitchen, Willem telling him not to smoke. Michel, Isa realized, had considered Willem a friend. And what had he seen in Willem's face on the street? Hatred? Revulsion and disgust?

If Michel had been a portrait in that moment, looking out the window, Isa would have named it *Pain*.

She reached out and took his hand, pulling it toward her on the black leather seat. She watched his brows come down as he stared, jaw working beneath the scratchy spot on his cheek. She couldn't see his eyes. But after a moment, he adjusted his grip and twined her fingers tight in his.

How long, Isa thought, does it take to un-become?

The car slowed. Isa looked up, and they were not near Museumplein yet. They were on a side street, an alley too small for the width of the car. They'd taken a wrong turn. Michel began saying something in German, probably about directions or backing up, but the car stopped. The engine turned off, and the driver pivoted around in his seat. Michel fell silent.

Because the driver was pointing a gun at his head.

23

ISA DIDN'T MOVE. She didn't speak, and neither did Michel. The driver was an older man, gray glinting in his side whiskers. Perfectly ordinary in his black chauffeur cap. Except that instead of his usual expression—sullen, impassive—his face was now animated, pink with satisfaction.

"You've had me driving all day," the man said, nudging the gun at Michel. "Do you know how hard it is, waiting on you all the time? It's damn boring, is what it is."

Dutch, Isa thought. He speaks Dutch. What had he overheard?

Absolutely everything.

She saw Michel's eyes slide once to her.

"I don't know what your game is. I don't care. But what I am sure of is that you don't want Gurlitt or Hofer knowing what you've been doing today. So I'll keep on driving you. I'll take you wherever you say. We can have a bargain on that. I'll even keep quiet about it. But you will have to pay for it."

Michel sighed. She was still holding his hand.

"How much?" Isa said.

"Five thousand guilders. Right now."

"That is ridiculous . . ." she began, but Michel squeezed her hand and shook his head once before he let her go.

"Five thousand is a large amount of money," Michel said, "and we will need some extra services for that. Like being ready at a certain place and time. Perhaps a word or two at the checkpoint. We could need you to know some things that are not true, and then be ignorant about some things that are. And it will be twenty-five hundred now, and twenty-five hundred when we arrive at our final destination. You seem fair-minded. You can see the fairness in that."

The man scratched his head.

"And really," said Michel, "there was no need for the gun. You could have asked and we would have made a deal."

The man seemed taken aback by this. The gun lowered, he tilted his chin and said, "We have an understanding."

Michel opened his jacket, showing the man that he was reaching for the envelope of bills. He counted out twenty-five and handed them over the seat. The man put the money away and started the car.

Their money, Isa thought, was water in a breached dyke.

But the three thousand they would have left after the driver's last payment was still so much more than she'd had before.

"Now where would you like for me to park?" the driver asked. "I don't mind waiting."

Michel had him park at the corner of the Museumplein, across the street from the Stedelijk, just before the checkpoint that barred the way into the soldiers' barracks. The place was nearly unrecognizable. The tram was still running, the concert hall and the Gothic facades of the museums still intact, but their roofs were covered in camouflage, dotted with anti-aircraft guns, with bunkers built all along the green, where the ice skating had been. It had become a place of concrete and barbed wire. Of khaki and olive. The red and black of the swastika.

Only the Stedelijk looked relatively the same, though it was not the same. The Stedelijk seemed to be holding an exhibition.

Its basement, Michel said, was holding art.

Michel straightened his tie. Isa tucked a straying lock of hair behind her ear. She should have brought the lipstick, but she hadn't thought of that. Michel had a word with their driver, the man tipped his hat, and then Michel came around and opened her door, offering her a hand. She stepped out into her city. Her city was enemy territory.

"Come," Michel said, voice low.

He took her into a café and found a table to one side, near the front window. It looked like a Nazi cantina, filled with smoke and soldiers, SS, police, and the occasional Dutch girl. The owners, Isa thought, were doing an excellent business. The waitress came, asking what they wanted in fluent German, winking at Isa like a co-conspirator. Isa ignored her. Michel ordered, and then he pulled a few coins from his pocket, explaining, nodding his head toward the parked car outside.

The waitress left and Michel lit a cigarette. Someone was playing a phonograph. Marching songs. Michel leaned forward. "You behave as if you do not enjoy being in a Nazi café."

It was true, but the comment did have the effect of making her smile.

"The paintings ready for shipment are being kept downstairs, somewhere beyond the boiler room—yes, I know," he said, replying to her look. "But they seem to think bombs are a greater danger than the damp. Show me the window that opens . . ."

They glanced out the café window together, toward the Stedelijk, and Isa saw their waitress taking coffee and a sandwich to their blackmailing driver on the corner.

"It is best to keep him happy, do you agree?" Michel said.

She agreed. Their sandwiches and coffee came next, and when the waitress had gone, Isa said, "You can't see the window from here, but just around the corner, on Potterstraat, the building will inset, and the window is in the farthest corner, just above street level. You'll find the right window, because that's where the coal is delivered. There should be a pile of it, unless they've run out. And . . . are you sure?"

"Yes," he said, "I am sure."

They'd argued about which one of them should retrieve the painting. Isa knew her way, knew the window, but Michel could use his letters of authority and even his brother-in-law's name to get past any guards. He could give the excuse of preparing the paintings, checking the paperwork. But these were memorable actions, easy to recall later, when a 1.7-million-guilder piece of art had gone missing.

"They cannot kill me twice," Michel said beneath his breath. Again. She didn't like his point any better the second time.

"You should have found a different place to hide," Isa commented.

She'd thought he might smile, but he didn't. "No," he said. "No, I found the right place."

Isa was getting some looks from the other diners while she ate. Sideways glances that would result in little whispered conversations beneath the music and noise. As if the nature of what she was about to do showed.

"What did he buy?" she asked suddenly.

Michel's brows came down.

"I mean what did Hofer buy? What did you write down in Gurlitt's book?"

"Ah. He didn't buy anything. It was the last entry on the page. A small line. I cut it away. You can only just see."

"Like you did my entry?" she asked, picking up her coffee.

"Do you mean the note I left beneath your pot? No, that was not from Gurlitt's books. Gurlitt's entry is still there. It had the wrong name and address, after all." He half smiled. "I knew I recognized you at the sale, but I was not certain from where, not until I saw the gallery. Then Theo's redheaded daughter came back to me. You had . . . grown somewhat, since you were eleven."

He studied her from behind his cloud of smoke.

"So what did you cut your note from?"

"My own book. Hofer and Gurlitt are not the only ones keeping records. Your information, at that point, was firm in my head."

Isa thought about that, about the little black notebook that had gone into Michel's jacket pocket at Oostermeer.

"Do you have money?" Michel asked.

He meant, did she have anything less than the fifteen hundred guilders still stuffed down the front of her dress? She shook her head, and Michel handed her what she would need for a ticket, causing another spate of staring. And some whispers.

Just how many people in the same week could think that she, Isa de Smit, a girl who had only ever been almost-kissed, was a prostitute? And a cheap one, too. She put the two guilders Michel gave her in her purse.

"Are you ready?" Michel asked.

She was. They left the café and she saw the looks. He did as well, two lines furrowed in his forehead. They parted ways on the sidewalk, Michel going back to the car to tell their driver where to be, Isa down and across the street to the Stedelijk.

She bought a ticket, giving the bored man in the booth a little smile, and stepped through the door. When she was young, the inside had been like the outside, sienna bricks with mahogany highlights, arches and niches and thin, horizontal stripes of buff stone. But Sandberg had had all the interiors painted a smooth, monochromatic white. So that the artwork could "be" and "speak." He'd changed the enormous yellow skylight over the grand staircase to clear glass, a thin vellum stretched lengthwise below it, veiling the daylight, painted with primitive figures of humans and animals in primary blue and red. A new creation story. Like the art he wanted to display. Modern, cutting-edge. Innovative.

Francina had loved it.

But Sandberg was somewhere on the run if he wasn't dead, and that was not the artwork being displayed here now. The Stedelijk was like seeing a favorite friend's Nazi twin. Isa clutched her purse, walking the first gallery. The exhibition was a celebration of the Dutch Labor Force, the polite name for the German slave labor program that had taken half the young men of the Netherlands and driven the rest into hiding. She meandered past paintings and watercolors, a few charcoals, all of handsome, shirtless Dutchmen—blond, healthy, and happy to a man—repairing dams and digging ditches, showering together and sharing meals. There were static poses as well, a boot on a log, the sun setting behind a torso where the muscles could be counted, punctuated by the occasional military portrait. When the young men of the Netherlands were dying by the hundreds. By the thousands. Of overwork. Of sickness and starvation. Buried in the rubble of bombed ammunition factories.

The level of fantasy was difficult to comprehend.

And what a slap in the face of the Dutch. A slap to every family who had lost a father or a brother or a son.

The air leaving her lungs felt red. Hot.

But the result was that the museum was practically empty. She'd seen only one German soldier patrolling—more of a stroll, really—and just behind the grand staircase, the door that led down to the basement stood quiet and unguarded.

Isa waited, gazing up at a bigger-than-life plaster cast statue of a male nude, the handle of a shovel balanced across his open palms like an offering to the gods. And the expression on the statue's face was so insipid, so self-satisfied at the apparent idea of shoveling without pants that Isa couldn't help but think that her mother would have laughed.

And probably gotten them arrested.

Footsteps came into the gallery, a brisk, military stride ignoring the art. She'd thought Michel would stand a little way away, pretend to admire the paintings while they talked. Instead, he came straight for her, forehead tense, a gaze of hard glass fixed on hers.

"Can you get in the basement?" he hissed.

She nodded. "I think . . ."

"Go. Hide. You are about to be arrested."

She stared.

"Run!" he whispered, hands flinching.

Isa moved. Fast on her toes, so her heels wouldn't click, trying not to announce her presence or direction. She turned left, hoping to come at the main central staircase from behind. Michel turned right around the corner, and immediately called something out in German.

Helping with a search.

Voices answered, echoing. Dutch and German.

Isa reached down and slid off her heels. And she hurried, heels in hand, fast and soft down the hall. She could see the opening to the main staircase coming on her right, the shaft of filtered light from the skylight and the creation story vellum.

And then she heard footsteps, coming quick from the opposite corner. Isa darted right and then left, into the doorway of the next gallery, stealing to one side and flattening against the wall. The sound of the alerted guard's boots echoed and passed her by. She could see his Nazi brown back, his rifle loose in his hands, heading for the same corner Michel had.

Isa listened. Breathed. And she ran.

Across and down the hall, and she was behind the grand staircase. She didn't know what she would do if the basement door was locked. There would be no key on the lintel this time.

She turned the knob.

The door was not locked.

She slipped inside, the talking, shouting only just around the corner, excitement raising the pitch. German and Dutch. One after the other, the words only slightly altered.

"Das Mädchen mit den roten Haaren."

The girl with red hair.

She shut the basement door behind her with the softest snick.

They thought she was the girl with red hair.

She heard Michel's voice, speaking Dutch, saying something about a side door, about a train ticket, but the voice replying wasn't listening, saying she would not get out. That she could not get out. There wasn't a lock on her side of the door. She went down the wooden stairs.

Into the dark, stockings catching on wood, listening for voices from above, voices from below. She could hear nothing over the rumble of the boiler, the hiss of steam and hot water through the pipes. There was a bulb switched on somewhere in the basement, a lessening of the dim as she descended. Her feet noted the change of temperature, the cold floor of concrete.

The hum of noise was unchanged.

It felt like she was alone.

When they didn't find her in the main two gallery spaces of the museum, they would be coming to the basement.

Isa bent down and put her shoes back on. She was in an open space with corners lost to shadow, iron columns supporting the beams, holding up the galleries, pipes of different sizes running with the joists above her head. She moved away from the steps, toward the Potterstraat side of the building, and found a corner room of tables, stacked chairs, scaffolding that was spiderwebbed, dimly lit from the barred, screened, half-oval window set at the street level outside. Hiding places that would not survive a light switch. Through an interior door and into a jumble room of posters, cast-off decorations, a few boxes in the gloom, and then in one wall, an electric glow shining in a line from below a door.

Isa put an ear to the wood. She slowly turned the knob. And then she opened the door fully, and stepped inside. Because she had found the art.

More than enough to fill a mansion. More than enough to fill a museum. The neatly wrapped, labeled packages were leaning against the walls, stacked ten and eleven pictures deep on racks that reached nearly to the ceiling. From pieces she could hold in one hand to a brown-papered frame that must have stood eight feet high.

Creativity. Beauty. Coerced and stolen.

She listened, straining to hear over the pervasive hum of the boiler. How had the red-haired girl, legend of the Resistance, become confused with Isa de Smit, art forger and thief? Had Gurlitt finally realized that the girl with the kohl around her eyes was the same as the girl with the orange hair sticking out of the hole in her cap? Or had they found her father's signature on the Rembrandt, the one Michel said was there? Or had Hofer found his signature on the Vermeer?

Now that she had been involved in a real forgery, she could see how inadequate the Rembrandt had been. The paper hadn't been right. It had probably smelled like ersatz coffee. But why would they suddenly think she was a seducer and assassin of SS officers? A blower-up of train tracks and the stealer of military secrets? Just because of the color of her hair? And how would she convince them otherwise?

She wouldn't.

Worse than a jail cell.

Isa stood, dithering. Their not-so-very-carefully laid plans to steal the *Vermeer De Smit* had almost immediately derailed. Their day had derailed. And there would be no carrying a painting down the street now. Not with her hair, in the heart of Nazism in Amsterdam. But the painting with her father's name on it, with their address, could not be loaded onto that truck. Could not get compared with the other Vermeer forgery.

If she couldn't take it with her, she would hide it. Right now. Keep it hidden long enough for the shipment to go on without it.

Isa knelt and began going through the leaning stacks nearest the door, flipping through the wrapped frames. The labels on the outside showed the name of the seller and who the painting was for, but not the title of the painting. Maybe that was a security measure. It wasn't much of a security measure. Somewhere in here, in a room by itself in the basement of the Stedelijk, was a 1.7-million-guilder painting, and no one had even locked the door.

She finished one stack and went to the other, and at the second painting from the top she paused. This one didn't have a frame, and its label read *Han van Meegeren*. Her father's masterpiece, the *Vermeer De Smit* they had sold just a few hours before, sold for a bad check. A new prize for Hermann Goering.

It made her sick to think of it.

Hofer must have run all the way from Oostermeer to get it here so fast.

She went through the pictures one by one, stack by stack, shedding her coat so she could use her arms faster. Van Meegeren's Vermeer forgery wasn't there. She tried the next stack, and the next, hoping she would be able to hear boots on the stairs. Voices or shouts. She climbed a shelf of the wood rack, praying she wouldn't tip it over, and off the top, she brought down a package that was labeled *Theodoor de Smit*.

Van Meegeren's forgery.

Isa held the painting and sighed, a sound that matched the hissing of the pipes.

And then she was curious. She went to the door that led out toward the stairs and opened it, listening. The boiler masked the noise of everything, but the light and the shadows were unchanged. Isa shut the door and hurried, reckless, balancing the painting on the edge of the wooden shelf, quickly working the knot in the string. It was stubborn, but she got it, carefully unwrapping the brown paper, lifting Van Meegeren's forgery from its folds.

And Isa gasped.

It was hideous.

Absolutely terrible. With the same composition as her father's, Christ in the center, flanked by Pharisees, the adulteress in front. But the colors were dull, the faces blank where they should have been serene, vapid where there should have been hope. Gaunt, almost skeletal in their corpse-like paleness. And the baking hadn't worked well this time, either. There were places along the edges that were flaking, peeling off.

Van Meegeren must have been ill when he painted it. Hungover. Under the influence. What could Gurlitt have been thinking, paying 1.7 million guilders for this? She might be doing him a favor by stealing it, before his Führer had a chance to see where his money had gone.

And this was the painting she got to keep, while her father's went to Hermann Goering, with his togas and firebombs. And for a moment she forgot about Nazis and the girl with red hair and things that were worse than a jail cell. Her thoughts had been burned by a burst of vermilion heat. She looked at the room full of treasures.

And why should Goering have them?

Why should Hermann Goering have her father's best work?

Isa walked back to the stack near the door and pulled out the package that said *Van Meegeren*, bringing it quickly to the wooden shelf, unpicking the string as soon as she had it propped upright. She unfolded the labeled butcher paper gingerly, no rips or extra wrinkles, took out her father's masterpiece, and refolded its labeled paper around Van Meegeren's terrible painting, tucking the Van Meegeren paperwork inside before she tied the string. Then she climbed, careful, and slid the package back onto the top shelf. Where she'd found her father's.

There. Goering could have that one.

She smiled. Mint. Blue ice. Satisfied.

And then a plane rumbled the building, shaking the bricks of the basement walls. And almost immediately following, the deafening crack and boom of flak, shaking the ground that was all around her.

A bomber.

And there were voices right outside the door.

24

ISA GRABBED HER coat, her purse, and her father's painting, spinning in one direction and then the other. The building rumbled, the flak cracked. A German command was barked on the other side of the door. Then she turned and tossed her coat and purse into the triangular space behind the eight-foot picture, set the *Vermeer De Smit* there, and put two fingers on the corner of the butcher paper she'd unwrapped, trying not to let it rustle. The doorknob turned, and Isa slid behind the painting, crouching, pulling the paper in with her inch by inch.

The hinges creaked, hot water hissing, a drain gurgling. Isa pulled the paper quietly. Slowly. The beam of a flashlight chased the corner shadows. Then the brown paper wrapping was with her, behind the painting. She held the air in her lungs, aching, listening to the sound of boots on concrete. At least two pairs. She wasn't sure if there were more.

The paperwork with her father's name on it was still sitting on the wooden shelf.

The crack and boom settled into a more distant, steady rhythm.

A German voice spoke, almost a whisper. A warning, maybe. They were frightened of her, the girl with the red hair. She could hear the tension in the voice. In the sharp crinkle of packaged paintings being suddenly moved. In the nervous play of a flashlight along the wall, another on the windowsill. A ray that shone back at the door. If she moved, she'd knock the tall painting forward and cause an avalanche. If they came around the way she had crawled in, one glance, and she would be found.

And panic, Isa decided, was a blend of red anger and yellow fear. Orange sparks that crackled and burst, exploding beneath her skin.

They were going to hear her ragged breath.

A beam of light came around the side of the tall painting, dancing along the shelf where her father's paperwork lay, playing over the concrete wall. And a German uniform stepped into view, a flashlight leveled at Isa's crouching knees.

She nearly screamed. An orange scream, erupting. A scream that didn't quite come out. Because the face above the flashlight was Michel. He looked into her eyes and put a finger to his lips.

She nodded. Breathing.

He bent down, like he was peering behind the painting, moving the flashlight. She could see the scratchy shadow on his chin. She could see the shadow beneath his eyes.

"Sie ist nicht hier," Michel said, full voice as he turned away.

The answering German was fast, excited. The man sounded relieved. She could imagine his forehead in a sweat.

Hers was.

Michel's hand was behind him as he walked away, palm out, waving her deeper into her hiding place. Telling her to stay.

She stayed. Listening as two pairs of feet moved toward the door, the hinges creaking closed.

The pipes ran. Even the sky had gone quiet. Isa closed her eyes.

Two sets of footsteps leaving the room.

Three beams of a flashlight.

Her heartbeat was the burst of a machine gun. Erratic flak.

She stayed where she was, counting long and shallow breaths to a slow three hundred, biding her time until her skin crawled orange. Sparking. Bursting. Until she wanted to scream. And then the door opened, brisk, and there were a few words in German. A question.

The voice at the door was Michel's. And Isa heard a sigh of annoyance, just on the other side of her enormous painting. And the third set of boots crossed the floor and left the room.

That soldier, Isa thought, liked to play games.

She let out her breath in silent, measured gasps, and counted another slow three hundred. Twice. Just in case. Until she finally pooled enough of her courage to get an eye around the edge of the painting stack and step out. The room was empty. Isa gathered the paper, as quietly as she could, glancing once at the beauty of her father's masterpiece, before she tucked in the paperwork that said *Theodoor de Smit*, wrapping it in the brown butcher paper that had begun its life around the other painting.

She didn't know what Michel intended her to do. She wasn't sure how long she'd been down here. If the search was over, the museum locked and closed. If the search wasn't over, and the galleries were crawling with police. Gestapo and soldiers.

What would Michel do?

He would do what she was supposed to have done, Isa decided. He would go to the window and try to get back to the car. Isa slid her mother's fur-collared coat back over her shoulders, picked up her purse, and then she looked at the wrapped painting, her father's name on the label. She couldn't leave it hidden. To be found.

She just couldn't leave it behind.

Isa grabbed the painting and flitted back to the door she'd come through, listening before she cracked it open. The room with the jumble of posters and boxes was murky, silent. She rummaged and found a big canvas bag, put the painting inside it, quietly stuffing old newspapers around and on top. It looked like a sack of rubbish. Then she crept back to the art room, sack in hand, and stood before the door to the corridor. She turned the knob slowly, an eye to the crack. The dim, open space was shadowy. It looked like it had before. It sounded like it had before.

Unless someone was waiting.

So she waited. Counting. For what felt like an interminable time. For anyone, at any moment, to spring out from the rubble and the gloom. When they didn't, Isa eased herself through the door and into the passage, farther into the building, looking for the way into the room with the coal. The room of her childhood adventure, when the world had been beautiful, and her mother had scolded her publicly and laughed the entire tram ride home.

It was just now occurring to her, how often her mother had laughed.

She found the coal room with ease. Exactly where she'd told Michel it would be, just before the back corner rooms, with a half-moon of a window high and level with the sidewalk, a wooden door made to fit its contours. And there was a gargantuan pile of coal underneath. A looming, lumpy shadow. She could smell it. And smell the boiler. The hiss of water was a constant drone.

Isa shut the door, set down her precious rubbish sack, pulled off her shoes again, and stuck them in her purse. She put her purse in the sack with the painting, put the sack as far up onto the pile as she could reach. And carefully, she began to climb.

It was dirty, slippery, delicate work, trying not to dislodge the chunks of coal. To keep the whole pile from spreading and disintegrating underneath her, leaving the window out of reach. Her stockings would never be the same, and neither would the coat, and probably the dress. She moved the sack farther up, and farther up, and then, at a slow stretch, extending the very tip of one finger as far as she could, Isa released the latch on the window.

The wooden door swung inward. She had to duck beneath it. And from somewhere in the maze of rooms behind her came the screeching, ratcheting protest of huge metal hinges, the swing of a heavy iron door. The door, perhaps, of the Stedelijk's gigantic boiler, which someone would need to stoke for the night. With the coal she was standing on. The coal she was half lying in.

She climbed higher, trying not to hurry, dislodging a little avalanche from beneath her heel. Through a screen of metal grate and iron bars, she could see a pair of legs in the azure blue-black of twilight, Nazi brown legs with polished boots crossed. Someone leaning against the side of the building. She caught a waft of cigarette smoke. Then the someone leaned down, as if adjusting a shoe, and the face that appeared upside down before her was Michel's.

She did not have time to contemplate what would have happened if the face had belonged to someone else.

Isa unlatched the false grate, lowering it outward. She slid down a few inches, and one or two lumps of coal went skittering to the floor. She could hear the voices of two men now, shouting over the noise of the boiler. She grabbed the sack and slid it up and through the window, felt the grip that took it from her hands. She heard the scrape of a shovel on concrete near the door. And then the heel of Michel's boot caught the edge of the grate and slowly shut it.

Holding it shut.

There was a shout from behind the door, and the shovel scraped away in the other direction. Cigarette ash fell in front of the window. Isa waited, legs aching, trembling from holding herself still. Two pairs of boots passed her field of vision on the other side of Potterstraat.

She didn't know how much longer she could hold this position.

Then Michel's foot came away. The grate fell open. Isa pushed and began to climb. The pile began disappearing from beneath her toes. But she got some momentum, got her chest onto the ledge, onto the sidewalk outside. Half-in, half-out.

She was not the same size as the last time she did this.

Someone shouted on the other side of the door to the coal room, an answer to a question. Isa scrambled, the top of the window scraping across her backside, knees scrabbling against the pavement. Michel's arms came down and helped to tug her through.

From high above, she heard the drone of a bomber.

"On your feet," he whispered. "Quick!"

She got upright, the front of her coat and the bit of skirt she could see were black—one soft smudge of coal—her stockings a series of ladders. She tried to get her shoes on. She put her left in her right and had to switch. Amazingly, her hat was still on her head. Michel shut the grate. It banged back down and he left it. He thrust her purse into her hands, flipped the fur collar up around the red of her hair, put an arm around her shoulders, and picked up the sack.

"Be ill," he said.

She immediately bent over, stumbling, and they began to walk together, awkwardly. The flak was going, distant, not the near guns, but it had the eyes on the street pointed upward. Isa watched their feet move past on the sidewalk, around the back corner of the Stedelijk. A German voice called, not unfriendly, a voice of concern, and Michel answered with something about a hospital and Westergasthuis.

She didn't look ill, Isa thought. She looked like she'd been to a party in a mine.

They came around the next corner of the Stedelijk, and Isa knew this would be the difficult part. The dangerous part. She could feel Michel's grip on her upper arm tightening. They got halfway up the other side of the building before he stopped.

And Michel let out a stream of soft German that Isa didn't know the exact meaning of but understood all the same. She risked an upward glance. She could see the street, emptying for curfew, the lights already gone because of the high-flying bombers.

An empty street.

"Bastard," he said. "The car is gone!"

She felt the shock of those words hit somewhere in her lower stomach.

And Michel's suitcase had been in there. With his clothes, and everything he owned. The picture of his family.

They had to get off the street, and they couldn't go back toward Museumplein. "Straight," Isa whispered, "toward the park."

They crossed the street, tripping over the tram lines. Just past the closed café, there was a little alleyway, a narrow lane, and they ducked in without being challenged. There was another wave of bombers passing, the firing from the airport taking over as they flew beyond the city.

The eyes were upward.

Now that they were off the main street, Isa stood up so they could walk faster, Michel with his arm still around her, ready to resume their ruse of needing the hospital. They crossed a bigger street, a tram line, and then back in the continuing little lane between the buildings. Out and left, where Isa bent double, and Michel talked quickly to a strolling guard.

Isa had never been so glad to be with a Nazi uniform.

Around the corner, and the entrance to Vondelpark was locked. Michel cursed again. They started up the street on the wrong side of the fence, in the shadows of the park trees. They could not keep going like this. They were too far from the gallery. Someone was going to stop. Inquire. Ask too many questions. Someone would question her hair. Ask why they were carrying a bag of trash.

They were going to be arrested.

They reached the end of the park and the full dark had come down, the paint pot of black tipped over. The street sat wide. Deserted. Except for the guard on the canal bridge at the Singelgracht, the first watery ring that half circled the city. There were five more between them and the gallery. They stood still beneath the last tree. The bridge was a two-lane road, wide to span the wide canal, its edges curving down and out and around to the cross street. The guard turned and walked the bridge, his rifle on his back, nearly disappearing beyond the bridge's gentle arch.

"Go," Michel whispered.

She didn't know where they were going. They were just running. Straight for the canal and the guard. But Michel veered left, to a little path beside the bridge, a track along the waterway. There was a grassy bank instead of a wall, a boat tied at a low wooden dock beneath a row of thick, gnarled trees. The boat wasn't large, but it was wide-bottomed, with a canvas top at one end, for the rain.

Michel stepped in behind the canvas and sat, a hand on the dock, steadying the rock of the boat, quieting the water's ripple and slap. He took the sack Isa handed him, then helped her climb in. The boat rocked dangerously. She couldn't see the guard. She dropped to her knees in the dark beneath the canvas top. Michel scooted to make room, legs stretched beneath the boat seat, the sack on his lap, while Isa turned carefully and sat, a pile of rope and tarp and things she couldn't see uncomfortably behind her back.

The boat settled, listing a little to stern. The water lapped. There was no rumble overhead, and the flak had gone quiet. Michel let go of the dock. The guard strolled back to their end of the bridge, leaned on the iron rail, and lit a cigarette.

They weren't even thirty feet away. Hidden by the blackout and the trees and a canvas canopy.

It wasn't safe to speak, even at a whisper.

Then Michel lifted his arm and put it around her shoulders, reaching for her hand to grip it against his chest. She resisted. She was going to get him dirty. And then Isa realized she was shaking. Enough to move the boat. Which was strange, because she didn't feel the sickness of her fear, or the heat, or even the little jolts of orange. Her body, for the moment, was separate. She concentrated on the warmth of the arm. The hand.

She'd lost her hat somewhere.

When the guard went to smoke on the other side of the bridge, she whispered, "What happened?"

Michel leaned close to her ear.

"After you went into the museum, I heard the guards at the check-point talking. Everyone was talking about the girl with red hair, how she had defrauded an agent of Hitler with valuable art and gotten away with a large amount of money. That she infiltrated a private residence to do it, where the agent only just escaped with his life."

Gurlitt. He'd finally put two and two together. And come up with six.

"He knows about the Rembrandt," Isa said.

"He must."

"Is that what they were meeting about today, at Herengracht?"

Michel nodded but didn't speak. He was watching the guard pause at the center of the bridge. When the guard moved to the opposite rail, Michel said, "It was the choice gossip of the day, of course, because a young girl has once again humiliated the Gestapo, and now, indirectly, she has embarrassed Hitler. There are men in the Gestapo right now who are losing their rank. And then a girl with red hair walked into a café with a German soldier just outside the Museumplein, and then she went to the Stedelijk and . . ."

"Someone called the police?"

He nodded. "Our driver must have heard as well. And Hofer will hear, if he has not already. He will not have missed your hair. Maybe he will even remember the Rembrandt, and my involvement now is obvious . . ." He stopped. The guard had come back to their side, staring down into the green-black waters.

Isa leaned close to his ear. "Van Meegeren," she whispered.

Van Meegeren knew who she was. He knew where she lived. And Gurlitt was telling the Gestapo that the girl with red hair had been in Van Meegeren's house. If Van Meegeren would try and pin his awful attempt at a forgery on her father, she couldn't imagine that he wouldn't save his own skin by sending the Gestapo straight to her door. And even if he didn't, there was a contract in his office. With her name on it.

When the guard strolled to the other rail, Michel whispered, "He will say nothing. You can expose him as a forger. There is too much money at risk."

But could they count on that? If the Gallery De Smit was searched, they would find two Resistance workers—one who had shot a member of the SS, the other a fugitive from one bombing, who had also bombed a building just yesterday—an addict artist with all the means to forge Dutch masters, and of course, a Jewish baby. And that was in addition to a deserting Nazi soldier and a young woman they could neatly pin as being the girl with red hair.

The Gallery De Smit was some kind of Gestapo prize.

Michel adjusted the grip on her hand. She wasn't shaking any-more, but she could feel the tension in his arm. He said, "I am more concerned about the leak."

Isa's eyes went automatically to the wood of the boat. And then back up to Michel. Was it a coincidence that someone turned in a family for the bounty, and that the searching officer, Klaus, came exactly when Truus was arriving with a Jewish baby? A plan that only Truus and Willem had known?

"I acquired some information," Michel whispered, "after I left you at De Dokter. There is to be a public execution, ten Resistance workers for Klaus. They have a preferred list for the executions, some are already prisoners, some they are still looking for." He paused. "Your friend Joop, who is watching the gallery, he is on it, and . . . so is Truus."

Isa stiffened.

Michel said, "They do not know that she is the one who shot Klaus . . ."

Isa hadn't known Michel knew it.

". . . but that is the point, is it not? The Gestapo had her name already. Someone is talking."

And there came her fear. Spilling.

"Did you tell Willem?"

He nodded. "Yesterday. He did not intend to tell Truus. But I would say that is why he was on Herengracht today."

But why wouldn't Willem tell Truus? Isa wondered. Truus should know if she was in danger. So she could protect herself. And what was Willem doing on the Herengracht, coming down the street after that arrogant Jew hunter? What had he been planning to do, by him-self on a street full of Nazis?

Isa shook the doubts from her head. Because they were ridiculous.

Surely, there was someone else in the Resistance who had known where Truus was taking Hildy that day.

And now Willem knew that Michel was a German soldier.

"He will think my information is a trap," Michel said. "Now that he knows who I am. But until they know who is talking, the gallery is not safe. Truus and the baby need to . . ."

Isa put a hand to Michel's mouth. They had gotten careless about the guard and their whispering, and now there were two guards. She could hear the soft back-and-forth of German. It sounded like conversation. Nothing more. She turned to tell him so.

And something shifted. In the feel of his hand. A mouth against her palm.

It was reckless, it was desire, and nothing like what she'd thought she would want.

She moved her hand from his mouth, a reluctant gesture. An unsure brushstroke. He waited. Hesitating. And then Michel closed his eyes and leaned his head back on the ropes.

"Someday, Sofonisba," he said, his brows dark, the words barely a whisper. "Someday I will not be wearing this uniform."

Isa breathed, unsteady. She wasn't sure exactly what that meant. But she could feel the starched wool of his jacket on the back of her hand like a barrier.

The arm that was around her pulled her in, just a little, so she could rest her coal-dusted head.

If the gallery wasn't safe for Truus and Hildy—for any of them—then it wasn't safe for Michel, either. And how would he survive this, with bridges blown to smithereens and nowhere to go? Truus would have to help him find a safe place. She would make her. She would make Truus listen and find a safe place for all of them. Just as soon as they got out of this boat.

They sat. Silent. Waiting to be noticed. To be caught. Watching the moon rise with a thin, chill fog. The two guards chatted.

And suddenly, Isa was waking, her hand still in Michel's, his arm warm against the cold that had crept up her legs. She lifted her head. The fog had thickened. Michel had his head back, eyes closed, mouth a little open. Asleep. There was only one guard now, and he was still staring at the sky. Where very high, very far away, Isa could hear the rumble. A shake of the air. They needed to get inside.

She jumped when Michel whispered, "Would you know your way to the gallery by canal?"

She nodded. "If I can see."

"Then should we steal the boat?"

They got the boat untied while the guard was on the other end of the bridge. Isa crawled cautiously to the front and lay down, to balance the weight, Michel using the dock to push the boat slowly backward, hand over hand into the darkness. The guard had his back to them, gazing, listening to the planes. When they'd moved all the way past the dock, deep in the fog beneath the trees, Isa sat up, and Michel passed her an oar.

They pushed and pulled the boat along the bank, clinging to the shadow side of the water, using the oars for the occasional splashless stroke. The planes had passed, and the city was silent. Fogbound beneath a watery moon. A cemetery of a city, full of buildings with dead eyes.

Underneath a small bridge, unguarded, and then Isa could see bricks rising to their right, very high, an oval curving out into the canal. The prison on Weteringschans, near the Leidseplein. The unspeakable place. She looked back at Michel, and he motioned for them to cross. To proceed along the murky water in the shade of the wall, rather than in full view of any guards.

It was risky, but they did it, cutting through the bank of fog, gliding, skirting the base of the prison wall. A sudden shot cut through the quiet. One discharge of a pistol that made Isa jump, echoing on the other side of the canal. She didn't look back at Michel. He was pushing them faster, faster with the oar, not caring if it splashed. Isa dug in and helped him. The prison bricks passed. And then she held up a hand, and they slowed to a stop, water lapping, in the moon shadow of a tree stretching out from the bank.

They were coming to their turn into the Leidsegracht, crossing the canal rings into the center of the city. She could just see the bridge ahead of them, blurry through the mist, three or four figures walking back and forth, talking. This was not the short, gentle arch of the bridges they had passed. The water here was wide, open, where two canals met, the bridge a major thoroughfare. They would need to approach it and turn underneath. And the fog was not going to cover them. Not enough.

Isa was considering whether they should abandon the boat, try the rest of the way to the gallery on foot. She wondered how far they would get, even with a uniform. She didn't think it would be far. And then came the drone of bombers. Again. Running high, moving east and north, but closer this time. The flak started up.

Closer this time.

And somewhere up above them, there was a little yellow starburst in the night, like a firework shooting sparks, quickly extinguished behind the clouds. It would have almost been pretty, if Isa hadn't known it meant fire and explosion, death in a machine of metal flying thousands of feet above the earth. But the faces of the guards had turned upward. Eyes fixed on the sky.

Isa looked back at Michel and he picked up the oar. They were going to make a run for it. They began to paddle together. Stroke. And stroke.

Faster. No longer worrying about noise. The flak was up again, the nearer guns, and the drone above them became a shake that made the water ripple.

Isa paddled for the last pier of the bridge, the turn. They were speeding through the fog, wind loosening her hair. The shake in the air became a roar. And Isa looked up at the belly of a plane, buzzing only just above the city. If the plane had paused, she could have counted its rivets. The machine skimmed the buildings at a tilt, listing, but gaining altitude over the skittering pop of the machine guns.

"Go!" she heard Michel yell.

She'd stopped rowing. She'd covered her head. She put in the oar and matched his rhythm. Five strokes and they were under the bridge. She didn't know what the guards were doing. Probably covering their heads like she had. They made the turn into the smaller canal, with walls instead of banks, going for speed rather than secrecy. Another wave of bombers droned above their heads. Another round of flak. The bridge was behind them. Michel steered them again into the dark of the wall, the side of the boat skimming and scraping the stones. But he kept their speed.

Isa's heartbeat sounded like the machine guns in her ears.

They passed the Prinsengracht and the Keizersgracht without seeing the first guard on a bridge. There were bombs dropping somewhere. The shock waves rolled across the surface of the water. South maybe, Isa thought, near the airport. They steered left into the Herengracht, so fast that they went wide, barely making the turn. Isa waved her hand right, and they turned almost immediately into a tiny canal passage between the buildings and into the Singel. They were nearly there. The gallery was close. Michel reached out, pulling them close to a wooden dock, and the machine guns stopped. Isa looked up.

Spotlights were in the air, bright white beams of vision, tracking the progress of five pale bubbles, like jellyfish in a dark sea, men dangling from the strings. Parachutists coming down, and they weren't being shot. They were being tracked. The Nazis wanted them. There were going to be so many soldiers in the streets. Michel was leaning out, trying to get a rope tied, and Isa stood, rocking a little, grabbing the dock to hold them steady. And then the rumble above their heads once again became a roar, a noise so intense it rattled Isa's teeth.

She stared up again at the belly of a plane, a leviathan filling the sky for the blink of an eye, listing. But this plane was not gaining altitude. It was whistling. Down, down, clipping the top of a church spire. Then came an explosion so loud she felt it inside her head. Inside her bones. The dock below her hands gave a leap. And something bright came through the air. A star. A flame. An arc of trailing light as it fell. Straight down.

And the boat disappeared from beneath Isa's feet.

"Thou shalt not kill."

—The Sixth Commandment, *Exodus 20:13*

(King James Version)

25

THE WATER CLOSED over Isa's head so fast she had no time to shut her mouth. No time to be surprised. The world was just suddenly without air or vision. A world of hiss and splash. Wet and cold. And it was too heavy. Her limbs were weighed down. Her dress, her coat, dragging and pulling.

Such a slow, slow fall.

Until the world changed directions, the water rushing past her ears. Until she broke the surface of the canal with a gasp, to a string of Dutch—and she presumed German—filth, Michel's hand full of the fur of her coat collar. She dipped down once more below the surface and came up sputtering.

"Get it off," he said. "Take it off!"

She got a hand on his wrist, wriggling her other arm out of the coat, and immediately felt the tug lessen. Isa kicked, freed the other arm, and then Michel was dragging her up onto the small dock. There was a flame-glow in the sky, low behind the buildings, and she could hear the fire brigade bell. She sat on her knees on the rough wood, coughing and dripping.

"Are you all right?"

She nodded.

"A piece of the plane came through the boat. Cut it in half. How did it not land on your head?" He sounded angry. Exasperated. "Look at me, are you hurt?"

She looked at him. And shook her head.

"Do you not swim?"

She shook her head again. Another string of German.

"You're dry," she whispered. Or he would be, other than one wet sleeve and a splash across his front.

"I had just stepped onto the dock."

That had been close. So close. Then she looked back at the canal.

Her coat was gone. And her shoes. Her purse was gone and the money inside it.

"The painting?" Isa asked.

"It was still in the boat."

She closed her eyes. She hadn't even told him it was her father's. There hadn't been time.

"Come," he said. "Quick. We have to get off the street."

Michel took her hand, pulled her to her feet, and she left wet footprints all the way up Spui and over to Kalverstraat, where she could see the coral and tangerine, the sunrise colors of an airplane burning, silhouetting the towers and the gables. The fire was farther away than she'd thought, but she could smell the smoke, hear the commotion on the edge of the city's silence. The parachutists must be down, because the spotlights were off, and the Gallery De Smit was dark, blacked out as it should be, no sleek shiny cars with German engines waiting in front.

They went the back way, down the narrow Rozenboomsteeg, along the convent wall, and through the crack between the buildings, where Michel stopped.

"Get on my back," he said.

He was right. There was rubbish. Glass. She would cut her feet to ribbons. She hiked up her wet, dirty skirt and got on his back. He bounced her once, to adjust her higher, to get an arm under each knee, and then they went stumbling through the dark, through the weedy, uneven stones. Isa lurched from side to side, clinging to Michel's neck, wondering where they were going to go now that the gallery wasn't safe. Marveling that she was alive. That Michel had managed to keep his hat.

"What about the uniform?" she whispered.

He turned his head just a little. "It cannot matter now."

He got the gate open, not bothering to shut it, and Isa slid down to the flagstone in front of the gallery's back door. Michel reached into his jacket pocket and brought out her key.

They'd gone from everything to nothing that day, but somehow, he still had a hat and a key to her house. He put it to the lock.

"We'll tell Truus and Willem about the money," Isa said. "Maybe they already know the last six children are taken care of. They won't like it, but it has to count for something, doesn't it?"

"Hildy," Michel said. "She has to be moved."

Isa nodded. They would just have to set aside their differences long enough to get the baby to safety. To get all of them to safety. And she would find a way to make her father comply, whether he felt like it or not.

He would not want to comply. Theodoor de Smit would want to stay in his garret until the Nazis came.

Michel turned the lock. Isa pushed the table out of the way, running ahead into the little gallery.

"Truus!" she called up the spiral stairs. "Willem? Papa?"

The treads felt soft, almost polished beneath her bare feet. She had no idea what time of night it was; the kitchen was too dark to see the clock. But she could see that the table was littered with bumps and shadows, like a storm had come through. They were probably all asleep, and it might be better not to wake her father until she knew what to tell him.

"Truus?" she said softly.

Michel was coming behind her, his feet slower. Reluctant. Through the dining room and into the poppy hall, and then she could hear Hildy fussing. There were no lights anywhere. She tripped up her own three stairs and called, "Truus, it's me," before she opened the door to her bedroom.

Hildy was in her drawer, legs kicking, unhappy, and Truus had her back to her, stuffing clothes into the leather bag.

"There you are," Isa chided. "Why didn't you answer?" She went to the baby and crouched down, stroking her head, still too wet and dirty to pick her up. And then Isa heard a click.

The click of a hammer being cocked.

Isa looked up. Truus was sitting now, on the edge of the box bed, her eyes red, her face a little blotchy. And she had the gun pointed at Isa.

"How could you?" Truus whispered. "How could you do it?"

But then Isa saw that the gun wasn't actually pointing at her. Truus was aiming at Michel, standing in the doorway in his Nazi brown, one hand gripping the doorjamb.

Isa had been prepared for anger. For argument. She had not been prepared for the gun.

"Truus, let me explain. He . . ."

"I don't need your explanation!" she said, sharp. Hildy's fuss crescendoed to a cry. Isa reached out again and Truus said, "And don't you touch her."

Isa stood. "He's deserting," she said. "He's been giving Willem information. Helping me get the money you need. For the children . . ."

"Oh, has he? Is that what he told you? Don't be so stupid."

Isa took a step. "We can't talk about this now, Truus. We need to get Hildy out. And you. We think the gallery might be searched. The police, maybe the Gestapo. We can't risk . . ."

"Coming here, are they?" Truus turned her red eyes on Michel, who was standing stiff, correct, and perfectly still. "Finishing the job?" she asked.

"What do you mean?" he replied. His voice was very cool. Hildy kicked and wailed.

"Truus! Put the gun down."

She didn't put the gun down. She kept her eyes on Michel. Two chips of cold sky. "I think you know exactly what I mean."

"Shoot me if you are going to shoot me," Michel said. "Or you can tell me what you mean."

"Willem," Truus said. "I mean Willem . . ."

"What has happened to him?"

Isa looked back and forth between the two of them.

"He's been arrested!" Truus dashed a tear from her face and steadied the gun. "Just like Greta. And it's your fault!"

Isa felt something sink inside her. But what had Willem been doing on a street crawling with Nazis?

"When?" Michel said. Sharp. "When was he arrested? Where?"

"What does it matter to you?"

"Where?"

"Herengracht." She looked at Isa. "He was taking care of a collaborator."

"And you think I made this happen?" Michel asked.

"You are the one who sent him there!"

"Truus!" Isa said. "Put the gun down!"

Michel said, "I gave him information about people who were

turning in Jews for the bounty." He tilted his head at the crying baby. "And I am glad I did it. Then I gave him information about Resistance workers who were being hunted. And I am glad I did it. I did not ask what he was going to do with the information, and I did not get him arrested. You have a leak."

"You trapped him! You collect names for your brother, people who can be blackmailed and turned into collaborators. And this time, you used one of the names to bait Willem! So they could catch him in the act!"

"Truus!" Isa said. "What are you talking about?"

"Because they want ten of us!" Truus yelled. "To execute! And Michel is helping them fill their quota." She put her gaze on Michel, realigning her aim. "Isn't that what your brother wants?"

"Truus! He doesn't even have a . . ."

And then Isa looked at Michel. He had his jaw clenched. His amber eyes closed. And when he opened them, the glass had gone dark, murky.

And Isa could feel something hardening inside her chest, like Van Meegeren's plastic paint.

"See?" said Truus. "He didn't tell you about his brother, did he?"

"No," Michel said. "I did not." He took off his hat. "How do you know about my brother?"

"You have a leak," Truus hissed. Her smile was something terrible. She turned it on Isa. "Ask him where he went before you two left this morning."

"I will tell her," Michel said coolly. "I went to see my brother."

Isa whispered. "You told me you didn't . . ."

"No. I said I had eight sisters."

He lied. That's what he meant.

"He went to inform on Willem," Truus said. She was triumphant in her tears, so eager to be right, so intent on her own pain that Isa's was invisible. "He went to tell the Gestapo where he was going to be, and what they could catch him doing!"

"I went to do the opposite," Michel replied. "I went to throw my brother off the scent."

"That is a lie. He has been using you, Isa!"

Isa ignored her. "Your brother is Gestapo?"

Michel turned his gaze on her. "Oh, yes. He finds me a very useful source. People who are desperate, who have stolen or sold art they shouldn't have, they can be so easily coerced into giving up their Jewish friends. It is interesting, though, just how many give false names. A false address. It makes finding them so much harder. It is very frustrating for my brother. You have met Franz, you know. He was sitting beside me at Van Meegeren's."

The arrogant boy-officer making Amsterdam Judenfrei. No wonder he'd been there. He was the brother-in-law of the Minister of Culture. Like Michel. And he'd been walking down Herengracht, right before Willem. Going straight-backed up the steps. Looking like Michel.

"My brother is kicking himself now, I would think," Michel said. "Missing his chance at the girl with red hair. But he came here to hunt Jews originally, not Resistance, and his mind that night was on . . . other things. I am certain he will find a way to forgive himself."

And standing there, in his Nazi brown, with his cold voice and hard eyes, he was someone she did not know. The blackmailer. The sneaky child.

Paintings, Isa thought, were not the only thing in the world that could be faked.

"Pick up the baby," Michel said. "She is not going to shoot me. Or not yet."

"Do not pick up . . ." Truus began.

But Isa scooped up Hildy, holding her upright against a shoulder. Hildy quieted immediately, hiccuping, not caring that Isa was damp and dirty and cold. She turned to Michel, and they looked at each other. He could have said he was sorry, that he should have told her. That his brother was not him any more than she was her father. But he didn't. He didn't say anything.

"Truus," Isa said. "If taking down a cell of the Resistance was what Michel wanted, he could have had all of us arrested a dozen times by now . . ."

"So true," Truus replied. "But he had a good reason to wait, didn't he?" She looked at Michel. "You had lots of reasons to wait, I hear. One-point-nine million of them."

Michel lifted a shoulder. "You should probably know that Heinrich will inform for anyone. Including the Gestapo."

And 1.9 million, Isa thought, was enough to kill for. Or to turn someone in.

Michel put his cool, smooth gaze on Isa. "I took ten thousand. At the bank. I said they gave me ten, but they gave me twenty. It's gone now. It was in the suitcase. Taking their money to start a new life seemed like justice, and I had . . . a little business I wanted to begin."

He shrugged again, and Isa felt the hardness in her breaking, little fissures, a spiderweb of craquelure. It hurt.

Why was it so hard to spot a fake?

"We have no more time for talking," Michel said. He stood up straight. Crisp. If Isa could have named his portrait in that moment, she would have called it *The Nazi*. "If Willem breaks," he said, "they will come . . ."

"Willem will never break," Truus said, the tears running fresh.

"Who else knew where Willem was going to be today?" Michel demanded.

"Only you!" said Truus.

"Who else did he tell about the names on the list?"

Truus shook her head. "As if I would tell you that."

But Isa thought Michel had a point. Michel might have lied. He might have been greedy. He might have used her for an enormous payday. But he had not been one of them at the dinner. And she had never believed he would hurt Hildy.

Willem was the one who hadn't told Truus about her danger. Who was lying about their relationship. Who wore uprightness like a mask. Who had a wound that made him pace the floors at night. A bleeding guilt for other people's deaths. Who was "paying for his sins."

Willem was the one with a father imprisoned.

Willem was the one who could be controlled.

What if he wasn't arrested on the Herengracht, following a Jew hunter? What if Willem had merely . . . gone to a meeting.

Michel tsked. German. Impatient. "Find your leak or none of you are safe!" he said. "But now I must go." He turned back to Isa. "When she is calm, make her think. Get to a safe place, or if you get caught here, hide in the garret. But do not go out onto the streets unless you have to. Cover your hair. Franz will recognize you. So will Gurlitt and Hofer. The Gestapo are looking, and you are the prize."

"What are you talking about?" Truus whispered. She sounded exhausted.

"And when you are calm," Michel said, taking a step closer. "Look at this." He lifted a hand toward his jacket, opening a palm to Truus, showing he meant no harm, reaching slowly into his inside pocket. He brought out the little black notebook. "Keep it for me. You will know what it is, and what it is for."

He reached out and set it on the dresser. And then he took another step, put a hand on Hildy's head, and kissed it, careful not to brush Isa with his hat.

"Where are you going?" Isa asked.

He looked surprised. "Do you really have to ask?"

She did. But he didn't answer.

He turned his back to the gun and walked out the door.

Truus sniffed. "And that," she said, "is the last we'll see of him until the Gestapo get here. And I was too much of a coward to shoot him!"

Isa looked at her friend, pink and blotchy with her ugly, ugly gun, and suddenly, she was in bloom. Fire-red, scarlet-orange, a poison heat that blazed through her blood.

"Shut up, Truus!" she said. "And put down that gun." Hildy started crying again. Isa kissed her head where Michel had. "Hold the baby, I have to change."

Truus sat the gun on the bed and took the baby, for the first time taking a proper look at Isa. "What happened to . . ."

"Shut up," she said, yanking down the zipper of her dress, pulling open drawers to find something dry to put on. She pulled out underthings—she had no more stockings—and dug the wet money from her bra, slapping it down on the dresser while the baby fussed. There was fifteen hundred guilders left. Out of three million.

"What have you been doing?" Truus asked.

"Getting the money for the children, like I said."

"Oh, Isaatje," Truus whispered. And she didn't sound angry anymore. Just sad. Brokenhearted.

Isa put a hand on her hip, half-dressed, wet and bedraggled. "What do you think I've been doing?"

And she saw the truth on Truus's face.

"I am not a prostitute, Truus! I've been selling art to the Nazis with Michel." She grabbed her blue-print dress and started pulling on her clothes. "I sold one to Hitler, though that hasn't gone so well. Today's was to Goering, and that didn't go so well, either. But I did get money and paid it for the children. And then a piece of a plane hit the boat, and I went in the canal."

"What?" Truus bounced the fussing baby. Hildy was very unhappy. "You were selling art? But that's illegal! The queen, the real government, says that anyone who sells to the Nazis is a traitor . . ."

"It was forged art, Truus. Fakes! But if I tell anyone that, then we can't sell them, can we?"

"Did you say 'plane'?"

Isa ignored her. "We were nearly caught, and now there's a whole group of Nazis who think I am the girl with red hair. Which I am, just not the one they think I am." She pulled her blue dress over her head. "I was nearly arrested."

"Fake art," said Truus, bitter. "And you thought you were going to get a million and a half guilders. I can't believe you let yourself get used like that!"

Isa straightened. "Like you haven't been used for the last three years?"

"What do you mean?"

"You know what I mean. You know Willem doesn't love you. And that he never has! Why do you go along with it?"

"What are you saying?" Truus said, quiet. Hildy was crying and squirming.

"Did he give them away at the Records Office, Truus? Is that why they died? Did he get Arondeus and the others killed?"

Truus narrowed her eyes, and Isa's gaze darted to the gun. She didn't think Truus would shoot her, but right then, she didn't feel sure about anything.

"You are the one who needs to shut up," Truus said. "You have no idea what you're talking about."

"He lies to you, Truus. His whole life is a lie! Did Willem tell you you're on the Gestapo arrest list? That you and Joop are two of the ten they want to execute?"

Her blue eyes went big.

"No, I didn't think he did. And how do you think they got your name?"

"Michel told them," Truus replied.

"Before he ever met you?" Isa countered.

"Willem is not the leak, Isa! He's arrested!"

"Is he?"

Truus stood with the crying baby, and then the anger froze on her face. "Joop," she said. "Joop!"

"What?"

But Truus only thrust Hildy into Isa's arms and darted to the window, pulling aside the blackout. Isa was surprised to see the dawn.

"Oh, no!" Truus said. "No! Isa, I missed the signal. I didn't check!"

"What signal? What . . ."

And then Isa heard a noise. A sound more unusual than bombers or an explosion. The sound of metal on metal. Sharp from the street.

The slam of a car door.

They hurried together, down the steps and across the hall to the blue room, where the windows looked onto Kalverstraat. Truus peered around the edge of the curtain, and then she turned to Isa.

"They're here."

26

THREE SECONDS PASSED where they stood, looking at each other. Then Truus dropped the curtain and ran, Isa right behind her with the crying baby, back to the bedroom. Isa put Hildy in the drawer, where she wailed, found shoes to put her feet into, while Truus threw the gun into the leather bag. Isa stuffed the wet money and the soggy identity card back into her dry bra.

"Where's her comforter?" Isa said. "Her bottle?"

"The bag. The milk powder is in the kitchen. She hasn't been quiet all night! She isn't feeling well . . ."

How were they possibly going to keep her quiet enough?

"Where is my father?"

"Asleep. In the garret . . ."

Isa ran out, then ran back in, past Truus, who was trying to get to the kitchen with the bag and the crying baby. She lifted her mirror from the wall and worked Elsa Groot's identity card from the back of it, tearing it a little at the edge. Then she grabbed her coat from the chair and the notebook Michel had left her, tucking it into the pocket, before she ran across the hall and met Truus again.

"Have you got the milk?"

Truus nodded, and they raced into the blue room, where Isa took the bag so Truus could climb into the wardrobe with the baby. Up and through, pulling up the step, shutting them into the meager light left from the bulb above the garret stairs. Isa ruffled the hangers of clothes, spreading them over the open back of the wardrobe before she shut the door in the wall and went up to the garret. Her father was turned over on his sofa, sleeping with his back to them, a sketchbook on the floor beside him.

"Didn't take him long, did it?" Truus said, sharp. She meant Michel, calling the Gestapo. She was at the front of the garret, where there was a round window that looked out on Kalverstraat, peeking around the curtain edge. Watching the Nazis gather in front of the gallery.

Isa ignored her. Hildy was screaming. Isa sprinted for the sink to get water in the bottle, listening for the pounding on the door. For the rifle butts. The breaking glass. Maybe Hildy would be quiet if they could get her to eat.

Hildy had to be quiet.

"You'll have to find a place to be still when they come in," she told Truus. "The floors creak. We won't be able to move."

She got the powder in, shaking the bottle, and Truus said, "Isa, look!"

Isa hurried to the round window and lifted a curtain tack, peering over Truus's shoulder.

The sleek, black cars were smudges in the smoky fog, lined up along the buildings, Nazi brown uniforms swarming in the dawn light with pistols, rifles, moving back and forth. Gathering around a door. A door to an abandoned shop across the street. Where the Groots had once lived.

"They've gone to the wrong house," Truus said, wondering.

"Yes. They have."

They'd gone to the house of a red-haired girl who had sold them a forged Rembrandt. Isa picked up Elsa Groot's identity card from where she'd thrown it on top of her coat and showed it to Truus.

"What I used when I sold Hitler a fake," she said. "With my picture on it, obviously."

Truus gave her a raised brow. "So he . . ."

"Michel didn't bring them. They got the address off the record of the sale."

"This is about forged art?"

"And the girl with red hair, yes."

There were other glints of light from across the street. People watching the Nazis batter down the abandoned door. They'd gone to the wrong address, but that didn't mean they weren't coming to the right one. For a different reason.

Truus dropped the edge of the curtain, pushing its tack back into the wall, and took the bottle from Isa. Hildy reached out with her hands and brought the bottle to her mouth, ready to take what she could get, warm or cold.

"Willem won't give us up," Truus said, glancing at Isa's father on the sofa and lowering her voice. "He would never. He punishes himself enough."

Isa turned away. She was afraid Willem had already done whatever he was going to do, and there was no way for any of them to alter it. For a moment, the garret was quiet, the only noise from the Germans outside and Hildy's contented sucking.

"Isaatje, what did you mean when you said you paid the money? For the children?"

Isa looked up. "For the bribe. You said that last night would be just in time, and it isn't safe for you to go out, so . . ."

"But who? Who did you give the money to?"

"Your friend. The one who was helping Willem. I've never known her name. She said she could get it into the hands of the ones who were . . ." Isa paused.

"Who are you talking about?" Truus whispered.

"The woman in the kerchief. That you've had following me."

Truus shook her head. Isa didn't like the look on her face.

"You know who I mean! She wears the green-and-gold kerchief, sometimes the sunglasses. A shopping sack. She's been following me ever since . . ."

Ever since Truus came to the gallery.

"I saw her talking to Willem on Kalverstraat. Right after he . . . when I was out at the café. And again, yesterday, she was behind Willem on Herengracht."

"Isa," Truus said slowly. "There are only three of us that work together in our part of the Resistance, now that Greta is gone. It wasn't . . . Joop that you saw?"

"Not unless Joop is a fifty-year-old woman with wrinkles." She almost laughed, but the significance of what Truus was saying was beginning to sink in.

"We don't have anyone else. I couldn't even point out another face in the Resistance. That's the way it's supposed to work, and no one knows about you but us." She could hear the panic creeping into Truus's voice. "Isa, if that woman has been following you, and she isn't one of us, then she has to be Gestapo."

That could not be right.

"What did you say to her?" Truus asked.

Isa pressed her fingers against her temples.

"What did you say?"

"I gave her the money and told her it was for the rest of the children. Could she get it into the right hands, and if they needed more, if they found more places, then I could get more . . ."

Isa felt an electric shock. Little pops beneath her skin.

There was only one place in the city where children were being kept, children who needed money and "places." Children the Resistance would be interested in.

Only one.

"Oh, Isaatje," Truus said. "They know." She had the baby in her arms, tears rolling from her eyes. "They know!"

And Isa was sick, yellow-sick and bloodred and a panicked orange. A pinwheel spinning. Because she had been so wrong about absolutely everything. And right about Willem.

Because she had seen Willem talking to the Gestapo.

But Isa was the one who had given up the children.

And she could see no way for this mistake to un-become.

She sat in a layer of dirt on top of years of dripped paint, arms clutching her middle. She could see her father's sketchbook lying on the floor in front of the empty easel.

Not her father's. That was her sketchbook. And then she lifted her gaze to her father's form, curled up on his sofa and extra pillows, staring at the curve of his back in the yellow satin shine of his smoking jacket. A shine that did change in the glow of the light bulb. A highlight still and static on the glistening cloth.

"Isa?" Truus whispered.

She was halfway across the floorboards before she knew she'd stood up. All that time they'd been in the garret, and Theodoor de Smit hadn't moved. He wasn't moving now. And she couldn't hear Truus anymore, or Hildy's fuss, or the sound of the Nazis across the street.

She was a frosted flower. A spiderweb of fractured, breaking paint.

She touched her father's shoulder. Dropped to her knees and put her fingers on his face. But there was no breath in him.

There was nothing in him.

And gray, Isa thought, was the color of grief. Gray with a tinge of blue. The color of loss. Of endings. Of cold stone buried in the dirt.

She took her hand from his face. There was a pillbox on the floor beside the sketchbook—a plain tin box—lying among some charcoal pencils. And she heard a moan. A sob. She thought it was Truus.

"I didn't flush them, Isa! I hid them under your mattress. In case . . . just in case someone got hurt. I never . . . I didn't know . . ."

And Truus hadn't gotten him a canvas, and so he had gone looking for a sketchbook. And found his Morpheus.

Her father had chosen. And his choice had not been her.

Isa sat. Blinking. Staring.

He had been such a brilliant artist. And such a wonderful father. And such a terrible father. The sun to her mother's moon to her distant star. Bright and beautiful and far away.

She picked up the sketchbook and opened it.

And there was her own face, her hair down, chin on palm, staring dreamy into the contents of a coffee cup. And there she was on the next page, in pajamas, lying asleep on her rug in a litter of sketches. Isa from the back, arms crossed in the empty gallery. Isa in profile, sitting crosslegged, laughing on her mother's bed. She was ten, she was eight, and then five, and there was one at the end that she thought must be her, though she'd been not much bigger than Hildy.

It was her life at every stage. In every mood and light. How could her father have made her hair look red with charcoal?

Because, Isa thought, it was a beauty felt.

And now she knew that her father had felt, and that he had also seen. And it was far too late for her to know that.

She closed the sketchbook and pushed it away. Someone was weeping, she just didn't know who.

Isa stood. She heard Hildy's fussing, Truus saying she was sorry, a snip of German from the street outside. She picked up her things, her coat and Elsa's card—the sketchbook she left behind on the floor—and she walked down the garret steps.

Her shoes were still untied.

"Isa?" Truus called.

Out of the blue bedroom, where no one lived now, down the straight stairs and into the empty galleries. Past the bricks that hid a Vermeer, and down again to Moshe's cellar, where she and Michel had forged a painting to save two very different kinds of treasure.

Isa laid down her coat. She didn't bother with a light. She picked up the broom handle propped against the wall. Marched to the mattress still tied to the column.

And she hit it.

Then she swung back, and she hit it again.

Again. And again.

She hit it again.

Gray-blue stone and linen.

Fire and panic and fear.

Scarlet and violet.

Heat and frost.

And blue. And blue. And blue.

Because she might drown in an ocean that was blue. Because blue was the color of regret.

And when Isa threw down the broom handle, she was sweating. And crying. And she knew what she should do. What she must do.

The only thing left that she could do.

She turned and found Truus sitting on the bottom step, waiting for her to finish, Hildy asleep in her arms.

"We have to go tell them," Isa said. "About what I did. Warn them and get the children out."

And she could see what Truus was thinking. That there were

six more children and only the two of them. That they had Hildy, a baby with nowhere else to go. But Truus didn't say any of those things. She just stood, back straight, patting the baby.

"All right, then," she said. "You'd better go tie your shoes."

Isa tied her shoes, then went upstairs to go through her mother's drawers. She found a scarf—light green, like spring pear and ferns—a scarf that could be folded into a kerchief, covering the bright copper of her hair.

She was a woman with a kerchief.

She buttoned up her coat, eating the bread Truus gave her. Then held Hildy while Truus ate and buttoned hers. While Truus checked the gun and the contents of the leather bag. Hildy was beginning to wake again. Fussy. And Isa could feel Truus watching her, wondering when she was going to fuss. Wondering if Isa was going to fall to pieces as soon as she needed her.

Isa didn't know, either.

It was ten after six in the morning.

"I covered him, Isaatje," Truus said. "So he wouldn't be cold." Isa nodded, and Truus checked the window, a peek around the curtain.

"They're going house to house," she said. "Police and three Germans. They've just gone inside the bakery across the street, and I don't think they waited to be—"

And then three shuddering bangs echoed from the front door of the gallery. A pounding fist. Almost straight below Truus, where she couldn't see.

A surprise after all.

Truus spun. "But they're still across the street!"

"They've split into two groups!"

Isa snatched up her purse, adjusting her hold on Hildy. Truus grabbed the leather bag, and they left the blue bedroom without a backward glance, hurrying across the hall and through to the kitchen. The bang came again. A rifle butt. A guttural shout of "Open!" in both German and Dutch.

The glass would break next, Isa thought.

Down the spiral stair, stealing through the dark of the little gallery, and around to the damp back hall. Truus was scooting the table out of the way when the front door of the gallery shook. When the glass shattered and the wood splintered around the lock. She reached for the back door, but Isa shook her head, holding the comforter in Hildy's mouth. Listening to the bark of orders and the scuffling of boots. Running inside. Running up the straight stairs.

She hoped they wouldn't find her father. That they would leave him in peace in his garret. Until she came back.

And when the stairs were protesting at their loudest, Isa nodded, Truus turned the lock, and they slid out the door and through the gate. Hildy began to wail around the comforter, jostling as they ran together down the uneven path, slipping out from the crack between the buildings.

The lane was chill, misted and tinged with the lingering smoke of a burning plane. "Which way?" Truus whispered.

Isa turned right, pausing to peer around the corner. Catching a glimpse of her own broken front door. Of her own brick street overrun with Nazi brown, teeming with the contrasting dark uniforms of Dutch police.

And then footsteps came running, heavy boots on the herringbone, coming from behind and too fast to avoid. A man veered into the alley, in thick pants and jacket, like he'd been skiing, a harness around his waist and legs. A parachutist. Was he British? American? He passed them in a flash. Around the next turn, and Isa heard the crack of pistols. Hildy cried.

"Which way, Isaatje?" Truus hissed.

She looked right again at the Nazis, some of them racing to the gunshots ahead, and they were probably behind, too, chasing the parachutist up the alley. She looked left, at the brick arch with its iron-nailed double doors. They were trapped.

Isa ran to the door and used her free hand to bang on the heavy wood. Then she turned her fist to the side and banged with everything she had. She didn't stop. She didn't notice the pain. They were in full view of the Gestapo on Kalverstraat, whenever one of them decided to look.

No one answered the door.

Hildy screamed. Isa heard a yell of discovery behind them, from between the buildings. The Germans had found the back door.

She banged harder, kicking for good measure. Truus's gun clicked. There were more shots from the street. Sharp shouts. Isa caught the word *parachute*.

She heard German orders from the gully.

She hit her fist against the door like she would break her hand.

And then there was a noise, a wooden bar being lifted. Hinges creaked, and one of the doors beneath her fist moved. A woman's face appeared in the opening.

"Help us!" Isa whispered.

The woman blinked, doe-eyed. "Well, all right," she said. A long scrape, and the door opened.

Truus pushed Isa and the crying baby inside, moving them down a passage between two buildings while the woman shut the door again, dropping its bar back into place. Hildy's cries echoed, the passage ended, and then they were standing in a large courtyard of autumn-gold grass, surrounded by tall, skinny houses sharing walls on each side. The noises of the city—Nazi shouts, guns, and glass—were oddly hushed. Almost erased. And the archway around the wooden doors, Isa realized, had never been anything more than a facade. A fake.

Hildy quieted, snuffling, watching the woman who came down the passage. She was young, slight, elf-like with a pointed chin.

"I was just going to morning mass," she said.

Isa saw Truus raise a brow.

"Would you like some breakfast?"

The elfin lady didn't wait for a response, just led the way with tiny steps, hands folded in front of her. They walked a path in the stillness, around the courtyard green, and a church tower Isa hadn't even known was there rose up suddenly beside them.

"Careful not to step on Sister Cornelia," the woman said, turning her pointy chin. Isa looked down, and circled a granite slab at the edge of the pavement, in the groove that was the gutter. There was a vase of purple pansies on it. Then they veered into an inset, where stairs climbed up the side of a house. Inside, there was a hall, and at the end of that hall, a little room that smelled of soap and tea.

The room had a bed with a plain quilt, two wooden chairs at a table, a small stove, and a bookshelf. There was a pot on the stove and a kettle, light just beginning to creep through two gauzy curtains. The woman lit the fire and a lamp.

"Please," she said. "Sit. And you probably won't be needing that."

She meant the gun in Truus's hand.

Truus said, "What will you do if the soldiers come? Or the police?"

The woman turned from the stove, surprised. "Soldiers?"

Isa caught Truus's eye, wondering if it was possible to have found the only woman in Holland who needed the Nazi invasion explained to her. Then the woman said, "They don't come in here. I think they're scared of nuns."

Isa looked at the woman's plain black dress, her black stockings. Her hair was cut in a not-unfashionable bob.

"Are you a nun?" Isa asked.

"Me? Oh, no." She went back to whatever she was doing on the stove, and Truus sat, exasperated, tucking the gun into her purse.

Isa sat in the other chair, bouncing a fussing Hildy. "My name is Isa de Smit. I'm your neighbor, from just down the lane."

"Neighbor? Really?" The little woman stirred a pot. Isa soldiered on.

"Yes. And . . . we've run . . . we've had some trouble. My father was . . . My father has . . . He died, and . . ."

And out of nowhere, her tears poured. Hot and stinging.

"Oh," the woman said. "Oh dear. I am so very sorry."

She set two bowls on the table. There was a gray lump of porridge in each, but with a large dollop of honey on top. Isa stared at it, wiping at her tears, and when she raised her eyes, the little woman was beside her, blinking, shy with her big eyes. "Could I . . . would you mind if I looked at your baby?"

Isa handed over Hildy, who thought about crying, but then Hildy's dark eyes locked onto the elf-woman's, and she decided to observe her instead, sucking on her comforter. The little woman cooed and talked nonsense, then laid the baby gently on the bed. Hildy acquiesced. And the woman said, "Do you have a diaper?"

Truus silently handed her the leather bag.

"Oopsie. She had a pin open," the woman commented.

Poor Hildy. No wonder she had cried.

They ate while the woman changed Hildy, the dirty diaper wrapped in a newspaper. The woman washed her hands and went back to the bed to stroke the baby's hair. Hildy's eyes were closing, her mouth working.

"Is she a little Jewish baby?" the woman asked.

Isa met Truus's gaze. So the woman did know something about the world outside her walls. Truus shook her head, warning Isa not to speak, but Isa set down her spoon.

"Yes. She is."

"Poor mite," the woman said.

"What is your name?" Isa asked.

"Sister Antonia." She had her eyes on Hildy.

"We need help, Sister Antonia. There are other babies like her."

She nodded.

"We need to go get them. Could I leave Hildy here with you?"

Truus watched, her mouth set in a line.

Sister Antonia didn't answer right away. And then she said, "Oh, yes. Of course. Take as long as you'd like."

As if Isa had said she was running down to the corner market.

Truus stood and began emptying the leather bag. They were going to need that. Isa pushed back her chair, went to the bed, and knelt down beside Hildy. She was relaxed now on the warm blanket, her arms thrown back, eyes closed, comforter just popped out of her mouth.

And love, Isa thought, has no color.

It is all the colors, blended into pure, achingly brilliant light.

Isa kissed Hildy's head, because her mother couldn't. And then she kissed it again, and followed Truus to the door.

"Wait," said Sister Antonia. "The other babies, like this one. Do they need . . . places? To go?"

Isa nodded.

"Then, if you wanted . . . if you thought I could . . . I wouldn't mind, if you brought one here."

Isa studied her earnest face and nodded again.

"Sister Amelia will show you how to get out."

And when Isa turned and Truus whirled, there was another woman in the doorway, heavyset and gray-headed, stooped with a cane. She led them out, past Sister Cornelia, past the church, and into a different passage. This one also had an archway, four steps up, covered and beautifully tiled. She unlocked the door, and they were on Spui.

Where it was loud with the world. Where the rising sun had colored the smoke and fog orange. Like panic. Where Isa's hair was red beneath her kerchief. Where something reckless bloomed hot inside her chest.

Truus took her arm. Like they were going to the cinema.

"Six more," Truus said, her mouth set.

Isa almost smiled, thinking of the convent. But she didn't. "Seven," she replied. "I think we can save seven."

27

THEY WALKED ARM in arm across Spui toward Rokin. Isa had the empty leather bag; Truus had her purse. Her other hand was clutching Isa so tight, she was leaving a bruise.

"When we take a child out of the city," Truus whispered, "we go straight to Centraal Station and get on the eleven o'clock or the four o'clock train to Amersfoort. The man who takes the tickets and checks the identity cards is Dutch, but he's National Socialist, and he knows us now. We always have children. It's safer at this point to keep him happy and paid. He wants us in the third car from the engine. Not another car . . ."

They crossed the street together, to avoid the German soldier coming to change shifts on the bridge, and stepped onto the number 14. The tram Isa shouldn't have taken, but had. They settled into a seat together, in the back, where no one could sit behind them. Where Isa's hair could remain unobtrusive.

The tram emptied and filled, a constant ebb and flow, but they didn't see any soldiers. The passengers were talking about the five captured American parachutists, the bomber that had come down on a school in flames. A whisper about the girl with red hair. The Germans, evidently, were busy.

"On the other end," Truus said, voice low, "we meet with a worker who delivers the children to their new families. Or sometimes it's the family that meets us, or sometimes we take them straight there. Someone calls ahead, and we're given instructions at the last minute. The hardest part is getting them out of the building."

Truus paused, making sure no one was listening.

"The theater is guarded and right across the street. Sometimes we hand them over the back hedge and come out of the teaching college instead."

Like the day she'd seen Truus. Waiting for the tram to come and block the guard's view.

"Then Henriette retypes the lists and leaves out that child's name. Or sometimes, she never puts them on there at all. It's like they never existed . . ."

Erased. And how many of them would never know who they were? Who they once were.

Damn the Nazis.

Damn the whole ugly world.

Isa loosened her friend's nervous grip. "And what about the five that I gave you the money for?"

"Four got out of the city. The fifth is Hildy. I've still got her money here." She tapped her purse. "And where, Isaatje, did that money come from?"

"I told you." Isa glanced at the empty seats around them. "I sold a fake Rembrandt to Hitler's art agent. It was supposed to be for the taxes."

Truus leaned back to look at her carefully. "You really did?"

Isa suppressed a smile. A little shiver.

Truus said, "Oh." Slowly.

And Isa saw Truus smile. Saw the moment when Truus realized who had paid for the rescue of those five children. Who was paying for the rescue of the last six. Or maybe seven. Then she sighed.

"But you didn't pay your taxes, did you?"

Isa watched the bare limbs of the trees pass by, their color wiped away, black and gray lines against the sky. Like a drawing in charcoal. That money was better spent where it had gone. To four children. And Hildy.

She would have to let the gallery go. And what was inside its walls. Moshe would understand. And her father didn't need it anymore.

She turned back to Truus. "There were six more with places?"

"Yes," Truus replied. "Or that's the last we heard. Two of the families got scared after Hildy. But I think they found new ones."

Isa nodded. "And who decides about . . . which ones?" She meant the children. "How do they decide?"

"I don't know. I don't know who's really in charge. Henriette is the director of the day nursery. Or that's what it used to be. Now she's in charge of deported children, by no choice of her own. She's Jewish, too. She just hands me the right one, all packed up, and tells me where to stop. I took one out in a milk crate, once. I've never seen any of the other workers who smuggle children out of the city, other than Willem. We . . ."

She didn't go on. Only looked out the window, swaying with the tram.

It was best not to talk about their differing opinions on Willem. Or Michel.

Isa knew who she'd seen Willem talking to, and what it meant. She could feel Michel's black notebook in her coat pocket, lying against her thigh.

Michel, who had lied. Who had used her. For money.

The thought brought the heat to her chest. A warm rush of scarlet-rose.

It was more than heat. It was a wound.

Truus was still staring out the window. Isa pulled the little black notebook from her coat, letting it open to a random page. The handwriting was perfect, a German engraving. She couldn't read most of it. Until she could. It was a list of paintings with dates. Prices and owners. She shut the notebook and slid it back into her pocket.

Buying and selling. He'd said he wanted the money to start a business. It was what he'd been raised to do. And he still had a 190,000-guilder check somewhere.

Isa didn't doubt that Michel would be able to make that check good.

Truus tightened her lock on Isa's arm again. "Are you all right?" she asked.

She wasn't. She was painting over her canvas, leaving the picture hidden underneath. She would strip it down and examine it later.

"I'll tell Henriette what happened," Truus said. "You don't . . . You just don't have to explain, that's all."

Isa shook her head. She would tell them that she was the one who blew their operation. She was the one who should be paying for her sins.

And when they'd saved the children they could, she would turn her attention to getting Joop and Truus out of Amsterdam. And out of the sights of a firing squad.

They got off the tram at Plantage and walked together, chins up, eyes up. Past the purple pansy pots. Past the flame-lit trees now bare and nearly burnt out. Past the cold, soot-smeared bricks of the ruined Records Office.

"Wait, Truus," Isa whispered. Around the corner she'd seen brown, Nazi brown—too much brown—gathered around the chained doors of the theater.

They waited, just beyond the cornerstones. And in another half minute, there was the tram, blocking the view of the soldiers. They hurried around the corner, down the sidewalk, and there were the steps of the teaching college. A good place, Truus said, where teachers could learn to teach, and not like a National Socialist.

They went up the stone steps, arm in arm. Two friends, arriving for an early class.

The tram pulled away and there was a truck across the street, waiting.

Inside, the receptionist at her desk took one glance at Truus and discovered some filing that needed doing. Across the hall, they could see a man in his office, an older man, gray hair wispy thin and balding, talking quietly on the telephone. He reminded Isa oddly of Van Meegeren. His movements as he wrote on a notepad were energetic, fast. And controlled. Serious and quiet.

Maybe not like Van Meegeren at all.

He lifted his gaze, saw them pass, and made a quick note.

They went straight through the building and out the back. Truus showed Isa a place where you could slide through the hedge, into the play yard of what had been a day nursery, a kindergarten. Only the children here weren't allowed to play outside anymore.

Isa could feel the heat rising, reddening. Reckless.

Inside the nursery was chaos. Children were crying, wanting attention. Needing to be fed, to be changed, in row after row of cribs and cots, many with three and four babies inside. There was a young girl trying to tend to them, obviously a prisoner. She was thin and dirty, but she was doing her best. Through the cribs and to one side was an office, a little crowd waiting on a woman who could only be Henriette.

She was heavy, grandmotherly, with a gold-link chain that held her sweater together, a bigger chain for her glasses. She was typing, frantic with concentration, and while she typed, she cried. Not a trickle, not a stream, but a dike that had burst, pouring down her neck to soak her blouse. Isa didn't know how she could see. The woman looked up.

"Thank God. Are there two of you?"

Truus looked at the people in the office, put a hand on Isa's arm, telling her to wait, and bent over the desk to speak to Henriette. Henriette replied low, quick, then went back to her manic typing. Her crying. Truus came back to Isa. "The money," she whispered.

Isa started digging the guilders from her bra, the last fifteen hundred, unworried about the stares.

"They got warned late last night," Truus whispered. "It could have been your woman with the kerchief, Isa, or something or somebody else. They don't know if the Gestapo knows everything, or only an inkling, but the children are being cleared out today. Henriette will probably be deported, too, now that they have no use for her. But she's not going to leave the children."

Truus had her mouth in a line, digging out Hildy's money to add to the stack. "They're calling everywhere for help to take the children out, but no one knows how to reach anyone, and Henriette is trying to match children with the money we've got, the families who can take them with the people we have to smuggle them out. Trying to figure out how many can be saved. She has a place for Hildy, and I told her about Sister Antonia. They're going to send a toddler to her, since toddlers are harder and they don't have to get as far."

One more child saved, Isa thought. Just because she had decided to knock on a closed door. She shook her head, wondering about leaving a Jewish child to be raised in the strange quiet of a convent that wasn't exactly a convent.

"At least it's life," Truus whispered, counting bills.

She was right.

Truus gave all the money to Henriette, and then they stood, tense, waiting. There were four women besides them. A girl with glasses, very young, who was helping Henriette with the lists; a blonde with two pins in her hair; a thin, hard-looking woman with threads of gray; and another girl, tall and skinny with a low-slung hat, who on closer inspection was actually a teenage boy. Forced labor, Isa thought. Everybody was hiding.

It was so hard not to go and comfort the children.

But it was so hard to choose which one to comfort. And which one to not.

Then a young woman burst into the nursery from the back hedge, sprinting up the steps. She was heavily pregnant. And ran like a track star. She dashed up to Henriette's desk, steadying her bulging stomach, and when she yanked up her blouse, there was a stuffed bag—not a baby—underneath. She unbuttoned the bag, pulled out a fistful of cards, handed them to Henriette, and sprinted back out the door again.

Ration cards.

Henriette waved over the girl with the glasses. She had a laundry basket in her arms. The girl got a card, tucked it in the basket, and handed it to the young man in the hat. He left without a word.

And there was a baby saved.

The man from the teaching college passed him on his way in—the one who had reminded and not reminded her of Van Meegeren—and as soon as he entered, Isa knew that he was the one orchestrating this. She could see it in the way Henriette and the girl with the glasses held their breath.

"Six," he said, pushing up his glasses.

Six more. Out of all these children. But with the baby who just left and Sister Antonia's toddler, it was two more than Isa had thought.

There was a scurry now, matching homes to babies, Henriette leaving the right children off the list. Typing. Weeping. Because every name she typed was a child not saved. Because every name she typed was a death sentence.

It was heartbreaking.

It was unbearable.

Three cribs away from the office door, there was a little girl, maybe one year old, with straight brown hair and blue eyes. She had nothing to play with, so she was playing with her toes, tears still wet on her cheeks while the other babies with her cried and pulled on the crib bars. The young girl who was a prisoner had a bag and a ration card in her hand, looking at the crib, evaluating the children, trying to decide.

She picked up the closest child and handed him to the girl with the glasses, who handed him to the blond girl with the pins. The blond girl took her ration card and money and left, her stride firm, determined, risking the child balanced openly on her hip. The little girl in the crib played with her toes.

And there was a child saved. And there was one not. As easy as that.

Isa breathed. She was burning. Bloodred.

Truus was gritting her teeth.

The woman with the threads of gray walked away with a newborn in a box. The man in charge from the teaching college had a child and a ration card in his arms. The girl with the glasses left with a baby in an overnight bag, and Truus was handed a sleeping boy in a shopping sack.

"I'll see you at the station," Truus whispered. "Third car. Be careful."

Isa nodded. Her words were choked. Truus hesitated, looking at her closely. Seeing something that gave her pause. But she had a baby in a bag, and so she shook her head once and hurried out the door.

Truus had been right to hesitate, Isa thought.

Because she was about to do something reckless.

Then the young girl who was a prisoner came and held out the leather bag. This child was smaller than Hildy, tiny, with a thick mop of dark and very curly hair. Sleeping with a ration card and a little stack of guilders at its feet.

Isa walked past the girl and the bag. She went to the third crib and picked up the child playing with her toes. The little girl didn't protest. Just wrapped her arms around Isa's neck. Isa grabbed a blanket to tuck around her, so she wouldn't freeze, then walked back and took the leather bag by its handles.

"But . . ." the girl began.

"Seven," Isa said. "It will be seven."

"Wait," said Henriette, scrambling with the cards on her desk. She picked up two and brought them, tucking them in the bag, zipping it halfway, so the baby would have air.

"I'll make a call about the little girl," she said.

"She can go to Hildy's family," Isa said.

Henriette craned her neck, like she was trying to hear.

"The little girl from before, who didn't get to go home. This child can go there."

Understanding dawned. Then Henriette went up on her toes, trying to see out the window. Watching for the soldiers. "Go," she said. "I'll make the call."

Isa tried to smile, to say goodbye. Henriette tried to smile back, but she was weeping.

Henriette, Isa thought, might be the bravest woman she'd ever known.

And then Isa was out the back door like a blaze, the children crying behind her.

Through the hedge in the backyard, the little girl squinting at the sun, careful with the baby in the bag, and into the teaching college, where the office was closed, dark beneath the door. Where the receptionist feigned disinterest. She was packing up her belongings. She was getting ready to run.

Isa stood at the window, watching for the tram. They were loading people into the trucks in front of the theater. Shouting and beating. The baby moved once in the bag but did not cry. The little girl clung while Isa shifted the weight on her feet. There was an officer, SS, instructing three soldiers, and they were looking at the other side of the street, toward the nursery. Isa measured her breath.

The tram came. And as soon as it blocked the view from the theater, she went out the door and down the steps, like Truus before her, only Isa turned left, walking back toward the Records Office. One glance behind, and she saw the tram pulling away, the four soldiers crossing the street.

The time to save the children was over.

Isa turned the corner.

Past the charcoal lines of limbs and the burnt-umber roof tiles. The lead-white shelves of an empty store. Eyes up. Chin up. With a child in her arms. With a baby in a bag.

Hot. Frosted. Painted over.

She was not invisible.

She was sweating before the next tram came. The little girl was sweet and docile, and so much heavier than Isa had thought. She needed a wash. And the bag had to be held so carefully, out and away from her bumping legs. Away from anything or anyone that might knock against it. Isa climbed gingerly aboard the tram.

It was full. The trams to Centraal Station were always full. There was no place to sit. She had to keep the bag level. She couldn't let it be pushed. Crushed. Have the baby start crying. She couldn't set it down. She had no free hand to steady herself. A man offered to put her bag on the rack above the seats and she shook her head. The tram swayed. The little girl laid a cheek on Isa's shoulder, and Isa leaned against the emergency door, trying to keep herself upright. Hoping the door didn't unlatch and tumble all three of them into the street.

The baby in the bag moved again but he didn't make a sound. Or not one that could be heard in the noisy crowd. He was sleeping like they'd given him something. She wondered if they had. The child in her arms was pulling at her kerchief, slipping it down, showing her hair.

She didn't have a hand to fix it.

A trickle of sweat ran down the back of her neck, underneath her coat.

A soldier got onto the train, riding in the front, the people moving back and away. His gaze ran over Isa, and ran over her again. And then he looked out the window.

The girl with red hair, Isa thought, was probably not expected to be carrying a baby.

Everyone stepped off the tram at the train station. A long, slow line. Isa waited until last, so as not to jostle her precious bag. The train station was designed much like the Stedelijk—Gothic stone and brick, niches and towers—with canals in front and the harbor behind. Boats drifted by with their sails up. Boats sped, belching steam. Trains spewed smoke over the rail bridges, and the sun hung pale in a hazy sky. The clock in the tower said 10:32 in the morning.

She needed to catch the eleven o'clock train to Amersfoort.

There were German guards everywhere. She walked past two at the front entrance—blending, fading into the crowd that filed through the doors—and there was another guard stationed at the back of the main lobby. This one gave her a second look, a long one with her kerchief slipped down. But Isa smiled at him, distractedly, playing with the little girl, nuzzling and whispering to her while they became a part of the background. The soldier's stance eased. He noticed someone else. He never looked twice at her bag.

Isa checked the boards. She had to go down the steps and up again to the center platform, coming out beneath the train shed, a beautifully designed half-barreled ceiling of iron and frosted glass. She picked up speed. The platforms here were not as crowded, and she threaded her way in and around the bodies, eyes up and looking for platform 6.

Faster. Faster, her back, her arms and neck aching so badly it was difficult to think of anything else. Difficult to pay attention, and she nearly walked over a woman coming down the platform from the opposite direction. A woman with a large hat half-covering her face, a brown plaid coat swinging at her knees. Their gazes locked, a thick line of perspective drawn from one set of eyes to the other.

And then they both looked away, Isa hoisting the now squirming child, looking at the sign showing destinations on the platform. But she was watching the woman in the wide-brimmed hat walk to the next platform, a small package in her hand, waiting for her train. The hair framing one cheek was black, soft, and dull as the coal smoke.

Then Isa realized that her train had arrived early. That the train in front of her was hers. Because Truus was sitting in the last seat of the third car, looking at the shopping sack in her lap.

Isa stepped up into the car, careful with her cargo. It was a third-class car, the door opening directly into the compartment, lined with high luggage racks and two rows of wooden benches with an aisle in between. Four or five people sat scattered among the seats. She saw

Truus see the child in her arms. See the bag in her hand. Watched her blue eyes widen before she looked away, staring out the window, absentmindedly patting her shopping sack.

Isa stopped two rows in front of Truus, laid the bag gently on the bench, and dropped down beside it. The little girl instantly pushed up and stood in her lap, reaching for the kerchief. Isa moved her hand and kissed her head.

The relief in Isa's arms and shoulders was its own kind of pain.

She settled the little girl back down and unzipped the bag just a little, to check on the unnaturally quiet baby. He was breathing. She zipped the bag halfway, fixed her kerchief, and started wiggling her fingers, so the child would play with those, using her other hand to comb through the head of soft brown tangles.

She didn't have the bribe money for this seventh child.

The older woman with the box from Henriette's office stepped onto the train, but her box had been exchanged for a pram with wooden wheels. The blonde with two pins sat a few rows ahead and across the aisle, her baby perched in her lap.

The time on the station clock said 10:46.

There was a commotion of talk on the platform, a little rise in the ambient noise. But it wasn't until she heard the soft gasp from Truus that Isa lifted her gaze to the window glass. Stared out onto the crowding platform.

And Isa understood, in the space of a heartbeat, that she'd gotten everything wrong. All of it wrong. About Willem's arrest and the leak. About Michel, using her for money and nothing more.

That she had been wrong about un-becoming. Wrong about beauty.

And right about the ugliness of the world.

A group of three Nazis had come onto the platform from the

stairs—two uniforms, one suit—and they had a prisoner with them. Big and blond, with puffed eyes and bloody lips, chalky skin smudged with olive and purple-black and blue. His wrists were handcuffed in front of him, and the four fingers of his left hand were obviously broken. Swollen. Disjointed and discolored.

Worse than a jail cell.

Willem had most certainly been arrested. His slitted eyes watched only the ground.

Gurlitt strode in front of him, smug behind his glasses, strangely eager in his hat and tailored suit. And on Willem's right side was Franz, Michel's brother, the boy-officer, the Jew hunter, impatient, arrogant, the insignia of the SS on his collar. But it was the soldier on the left who held tight to Willem's injured arm, straight and square-shouldered and repugnant in brown, chuckling at a comment whispered low in Willem's ear. Willem's shoulders drooped. And the smiling Nazi raised his eyes to the train car.

Two cold pieces of murky brown glass.

28

ISA SHARED A long look with Michel as he passed, pulling Willem roughly to the platform directly opposite. Willem hissed in pain.

At first, she'd thought Michel was trying to blackmail her. Then she'd thought she'd found a friend. Or maybe more. Then she thought she'd been used for money. A lot of money.

When Truus had been right all along. Willem had been right all along.

Nazis who will make you collaborate. Nazis who will pretend to be your friend.

Isn't that exactly what a Nazi would do, to gain someone's trust?

There had been no leak. Michel was the leak. And what she had been used for was to bring down a very effective cell of the Resistance.

Had she seen what she wanted to see? Been so ready to believe?

How could she have been so fooled by a fake?

And he had almost made her believe in beauty again.

And now Willem was arrested, and Willem had broken, and told them too much. Because they were here, at this train car full of Jewish children. And she was here, with her red hair underneath her kerchief. And what did it matter to them if she really was the girl with red hair or not? A lack of truth wouldn't lessen the honor of catching the prize.

And there was more than one kind of prize.

Isa held tight to the child in her lap, one hand on the leather bag.

She was frosted and fractured. A red wound and a flame.

She was vermilion to the very marrow of her bones.

Damn these Nazis.

Her father had chosen. And now so would she.

Isa picked up the little girl and the baby in the bag. Truus had tears streaking the dirt on her cheeks.

"Take her for a minute, would you?" Isa asked, putting the child in Truus's lap before she had a chance to say no. The little girl immediately scrambled to pull upward, keeping Truus's hands full, allowing Isa to snatch away her purse.

"Stop!" Truus whispered. "Isa!"

But Isa had already gone back down the aisle, past the scattered passengers whose attention was riveted by the three Nazis and their prisoner.

"Could you look after this for me?" she asked the woman with the pram. The woman was surprised. Alarmed. But she took the leather bag. Gently. She knew what it was.

Isa walked up the aisle of the train and pulled off her kerchief. Her hair was mostly down, anyway. Out of any pins she'd managed to get in it. And now the gun was out of Truus's purse and in the pocket of her coat, the purse tossed on a seat with her kerchief. Isa stepped down and out of the train car.

And they didn't see her coming. Not until the last second. Not until she had walked up to Gurlitt and pushed the barrel of the gun—still in her coat—straight into the soft, tailored seam of his suit jacket.

"Hello," she said.

Gurlitt froze, trying and failing to look over his shoulder, heavy eyes opening wide behind the glasses. Franz took a step, hand on his pistol, but Gurlitt raised a palm, forestalling whatever he was going to do. She saw when Franz recognized her. Open-mouthed. Flushed. And a little terrified. He took a step back, holding hard to Willem's good arm. Willem was slumped over his handcuffs, bloody and broken and the picture of defeat. But one glance came from beneath his swollen lids, and Isa saw awareness. Energy.

And then she had to look at Michel, standing cool and quiet, waiting for her next move. She tilted her head, beckoning him forward. He left Willem with Franz and came, hands neat behind his back.

"Shall we talk?" Isa asked. Michel translated, walking with them as Gurlitt allowed himself to be moved a few feet down the platform, a safer distance from Franz. The train on their side had not arrived, only a short drop onto the graveled track behind them. Franz was watching her, frightened, and possibly fascinated, by the girl with red hair. She would try to keep it that way.

It would distract him from the children in the train car.

Isa kept the gun in Gurlitt's back, discreet with her coat, like she was giving him a hug from the wrong direction. They were nearly the same height. She looked over his shoulder at Michel.

"How nice to see you again, Herr Gurlitt," Isa said. Michel began translating while she spoke. "I'm sorry it's not under better circumstances. But your prisoner is getting on the train with me, and I need you to tell his guards to let that happen."

She glanced up at the clock. It was 10:52.

Michel listened then said, "Herr Gurlitt would like to know why he would allow this, when he has the girl with red hair right here? And we are both getting on that train with you."

Her gaze cut to Michel at that last sentence, a sentence she was certain Gurlitt did not say. "Tell Herr Gurlitt he will allow the prisoner onto the train, and you and your brother will stay back. If he does not, I will send a letter informing his Führer that the paintings purchased for his new museum are forgeries. And why would I want you on that train?"

Michel didn't answer her. He translated, listening to Gurlitt talk, but his eyes were on hers. He said, "Gurlitt says his Führer will not care about the Rembrandt, a small purchase in a small auction house in the backwater of Europe."

"Ask him if his Führer will care about the Vermeer?"

This pleased Michel, Isa could see it at the edge of his mouth. Which she did not understand. It did not please Gurlitt.

"Tell him that I know *Woman with a Wine Glass* is a forgery. That it was signed in the same way the Rembrandt was signed, and if he wants to explain to Hitler that he paid one-point-six million guilders for a fake painting, then please be sure and not let me or the prisoner on the train."

Michel translated, and now Gurlitt squirmed. Isa pushed the gun more firmly into his back. He said something short.

"He says this is a lie." But then Michel spoke to Gurlitt, a quick string of words, and turned to Isa. "I've told him that I had doubts myself, and that it might be best to have the paint scientifically tested, and I am getting on that train with you whether you say so or not."

Gurlitt replied, and Isa could see Franz, absorbed, his grip on Willem loosening. Willem was watching, too, alert beneath his puffy lids. She wondered if the train car behind her had faces to the glass.

"Herr Gurlitt says the Führer will not believe such a letter from a stranger and that he has nothing to fear from you."

"Tell him the letter is not addressed to Hitler. Tell him it's addressed to Hofer."

And there it was again. That pleased look. Michel translated quickly. And this was the threat that shook Gurlitt. He almost went limp beneath her gripping hand.

"Willem and I are working together," Michel said in Dutch, no longer worrying about Gurlitt. "We're going to try to get on the train, but one of us is going to get killed unless you give me your gun."

Isa felt her mouth fall open. How gullible did he think she was?

Gurlitt's eyes had darted to Michel. He'd understood "Willem."

Isa said, "Tell Gurlitt that he will instruct his guard to let the prisoner on the train. And he will misdirect any pursuit that might come. That if one of us is caught, the letter will be sent."

Michel told him and then said in fast Dutch, "My brother has no idea about the children. He is ambitious and thinks these ten executions are his opportunity for fame and promotion. He hates me, and he detests Willem. He will kill one or both of us before he lets us on that train, and I am getting on that train. I need the gun."

She shook her head. "You can tell Gurlitt that he can be assured the letter to Hofer will be sent because I, unlike others here, am not a liar."

Michel's jaw clenched. Gurlitt looked back and forth between them, Franz watching his brother with a dawning suspicion. And when Isa stole a glance, Willem gave her an almost imperceptible nod of his head.

She had no idea what that meant. Michel took a step forward. "Did you look at the notebook? Do you know what it is for?"

She shook her head again. Why would he be bringing up a list of clients right now?

"Look at me, Sofonisba, and tell me what you believe is real."

She wouldn't look. She gazed pointedly at Franz. Gurlitt moved, and she poked him with the gun barrel. Franz was slack-jawed. Michel came a little closer.

"You knew what was real the day you brought home Hildy. Tell me how you knew that you could trust me that day."

But she hadn't known. That was the point. She hadn't been sure at all. She'd only felt it.

Ah, but beauty is not a thing one sees, she heard her father's voice say, with his slippers and his cigarettes and satin. *Beauty is a thing to be felt . . .*

She looked up at Michel. He looked back.

And . . . damn him. Damn, damn, damn him.

Why was he able to make her believe?

She sighed. She didn't know why anyone did anything in this ugly world anymore. Except for one thing.

She had just understood the purpose of Michel's black notebook.

Gurlitt was talking, Franz was talking, and Isa hadn't been paying attention. There was a train station in motion around them. People passing. Staring. Truus's face pressed against the window. A sharp, shrill whistle and a release of steam. Isa looked at the clock over Willem's head. It was 10:55.

Her gaze dropped, and Willem inclined his battered head a fraction of an inch toward Michel. Isa blinked and nodded. Just a little. Franz and Gurlitt were squabbling back and forth across the platform divide.

"Quiet!" she commanded. Neither of them needed a translation. They quieted. She looked at Michel. "Ask Herr Gurlitt if he's ready to comply."

"He's ready," Michel said, without asking. He wasn't sure what she was going to do.

Neither was she.

"Then tell him we are walking to the prisoner. That he will speak to his guard and I will make an exchange."

They began an awkward shuffle toward Willem and Franz, Isa's coat pocket held tight against Gurlitt's back. Gurlitt threw a word at her. Michel didn't bother to translate.

He said, "When we get there, give me the gun and take Willem to the train. I will keep Franz occupied and make sure his attention is focused elsewhere."

He'd said it loud enough to be certain Willem would hear. But Franz had heard his name. His brows drew down, exactly like his brother's. Which was disconcerting.

And what, Isa wondered, would Franz the Jew Hunter—so fully focused on the glory that executing Willem and catching the girl with red hair would bring—do if he actually stopped to consider the train in front of him? Full of Jewish children and Resistance and even the killer of Klaus? All he had to do was notice the number of babies. To start asking for identity cards.

They stopped in front of Willem. She could see Franz itching for his pistol, waiting for an order from Gurlitt. Isa reached out and pulled Michel roughly by the arm, close, as if she was covering them both with the gun. A nudge, and Gurlitt started giving Franz his instructions, while Michel's hand came slowly, gently around her back to find the pocket of her coat.

His hand slid over hers. Warm.

And she let him take the gun.

She could almost hear Truus's frustration. She kept two fingers pointing in her pocket, pushing against Gurlitt's back. Like a child playing robbers.

The whole train car must have just seen what happened. And

since it was mostly full of Resistance workers, she wasn't sure whether Michel was about to be helped or attacked.

Gurlitt was still talking. He was always talking. Franz reluctantly got the key and unlocked Willem's handcuffs, arguing while he did it. Almost whining. Darting fearful looks at Isa. Michel spoke, and Franz snapped back. Gurlitt snapped at both of them.

Isa took some cautious steps, fingers pointing in her pocket, and said, "Come on, Willem."

He moved. But Franz didn't want to let him go. Gurlitt spoke again, sharp, and Willem jerked his good arm free, wincing. The train whistle blew. It was 10:57.

And Isa watched Franz frown as Willem walked away, mouth pressed into a sullen line. A little boy angry. Angry, perhaps, because he was afraid of being seen as small. Franz balled a fist and yelled at Michel. Accusing. Michel replied, cool to his brother's hot, hands held neatly behind his back.

Only now, one of his hands held a gun.

Isa followed Willem, moving backward toward the train. Franz came forward, gesturing, yelling, arguing with Michel while Gurlitt shouted "Nein! Nein!" over and over again.

Herr Gurlitt really was afraid of facing the consequences of that letter.

While Franz, Isa thought, after losing a prisoner and the girl with red hair, seemed to be more afraid of facing ridicule.

The brothers' argument was drawing a small crowd on the platform, mothers, travelers, the woman with the package and the wide-brimmed hat. One of the babies on the train cried. Michel took a step back, and another, as if pushed by his brother's onslaught.

Isa stepped into the train car without turning, fingers still pretending, Willem beside her at the doorway, his feet on the platform, waiting for Michel. A steam cloud burst from the engine. It was 10:58.

And then Franz looked at Isa, and his mouth opened.

Her fingers must not have been pretending very well. Because Franz had just realized she didn't actually have a gun.

He looked at Gurlitt, who shook his head. At Michel, impassive, and halfway to the train.

"Resistance!" Franz yelled, looking around for someone—soldiers, police, anyone. "Resistance!" And he pointed to the train, as if the gathered crowd should help with the arrest. For once, there didn't seem to be a collaborator in sight.

Gurlitt told him to stop, but he didn't listen.

"Resistance!" Franz shouted. "Das Mädchen mit den roten Haaren!"

The girl with red hair.

The people didn't react.

Franz flung up his arms. He was losing a promotion and his pride.

"Homosexuell!" he yelled, the word so close to the Dutch that Isa knew exactly what he was saying. "Lassen Sie den Homosexuellen nicht entkommen!"

Homosexuell.

Don't let the homosexual escape.

And he'd been pointing at Willem.

And everything Isa had never understood about Willem fell suddenly, naturally into place. It wasn't Arondeus who had been in love with Willem. Willem had been in love with Arondeus.

Willem stood stoic on the platform, motionless at the open door, holding his broken hand. Michel was only steps from the train, while Gurlitt had retreated, cringing behind a bench. The warning whistle sounded. The chug of the engine. Franz searched the crowd, looking for a sign of agreement. For condemnation. For anything. No one moved.

Only Franz, Isa thought, was the one feeling condemned.

His mouth clamped down. Isa blinked.

And in the split second of darkness that flashed behind her eyes, Franz had drawn his gun and pointed it at Willem.

And Michel had his gun pointed at Franz.

There was an almost instantaneous emptying of the platform, a scramble behind Isa in the train. People moving for distance. For cover. Bending below the levels of the windows to move babies to the safety of the floor.

Franz looked surprised at the gun in Michel's hand. And then unsurprised. And then betrayed. And angry. Small. He swung his arm around, and now the gun was pointing at Michel.

They stood there, brothers in the same uniform. But underneath, they were two very different colors.

Isa heard the second chug of the engine. The train lurched once and she stumbled, grabbing the side of the open double door. She'd forgotten about safety. She'd forgotten to breathe. She wasn't capable of looking anywhere else.

And then Michel's head gave a little shake, brows down. He released the hammer and lowered the gun. Franz called out, shouted, following his brother's progress with the barrel of the pistol as Michel walked slowly to the train, gun slipping back into his pocket. He stepped into the doorway, turned, and extended a hand to Willem. Willem took it.

Franz tensed. His mouth set in a determined line.

"Stop!" Isa cried.

Willem spun. Took a step to the left. And Franz fired.

Once.

And Willem and Michel both fell backward onto the floor of the train.

Truus screamed. Someone else screamed, and Isa was a pop of orange shock. And when she raised her head, she found the gun aimed at her.

Franz looked her in the eye. Stunned. Panicky. His lips pressed down into a line.

He was going to kill the girl with red hair. And she was going to die on the same day as her father.

Isa stepped back. She put out a hand.

And the shot fired.

Once.

Twice.

Isa clutched at the buttons of her dress.

And Franz fell face-first to the platform.

Now the screams were a chorus. The train wheels began to turn, and Isa was looking down at her chest, her stomach, the palm of her hand. But she was whole, un-shot. And the woman with the wide-brimmed hat was tucking a gun back into the pocket of her brown plaid coat.

The woman walked away, calm, package still beneath her arm. Past Gurlitt, huddling behind his bench, past Franz, unmoving in a small sea of flowing blood. Isa's train picked up speed, keeping up with the woman's pace, and then the train on the next track came in like a hurricane of hot metal and squealing brakes. The hat flew off the woman's head like a kite.

She was younger without the hat, hair dark and dull like it had been rubbed with coal. The young woman looked up and met Isa's gaze. She had a sprinkle of freckles on her nose. But now Isa could see the hair growing out from her scalp, a bright stripe of color on either side of her neat part.

The young woman's hair was red.

And so was the puddle spreading beneath Isa's shoes.

Because Willem had a hole in him.

And so did Michel.

29

ISA DROPPED TO her knees. Truus was there, trying to help Willem roll off Michel without the use of his broken hand. He was shot straight through his upper shoulder, a neat hole through his shirt in the front and back, oozing blood. Isa helped sit him up, Truus muttering and cursing and kissing Willem's cheek.

The same kind of kiss she would have given Isa.

Isa looked down and found Michel blinking up at her, his face an odd shade, as if his skin had acquired an underlayment of ivory. He had a hole in the shoulder of his jacket, and there was blood all over him, though some of it looked as if it might belong to Willem.

Isa yanked off her coat, threw it onto the nearest seat, and got Michel upright. He cried out when she did it, and then she was opening his jacket as fast as she could manage the buttons. He was shot like Willem—almost exactly like Willem—a hole through the upper left shoulder, front and back. With Willem standing on the ground and Michel on the train, the bullet had gone right through both of them, and in nearly the same place.

"Get it off," Michel said. Meaning his jacket. "Take it off me."

She slid his left arm out as gently as she could, but he was hissing, sweating. She unbuttoned his shirt, tearing some away in her hurry, pulling the cloth gingerly away from the wound.

Such a perfectly round hole, front and back, pulsing blood.

She found the scarf she'd used as a kerchief and pressed it to the bleeding in the front, wadded up his Nazi brown coat and stuffed it behind him, between the wound and the wooden wall of the seat compartment. Then she hiked up her skirt and sat on him, straddling his knees, pushing back as hard as she could, trying to get pressure on both the wounds.

The woman with the pram came and shut the train doors. Isa hadn't even noticed the roar and blow of the wind, the city racing by just outside, until it was gone. There was still a baby crying somewhere, and their conductor had not come. The people not working for the Resistance seemed to have all moved to the next car.

Isa didn't blame them. Blood was soaking through her fingers. There was blood all over the floor. When Michel raised his head, he was so pale, his eyes were almost a different color. Raw sienna, tinted dark.

"You gave me the gun," he said.

"And you didn't use it properly," she replied, instantly regretting it.

But he'd almost smiled. Before he grimaced. "Do you have to push so hard?"

"Do you have to keep bleeding?"

She wanted to say she was glad he was alive. That she was glad she was alive. That she understood now, why he'd wanted the money. But she was like an overused palette, so speckled with shades and hues that it was impossible to focus on just one color.

Willem and Truus were on the other side of the aisle, a mirror of Isa and Michel, Truus holding the old farmer's jacket over Willem's wound, cushioning his broken fingers with her coat.

Isa looked down. "You didn't leave," she whispered. "You went to get Willem."

"I told Gurlitt the girl with red hair was raising money for the

Resistance with art." His eyes were closed again, breath coming hard, fist clenched against pain. "I said there was a shipment going out that could be confiscated . . ." He winced. "A trainload of art . . . he could get his hands on for free, and that Willem knew where to find it . . ."

Gurlitt would have jumped at that. No wonder he'd been so eager. A fish that had never understood about hooks.

And it had kept Willem alive. And well enough to walk and talk.

"Willem took us to a train car with a conductor he knew could be bribed . . ."

Where they'd all been sitting, smuggling babies.

"We were just going to . . . jump on, when the train went . . ."

And one of them would have been killed, like he'd said on the platform. Or both.

Isa held on to the back of Michel's neck, pushing on the wound. The scarf wasn't enough. It was soaked. When he spoke again, his voice came low beneath the rattle of the train.

He said, "I heard . . . two more."

Isa knew what he'd heard. "She shot your brother," she whispered. "Who did?"

"I think it was her. The girl with red hair."

Michel reached up and touched a piece of hair hanging loose on her shoulder. "Not you?"

"No. Not me."

"Is he dead?"

She hesitated. "I think he is."

She let him rest his forehead on her chest, the prickle of clipped hair against one hand, the flow of his blood on the other, head underneath her chin. There was another baby crying now. Isa could see the blond girl with the pins near the back, bent over, maybe changing a diaper, while the girl with the glasses—from Henriette's office—was bouncing a child on each hip. Isa hadn't even known the girl with the glasses was on the train.

Michel said, "Did Willem get shot?"

"No worse than you," Willem replied. Isa hadn't realized he could hear.

"Where is Hildy?" Michel asked.

"She's safe." And without a family to take her. Because Isa had given her family to the seventh little girl.

"And Truus is . . ."

"She's here on the train. She's safe, too."

"I hear . . . babies . . ." Michel's question trailed off. His head was loose against her chest, moving with the rhythm of the tracks. She exchanged a quick glance with Truus. Truus had a trail of blood to her elbow, but Willem's bleeding had slowed. Michel's had not. Isa leaned back and tapped his cheek, making his eyes open.

"We got the last ones out," she said, answering his question, trying to keep him awake. He blinked, bleary. "Nine more children. Six of them are here now. But the woman in the kerchief wasn't Resistance. I gave her the money and I ruined everything."

Michel shook his head. Swaying and slow. "She was an informer for the Gestapo. But . . . they were already going to take the children today. They were talking about it . . . at headquarters. But getting the network . . . would have been a feather in my brother's cap . . ."

She held his head, trying to keep it still.

"I should have told you about . . ." His voice was sinking to a murmur. "I should have said . . . about the money . . ."

"Michel," Isa whispered. "I know what the notebook is for."

But his eyes had fallen closed, and this time when she tapped his cheek, he didn't open them.

And Isa felt the frost of her fear, prickling. She hadn't said what she needed to. Asked what she wanted to. She hadn't even told him about her father. And then the woman with the pram came through the connecting door of the train car, a man with a grizzled beard behind her. She looked triumphant.

"Not a doctor," she announced. "Better. A medic. From the last war!"

The old man came to see what he was up against. Then he said, "Find me some bandages."

He looked beneath Isa's soaked scarf, told her to keep the pressure on, and went to work on Willem. The woman with the pram had a vise grip, holding Willem's lower arm while the medic set the fingers. Isa shuddered to hear it. Truus fled to the back of the train. But Willem didn't make a sound, the pain on his face patient, and terrible, because now Isa could see that somewhere inside himself, Willem thought he deserved that pain. Because there was something wrong with him.

When there was nothing wrong with him.

She was sure he'd stepped in front of Michel on purpose.

The girl with the glasses had two baby blankets that could be spared and ripped them into strips, managing this feat with a penknife and her teeth. The grizzled medic splinted each of Willem's fingers with a piece of broken pencil, wrapping his hand and then the shoulder. He must have known what the fingers and the bruises meant. He moved on to Michel, examining him front and back, poking and prodding where the bleeding had finally slowed. Michel woke up for this, groaning.

"Hush," the medic said. "You fellows are lucky not to have a bullet left in you."

And then the compartment door opened, and the conductor came in, surveying the children and the bloody mess they'd made of his train car. Truus ran forward, and they had a consultation. And when the man left, Truus came back down the aisle with a face as red as the stains on her blouse. Isa went to her. The blonde with the pins came to hear what was happening, her baby on her hip, the girl with the glasses jiggling Isa's little girl. The woman with the pram had the four little babies lined up on a bench in their bags. She leaned in, and they all put their heads together.

"The louse says a shooting on his train is going to cost us," Truus hissed. "And I don't dare tell him this is the last time or he'll turn us in for the bounty as soon as we pay."

"How much does he want?" the blonde breathed.

"Two hundred each," said Truus. "And that includes the two wounded."

Sixteen hundred guilders.

The woman with the pram gasped.

"He says we have ten minutes. Before we hit Amersfoort."

The girl with the glasses crossed her arms. "So, what have we got?"

"We should have two hundred and thirty each," Truus said. "Henriette doled out the extra, for the families . . ."

"I've only got a hundred and fifteen each," Isa said. Because Isa had taken an extra child. "We're . . ." She put a quick finger to her temple, doing the math. "We're four hundred and fifty guilders short. Will he count it?"

"Oh, yes," Truus replied. "He counts."

"And what will he do when we don't have it?" Isa asked.

"I don't know. We've never tried him."

A man who took bribes not to turn children over to the Nazis did not have a character Isa wanted to test.

"Empty your purses," said the girl with the glasses. "Find everything you can."

They gathered—pockets emptied, bags checked, and even the pram—anything, everywhere, giving it all to Truus. Isa turned out the pockets of her dress, though she knew there was no money there. She even turned her back and checked her bra. Truus was adding, counting. Four from the woman with the pram and seven from the blonde. These were the train tickets home, Isa thought. They went into the pile.

Willem, being straight from prison, had nothing. The girl with the glasses had two guilders to her name and was trying to mind all the babies at once. And then Isa saw the bloody Nazi jacket on the floor.

"Michel, quick," she said, searching around the gun still inside his sticky pocket. "Do you have any money?"

His lids were heavy, eyes closed. But the edge of his mouth turned up. "Are you really asking me that?"

It was true. Between the two of them, they could lose money by the bucketloads.

She'd had so much more yesterday than she had today.

The blonde with the pins searched frantically beneath the seats. The woman with the pram gave the gun back to Truus and used Michel's jacket to vigorously wipe blood from the floor. As if a cleaning might get them a discount. She'd never even asked how a Nazi had come to be fighting on the side of the angels. None of them had. Isa caught Truus's eye, and Truus shook her head.

To get this far and lose to a greedy train conductor was infuriating. The lucky few, whose names Henriette hadn't typed, the last children to be saved, caught and sentenced to death because of a few guilders. It was maddening. Heartbreaking. It brought tears to her eyes.

Isa looked down at her hands. She was vermilion beneath her fingernails.

She grabbed the coat she'd thrown over the seat and dug for a handkerchief. The elusive handkerchief. It was confounding how she could never find her handkerchief. And then she checked the inside pocket.

And came out with a wad of bills.

The Dürers. Isa jumped to her feet and shouted, "The Dürers!"

"What?" said Truus. But Michel was smiling, his eyes closed.

Isa scrambled down the aisle, holding out a fistful of cash. Truus's blue eyes widened. They went soft like a summer sky. She grabbed the money and counted.

It was four hundred, Isa knew it was. Plus twenty-five for her ill-fated modeling.

Truus finished counting and counted again. She stared at the money in her lap, stricken.

"Twelve guilders! We're twelve guilders short!"

And Isa looked over her shoulder.

The medic she'd nearly forgotten was sitting in the corner, waving a ten note. And when Truus came to get it, he dropped two one-guilder coins into her palm. She kissed the grizzled man on the cheek.

Truus paid the conductor, waiting while he meticulously counted. Whistling. Isa wanted to spit on him. And on his way through the car, as the train went around a bend, Isa bumped him hard and made him drop—and then pick up—the scattered money. Every bill of it.

Only a little reckless. And satisfying.

The train slowed and squealed into Amersfoort, a much quieter place than Centraal Station. Gurlitt must have been very afraid of his Führer—or Hofer—because, true to their bargain, there were no Nazis waiting for them, the guard on the platform bored and indifferent. The medic, the woman with the pram, the girl with the glasses, and the blonde all got off with the three children they had rescued.

And then they were gone. Disappeared. Melted away, like a scraped canvas whose picture was lost.

Isa had never even known their names.

Truus said this wasn't their stop.

The whistle blew and the train picked up steam, speeding out into the flats, the long, wide landscape where the cerulean of the sky met the wheat gold of the field grasses. Where the windmills creaked at the mirroring edges of quiet canals. They had the train car to themselves. Isa opened the window and tossed out Michel's jacket and hat—Nazi brown, black and red, bloodstained. Scattered and gone.

He didn't even know she'd done it. He was floating, in and out, groaning softly every now and again with the bumps of the train. The medic had said not to worry. That he'd lost blood, that was all. His body would make more. To clean the wounds as soon as they could. The makeshift bandage was bloody. His undershirt was bloody. The freckles she could see scattered on his shoulders stood out unnaturally on his waxy skin. Isa folded up her coat and made a pillow for his head.

And she was frosted. Fractured. A web of open cracks.

Truus was watching her.

Isa went across the aisle to pick up the baby from the leather bag, a tiny boy who'd finally woken. Truus's baby had gone back to sleep in his shopping sack, Isa's seventh child crawling up and down and all over Truus's lap. Isa sat on the wooden bench beside her, settling the baby in her arms, rocking with the rhythm of the train. Truus, she could see, had something to say.

"Willem says that Michel stayed with him the whole time, even when they were breaking his hand," Truus began.

Isa winced.

"He said Michel kept prompting him to say the right things, so he could feed the interrogators what they wanted, which was information about the girl with red hair. They were making things up, of course, but it spared him the worst. It saved him."

Isa looked at Willem, two rows away, propped upright against the train wall, leaning to his good side against the bench. His bruised and swollen eyes were closed, the bandaged arm cradled. If Michel hadn't done what he did, Willem would have been executed. Taken to the dunes like Arondeus. Or hanged in public with nine others. She glanced back at her friend. It was unusual for Truus to admit when she'd been wrong.

"You know, Willem knew Michel was a German soldier from the beginning," Truus said, grappling with the curiosity of the little girl.

Isa shook her head.

"Something about polished boots and a military haircut. Even when we found out about the brother, he was certain Michel could be trusted. It's disgusting, how often Willem is right." She said it fondly. "He thinks your woman in a kerchief must have been following us for a long time. That she must have been a regular informant with pay. That she's what . . . happened to Greta. Joop and I were next, but she caught Willem out and in the act—setting fire to a boat in the Herengracht, one of the names Michel had given him—so they got him first. That woman must have thought she won the lottery when she saw your hair . . ."

The memory of handing that woman money made Isa's skin crawl. She pulled the blanket tighter around the baby and said, "So why was he talking to her?"

"Talking to who?"

"Why was Willem talking to the woman in the kerchief?"

"What? No, he wasn't. When?"

"The day I was at the café with Michel. When Willem blew up . . ." Isa waved a hand.

Truus shook her messy hair. "Are you sure that wasn't Joop? Joop got conscripted for labor, you know, so he's been hiding for over a year now, wearing dresses so he won't be picked up on the street. He grew out his hair and pins it up. Joop probably does wear a kerchief, now that I think of it, when he hasn't had time to do his hair."

Isa tried to picture the scene from behind the rose pots. Tried to imagine Joop Janson not having time to do his hair. Maybe the kerchief on Kalverstraat that day hadn't even been green and gold. Isa sighed. "Is Joop all right?"

"He left the city as soon as Mrs. Breem got the call."

Mrs. Breem. With her illegal newspaper. Her telephone, passing messages to an empty house next door. And with such an excellent rear view of the Gallery De Smit. Had Mrs. Breem, Isa wondered, ever seen a Nazi go back and forth down the gully? Had the woman in the kerchief ever seen? Could Michel's repellent uniform have actually bought them time before a Gestapo raid? Or had the woman in the kerchief never actually pinpointed her address, and that's why the Gestapo went door to door?

She'd probably never know. Except for how close they'd all come.

There had been so many different ways to die.

And yet, they hadn't.

"What I really want to say is that we brought a lot of trouble to you by coming to the gallery, and . . . oh, Isaatje, I just really am sorry. About all of it."

Isa rocked the baby, a little peach with fuzz for hair, surprised again by the sting of sudden tears. She knew when Truus meant what she said. She knew what Truus meant by "all of it."

But Isa wasn't ready to strip down the portrait of her father. For now, it was painted over.

She stole a look at the two wounded, at the field and sky passing on the other side of a bullet hole. Truus holding out a hand for the seventh child to play with and pat. She lowered her voice. "I wish you could have told me. About Willem."

"I know. And I said so more than once. But it was Willem's decision. And, Isaatje . . ." Truus hesitated, glancing once at Willem's still form. "You've lived in your gallery a long time. I think you didn't realize, maybe, how hard it was at school if someone suspected, if the thought even crossed their minds. Remember when Willem asked you to the cinema?"

She did. She'd been horrified. Fourteen years old and more dramatic than Moshe. And Willem had asked her to the Corso, where she and Truus had not been welcome since *Blonde Venus*.

"He was looking for a friend. And he knew what kind of people were at the gallery. He thought you would help . . ."

And she'd misunderstood. And rejected him. Thoroughly.

"Pretending to be with me made everything all right," Truus said. "Kept his family happy. But things were never going to work that way for Willem. And he's such a do-the-right-thing rule follower. And then, when he finally did allow himself . . . well, Arondeus was a tragedy, wasn't it?"

It had been.

"Willem was the lookout. He thought he should have seen, prevented them from getting caught. But they were betrayed, Isa, and the only reason Willem wasn't shot was because Arondeus didn't give him up."

And so Arondeus died. And Willem didn't.

Damn the Nazis. Damn them straight into the mouth of Botticelli's Satan.

Isa held the baby tight.

"His family found out about Arondeus, you know. They won't have anything to do with him. So you can see why Willem might hesitate. To say anything . . ."

She could.

The train leaned around a curve, and Michel tried to move. Made one soft, sharp cry without opening his eyes.

"They'll get him out to Switzerland now," Truus said. "Willem was already working on it. I hope they'll have him out of the country before the end of the week. In the meantime, the farm is safe."

Isa watched the baby in her arms. Truus was giving her the side-eye. Looking for a reaction. Isa wasn't going to give her one.

Because she was an overused palette.

A pinwheel spinning. A twisting maze of darkest purple.

Because she hadn't decided yet. How she would let go.

"Are you all right, Isaatje?" Truus asked.

Isa didn't answer. Because she wasn't.

When the train squealed its way into Apeldoorn, Truus left Isa in charge while she went to the station to find out what was happening. The train would wait for an hour, she said.

It was dangerous, sitting alone on the empty train with a smuggled child in her lap. Conspicuous. Almost forgivable to think that a traveler might step into a train car, see an imperfectly cleaned floor, two men with bullet holes, and two babies stored in bags, and decide to call a policeman.

But Truus came back quickly. She had two coats over her arm.

"Stolen from the cloakroom," she whispered. "Walked right past the guard and he practically yawned. And I made a telephone call. There will be a wagon in half an hour, and they are going to take both of the little ones, and Hildy's family is still coming, so I guess they'll just be taking this one instead."

Isa looked at the little girl on the bench seat grabbing at her toes. She wanted to touch everything. Know everything. And it was so haphazard, the way they were playing with her life.

"Henriette was arrested," Truus said. "Just after you left. They took everyone. All of them. We knew they would, but . . ." Truus rubbed the back of a hand impatiently across her eyes.

But Henriette, Isa thought, had known what was worth the risk. Hildy, and this little girl, the two baby boys in bags, they made it easy to believe in the beauty of the world. Truus sighed.

"Take the little girl into the ladies' toilet. There will be a woman with cherries on her hat. Give her the baby. Wait five minutes and leave. If there's anyone else in there, she'll go in a stall and wait."

"When?" Isa asked.

"Now. We have no time. I'm going to try and get Willem into this coat. Hurry up, Isaatje! And comb your hair. And wash your hands while you're in there. You're bloody."

Isa put on her coat to cover her stained blue print, found two pins in her pocket and stuck them in her hair. Surely, so far outside Amsterdam, they wouldn't be looking at her hair. She wrapped a blanket around the little girl and scooped her up, hiding her hands. The child wrapped her arms around Isa's neck. Trusting.

Isa stepped out of the train and walked straight to the ladies' toilet without getting a second glance.

It was empty. For two minutes. And then a woman opened the door. Isa saw a sun-worn face, wrinkles around her eyes. Strong-looking hands. A hat with cherries on it. The woman smiled politely, a little grimly, and held out her arms. Isa put the little girl in them. The woman tucked the blanket, turned, and left.

And there was a child saved. And, Isa couldn't help but think, a little girl lost.

She washed her hands. And when she got back to the train, Truus had both Michel and Willem awake and sitting up, coats covering their bloody shirts and bandaged wounds. Willem's left arm was out of the sleeve, hidden beneath the cloth. Truus put a comforter in the mouth of the smallest baby, while Isa combed her fingers quick through Willem's hair. There was nothing much to be done about his face. And then she knelt down to clean up Michel, rubbing the dried blood on his cheek, with her coat sleeve.

And Michel grabbed her hand. He was heavy-eyed, almost drunk. He brought her knuckles to his mouth and kissed them. Like he had at Hofer's. And then he opened her palm and kissed that and it was not like Hofer's.

It was a thrill. And a shiver. Reckless.

He was smiling, swaying in his seat. Possibly unaware of anything he'd just done.

She stood, looking down, thumb still at the corner of his mouth, and Truus said, "Oh, Isaatje." Very softly.

Because she knew now, what Isa was going to do.

They got Willem on his feet first. He was steadier than Michel, patient in his pain. Isa got between and put an arm around them both. Truus took Michel's other side, a bag in each hand, and when they walked, they all steadied each other.

They looked like they'd all been to a very bad party.

They stepped together from the train car, stumbling. The platform was deserted, but it was a small station. They were nothing close to invisible.

"Head up, Michel," Truus said.

Then she marched ahead, careful with her bags, and walked into the building. Isa tightened her grip. She was afraid Michel was going to fall. Willem got the station door open with his good arm, and they sidled through. Truus was talking to the guard about directions, animated, with two bags full of babies. Pointing the guard's attention toward the trains and away from the doors. Truus really was pretty. Even with her messy hair and a night like they'd had. The guard looked at her face and nothing else. The ticket seller shook his head and went back to his book.

He also seemed to think it'd been a very bad party.

Outside the doors was a town rather than a city, a place the war had lightly touched, dim beneath slate clouds that tinted to blue. It was going to rain. They got a few looks from the sidewalk. But Willem knew where they were going, leading the way to a side street, where a wagon waited, hay in its back, a man on its front seat with a woman beside him, holding the reins of the horses.

The man climbed down when he saw them, a no-nonsense farmer who understood his business. He let down the gate of the wagon. It was the tilted kind, low for spreading hay or manure in a field. The farmer threw out a quilt and they got Michel sitting. And then Truus came down the street, trying to run without jostling her bags. One of the babies was crying. The woman tied the reins and came around to help her.

If anyone in the town was looking, they seemed to be looking the other way.

Isa turned to Willem. And then she reached up and hugged him, careful of his hand and shoulder. He hugged her back with one arm. And there was no need, Isa discovered, to say anything. They were perfectly understood.

"Take care of him," she said, looking at Michel.

"He'll get to Switzerland," Willem replied.

"And her," Isa said, nodding at Truus.

"I always have. But we won't be back in Amsterdam. Not until the Allies win. Or the Nazis lose. Or the world has changed."

An ugly world. And it really didn't have to be. But it was.

Truus came around to the back of the wagon. "I wish you would come, Isa," she said.

"Hildy needs me."

Because Hildy was hers now.

"And I have to bury my father."

She didn't even know if the Gestapo had found the garret. What they would do if they'd discovered a dead man inside. She had to make sure her father was at peace. And if she was going to lose the gallery, there were things to be done. To be moved.

Maybe Moshe's Vermeer would like to rest with Sister Cornelia.

Maybe even in this ugly world, there was something beautiful she could build. Something of her own.

"Do you have any money?" Truus asked.

Isa reached down her dress and held up a ten-guilder note, stolen from the conductor when she'd knocked his ill-gotten gain all over the floor.

Truus shook her head. "Is there a train?"

"Fifteen minutes."

Then Isa turned to Michel, kneeling down on the wagon gate, where he could see her. He had his good arm clinging to the wooden rails, trying to hold himself up. Isa reached in her pocket and brought out the little black notebook. His eyes found it and focused.

"I know what this is for," she whispered.

"Do you?" His voice was slurred.

"You're going to give them back. That's what the money was for. You're going to find the stolen paintings and give them back."

He smiled. It was a lovely smile. And a little drunk.

She went to tuck the notebook into his new jacket, but there was a folded paper sticking out of its cover. A creamy edge. Isa opened it.

And found a check. For 190,000 guilders.

Of course he had left her a check for 190,000 guilders. She closed it back inside and tucked the notebook into his new jacket.

"Look at me," she said.

He raised his eyes.

"Get them back."

He smiled. And nodded.

And love, Isa thought, has no color. It is all the colors.

Pure brilliant light.

She stood. And then Truus said, "Wait!" Running around to the front of the wagon, coming back with a scarf. A bleached linen kerchief with a printed pattern, stiff with dirt and wear. Truus wrapped it firmly around Isa's hair, kissing her once, twice, one cheek and the other.

Pale linen. The color of sadness. With little spring ferns all over it.

Michel was swaying where he sat. Isa leaned down.

"Michelangelo," she whispered in his ear. She felt the scratch of a cheek. The brushstroke of lashes. "I think you are beautiful."

And Isa turned away and walked alone, back to the train station.

"The beauty you create shall be known as compassion and shall console the hearts of men."

—Commandment VII, from *Decalogue of the Artist*,

Gabriela Mistral

30

Amsterdam, The Netherlands
— February 1946 —

ISA DE SMIT climbed the grand front steps of Keizersgracht 321, the former mansion of Han van Meegeren, and did not bother to ring the bell. She stepped quickly inside the elegant white hall and shut the door against the cold. The house was warm with bodies, with the rising smoke of cigarettes, buzzing with the hum of conversation. With rumor. Speculation. Who? And how much?

She smelled old things. And money.

The walls were crowded with framed art.

Isa bent down and loosened the fur hood around the face of the little girl with her, letting it fall back from a mop of soft brown curls.

"Your coats?" said the man at the front register. He looked askance at the child, but Isa brought her to all the auctions. She unbuttoned her coat, an old, timeless fashion, like her mother's navy dress underneath it, her bright hair knotted in a chignon. She handed the coats to the registrar, signed her name, and got a number.

"Are you ready, little imp?" Isa asked.

Hildy took Isa's hand, and when they got to the first painting, raised her arms to be picked up.

"Now remember, darling, we look at them all, a good look, and then we look again, and you will tell me which ones you think the people will buy first."

Hildy nodded, serious about her duties, gazing at the paintings with a finger against her mouth. It was slow going. Because the auction was well attended, because curiosity was rampant. Because when Amsterdam was liberated in May 1945, just before the fall of Germany and Hitler and the entire Third Reich, the new Dutch government had immediately begun a program of pursuing collaborators.

Arrests. Public humiliations. Loss of property. Reputation. Trials that carried a death sentence. And Han van Meegeren's name had been found on a receipt in the files of Hermann Goering, a receipt that named him as the seller of a painting called *Christ with the Adulteress*. A previously unknown Vermeer, Goering's prize possession, taking pride of place above the desk in his office.

An unknown Vermeer was a painting of immeasurable importance to the Dutch.

Van Meegeren had been arrested for collaboration. Van Meegeren had a death sentence hanging over his head. Van Meegeren was in the unenviable position of having to prove that he could not be a hated collaborator, because had not actually sold Hermann Goering a priceless Vermeer. Because the painting, *Christ with the Adulteress*, wasn't a Vermeer. The painting was a fake, and he, Han van Meegeren, was its forger.

It had been easy to prove, because it was true. He was found not guilty. He was also found to be the clever Dutchman who had pulled the wool over the eyes of Hermann Goering. The canny forger who had managed to hoodwink the Nazis.

Han van Meegeren had become a hero.

He was probably wondering how it all came to be, since Goering's prize painting had actually been sold to Gurlitt.

But heroes still needed something to live on, and Van Meegeren had spent all his money. So today, he was having an auction. A little housecleaning before his new trial. This time, as an art forger.

It was a trial, Isa thought, he really couldn't help but lose.

"This one!" said Hildy, pointing.

"You're supposed to wait until we've looked at them all," Isa chided, but without much conviction. The picture was oil on canvas, a young woman with copper-flame hair, holding out a severed head. *Judith with the Head of Holofernes.* Only the head of Holofernes held a striking resemblance to a leering Van Meegeren. The colors were magnificent, the hair almost taking on the movement of fire. He must have done it from memory. And it was hanging on the unobtrusive door to his cellar.

She hadn't seen Van Meegeren since that day in her dining room, when he left the pills that killed her father. And she didn't expect to see his face here today. He might be a hero to the Dutch, but in the art world, he was an anathema.

She was sure he'd hung that painting there on purpose.

"Perhaps you're right," Isa said, giving Hildy a kiss. She giggled when the lipstick mark was wiped from her cheek.

The auction was held in the living room, not as pristine as it had once been, the furniture moved to make way for chairs. Isa found a seat all the way to one side, just in case she needed to leave with Hildy. She never had to.

She could see into the dining room, where tall vases had overflowed with storm clouds of roses. Where the toe of a sock had passed her a key.

It was beautiful, in a way, Isa thought, that something so pure and brilliant could never really burn itself out.

Beautiful.

And cruel. Because the ache never healed itself, either.

She kissed Hildy's curls.

The auction started, and Isa gave Hildy the paddle with the number. Some people found this cute. Hildy would have been offended. But they weren't buying much today. There wasn't much here that was right for the gallery, and she was sure the prices would run high. Everyone, ironically, wanted to own the paintings of a famous forger.

"Here it comes, darling," whispered Isa.

An auction always gave her a blue-and-green thrill.

"We have for sale an original Van Meegeren, *Judith with the Head of Holofernes*, signed upper right. Shall we begin at one hundred?"

Isa poked Hildy, and she raised the paddle.

Someone said "one hundred twenty-five," and Isa poked Hildy again. "One hundred fifty," Isa said.

"Two hundred, please."

Isa didn't move. The voice had been directly behind her. A voice she hadn't heard for two and a half years. She nearly missed her bid. She poked Hildy and said, "Two hundred fifty."

"Three hundred."

Damn him.

Isa poked. "Three hundred fifty."

"Five hundred."

And she felt the fire-flower. Hot. Scarlet. A full bloom she hadn't experienced since the Nazi occupation. It made her reckless.

"One thousand," she said. Forgetting to poke Hildy. Hildy gave her a look.

Damn, damn, damn him. That was her budget for the month. And she couldn't sell that painting in the gallery. It wasn't in fashion.

She didn't want to sell it. She loved it.

She just didn't want to give Van Meegeren a thousand guilders.

The voice behind her stayed quiet and the gavel came down at one thousand.

"Come, love," Isa said.

Isa picked up Hildy and swept out of the room, careful not to look at the seat behind her. She went to the registration desk and said, "Lot nineteen. Could you have it delivered . . ."

"Could you wrap it, please?" said the voice from behind her. "We are going to the same address."

Isa bit her lip. But she didn't say anything. This was something that was better faced.

She couldn't face it. She was hot like her painted Judith hair.

She watched the registrar wrap the painting in brown paper while the auction went on in the living room. He glanced at the picture, and then up at Isa.

"Hello," said Hildy, whispering for the auction. "Are you coming to my house?"

Isa could hear the rustle of a suit. Of someone crouching down. "Hello, Hildy. What makes you think I am coming to your house?"

"Because you said you were going to the same address, and I am going to my house next."

Hildy was an astute three-year-old. Or that's how old the doctor thought she might be. Hildy, the doctor said, had started life small and malnourished.

"Our coats, please?" Isa whispered.

"How do you know my name?" Hildy demanded. Just a little loud.

"Because I knew you when you were a baby."

"Did you know my real mommy?"

"No," he said quietly. "Only Isa. You were so little, your whole hand could wrap around this finger."

"Did you feed me bottles?"

"I did."

"Did you change my diapers?"

"Yes."

The coats came and Michel stepped forward, took Isa's coat, and held it out. She managed to get it on almost without looking at him. Instead, she watched Hildy studying the stranger who had changed her diapers. Michel helped Hildy into her coat next, tying up her fur hood. And then she looked up and raised her arms to him.

Hildy always had liked Michel. Even as a baby.

Isa lifted her chin and let herself look. Michel was older, a little thinner, but wasn't everyone after 1945? He was wearing a very nice suit, browns and cream, with a dark overcoat that brightened the amber of his eyes.

She'd told him he was beautiful. And she hadn't heard from him since.

Except for once. And in Isa's opinion, that time didn't count.

She was vermilion, but it was a muted tone, tinted gray-blue with loss and with a lilac uncertainty, contrasted with the deep, deep cobalt of regret.

Loneliness, Isa thought, was so many things.

They went out the door and down the steps, Michel carrying Hildy and the painting. The wind was whipping bitter off the Keizersgracht, the canal half-frosted, a world smoke-gray and edged with coal soot. It had its own bleak sort of beauty.

"Let's take the car, shall we?" said Michel.

She looked at him sidelong, at the car parked beside the canal and across from the steps. He leaned the painting against the wheel, opened the door for Isa, handed her Hildy, and put the painting in the trunk. Then he came around with the keys and slid behind the wheel.

"It is not mine," he said. "I just have it for the day. And if I use all the petrol, my client will have my head. But I had items I did not want to transport on a tram."

His client. His client with a car. Items he didn't want on a tram. Chatting like they'd seen each other yesterday. But the trouble with un-becoming, Isa decided, was that you inevitably became something or someone else. She had no idea who Michel was now.

Isa looked out the window, cuddling Hildy. She was so hot she was going to cry.

"Don't be mad, Isaatje," said Hildy.

"Is Isaatje mad often?" Michel asked.

"Only when it's very serious," Hildy said, seriously. "Isaatje is sad more than she's mad."

"Ah," Michel replied.

Far, far too astute. Why had no one mentioned how troublesome children are?

Michel drove straight to the Gallery De Smit, parking close to the windows, so as not to block the narrow Kalverstraat. Isa didn't wait for him to come around for the door. She opened it and let Hildy out, following Hildy's headlong rush for the gallery.

"Hello, doll!" said the woman at the desk.

"Hello, Marja!" said Hildy. And she took off down the length of the gallery, doing somersaults, using the fur of her hood as a cushion.

"Did you buy anything— Oh, hello. You're back!"

Isa turned to see Michel in the doorway. For one moment, she remembered the echoes of an empty room. The blackout. A brown hat.

"Hello again, Marja," said Michel, shutting the door. "She was just where you said."

Marja smiled, completely missing the look Isa gave her. Michel watched Hildy somersault, then run pell-mell up the spiral stairs.

"Could I give this to you while I look, Marja?" he asked, handing her two wrapped paintings. "I was in a hurry before."

"Of course," she said, sweetly, drinking him in while he

unbuttoned his overcoat. Isa slid her hands into her pockets, leaned against the yellow bricks between the galleries, and crossed her heels. Looking at Michel while he looked at art.

Michel studied each piece. Thought about each piece. Traditional landscapes and portrait oils, gilt-framed and gold-leafed, watercolors in a simple square of crisp solid black. But there was also a collection of teal-glazed pottery. Three woodcuts, a collage, and a Japanese print. The Gallery De Smit was bright with bulbs and window light, lavish in shades of chartreuse and shamrock, citrine and seashell, lime and lazuline and the purest white. It was alive. Growing.

Unique.

It was beautiful.

And it was hers. Her created beauty, carved from the ugliness of the world.

Michel gazed up at a row of framed charcoal sketches, hung high and not for sale. A dozen versions of Isa's face in every mood and every light. Signed, if you knew where to look. He studied these for a long time.

Marja was fascinated. Isa wished she'd go home.

Michel proceeded to the little gallery, where the work was riskier, more avant-garde, lifting a hand to touch the yellow bricks beside her on his way. Isa turned the corner, examining while he examined. He stopped in front of a color study, large, half the wall, a pattern of color and contrast that tricked the eye, undulating where it should have been straight, angling when it should have curved, its center erupting in an enormous, red geometric flower.

"This is nice," he said.

"I painted it."

"I know." He turned, and now he examined her.

And she was ablaze, a brilliantly aching fire. It was cruel.

He said, "Could we talk, please, Isa?"

She lifted a hand toward the stairs. Michel stepped to the desk and got the paintings, Marja craning her neck around the bricks to see them go around the spiral.

In the kitchen, there were easy chairs where the sofa had been, new cabinets above the tiles on the marigold walls, and a new table, blue, sleek, Formica-flecked. Hildy was climbing into one of the chairs at the table, Willem pouring her a glass of milk. Willem looked up, and his face lit.

"Michel!" he said, coming out to offer his hand. Michel set down the paintings and shook. Willem clapped his back, pulling him briefly into a hug. "What are you doing? Can you stay?"

Isa slid her coat from her shoulders, watching Michel take in the scene. Willem barefoot in the kitchen with his shirt untucked. Pouring milk.

"Willem lives here," she said. "While he's back at the university."

"Willem!" said Hildy, bubbling her milk. She had no manners outside an auction house.

"Where is Truus?" Michel asked, pulling out a chair.

"Married," Isa replied. "She's a teacher now in Utrecht." She turned to light the flame under the coffeepot. She could feel eyes on the bare nape of her neck. "Willem needed somewhere to stay, and I had the space. We're quite the controversial little family."

"People can be narrow," said Willem. "But Isa gets the worst of it. Most of them think Hildy is . . ." He shrugged.

"German?" Michel supplied.

"Or mine. Or somebody else's."

Willem was avoiding the word *prostitute*.

Michel raised a dark brow. "Cigarette?" he offered.

"Why not?"

They lit up, waiting for the coffeepot to boil. Hildy finished her milk.

"Can I go play with Sister Tony and Tomas?"

Isa shook her head. "It's late, love. We'll go over tomorrow." Hildy slid down from the chair, lifted her arms to Isa, got picked up, got a kiss, and took off at a run through the swinging door of the kitchen.

"She is a beautiful child," Michel said.

"Yes," said Isa. "She is."

She put an ashtray on the table. A little too hard.

"How is the hand?" Michel asked.

"Working," Willem said, stretching his fingers. The pinky was a little crooked. "How's the shoulder?"

"Stiff now and again. Yours?"

"Same."

They smoked. And Isa saw Willem studying her rigid stance, then over to Michel, who was fascinated by the tabletop. Back and forth above his cigarette. He caught Isa's eye and gave an almost imperceptible nod of his head toward Michel. She ignored him.

"You've redecorated," Michel commented.

"We spent the fall and winter of forty-four at the farm with Truus and Willem," Isa said. "We would have starved, I think, if we hadn't. When we got back, everything made of wood had gone into somebody's stove. Down to the kitchen cupboards. We're lucky to still have the floors."

Michel lifted his eyes. "And the art?"

"Packed. In a vault in the convent."

"All of it?"

Isa straightened. No, not all of it. There had been one left behind, safe in her wall. But Michel Lange didn't need to know that.

His eyes dropped to the ashtray. "I am sorry. About your things."

"Maybe they kept someone alive."

Isa winced. She sounded cold, even to herself. When she was hot. When she was ablaze.

The coffee boiled, and then Willem leaned his elbows on the table. "So, where have you been, Michel?"

And there it was. The question. Isa's hand gripped a cup.

"In Switzerland until the end of the war," Michel replied. "Then back in Vienna for a time, for some family matters . . ."

She couldn't imagine what his family matters might have looked like.

". . . and then I was asked to Berlin, to help catalogue art. It was urgent, before pictures and paperwork began to walk away. As many of them already had. I worked on Goering's collection, among others."

Isa glanced up. Had Michel been the one to find Goering's receipt for *Christ with the Adulteress*? Responsible for getting Han van Meegeren put on trial for collaboration?

She could ask him, but she poured coffee instead. It was still ersatz.

Willem stubbed out his cigarette. "None for me, Isa. I'm going to play with Hildy for a while."

"Is Markus coming?" she asked.

"Later." He pushed back his chair. "And Michel . . ." Isa saw Willem give him the tiniest of nods. "You really should stay."

Traitor, she thought, watching him saunter off into the dining room.

She put two cups on the table, sat, and crossed her arms and her legs. Michel lit another cigarette, gaze on the ashtray. Cool and composed in his jacket and tie. She might have named his portrait *Business Deal*. Except that she could see his knee jiggling.

"It is good to see the gallery open again," he said finally. "It is better even, I think, than what it was." He hesitated. "I suppose you received my check?"

"Oh," said Isa, feigning surprise. "Was that from you?"

She had been stunned when the letter from the bank announced a deposit of fifty thousand guilders, running for the tax office the very next day like she'd entered a race. But when the days slid by without a call, a knock—not even a note beneath the flowerpot—Isa knew what that money had been, and she knew what she was to Michel Lange. A debt paid off. A business transaction now ended. And with the brilliance of her light still burning.

Cruel.

She reached for her coffee cup. "It's just so difficult to keep up with who is paying me money these days. Especially when they don't bother with names. I'll check the ledger book, shall I?"

Michel's brows were down, still staring at the ashtray. "Would you like to ask me a question?" he said. "Would you like to ask me where that money came from?"

"I assume you had better luck with Hofer's check."

"No, Hofer's check was bad."

He waited. Smoking. Teasing out the moment.

Reeling her in.

"All right, where, Michel? Where did the money come from?"

She saw the softening, just at the edge of his mouth, before he said, "Gurlitt."

"Gurlitt? Why did he pay you money?"

"Because I told him that if he didn't give me one hundred thousand guilders, I would tell Hitler about the art he was pilfering."

"What art?"

"The work of degenerate artists that Gurlitt was collecting instead of burning. The art he was charging Hitler inflated prices for, so he could skim off the top and buy. And at the end of 1943, Gurlitt was very grateful for his Führer to not have this information."

Isa set down her coffee. She'd never even tasted it. "You blackmailed Gurlitt?"

He nodded. And so Gurlitt had paid for the taxes and for the restarting of the Gallery De Smit. He'd paid for keeping a genuine Vermeer safe and hidden.

Michel knew that would give her a thrill, damn him. She wasn't going to let him see it.

"Is that the new business you've started, then?" she inquired. "Blackmail?"

Michel shook his head. "Enough."

"You weren't very good at it the first time you tried. I wouldn't have thought it was your chosen line of—"

"Enough!"

Isa closed her mouth, waiting. He lowered his voice again.

"I did not write to you, Sofonisba, because I did not know that you would want to hear from me. And the taint of that uniform stayed with me like a smell . . ."

"I threw your uniform out the window."

"And you left—"

"I had to leave!"

". . . and you were gone without a word, after I had lied to you . . ."

He'd been forgiven. And she hadn't left without a word. Could he really not remember?

". . . and you never even told me about Theo. And I said to myself that I had no right to expect anything from you. That you might wish to forget someone you had known for a painful eight days in the middle of a war . . ."

Eight days that had blown through her life like the north wind.

". . . and I said to myself that it was a kindness, not to write. That it was not fair, to think you could have known me as I am. You did not even know me . . ."

"Yes, I did. I knew you."

He sat back. "I think that is true."

It went quiet in the kitchen. Willem and Hildy were somewhere upstairs, chasing and making the light fixture rattle.

"I said goodbye to you," Isa whispered. She'd said goodbye in a way that she'd thought was telling him to come back.

"Did you? It seemed . . . like a dream." He reached out, playing with the burning cigarette in the ashtray. "I thought it was a dream. And then, in Antwerp, something happened. And since then, I have told myself that perhaps we could become friends. That you and I could be good friends. But I see now that I have made a mistake, and we cannot be that."

He stubbed the cigarette. Stubbed and stubbed it.

"Why?" she said. "What mistake?" The heat in her chest was leaking from her eyes.

"I see now that we cannot be friends because you love me."

Isa felt her lips part. "What?"

He almost smiled. "Well, you are not indifferent. And I am also . . . not indifferent and never have been, but you know that perfectly well."

"No. I do not."

"No? Then it is just as well that I have come all this way to prove how not indifferent I am. I have brought you a gift. Two gifts, though one you may like more than the other."

He pushed back the chair and brought the second wrapped painting—much smaller than *Judith*—laying it gently on the table. "This is for you."

And he sat back down. Knee jiggling. Watching her. Amber-eyed.

Isa looked at the package, swiping once at her cheek. Trying to decide if Michel Lange had just said he loved her. The brown paper was reused, a road map of wrinkles from previous foldings, the string in a tiny hard knot. She had to pick with her fingernails. And when it finally came loose, Isa opened the paper and turned over the picture.

And saw *Christ with the Adulteress*. Her father's version. Theodoor de Smit's masterpiece in baked paint. It was a little damaged on one corner, but nothing that would mar the power of its composition. Its emotion. Its expression. Its luminescence and light.

Isa blinked. She stared.

"It is still beautiful, is it not?" Michel said.

She looked at him and not the painting. "I think it might be beautiful."

She knew it was. Because she could feel it. She'd forgotten, for a moment, how pain can mask the feel of beauty.

How pain can make you forget to believe in beauty at all.

She touched the tint of ultramarine in the face of Christ. The spiderweb of craquelure. "But . . . I don't understand."

"Neither did I, not until I saw the trial and a picture of what had been in Goering's office. You switched the paintings, Sofonisba. In the basement of the Stedelijk."

"I did."

"You did not tell me."

"I was busy." The surface they had created looked so genuine. "Where did you find it?"

"This is the something that happened in Antwerp. I could not believe my eyes when I walked past the shop. There is some small damage. Someone has put it in a bad frame. But time in a canal does not seem to have done Van Meegeren's paint any harm. I took it as a sign. To try my luck, as the Americans say." He shrugged. "It is a painting about forgiveness, after all."

She'd liked to think that was why it was her father's last painting. That he'd been asking her forgiveness. She knew this wasn't the reason. But still, the painting had come back to her, and she'd forgiven Theodoor de Smit a long time ago.

The only one who needed to forgive Michel was himself. But only he could decide that.

She touched the headdress of the adulteress, glowing in the hope that lit her face.

Michel was still watching her, wary. "Would you like your second gift?" he asked.

He pulled an envelope from his jacket pocket and slid it across the table. It had a name on the front, in handwriting of copperplate.

Rebeka Franken

"Rebeka," said Michel, "is the only surviving member of the Franken family."

"Moshe's sister?" Isa drew a breath. "I thought they had all died."

"She was in hiding."

Isa held up the envelope. It was sealed. "And what's inside?"

"The paperwork showing Rebeka's ownership by descent, of a painting titled *Woman with a Wine Glass* by Johannes Vermeer. She would like to come here tomorrow, to the gallery. To meet you."

"Yes," Isa said. "Yes, of course."

She looked at the envelope. Remembering a promise made to haunted eyes. She remembered the contents of a small black notebook.

"Is this what you're doing now?" Isa asked. "Tracking down the owners of lost art?"

"Yes, or vice versa. A client will sometimes ask me to find a certain painting. I also buy and sell, thanks to Gurlitt, which so far has provided the funds to repurchase pieces, if needed. I do not charge a client for their own art."

Gurlitt funding the return of stolen art. The idea shivered down her back.

What a shame they didn't get their three million.

"You can see," Michel said, "why I was not certain you would like your gift. You will be sad, perhaps, to see the Vermeer go?"

Isa shook her head. "No, it's what he would have wanted. It's her birthright."

It would have made Moshe so happy.

Isa set the envelope beside the untouched coffee, finger tracing the writing of the name.

"How many times have you looked closely at a genuine Vermeer?"

Michel leaned his elbows on the table. "I have only seen a genuine Vermeer in a museum."

"Would you like to see one?"

He reached out with a finger, just brushing a lock of hair from her neck. "Do you have one that you would like to show me?"

"Yes. Do you want to see it now?"

His eyes were amber glass. "Yes."

"The tools are upstairs, in the storage closet."

Michel stood, climbing straight up the spiral stairs as if he'd been summoned. Isa took her father's painting down to the gallery and told Marja they were closing early, hustling the woman and her curiosity out the door. Isa turned the sign. She turned the lock, found a nail, and hung her father's painting on it, bad frame and all. When Michel came down, wooden stairs creaking, toolbox rattling, she was pulling the last of the gallery's drapes closed.

Michel took off his suit jacket, tossed it on Marja's desk, loosening his tie and his top shirt button. He went to the wall of Jacobean brick and ran his eyes over it, ran his hands over it—deftly, delicately— trying to feel a joint, the place where the mortar was new.

And he was imperfect. And beautiful.

And the blaze in her was pure, achingly brilliant light.

Because light is made of all the colors.

Isa walked across the gallery, heels sharp on the wood. Michel looked back when he heard her come. He turned, and she took his face in her hands and kissed him.

He didn't even seem surprised.

He didn't let her go. He covered her mouth, her face, and her neck, and back to her lips again. Held her by the knot in her hair. It wasn't enough. And she was reckless. And he was reckless, and she could feel the shape of his skin beneath the shirt and tie, the bricks behind, the edge of his lips, the hand on the curve of her hip, the back of a calf against her leather heel. Her breath was short. The knot was down.

And then a finger was on her mouth, a feather stroke of hush, and Michel said, "Hildy is in the kitchen."

"Hildy," Isa breathed, "will go to bed right after supper."

She could feel the smile. The laugh. Warm and unexpected.

"Get the chisel," he said in the space below her ear.

Isa got the chisel. Knelt in front of the wall in her disheveled navy dress. She found the soft spot in the mortar, the last tapped brick. She placed the blade and hit it with the hammer.

And she hit. And hit. Four sides until the brick was loose. She swung, hammered, chiseled, and Michel stopped her progress with an arm around her waist, a mouth on the nape of her neck. And then he let her work and the dust flew, and they got dusty, and the bricks came down, and the dress came down from a shoulder. And then Willem came down, only to climb back up again, shaking his head while she hammered.

And beauty, Isa thought, had no imperfection. Because beauty was imperfection. Like art. Like people. Like the world. Creating and re-creating, becoming and un-becoming. Something to find, even when it's hidden. To feel when it isn't known. Making it. Breaking it, and chiseling it free. And when the hole between the bricks was wide enough, Isa could see into the strange, dark space between two ancient studs, an ugly place of grime and forgotten things and dirt, where a package lay, square and wrapped in moldering canvas.

She reached in, feeling, stretching for the frame, and Michel helped guide it out between the bricks' ragged ends. She set the package on the floor, in the chips and the mortar dust.

"Open it," Michel said.

Isa unwrapped the canvas.

And they beheld the hand of the master.

AUTHOR'S NOTE

Artifice, like many stories I find myself writing, begins with a cross-roads, a place where one fascinating life intersects with another in a landscape of some of the world's most extraordinary times. These pathways walked are captivating, their junctions irresistible. They make me want to write books. Here are some of the roads that crossed to create *Artifice*.

Han van Meegeren and Johan van Hulst

Han van Meegeren was one of the most clever and successful art forgers in the world. But in 1943, no one knew that.

He was born in 1889 in Deventer, the Netherlands, and made a reasonably successful living in art, working as an assistant to an art professor, supplementing income with still lifes, Christmas cards, and, increasingly, portraits. He wanted much more. When Van Meegeren finally realized the dream of his first public exhibition, the critics were not kind. Modern art was popular; Van Meegeren's love of the Old Masters was considered gauche and unoriginal.

Perhaps this was a catalyst.

By 1932, Van Meegeren was experimenting with forgery, using scraped-down seventeenth-century canvases and period upholstery nails. He made his own badger-hair brushes and mixed authentic pigments. And into these pigments, he added a mixture of carbolic acid and formaldehyde, the base formula for Bakelite, an early plastic that was used for everything from radio knobs to hair dryers. When heated in an oven, the surface of Van Meegeren's plastic paint could be cracked, then rubbed over with India ink, creating an authentic craquelure. He also did his homework, studying painters with gaps in their histories, with few known early works, looking for subject matter and style that would support the pet theories of critics and historians. Because who doesn't want to believe when they're being proven right?

In 1937, Van Meegeren sold a plastic paint Vermeer, *The Supper at Emmaus*, for 520,000 guilders. It was hailed as a masterpiece. More forgeries followed, and in 1941, he sold two more previously unknown Vermeers, *The Last Supper* for 1.6 million, and *Issac Blessing Jacob* for 1.25 million guilders. They were admired and authenticated.

Van Meegeren's takings in 1941 alone would compare today to $28 million.

But his lifestyle was lavish and out of control. Van Meegeren had a drinking problem and a dependency on morphine. The quality of his forgeries suffered. But the Nazis were in the Netherlands and they were buying. So in 1943, he sold a "newly discovered" Vermeer, *Christ with the Adulteress*, to the avid collector Hermann Goering, second-in-command of the Reich.

Goering hung *Christ with the Adulteress* on his office wall, the jewel of his collection. But he stiffed Van Meegeren on the deal, paying with paintings instead of cash, a reputed 137 confiscated pieces of art that he had no room to store or display. In the summer of 1945, after the fall of the Reich, when Goering's vast collection was being catalogued, Han van Meegeren's name was found on the receipt for

Christ with the Adulteress. He was arrested for collaboration, and in the face of a death sentence, confessed instead to forgery.

They didn't believe him. Van Meegeren had to prove himself a forger or be executed. So he offered to paint a Vermeer while in custody, demanding his exact ingredients and correct conditions for painting, including alcohol and pills. Van Meegeren painted his prison Vermeer, *Christ among the Doctors*, and in one of the most embarrassing moments of the art world, his painting was authenticated.

Van Meegeren became a legend in Holland, the artist who hoodwinked the Nazis. In the art world, he was a pariah. Van Meegeren forgeries were turning up everywhere, and museums, collectors, and critics alike were professionally and personally embarrassed.

Unsurprisingly, Han van Meegeren was convicted of forgery in November 1947 and sentenced to one year in prison. He never served a day. Van Meegeren died of a heart attack, likely brought on by morphine withdrawal, on December 30, 1947, at the age of fifty-eight. Now, ironically, his work is in demand and often forged. Sometimes his forgeries are forged.

Johan van Hulst, on the other hand, was also clever and successful in his chosen profession. He was slight, balding, with a thin face and nose, much like Han van Meegeren. And in 1943, he, too, had a secret. He was running one of the most successful rescue operations for smuggling Jewish children that ever took place during the war.

Van Hulst was born in Amsterdam in 1911. He was a quiet man, intelligent and unassuming, with a master's degree in psychology and pedagogy, and a PhD in the humanities. By 1938, he was an assistant principal at a teacher's college. By 1940, during the Nazi invasion, he was made director, discreetly training teachers how not to teach the new National Socialist curriculum. Van Hulst's teaching college was located directly across from the Hollandsche Schouwburg theater, which had been converted into a temporary prison for Dutch Jews awaiting deportation. And in the day nursery next door to the college was another kind of prison: a prison for Jewish children, destined for death in the concentration camps.

For Johan van Hulst, this was utterly unacceptable.

Van Hulst began working with Henriette Pimentel, the Jewish director of the day nursery, and Walter Süskind, a member of the Jewish Council now put in charge of the prison theater, both of whom were slated for eventual deportation themselves. Together, the three quietly found homes willing to hide a Jewish child. When a place was found, a child was "mistakenly" left off the transportation list, or the list might be retyped. Then children would be handed over the back hedge to the teaching college, where they were housed in classrooms, taken out the front door in shopping bags and laundry baskets by students and Resistance workers, spirited out of the city as far away as Friesland. It was a monumental task, a risky and heartbreaking business. Only a few children at a time could be saved or they would all be caught. The rest, they had to let go.

By the end of July 1943, their operation was blown. Henriette Pimentel and Walter Süskind were arrested, Henriette to be murdered two months later in Auschwitz, while Walter would die in February 1945 on a death march. Van Hulst only just escaped with his life and spent the rest of the war in hiding. An estimated six hundred Jewish toddlers and babies had been saved. It was probably more.

But they were also six hundred children lost, cut off from their Jewish identity and even their former names, never to be reunited with family. Due to collaboration, excellent prewar record keeping, and the direct control exercised by the occupying Nazi government, about 94 percent of Dutch Jews did not survive the Holocaust, the highest percentage in Europe.

It was probably more.

Johan van Hulst went on to become an author, a university professor, a senator of the Netherlands, and a member of the European Parliament. He was honored as Righteous Among the Nations by Yad Vashem in 1970. An avid chess player, he won tournaments at the age of ninety-five and at ninety-nine. Until later in his life, very few people in his home country knew what he had done during the war. Van Hulst died in 2018 at the age of one hundred seven. His former teaching college will open as the Dutch National Holocaust Museum in 2024.

Van Meegeren and Van Hulst were two Dutchmen who looked vaguely similar and lived through the Nazi occupation of the Netherlands. They couldn't have spent their time more differently. Van Meegeren declared himself a national hero for hoodwinking Hermann Goering. Van Hulst, when asked, said he didn't believe he was a hero. That there was only one question he could ask when saving those last twelve children before the soldiers came, a question he asked himself all his life. And that question was: Why not thirteen?

As an author, thinking about crossroads, I can't help but ask my own question: What if the situations had been reversed, and Van Hulst was the one with $28 million? At least one part of our world might have walked a very different path.

Willem Arondeus and the Girl with Red Hair

The Dutch Resistance was a loose organization of individuals and groups that sometimes banded together, and sometimes found their own way to resist the German occupation. **Hannie Schaft**, who came to be known as **the Girl with Red Hair**, was born into a family of

Communist leanings with no love for Fascism or the Nazis. She was nineteen when Germany invaded the Netherlands, and with her friends, the sisters Truus Oversteegen (sixteen) and Freddie Oversteegen (fourteen), she immediately began training with weapons and explosives.

The three girls formed an unusual squad of female assassins and saboteurs. Freddie was the first when she shot a Nazi from her bicycle. Truus killed a soldier she was passing, a man about to execute a family on their own doorstep for hiding Jews. The three together would lure SS officers into the woods with the promise of an assignation, and leave them buried there. Hannie, however, was the most active, mapping military sites, transporting weapons, and personally assassinating German intelligence, Dutch police, and collaborators. "The Girl with Red Hair" was on the top of the Germans' most wanted list, the most feared member of the Dutch Resistance, partially because she was the most recognizable. Hannie dyed her hair black and carried on Resistance work even after the arrest of her parents, hiding Jewish people, gay people, Communists, anyone who was on the Nazi deportation lists.

On March 21, 1945, Hannie was arrested at a checkpoint for distributing an illegal Communist newspaper. After beatings, torture, and solitary confinement, all without giving her true name, the Girl with Red Hair was finally identified by her roots, just growing out from the dye. Hannie Schaft was taken to the dunes for execution by machine gun on April 17, 1945. When the first bullet only grazed her head, Hannie was reported to say, "I shoot better." The second round killed her, eighteen days before the liberation of Amsterdam. Truus and Freddie Oversteegen both survived the war, and Truus named her daughter after Hannie.

Willem Arondeus was a man also finding his own way to resist the Nazis, as he had been finding his own way most of his life. Born in Naarden, the Netherlands, in 1894, Willem was an artist, specializing in illustration and graphic design, and he was an author, publishing his own books and illustrating others. He was also openly gay. While being gay in the Netherlands had been legal since 1811, it was still not socially acceptable, and Willem was rejected by his family. When the Nazis took over the Netherlands, being gay was once more outlawed, and "homosexuals" were sought out and imprisoned.

Willem joined a Resistance group of students, artists, musicians, and dancers, primarily producing illegal newspapers and false identity cards. False identity cards saved lives by allowing people to move about the streets and avoid arrest and deportation, to get coupons for goods and ration cards. But the Dutch themselves had created a barrier to this help: the Civil Records Office, where information cards had been meticulously kept for each citizen for decades. This system was an enormous help to the Nazis, especially in identifying Resistance workers and Jews. So Willem Arondeus decided to blow it up.

On March 27, 1943, with the help of two medical students, a sculptor, a tailor, an architect, a lesbian musician, a lawyer, and Willem Sandberg, the curator of the Stedelijk Museum, Willem and thirteen others went dressed as policemen to the Records Office, where they were let in on the pretense of looking for explosives. They drugged the guards, dragged them outside, doused the records with accelerant, and set off a bomb. They managed to destroy about 800,000 records, which, unfortunately, was only about 15 percent. They were almost instantly betrayed by an unknown informant.

Willem Arondeus was arrested and convicted of the bombing along with twelve others, including his partner, Sjoerd Bakker. They were executed by firing squad on July 1, 1943, on the same dunes where Hannie Schraft would die. Willem Arondeus's last words were said to have been, "tell the world that homosexuals are not cowards." Willem Sandberg, who returned to the Stedelijk after the war, designed the memorial plaque for Willem Arondeus in 1946.

While the historian in my heart wants to believe the last words of Hannie Schaft and Willem Arondeus, the historian in my head isn't so sure. I think those words say more about what others wanted to remember about them than what was actually said. And maybe that says something in itself. Two individuals honored as Righteous Among the Nations, who lived out the courage of their convictions. But because one was a Communist and one was gay, neither was celebrated as freely as they could have been. But that's a road that seems to be changing its direction.

Gurlitt, Goudstikker, and Hofer

I might, perhaps, be doing Goudstikker a disservice by placing his name between Gurlitt and Hofer, because for anyone who loves art, the story of Goudstikker is a tragedy. Here are three paths that should have never crossed, even if it was only with artwork.

Jacques Goudstikker was a Dutch Jewish art dealer in Amsterdam. This is probably also doing him a disservice. Goudstikker owned a preeminent international art gallery, several residences, and one of the most impressive and historically important art collections in Europe. His collection numbered around 1,400 pieces, all organized and numbered in a little black notebook filled with names like Goya, Bellini, Rubens, and Rembrandt. He married a glamorous opera singer and had a son. In May 1940, when German parachutists dropped from the sky, Goudstikker might have been better informed than many, because he immediately fled with his family, leaving his gallery and his art collection, his car still running on the dock. On that same night, crossing the English Channel in the pitch dark of the blackout, Goudstikker left his cabin for some air and fell through an open hatchway, breaking his neck.

Back in Amsterdam, vultures in the shape of the Nazi eagle descended. Goering confiscated eight hundred paintings from Goudstikker's collection, acquiring his business on Herengracht and his estate at Oostermeer in a forced sale for a fraction of its worth. The business, still being run as Galerie Goudstikker, was taken over by Goering's henchman, Alois Meidl, who was also involved in acquiring Van Meegeren's fake *Christ with the Adulteress*. But Goering still needed to fulfill his voracious appetite for art, and for this, he used Walter Hofer.

Walter Hofer was a German art dealer who got his start in his brother-in-law's art gallery in The Hague, the Netherlands. But his brother-in-law was Jewish, and Hofer arranged for a divorce for his sister and a visa for his brother-in-law, effectively taking over the business. He was appointed as the personal art agent to Hermann Goering and the director of the ever-growing Goering Collection, traveling Europe on Goering's art trains, often using Goering's authority to collect for himself. Unfortunately, "collecting" almost always meant forcing a sale, or outright stealing, but even this became increasingly difficult. The second-in-command of the Reich was not easy to please, and insisted on buying for nearly nothing, or for ridiculously inflated prices that also inflated his ego. It made it difficult for Hofer to compete, especially when his rival was Hildebrand Gurlitt.

Hildebrand Gurlitt was also German, born into a family of artistic scholars. But one of his grandmothers was Jewish, a problem that was mostly overlooked when Gurlitt was appointed by Hitler as one of four agents to curate "degenerate" art. Gurlitt helped decide what was burned, or sold to collectors outside the Reich, and soon after, he was authorized to begin "collecting" for Hitler's favorite project, the

Führermuseum. In 1944, Gurlitt bought two hundred paintings in Paris for the Führermuseum, though according to the paperwork, only 168 actually got marked for shipment to the proposed museum. He did this in every major city in Europe, but especially in the Netherlands.

In June 1945, after the fall of the Reich, Gurlitt was arrested with twenty boxes of art. He was able to convince his interrogators that he had been persecuted by the Nazis for his Jewish heritage and that the art was actually his. They let him go. Hofer continued to give tours of Goering's vast collection to visiting American generals like nothing had happened, receiving compliments on the beauty of the collection and getting his picture in *Life* magazine. Both men became respectable dealers (and rivals) in Munich, shaking off the taint of stolen art without a trace. Only the declassification of documents in the 1990s began to show the real extent of their involvement in stolen art.

But it was too late. Hofer had died in 1971. Gurlitt had died in a car crash in 1956. Goudstikker's wife had begun suing to get her late husband's collection back in 1946. But because the auction house had still continued to operate under the occupation, she was treated as a collaborator. In 2006, for the first time, 202 paintings of the Goudstikker collection were finally returned to the family. And in 2012, an incredible discovery was made. For more than fifty years, in a tiny apartment in Munich, the son of Hildebrand Gurlitt had been living like a hermit with 1,700 pieces of art: Matisse, Otto Dix, and Degas, much of it considered "degenerate" and lost to the war. Gurlitt's secret collection. Gurlitt's pilfered art is estimated to be worth somewhere in the tens of millions. It is actually priceless.

And so why do these stories of Nazi looted art never fail to fire the imagination? I think it's because of the way a path of beauty can intersect with ugliness to make such an incongruous crossroads. So much about Nazism professed to love the beautiful. Beautiful people, beautiful art, health, and nature. But like the Nazi-occupied Stedelijk's exhibition in 1943, Kunstenaars zien den Arbeidsdienst (An Artist's View of the Labor Service), the exhibition Isa was so offended by, the beauty that Nazism seemed to profess glossed over an ugliness that could not be denied. How can these two things lie side by side in the same person?

Like Van Hulst, it is the question I continue to ask myself. And the only answer I can give is that the beauty seen is not the real beauty. That the true beauty of the world is felt. And the best way to create it is to always be finding, building, and rebuilding my own.

To view high-quality images and an incredible in-depth study of Vermeer's history and catalogue, including the fakes, go to essentialvermeer.com. You won't find *Woman with a Wine Glass*. I made that one up. You will find its pretend companions, *Girl with a Wine Glass* and *The Glass of Wine*.

For more on Van Meegeren, those who are currently faking Van Meegeren's paintings, and a fun "spot the fakes" exercise, go to meegeren.net There are many very good Van Meegeren paintings shown, but I stand by my opinion that *Christ with the Adulteress* isn't one of them.

For more information on the Begijnhof, Amsterdam (located near the intersection of Spui and Rozemboomsteeg), the religious order of women that ran it, and the legend of Sister Cornelia, the website amsterdam.info/sights/begijnhof is an excellent starting place.

For more information on the crash of the American Flying Fortress bomber into a school in Amsterdam on March 22, 1944 (about six months later than the action of this story), the parachutists who bailed out, and the piece of wing that landed directly on top of a horse and cart, emielros.nl/bommenwerper is a website with detailed information and an English translation.

For more information on the history of drug use in wartime (and after), visit recovery.org/addiction/wartime. For more information on America's continuing opiate epidemic, please visit the Substance Abuse and Mental Health Services Administration at samhsa.gov.

Finally, if you visit Amsterdam, be sure to drop by Café De Dokter on Rozenboomsteeg, run by the Breem family since 1798.

ACKNOWLEDGMENTS

Would the following please accept all my love and thanks:

My critique group: Ruta Sepetys, Amy Eytchison, Angelika Stegmann, and Howard Shirley. You taught me to write, and you have continued to love me and support my journey for the past seventeen years. I can't imagine a better definition of "friend."

The Rijksmuseum, Amsterdam: Thank you for all your beauty. And for answering all my questions!

The Stedelijk, Amsterdam: Your amazing online, detailed, and translated archives were a godsend. Thank you.

Verzetsmuseum (Dutch Resistance Museum), Amsterdam: There is not enough thanks for your work in keeping these stories of courage and conviction alive. It is so meaningful. Thank you.

The family of Jan van Eys: Jan's kindness to me in the last weeks of his life could not have been more treasured. His stories of the Nazi occupation in Amsterdam, of hiding his Jewish cello teacher, of being hidden himself from forced labor conscription for two years, were surprise enough. Discovering that his father had been Han van Meegeren's accountant and the executor of his will, getting personal descriptions of Van Meegeren and his studio on Keizersgracht, were shocks I will never forget. Jan was a beautiful and accomplished man, and he will be missed.

My Scholastic team and family: Elizabeth Parisi, Aleah Gornbein, Rachel Feld, Daisy Glasgow, Lizette Serrano, Emily Heddleson, Sabrina Montenigro, Maisha Johnson, Janell Harris, David Levithan, Erin Berger, Seale Ballenger, Ellie Berger, Lori Benton, John Pels, Leslie Garych, Brittany Schachner, Dave Ascher and the Trade finance team, the phenomenal Scholastic sales team, including but not only Elizabeth Whiting, Jacquelyn Rubin, Savannah D'Amico, Jarad Waxman, Daniel Moser, Caroline Noll, Roz Hilden, Jody Stigliano, Jennifer Rivera, Holly Alexander, Sarah Herbik, Brittany Lowe, Sydney Niegos, Kelsey Albertson, Sarah Sullivan, Deborah Owusu-Appiah, Nikki Mutch, Tracy Bozentka, Chris Satterlund, Terribeth Smith, Barbara Holloway, Betsy Politi, Brigid Martin, as well as Jennifer Powell, Rachel Weinert, Tori Simpson, Mona Tavangar, Jazan Higgins, and the Scholastic Book Fairs and Book Clubs. Thank you for all your love and support and for having my back!

Lisa Sandell, my beautiful editor, and Kelly Sonnack, my beautiful agent: I say this for every book, and yet, with every book I mean it more. Lucky. Blessed. Lucky. Blessed. I really can't believe I have the pair of you. Thank you for being my career's guiding light and my heart's dear friend.

Lindsey, my assistant: Should I thank you or apologize? I think I'll thank you.

Aunt Brenda: You let me have a writing retreat in your house again. For a month. With my own coffee maker. While I untrained your dog with too many treats. Everybody should have an Aunt Brenda.

Stephen, Elizabeth, Chris and Siobhan: Thank you for being my family. I love you.

And for Philip. For everything. All the time. Always.

ABOUT THE AUTHOR

Sharon Cameron's debut novel, *The Dark Unwinding*, was awarded the Society of Children's Book Writers and Illustrators' Sue Alexander Award for Most Promising New Work and the SCBWI Crystal Kite Award and was named a YALSA Best Fiction for Young Adults selection. Sharon is also the author of its sequel, *A Spark Unseen*; *Rook*, which was selected as an IndieBound Indie Next List Top Ten Pick, a YALSA Best Fiction for Young Adults selection, and a *Parents' Choice* gold medalist; *The Forgetting*, a #1 *New York Times* bestseller and an Indie Next List selection; its companion, *The Knowing*; the widely acclaimed World War II thriller *The Light in Hidden Places*, which was a Reese's Book Club YA Pick; and the *Publishers Weekly* bestseller *Bluebird*. Follow her on Instagram at @sharoncameron-books or on Twitter at @CameronSharonE.